SIGHT BEYOND THE SUN

ALSO BY MELODY JOHNSON

Love Beyond Series

Beyond the Next Star

Sight Beyond the Sun

Night Blood Series

The City Beneath

Sweet Last Drop

Eternal Reign

Day Reaper

Anthologies

Romancing the Holidays, Vol. 1

Romancing the Holidays, Vol. 2

Romancing the Holidays, Vol. 3

SIGHT BEYOND THE SUN

MELODY JOHNSON

INCENDI PRESS, LLC

Cover design by Trif Book Designs: https://trifbookdesign.com

Names: Johnson, Melody, 1988- author.

Title: Sight beyond the sun / Melody Johnson.

Description: [St. Mary's, Georgia] : Incendi Press, LLC, [2023] | Series: [Love beyond] ; [2]

Identifiers: ISBN: 978-1-7351499-3-6 (paperback) | 978-1-7351499-4-3 (hardcover) | 978-1-7351499-5-0 (ebook)

Subjects: LCSH: Women prisoners--Fiction. | Spies--Fiction. | Human-alien encounters--Fiction. | Undercover operations--Fiction. | Military missions--Fiction. | Space ships--Fiction. | Man-woman relationships--Fiction. | LCGFT: Romance fiction. | Science fiction. | Spy fiction. | Action and adventure fiction.

Classification: LCC: PS3610.O36633 S54 2023 | DDC: 813/.6--dc23

ACKNOWLEDGMENTS

To the usual suspects, including my beta readers, Abby Sharpe, Leah Miles, and Margaret Johnston; and my fellow First Coast Romance Writers. Thank you for the unconditional support and invaluable advice—year after year, book after book. My craft and knowledge of the industry has exponentially improved in your company.

To the best team a writer could find, including my editors, Nicole Klungle and Linda Ingmanson, and my cover designers, Paul and Andrei Trif. The beauty of your words and art brings my book to life. It's amazing how many wrong turns it takes to finally reach a story's conclusion. Thank you for helping me find the way.

To my readers who gave "that crazy alien book" a chance and fell in love with Delaney and Torek as hard as I did. *Sight Beyond the Sun* was the Mount Everest of writing journeys, but your voracious requests for a second book gave me the strength, determination, and confidence to climb to its peak. Thank you for wanting more.

To my husband, Derek. Always.

PART 1

vivsheth (verb): to chase something with purpose. (noun): pursuit.

PROLOGUE

Of all the many distasteful missions Raveno Hoviir had completed in service to his people, he'd never been required to commit murder to maintain his cover. It probably wasn't required now, but for the first time in ten years, five months, and seventeen days, he was happy to embrace the monster he pretended to be.

He and his crew had traveled across three galaxies for this meeting. He'd hoped that Dorai Nikiok had finally decided in favor of their alliance, and he'd anticipated meeting her, or her military commander, Torek Renaar, face-to-face. Neither were aboard their ship now, and apparently, neither could be reached to confirm if this was truly their official stance: the planet Lorien and its citizens, the *lorienok*, condoned the trade of sentient people.

"Each human is worth fifty," the *lorienok* captain said, "but Dorai Nikiok is willing to part with them for thirty-seven."

Oh, they're willing to barter? How diplomatic of them. Raveno tried and failed to keep the telling spines of his *vresls* from flattening as he agreed to the deal, every word of his negotiation like vomit on his tongue.

The humans were transported from the Lorien transport vessel and onto his, but despite his burning temper, Raveno remained patient. He waited until the humans were boarded and secure. He exchanged *lasvik* with their captain, brushing his fang carefully across the man's throat, thereby solidifying their deal and his departure, and he continued waiting until every lorienok had returned to their ship before giving the order.

Really, Raveno was the very definition of calm reason.

"Fire the *lir s'flis*."

Tironan stilled in the copilot's chair, his claws hovering motionless above the control panel. "Vri C-C-Cilvril?"

Raveno inwardly cringed at such a formal address stuttering from his brother's mouth. "You heard me. I want that ship and all the lorienok inside nothing but ash floating in our wake."

"B-b-but we are w-within range."

Must he order him to breathe as well? "Fire the lir s'flis, *then* get us out of range. Or, get us out of range first, if you must, and then fire. I'm not paying for those humans."

The monsters who bought and sold people like livestock might receive their retribution in the next life as they deserved, but he'd ensure they received it in this one.

Raveno didn't clarify his reasoning, however, and Tironan stared at him wide-eyed. Where he'd once looked up to a brother, he likely now saw only a stranger: a ruthless, honorless man who agreed on a price in one breath and ordered murder to escape from that price in the next.

"I—I—I—"

"I can maneuver us out of range, Vri Cilvril," Dellao interrupted from the pilot's chair.

From tips to lobes, Tironan's ears flashed a bright blue.

Ignoring Tironan's embarrassment, Raveno nodded at Dellao, then turned to Zethus, the only other officer besides Avier within his fifteen-man crew who knew the true nature of his meeting with the lorienok. Or rather, his true hopes for that meeting.

"Take a solo cruiser and stay on Earth," Raveno whispered. "It's been how long since your last scouting mission?"

"On Earth? Ten *thesh*," Zethus answered, already selecting and fueling a cruiser with a few keystrokes.

Raveno sighed. "Too long. I'll be relying on you for updates, especially on communication and nutrition, as quickly and regularly as possible. We may need to update our translators. And I need to know if this"—Raveno gnashed his teeth—"*incident* was noticed. If we need to prepare defensive maneuvers."

"Your will by my hands, Vri Cilvril." Zethus clicked his heels in formal salute, about-faced, and ran for his cruiser.

Avier cleared his throat.

Not now, Raveno thought, but as brilliant a physician as Avier was, he hadn't managed to add mind reading to his skill set.

"We're keeping them?" Avier asked under his breath. "We're really transporting thirty-six people against their will to Havar?"

"Per Josairo's orders," Raveno hissed from between his clenched teeth. "And we follow every word of Josairo's orders, do we not? *His will by our hands?*"

Avier's lip curled. "Technically, he ordered we transport at max capacity."

"You want to abduct another one hundred and sixty people?" Raveno waited until Zethus had disembarked, and not a second longer, before firing the lir s'flis himself.

"Cry m-mercy," Tironan whispered.

True to his word, Dellao maneuvered them out of range without incident. Raveno grinned, the dark pleasure in his expression genuine this time as the lir s'flis detonated on impact, leaving the lorienok exactly as he'd wanted and they'd deserved: nothing but ash.

ONE

Before noticing the existence of boys, before developing a sense of sarcasm and a taste for adrenaline, Kinsley "Switch" Morales fell head over heels for explosives. Lighters and sparklers when she was young. Firecrackers and fireworks in grade school. At eleven, she'd built her first homemade bomb with a watermelon set to a kitchen timer. Her parents' back porch still sported pulp stains. At thirteen, she'd branched out into more sophisticated triggers, magnets and cellphones, and was sure to clear her internet history before putting her research to practical use.

Some experiments didn't go as planned—which is why they were called *experiments*—but at sixteen, when one of her pressure-sensitive triggers happened to be a bit too sensitive, nearly taking out Sir Whiskers in addition to the barrel she'd been intending to blow, suddenly everyone questioned her motives. Suddenly, she intended to hurt people, and she needed doctors and counselors to reveal why. That's all anyone ever wanted to know: Why the cat, why pressure triggers, why explosives? Why couldn't she just join the soccer team like Reece and make friends and play nice like a "normal" teenager?

Her parents would never understand because it had absolutely nothing to do with why. She didn't want to hurt anyone. She didn't want to hurt herself. She didn't want to destroy her future or their lives. And she most certainly did *not* want to do anything like her sister, soccer or otherwise.

She wanted to press a button and watch the sparks fly.

By seventeen, Kinsley could construct and defuse time-switch, command, and remote detonated bombs. She could dismantle and reassemble three-, four-, six-, and eight-cylinder combustion engines and hotwire nearly any motor vehicle. And according to the flight simulator she'd worked like a dog at Mickey's Body Shop the previous summer to earn, she could land a Cirrus SR22 as well as she could take off. Her parents were enthusiastically supportive of her side passions for engines and aviation—anything that didn't risk burning the house to the ground—but it wasn't until she joined the army that her unconventional talents were truly appreciated.

Two years in, Sergeant Colt Brandon, Special Forces, recruited her to join his ops team, and from that moment forward, for the first time in twenty years, Kinsley felt something inside her click into alignment. Brandon had never cared about the whys of it all as long as she blew up what and who he wanted, how he wanted, when he wanted it.

And Kinsley was thrilled to oblige.

Little did she know at the time that her proclivity for danger, her obsession with explosives, and all that field experience would come so in handy after being abducted by aliens.

Abducted by aliens.

Of the many ways Kinsley had envisioned herself leaving Earth, an alien abduction had never been one of them. Exploding in an IED of her own making, sure. Exploding in an IED of someone else's making, absolutely, particularly during that last especially hairy mission in Yemen. Of old age, not as possible and not her preference, but certainly more likely than being *abducted by aliens.*

She and her fellow three dozen human captives had had the great misfortune of getting caught in what Kinsley suspected was some sort of intergalactic human trafficking ring. Who knew the Georgia stretch of the Appalachian Trail was so rife with danger? She'd survived fire fights in Afghanistan, for Heaven's sake, but hiking in the deep woods of North Georgia, *that's* what did her in. She'd fallen asleep, in peace if not complete comfort, snuggled in her tent, and woke up the next morning suffering from the worst hangover of her life.

From inside a cage.

It hadn't been a hangover. It hadn't been the next morning. And after being herded from one cage to another—from one *spaceship* to another—she didn't intend to allow herself to be trafficked for much longer.

Within a week on the second ship, Kinsley had discovered a convenient, if questionable, escape route from her prison cell: a network of ceiling shafts. Similar in form if not function to ventilation ducts, the shafts carried fire instead of air through the ship. A vent was positioned in the ceiling of each cell, including her own, the easier for the aliens to threaten execution by incineration and achieve their unwavering obedience.

The easier for Kinsley to escape from her cell when the shafts weren't in use and explore the ship.

Although perhaps "easy" was downplaying the near paralyzing fear she overcame with every escape. Even now, after fifteen weeks and nearly one hundred escapes, she still had to remind herself that the incineration shaft walls only *felt* like they were closing in. Her lungs weren't *actually* being crushed. She wasn't trapped, not this time, and considering the danger the shafts posed, she was more likely to fry like Riley than suffocate like Brandon.

Funny how that morsal of logic didn't comfort her throbbing heart.

But she did take comfort from the fact that fire vents were positioned above the infirmary, galley, training room, even the cockpit—identical to the ones in the brig. Someone had constructed this spaceship with the ability to deliberately incinerate *everyone* inside, the crew as well as their prisoners. Obviously, a thorough someone. A paranoid someone.

Kinsley's kind of someone.

A few loose screws here, another warning example there, and bam! Everyone *outside* the brig would be reduced to ash.

Kinsley smiled at the thought. Her Special Forces team hadn't dubbed her "Switch" for nothing.

Reel it in, girl. One phase of her plan at a time. Until she finished learning how to operate, pilot, and maintain the spacecraft, she wasn't instigating a mass incineration and commandeering the ship. Not on purpose, anyway.

Not yet.

Thus far, she'd mapped the aliens' ship, ascertained their military-like chain of command, and tracked their routines. The guards worked three shifts per twenty-five hours and rotated shifts every five days—if one could technically still track the passage of time in days without the sun. The aliens were on duty for one shift, trained for a second shift, and rested for a third, on repeat. But despite such a rigorous regimen, they were just people, and people weren't perfect. They skipped their guard assignments, allowing Kinsley the opportunity to escape. They chitchatted on duty, revealing insight into their personalities and rank dynamics. But best of all, they suffered injuries during training sessions, giving Kinsley a front-row seat to alien first aid, the drugs they sometimes administered to anesthetize patients during healing tube sessions, and the punch codes they used to access those medications from the dispensary.

Punch codes that worked just as well for Kinsley as they did for the aliens.

She still needed to better understand their culture and objectives to anticipate their movements, but today's mission was more hands-on than observational. During her previous escape to the cockpit, she'd determined that pressing all six blue buttons in the left quadrant of their instrument panel, lo and behold, steered the ship ninety degrees left. Today, she'd confirm if pressing all six blue buttons on

the right quadrant of their instrument panel steered the ship ninety degrees right.

Kinsley strained to hear past the metal walls, whirring engines, and air filtration systems to spy on the room below. The cockpit was quiet but not silent. Hisses and rattles of conversation and the *click clack* of claws on the control panel filled the room. By the dim glow of their instruments, Kinsley could just barely distinguish the two aliens from the darkness. They sat directly below her in pilot and copilot ergonomic swivel chairs, the shine of their opal scales highlighting the prominence of their bold features.

The pilot was a dirty blond, his long hair braided at the temples and away from his face. She'd seen it all now: reptiles with hair. Or perhaps they were mammals with scales, considering how disturbingly humanlike their faces and bodies were if one ignored the fact that both were covered in scales instead of skin. They had talons instead of fingernails, two thumbs on each hand, and a slithery, bifurcated tongue. Kinsley shook her head—no matter their taxonomy, she recognized the pilot by the lightning bolt-shaped scar through his bottom lip. He'd taken the blame for her resetting their autopilot systems last week. She didn't know his copilot—strawberry-blond hair and a less prominent browbone. He was missing one of the thumbs on his right hand. The opal scales around the missing appendage were gone as well, the exposed navy skin raw.

Like all the aliens, these guards were Conan the Barbarian–esque, complete with obscene muscles, claw necklaces, and, in the case of their uncompromising captain, a legit, bone-studded Conan headband. Unlike Conan's, their ears were pointy-tipped, their mouths contained retractable fangs, and inexplicably, their wrists glowed with a pulsing blue dot, not dissimilar from the pulsing blue buttons on their ship's control panel.

The possibility that the aliens weren't living people but androids was a popular theory among her cellmates who had yet to escape their prison.

The aliens' uniforms were stiff and gladiator-like, studded with metal accents and designed more for the holstering of weapons than for modesty. Just the two aliens currently piloting the ship carried over a dozen ice pick-like weapons of varying lengths and sizes strapped to their hips and what appeared to be—but probably wasn't —a two-foot decorative kaleidoscope slung across their backs.

By far, the aliens had Kinsley on height, weight, and weapons. She was no match for them physically, but the one advantage that Kinsley did have was a lifetime of blowing up people's expectations. Literally.

And a sports bra full of injectable sedatives stolen from their infirmary.

Two syringes in hand, Kinsley dropped from the incineration shaft. She landed on her feet, immediately twisted her left ankle— what she wouldn't give for sneakers!—and stabbed both aliens in the neck. The needles slid deftly and swiftly between the layers of their protective scales to the soft skin beneath. She hit the plungers, dodged back, and held her breath.

The pilot stiffened. He turned, but even as his head rotated toward Kinsley, his eyes were rolling back in his head.

The copilot only blinked. His expression never even wavered as he dropped headfirst onto the control panel. The pilot's collapse was only a second behind. He fell back, boneless, his ergonomic chair very helpfully cradling his limp, unconscious body.

Kinsley minced forward, stretched out a cautious hand, and shook the pilot's shoulder.

His head wobbled. He released a rumbling snore.

He remained unconscious.

Kinsley remembered how to breathe.

One day she might mis-aim and break the needle on their scales. One day they might spot and spear her before she could disable them. One day they might realize what she was doing, anticipate *her* movements, and catch her red-handed.

But one day was not today.

Kinsley tossed the used syringes up into the incineration shaft, then swiveled the aliens' unconscious bodies out of her way as she approached the instrument panel. The dozens of flashing buttons and shiny switches called to her. *Press me, and I'll take you home,* they said, and as much as she resented the aliens for uprooting her life, as much as she hated the unending blur of days and nights caged in darkness with the bleating complaints of her four cellmates (well, three now), this challenge—spying on her captors, learning their technology, commandeering their ship, and returning three dozen civilians home to Earth—was the greatest mission of her life. Maybe her *last* mission, but she would be successful. She had to be, or she'd never see Reece again.

Not making amends with her sister, more than anything else she'd suffered, was unacceptable.

Above the instrument panel was a huge wall-to-wall digital screen divided into monitoring segments. Some were simply exterior views of the ship and others were probably ship stats. Flight path, speed, and exterior and interior temperatures had been easy enough to decipher with some experimentation, but there were still symbols and screens and flashing dots she needed to demystify, including their defense systems, which sported what she suspected (*hoped*) was some sort of rocket launcher.

She focused on the exterior views of the ship: The coast was clear. No asteroids, space stations, or satellites in their way—nothing but wide-open space for experimenting.

Kinsley cracked her knuckles, took a deep breath, and pressed all six blue buttons in the control panel's right quadrant.

The ship began to turn right.

She reined in her enthusiasm, still waiting, and then outright fist pumped as the ship stabilized itself at ninety degrees and continued on its new trajectory. Success!

Mission complete.

The glowing buttons on the instrument panel continued pulsing at her.

Kinsley caressed her finger lightly over the orange button that she suspected controlled the cylindrical, bullet-tipped defense weapon. It was a rocket. It had to be. What else could it be? She hadn't fired a weapon, lit a fuse, or built a bomb in months. After everything that had gone wrong in Yemen, after her life had figuratively blown up in her face following the literal blowup, and then after *this* unforeseen catastrophe—*aliens* for God's sake! Who could have seen that one coming?—she needed a little joy in her life.

It probably wouldn't feel anything like pulling the trigger on a real rocket launcher, like the MATADOR. She wouldn't need to brace against the kickback. She wouldn't get to feel its power surge from her hands through her whole body as her target exploded.

Still, it was a button to press.

Its pulsing glow filled her whole vision. Her finger itched.

Oh, but she deserved to watch *something* explode!

She curled her fingers into a fist, resisting temptation, just as the power on the instrument panel and all the digital monitors cut to pitch black.

What the hell? I didn't touch it!

A rattling hiss spiked through the room.

Shit. She was made.

Think, think, think!

She could wait and let the alien make the first move. But he wasn't a T-Rex; his vision wasn't based on movement. In fact, with his nocturnal eyes, he had the advantage of sight.

She could fight, but even if she managed a miracle and overcame this one alien, she was one against fourteen outside the cockpit.

She could run, but would she reach the incineration shaft before he reached her?

Something moved.

Adrenaline jump-started her instincts. She lunged for the control panel and slammed both hands on the console, pressing random buttons simultaneously.

An alarm whooped over the intercom. The control panel and all its monitors sprang back to life. One of the monitors in particular, the one that controlled the rocket launcher, flashed a series of symbols. A countdown.

Maybe she'd get to blow up something after all.

Before she could get too giddy at the prospect, she whipped around. Yellow warning lights strobed through the room, illuminating an eight-foot-tall alien blocking the cockpit's open doorway.

A massive, rage-filled alien, if his snarling expression was anything to judge by. His glossy platinum hair cascaded down his back to his waist. The tips of his pointy ears poked through that perfect hair, and a few locks at his temples were braided into a bone-studded headpiece that encircled his head.

The Conan headband. Their uncompromising captain.

The thin circle of his blood-orange irises met hers. His pouty upper lip curled back on a rattling hiss, and Kinsley barely had enough time to think *I'm dead* before he dove for the control panel.

Kinsley shoved the unconscious pilot out of her way and leapt onto his chair.

The captain click-click-clicked several buttons with all eight of his claw fingers and four thumbs in a flurry of machine gun-style efficiency.

Kinsley jumped off the chair and caught the edge of the shaft's vent with her fingertips. Shit, she'd almost missed it.

The click clacks of his typing stopped. The alarms cut. The lights died.

Damn, he must type over 120 words a minute!

She pulled herself up, straining her biceps, triceps, and every little 'ceps in her fingers from knuckle to nail, and hooked her right knee into the shaft. She was going to make it. She—

Something gripped her left ankle.

No.

The alien yanked her from the incineration shaft, swung her through the air, and slammed her to the floor, square on her back.

Oof, there went her breath and elbow and maybe two ribs. One, if she was lucky.

She squinted up at the monitor that controlled the rocket launcher. It had frozen on a symbol, no longer flashing. No longer counting down.

No longer about to blow anything up.

"*Fuuuu*," Kinsley croaked. "Couldn't even leave me that one last little joy, huh?"

The alien pinned her under him, one hand at her thigh and the other on her opposite shoulder. Just two points of contact, and she was trapped. His strength was incredible. She kneed his kidney—well, the location where his kidney should be, assuming he had one—but he didn't flinch. He wasn't even winded. A glossy inner eyelid swept across his eyes, and for a moment that was his only movement as he glared at her, his gaze incendiary.

When he spoke, his long, thin, bifurcated tongue flicked out with each consonant of his rough but perfectly understandable English: "Who says the joy I give you will be little or your last?"

TWO

Raveno Hoviir didn't suffer incompetence. He didn't suffer anything without consequence, a policy his crew was testing time and again lately and without any perceivable sign of becoming more competent. His reputation, carefully cultivated over a long and brutal career, was usually incentive enough to inspire obedience. He couldn't let that reputation crack, not for anything: not for his morals as he punished decent soldiers for mistakes that didn't warrant such severity; not for his soul as he led abominable missions to maintain alliances with Bazail, Iroan, and Fray; not for his body as he'd gone to unmatched extremes to prove his loyalty to Cilvril s'Hvri Josairo.

He played the villain in service to his people, a role as necessary as it was revolting.

During Josairo's early reign as Cilvril s'Hvri, the killing hand of Havar, he'd been the strength and armor their planet had needed to survive what historians now referred to as the War of Wrath's Will. After bolstering their military forces and gaining the autonomy to wield them as he deemed necessary, Josairo achieved what four previous Cilvrili s'Hvri had died failing to accomplish: He'd secured

Havar's independence from her sister planet, Haven, and ended years of oppression and tyranny.

Or so the historians claimed and the schools taught. Based on Raveno's first-hand experience, he often wondered if Josairo hadn't simply murdered historians until he'd found one willing rewrite the war to his liking.

Nevertheless, however he'd managed to wrest unilateral control of their military and judicial systems, Josairo's unmatched combat skills ensured he kept it, even as he modified their fleet of luxury destination ships into prison transport vessels. Even as he ordered the abduction and trafficking of innocent, sentient people. Even as the peace and prosperity he'd supposedly achieved following their victory against Haven soured into fear-filled obedience. In earning their independence, the havari had traded a foreign tyrant for a domestic one, and every warrior brave enough to challenge Josairo to a frisaes and legally end his rule had thus far lost.

When Raveno ended his rule, it wouldn't be legal. But he would win.

Until then, the weight of Raveno's sins were his to bear or be crushed by. Which made confronting the horrific results of his own undercover operation insufferable, knowing his reputation would demand he deliver swift and harsh punishment when faced with his crew's greatest incompetence to date: a human outside her room and tampering with the equipment in their control room, of all places.

Dellao and Tironan were asleep in their seats, and the woman, cry mercy, the woman was fierce as only a mother could be, all snapping eyes and straining muscles. Some people withered from the poison of oppression, but not her. She seemed fueled by it. She gritted her square teeth with determination. Her soft cheeks flushed a deep crimson from her efforts, and her scent—Raveno sealed shut his nostrils, cutting short that disturbing thought before it could fully form.

"Who do you work for?" *Thev sa shek*, a traitor on board *Sa Vivsheth* was the last thing he needed.

Her jaw fell slack. "Y-y-you speak English?"

"Obviously." His English was rusty and not quite as good as his Mandarin, but still good enough for interrogation. "Who sent you?"

"I think we got off on the wrong foot." She licked her lips, and deep indents on the corners of her mouth dipped into her cheeks. "My name is Kinsley Morales, but my friends call me Switch."

He stared at her a moment. Had she just introduced herself? Didn't she realize she was being interrogated? To *death*, if she didn't cooperate.

Please, just cooperate.

"My mother named me after my paternal grandmother. An 'apology' name, I always said, because she'd named my sister in honor of *her* mother, which caused quite a stir on my father's side of the family. But everyone's ruffled feathers settled after she named me. The only time my presence had settled anyone's feathers." She ran out of air and inhaled a deep, trembling breath. "What's your name?"

Ah, he might have believed her composure if not for that tremble. She knew her predicament precisely and was attempting to save herself by appealing to his compassion.

The man he'd become to overthrow Josairo couldn't afford compassion. "Did my brother recruit you with the promise of freedom? What are your orders?"

The woman flinched. A pained whine escaped her clenched teeth.

Svik, was he hurting her? Raveno loosened his hold, just in case. It might come to that, but not now and certainly not by mistake.

Yet, even beaten down, in pain, and defeated, the gleam of calculation sharpened the woman's gaze.

Strong in mind if not in body, he thought warily, knowing the terrible efforts it took to break the strong of will. His own physical wound had long since healed, but the muscles of his residual limb often pained him as if his left calf still remained, twisted foot and all.

"Must I repeat the question?" he asked. If not Tironan, *someone* on board had released her.

The furry tuft above her right eye lifted. "How should I know if I know your brother if I don't even know *you*?"

Ha! Fine. He spoke his full name and rank for her in traditional Hvrsil, just for the pleasure of matching her obstinacy with his.

"I...I'm not sure I can pronounce that," she admitted.

"Considering the deficiencies in the form and function of your tongue, I expect not."

She narrowed her eyes, clearly unsure if she should be insulted. "Do you have a nickname too? Something less, er, taxing on the vocal cords?"

"No."

"What do your friends call you?" she tried.

"I have no friends."

"Something I can call you while I beg for mercy, then," she snapped.

A laugh overtook him at that, as swift, unwanted, and jarring as a seizure. Oh, this woman was a little firework: all sparks and fierce light wedging lethally beneath his scales.

"When you beg for mercy, you may call me by the modern Haveo version of my name," he relented. "Raveno Hoviir."

"A pleasure to meet you, Raveno Hoviir."

He was certain it wasn't. "I warn you now: Beg all you want, but only information—truthful, valuable information—will earn you that mercy."

If he wasn't mistaken, her heart physically skipped a beat as she nodded.

"Who unlocked your room?" he asked.

"No one. I escaped on my own."

He tilted his head. "You escaped from your guarded room with its locked door on your own."

"Yes."

"Are you—how would you say it?—a Houdinian?"

She blinked. "A what?"

"A man of magic."

"Um. No. I escaped through the incineration shaft."

Raveno blinked. "The what?"

"The network of ceiling shafts that ventilate fire."

Ah, *thev sa shek.* The heating ducts. One of the many questionable modifications Josairo had commissioned for their fleet of luxury destination ships.

He must have misheard her. "You do not refer to *that* ceiling shaft."

Her eyes darted to the heating duct in question. "Yes, I refer to that ceiling shaft."

Raveno reared back. "Did you not witness the public execution?"

"How could I miss it?" Her cheeks darkened. "Riley was my cellmate."

"And you thought it wise to crawl through those same heating ducts that killed your fellow human?"

"Heating ducts?" She laughed bitterly. "They do significantly more than just heat."

He released a low hiss, willing her to squirm, but her expression remained earnest. Like all humans, the woman's fleshy exterior—skin, they called it—was disturbingly vulnerable. The most miniscule change in temperature burned it. Even their planet's sun could burn it. Stab it anywhere, and it bled. Burn it long enough, it blistered, *then* bled, so he hadn't considered Josairo's heating ducts a liability other than to his sanity.

He should have known. Everything Josairo's hand touched eventually pierced between his scales.

Who in their right mind would willingly crawl into such a space knowing that with a flick of a claw, whether by accident or deliberate intent, their body would disintegrate?

"Are you brave or insane?" he heard himself ask before he'd even formed the thought.

"Desperate," she muttered.

Raveno shook his head. "For what purpose did you leave your room?"

Her lips flattened: against the truth, against the pain of his hold, against betrayal? "To spy on your crew, devise a means to kill them—and you—commandeer the ship, and return home to Earth."

Another laugh overtook him, more forceful than the first. Oh, but he couldn't afford to like her. Not her fire and not her bravado. Not any of her.

He could only afford to follow through on his word.

"Only truthful, valuable information, remember?" Raveno flared the spines of his vresls and bared his fangs.

Her eyes dropped to his chest and widened. "Not a claw necklace, then."

Necklace? "Is Tironan working directly with your government or only with you?" Raveno tightened his grip, hoping to reestablish focus. "Did he—"

Something inside her shoulder popped. A wet crunch, and her eyes rolled back into her head on a high, keening shriek.

Svik! What kind of bones and ligaments separated from such little pressure?

She could be someone's killing hand, he reminded himself. She could be *Tironan's* killing hand, and if that was the case, she could have the power to unmask him and unravel the entire operation he'd sacrificed so much, to complete.

"Look at me," he spat. "Look at me, or I will break your other shoulder to match the first." His stomach curdled at the thought. *Just look at me!*

Her eyes squinted open, and she glared at him through pain-fogged slits.

"I have the technology on board to heal you. Convince me to use it."

Her breathing was heavy now, not just trembling, and her skin had become sticky with moisture. Clammy, her people would say.

Not indications of good health in her species.

"I don't know Tir-Tiro—man?" she panted. "And I don't know your brother either."

Raveno tightened his grip, more carefully than before, but enough that her body spasmed with pain and panic.

"But, but," she added quickly, "the alien who recruited me did promise my freedom."

Ah. Perhaps Tironan hadn't revealed his name or their relationship. Or perhaps his traitor wasn't Tironan. Or perhaps the woman was simply telling him what she thought he'd want to hear.

Traitors did seem to abound ever since he'd become one.

"What are your orders?"

"My orders. Um. My orders are to...to cause chaos on this ship. To make you and your crew look incompetent."

And she was doing a stellar job of it. Raveno shook his head. "Are you loyal to the man who recruited you, or is freedom your true motivation?"

The woman jerked her head up and down but didn't speak.

"Which is it? You must speak your truth."

"My only motivation is to gain my freedom," she rasped.

"The man who recruited you. What is his name?"

"He...he didn't give me a name."

Of course not. "Describe him."

"Er, well, he's tall. Scaly. Muscular. Sharp claws. Lethal fangs. Prominent chin and cheekbones."

"Those are common characteristics of all male havari and everyone on this ship," Raveno said dryly. "You could be describing me."

She shook her head, and the jaw-length strands of hair framing her face slapped her wet cheeks. "If I were describing you, I'd mention the headband."

Headband? "What color was his hair?"

Again, that shaking head. A lock of her wild hair stuck to her cheek. "It was too dark for me to see him clearly."

Raveno tore his focus from that defiant lock of hair. "Are you saying you know nothing? That you are useless beyond causing me grief?"

Those square blunt teeth sank into her bottom lip. "I would recognize his face. If I saw him again."

If only that were true! She was in pain and terrified and would likely say or do anything to gain his favor, but if she really did know who was betraying him and could truly identify him... "I am inclined to heal you."

The woman stared at him. Her breathing was becoming increasingly labored.

"You will continue the pretense of serving him, but in doing so, you will report his orders and objectives back to me. You are *my* killing hand now."

"Killing hand? You expect me to *kill* for you?"

"It is an expression. Akin to your *right-hand man*, but on Havar, handedness and gender do not qualify one for the job. Only intent. You will do my bidding, whatever that bidding is, with precise, end-all, unthinking intent."

She exhaled a shaky breath. "And in exchange, *you'll* promise my freedom?"

Raveno leaned in close, careful of his grip and very careful of his teeth. "In exchange, I promise to let you live."

Her throat swelled and contracted as she swallowed.

Raveno glanced down, momentarily distracted by the movement. That lock of stubborn hair was still affixed to her cheek. Unthinking, he inhaled.

Oh. Ecstasy.

"Got it," she rasped.

Raveno snapped his eyes up to meet hers, his ears burning. By will alone, he would cease scenting her! "If I find you lying to me, now or ever, I will—"

She made a gurgled, choking sound in the back of her throat. Her eyes rolled.

His gut twisted. "Calm yourself!"

"Or what? You'll pop my arm off entirely and beat me to death with it?"

"Not to death." He forced a grin. "Just until you confide the truth."

She huffed, and the fringe of short hair over her forehead fluttered.

"Are we agreed, then? You are now *my* killing hand?"

"I'll be whatever hand you want me to be, just *please* pop my shoulder back into its socket. It's killing me." A pause and then she added, "Figuratively. Don't want to lose a limb over a little exaggeration."

"No, we certainly do not want that. If I dismember you, I too would want the punishment to fit the crime."

She widened her lips, and the indents on either side of her mouth deepened. "Glad we agree on *something*."

Raveno had accepted long ago that he'd need to become a worse monster than Josairo to overthrow him, but such sacrifices didn't prevent his heart from aching. He wondered if Josairo suffered the same pangs of conscience. If perhaps he too had convinced himself that the atrocities he committed were for some greater good.

He hoped not, because if not their intent, what truly separated him from his father?

THREE

Kinsley curled on her side, trying to ignore the sheep she was caged with—*her* sheep, she reminded herself. But the reminder was more burden than comfort as the inanity of their conversation progressed.

"How'd your mission go?" Benjamin asked.

"She returned alive, didn't she?" Despite his gruff tone, Martin's hand was gentle on her forearm. "It went well enough."

Leanne sniffed. "She doesn't look 'well.'"

"We've been caged in here for months." Martin scratched at the rough underside of his beard. "None of us are 'well.'"

Benjamin smoothed his hands over the furry blanket he wore like a robe over his shoulders. "Considering the luxury of our accommodations, it could be worse."

"We were kidnapped by aliens and are being trafficked across the universe to who knows where or how far from Earth for God knows what purpose," Martin said flatly. "How much worse could it get?"

"It hasn't been months, has it?" Leanne asked.

By the dim glow of the hallway baseboard lighting outside their cell, Kinsley could just decipher the outline of their bodies. Leanne, resplendent in a purple lace teddy, slumped on the velvety cream chaise longue, her twig arms locked around her knobby knees. Despite the wide, unused cushion to his left, Benjamin sat hip to hip with her. His glasses reflected a little of the hallway light, illuminating the straggles of his face's attempt at facial hair. Martin sat beside Kinsley in black boxer briefs, his muscles occupying nearly as much square footage as Benjamin and Leanne combined. If not for Kinsley, he probably would have propped his back against the soft mattress pillows instead of the hard box spring, but Kinsley preferred to rest on the reality of the cold, uncompromising floor rather than the bed.

This wasn't a hotel suite. It was a cage.

No matter the couch and its cushions, the furry blankets, the soft mattress with its even softer pillows; no matter the opulence of their spa-like bathroom with its many not-so-mini shower gels and body scents; no matter the impressive technology of their adjoining personal gym, complete with digitally adjustable dumbbells, a treadmill sleekly imbedded in the floor, and what resembled but couldn't be a Wing Chun dummy for combat training—the "luxury" of their "accommodations" was behind a door that locked from the outside.

Kinsley shivered.

Martin leaned in. "If you're cold, I could—"

She pulled her arm away and out of reach. "I'm fine."

Martin stiffened, but really, what was the point of becoming familiar—or heaven forbid, *reliant*—on someone who could lose his sense one day, ask for more rations, and be gone the next?

"It has been..." Benjamin paused to consult the time and date on his mechanical watch. Everyone else's smart watches, cell phones, and various electronics had died after two days, but not Benjamin's stupid watch, as they were reminded of every morning for the last "One hundred and thirteen days. So, sixteen weeks and one day, which makes it..."

"About four months, Einstein," Martin grumped.

"It *has* been months." Benjamin confirmed, as if anyone besides Leanne needed confirmation of this.

"But not so many months that it's almost years," Leanne said, sounding bafflingly reassured by this concept. "We can still count it in weeks and it not be ridiculous."

Benjamin cocked his head speculatively. "How can a measurement of time be ridiculous?"

This conversation is ridiculous, Kinsley thought.

"This conversation is ridiculous," Martin muttered out loud.

Kinsley smirked. Maybe the aliens were experimenting and had somehow managed to meld Martin's brain with hers.

Leanne only ever heard what she wanted to hear—in this case, Benjamin's interest—and blundered on. "When the number of weeks no longer makes sense, it becomes ridiculous unless we convert it up to months."

"Hmmm." Benjamin gave her rambling serious, philosophical consideration. "That's an interesting supposition: a person's immediate understanding of a number's value giving that number relevance. I think—"

"Oh, here he goes, thinking again," Martin moaned.

"I'm serious. She—"

"We know you are." Martin rubbed his eyes. "Whatever you're about to say, don't, and leave the rest of us to rot in peace and quiet."

A pause, and then, surprisingly enough, Leanne was the one who spoke up. "I like Benjamin's thinking."

Another pause. "You do?"

Kinsley choked back a sigh. Oh, Benjamin. So hopeful.

A longer pause. "Well, I don't like the quiet," Leanne admitted.

Martin chuckled. "Not the same thing. Sorry, Romeo."

"I didn't—"

"We're not—"

Something heavy pounded against the clear viewing pane of their cell.

Everyone, even Leanne, froze. Waiting. Praying.

A guard was watching them. They couldn't hear anything outside the cell through the soundproof viewing panels, but who knew if the guard could hear them? His wide, reflective pupils flicked from Benjamin to Leanne to Martin to Kinsley and back to Benjamin.

Kinsley tried to remain calm, but Riley's execution was still too present. The moment rushed back, identical to now, just before the door had slid opened and a scaly hand had reached in, then dragged Riley out. Then and now, her thoughts screamed in pounding sync with her racing heart: *Don't let it be me. Don't let it be me.*

Don't let them take me.

The hatch at the bottom of the door lifted, and a food platter heaped with unidentifiable plants and meat slid across the floor.

Benjamin, Leanne, and Martin converged on the platter.

Kinsley slumped for a boneless moment and remembered how to breathe.

Someone squeezed her shoulder.

She peeked up.

Martin was dangling a grilled wing the size of her head above her face.

"Do you need me to force-feed it to you?"

Kinsley wrinkled her nose.

"Fine, pass on the grilled ostrich, but at least have some of those blue beans you like." He gestured to the food platter with the giant wing. "You need the protein."

"Too late." Leanne scooped up the final helping of the blue whatever they were.

Martin shook his head, annoyed, and forced the wing into Kinsley's hand. "Choke it down, or I'll ask them for more rations."

Kinsley sat up on a wince. "You would not."

"Eat or find out."

The bird—whatever its actual species—was already dead. Martin was still alive, and although she doubted he was dumb or crazy enough to repeat Riley's mistake, she wasn't willing to risk his life over it.

And she *was* hungry.

Kinsley screwed her eyes closed and took a bite.

Her mouth flooded. Her tongue sang. Her stomach rejoiced.

She swallowed, and the poor bird nosedived into her gut.

"The aliens must have a higher purpose for us." Benjamin mumbled, his mouth full. "Why else would they keep us in such comfort and feed us so well?"

Kinsley snorted. "Farmers feed livestock well too, before the slaughter."

Leanne dropped her wing. "Are you implying the aliens are going to eat us?"

"No." *Maybe.* "I'm implying that food and luxury are just illusions to lull us into complacency. Whatever purpose they have for us is nothing to get optimistic about."

Benjamin finished his ostrich. "It's not just the food. They clean the room. They wash your clothes. They..."

Kinsley bit back a laugh at that. It still amazed her that of the five of them, Riley included, she'd been the only one wearing actual clothes during their abduction. Who camped on the Appalachian trail in nothing but a purple teddy or boxers?

"...and the bathroom is pristine."

Martin elbowed her side. "The bathroom *is* admittedly better than the one in my shit apartment on Earth."

"I'd trade the seven options of scented body soap for my freedom, thank you very much," Kinsley muttered.

"And they provide you and all the women with, er..."

Kinsley tilted her head and waited to see how he'd spit that one out.

"Sanitary napkins. And—"

"Oh, yeah, they're running a five-star establishment here."

"I'm just saying, it stands to reason that if they care about our health and comfort, maybe their purpose for us isn't as horrendous as we keep imagining."

"I wasn't certain of God's 'purpose' for me on Earth," Kinsley said. "I'm certainly not on board with whatever the aliens have planned for me across the galaxy."

"Amen to that," Martin chimed in.

"In any case, I felt the ship turn ninety degrees. Just like you said it would," Benjamin said, tossing his polished bone on the carcass platter. "So *that's* something to be optimistic about, right?"

Leanne leaned back, licking her fingers. "But I felt the ship turn back on course. We're still not headed home."

"I didn't expect to fool the aliens into navigating us back to Earth." Kinsley forced down another morsel of wing. "The purpose of yesterday's mission was to experiment with the control panel. Which I did."

Leanne raised an eyebrow. "Did you figure out the purpose of that glowing blue dot under their scales?"

Kinsley kept chewing. "Nope."

"I maintain they might be androids," Benjamin said, as if anyone wanted to hear his opinion.

"They bathe and eat and bleed and breathe," Kinsley reminded him. Again. "They're not androids."

"But if they were, we could unplug them, destroy their charging stations, or remove their batteries. We could—"

"*But they're not.*"

Leanne set her polished bone back on the platter. "Did you figure out how to unlock the cell doors?"

Kinsley gritted her teeth. "No."

"Did you—"

"I turned the ship ninety degrees right, Leanne. That was the purpose of my mission, and that's what I did."

Leanne compressed her lips into a thin, quivering line.

"What have *you* figured out lately?" Martin interrupted. "Besides new and inventive ways to complain."

Benjamin straightened. "Hey now, that's not necessary."

Martin chopped his hand through the air. "We should be grateful that Switch is willing to..."

Kinsley finished her wing, tossed the bone onto the platter along with the rest of the mutilated bird's carcass, and curled back into her fetal position. Let them argue. What else would pass the time? They craved healthy mental stimulation, some medium between boredom and terror, so let the three of them debate her missions as if she was the lead in their new (only) TV show.

What was Kinsley's next mission? Would she fail or succeed? Would she be captured, tortured, and die, or would she single-hand-edly kill all the scaly aliens, fly their spacecraft back to Earth, and save her fellow captives from a fate worse than death? Tune in next week for another episode of *Game of Galaxies*.

"She might not look well, but the mission *was* successful," Benjamin insisted. "Right, Switch?"

How to define success? Was getting caught and agreeing to spy on a traitor who didn't exist a success? Were a dislocated shoulder, two broken ribs, a fractured collarbone, a cracked scapula, and four ripped fingernails—all rapidly repaired via magic healing tube—a success?

Was simply surviving a success?

Kinsley closed her eyes, but the thin, glowing ring of Raveno's blood-orange irises stared back in her mind. She could still see his talon-tipped, rattling chest flap that wasn't a necklace at all—*it moved* —and hear his hissing, bifurcated tongue demanding the truth, but believing only lies.

But hey, she'd steered the ship, as intended.

"You felt right," Kinsley murmured. "The ship did turn ninety degrees."

"What happened?" Martin asked gravely.

"I told you: I pressed all six blue buttons in the right quadrant of their instrument panel. We have official confirmation on navigating the ship in lateral directionality."

"I mean what happened to *you*. Usually, you return on a mission high, all suppressed excitement and adrenaline. This time, you, well..." Martin eyed her like one might an overripe fruit.

"This time you look sick," Leanne leaned back, as if whatever Kinsley had might be contagious.

"I'm fine."

Benjamin frowned. "You don't look fine."

Kinsley shrugged. "We've been caged in here for months. None of us are really fine. Right, Martin?"

Martin, who had just said nearly the same thing not five minutes ago, grunted. "You look worse."

Typical. "Well, I'm as fine as I'm going to get. Listen, I learned something else today that might affect how we conduct our missions going forward."

Leanne scrubbed both hands over her face. "Oh God, what now?"

"I discovered that, as unlikely as it might seem, we aren't the only people on this ship who speak English. At least one alien does too."

A beat passed in silence..

Leanne dropped her hands and glanced at Benjamin.

Martin leaned in. "Did you hit your head during this last mission?"

"I did, but— Stop that." Kinsley batted away Martin's probing fingers. "One of the aliens spoke to me."

Martin studied her for a long moment. "An alien *spoke* to you."

"Yes, and he spoke English. He caught me right after I'd steered the ship, and—"

"You were caught?"

Leanne slapped a hand over her mouth.

Benjamin looped an arm around Leanne's shoulders, as if *she'd* been caught and needed comforting.

Not that Kinsley needed comforting.

Kinsley rubbed the back of her neck. Raveno had healed her, so why did her left scapula suddenly still ache? "He offered me an ulti-matum. In exchange for not killing me, I agreed to be his"—*Killing hand* sounded a bit too ominous—"spy."

Leanne made a squeaking noise from behind her hands.

Benjamin leaned forward, ignoring Leanne for once in favor of logic. "His *spy*?"

"Keep it down," Kinsley shushed. "We don't know how many others also speak English. We need to play this close to the vest which means no more loose lips from you three. Covert missions need to remain *covert*."

"What does all this even mean?" Leanne was rocking slightly, side to side, as if her entire body, not just her mind, was in denial.

"It means that we need to be more careful about what we say and how we say it," Kinsley explained. "Like when I leave on a mission, maybe I'm 'grocery shopping' instead of, you know, what I'm really doing."

"You want us to talk in code?" Benjamin asked, clearly excited by the prospect.

Leanne stopped rocking. "What?"

"We could talk freely when we thought no one could understand us," Martin said, quick on the uptake, as usual. "But if one alien speaks English, then we can assume that a few more do too. And if any of the English-speaking aliens overhear our conversations, we wouldn't want to compromise Switch when she goes...*grocery shopping*."

Silence, and then Leanne turned to Benjamin.

"When they say grocery shopping, they mean *her missions*," Benjamin whispered.

"I'm not an idiot. I understand the concept of and logic behind speaking in code." Leanne ducked out from Benjamin's arm, and he physically deflated. "But we've been talking about *grocery shopping* for months, and only *now* we're worried about giving the aliens a heads-up?"

"Obviously not *all* the aliens speak English, or I'd already be dead," Kinsley said darkly.

Martin reached out, slowly this time—probably anticipating another rejection—but when his hand found Kinsley's, she let their fingers interlock.

"We can't be the only captives talking about returning to Earth," Leanne reasoned. "Maybe *all* the aliens speak English, and they don't care what we talk about. It's just talk, and they don't see us as a threat."

"Maybe," Kinsley conceded, "but the one I spoke to definitely cares."

Ignoring Leanne and Benjamin, Martin shifted the full force of his disapproval on Kinsley. "I thought you were being careful."

"I was," Kinsley said, taken aback by the vehemence in his tone. "I mean, I *am*."

"Agreeing to spy for one of the aliens who abducted us doesn't sound like being careful to me."

"The alien wasn't exactly in the mood to negotiate," Kinsley snapped. "It was either agree to spy or die. I didn't have much of a choice."

"The—" He hesitated, thinking. "*Candy* you found works like a charm. Why didn't you—"

"I'd already used both *candies* on the pilot and copilot." Kinsley slumped back against the box spring to glower at the ceiling. "It's not as if I *wanted* to get caught."

"Losing Riley was...and watching his body as they..." Martin coughed, clearing his throat.

"I know," Kinsley whispered. She closed her eyes, but the darkness behind her lids was nearly as complete as the darkness of the room and couldn't ease the recollection of those memories.

"Can we not talk about this?" Leanne said hoarsely, her voice thick with tears.

Martin's thumb stroked across Kinsley's knuckles. "I can't lose you too."

Was her pounding heart as deafening to everyone else as it was to her in the silence?

Kinsley tried to pull away from Martin, but this time, he held on tight. "What were the terms of your *grocery list* with the alien?"

Kinsley straightened on a long exhale, feeling bruised. "He wants me to identify a traitor on his ship."

"A traitor?"

"Yep. You know, the alien I've been working with who promised me freedom in exchange for running his missions."

Benjamin scratched the scruff on his cheek. "But you haven't—"

Kinsley kicked his shin.

"Ouch!"

"In exchange for *my life*," Kinsley said, "I'm more than happy to point a finger at whoever he wants identified."

Martin raised his eyebrows. "That's a dangerous game."

"Someone has to play."

For a long moment, there was no bickering or complaining. Nothing but breathing in the darkness.

"When we get back to Earth," Martin whispered, "the first round is on me."

When, he said. Even cynical, gruff, no-nonsense Martin thought in terms of *when*, not *if*. Only one other person in her entire life had had that kind of confidence in her abilities.

Kinsley slipped her hand away, and Martin, having allowed his grip to loosen, couldn't stop her.

"When we get back to Earth, I'm booking a spa treatment," Leanne murmured, her voice soft. Dreamy. "Mani, pedi, facial, massage: the works."

"After our celebratory round, I'm grilling up a steak," Martin added. "Outdoor barbecue on a sunny day, a cold Yuengling in hand. Hell, in both hands." Kinsley felt the weight of his regard. "What do you want me to grill up for you?"

"A burger," Benjamin answered, "with bacon and fried onion rings and mushrooms and swiss cheese and barbecue sauce."

Leanne groaned, wrapping her hands around her stomach. "I'll book a hair appointment too. Cut and color, *and* a deep conditioning treatment."

"We'll finally get to see how *Game of Thrones* ends," Martin added.

"I already know who ends up on the throne," Benjamin said, a smile in his voice. "Tyrion is too smart to die."

"He might not die, but that doesn't mean he'll end up on the throne," Leanne pointed out.

"'When you play the game of thrones, you win or you die,'" Martin reminded her. "But he's wrong. Jon Snow is the hero of the story. He ends up on the throne."

"In your dreams," Kinsley said. "Daenerys is the hero of the story. She's fire-resistant and has three dragons."

"Two, now," Benjamin countered.

"And great hair," Kinsley added.

Benjamin laughed. "What does that have to do with anything?"

Leanne sighed wistfully. "Great hair is everything."

They fell into silence again.

Martin searched for Kinsley's hand, found her knee instead, and settled for that with a squeeze. "Thank you for grocery shopping for us. We're all hungry, and you're the only one with enough money to buy what we need. So, thank you."

"I'm hungry too," Kinsley whispered through the sudden constriction in her throat.

"I know. Believe me, I know."

"How can either of you be hungry?" Leanne asked. "We just ate, and they feed us constantly."

Kinsley covered her face with her hands, holding back the insane urge to simultaneously laugh and cry.

Benjamin sighed. "I miss the first aliens. The ones with all the fur."

"We're aware of which aliens you're referring to, Einstein," Martin grumbled. "They were just as bad."

"Not nearly. They were gentle and kind, and they seemed like they—"

"They abducted us," Martin said, his voice gone flat and cold.

"They took us from our home without permission and caged us against our will. It doesn't matter what they *seemed*."

Kinsley dropped her hands to her lap and nodded. "It's better this way. Their cruelty will make it easier to k—" She coughed. "To go through checkout. At the grocery store."

Martin stroked a gentle thumb over her kneecap, and that was it. Tears sprouted.

Kinsley jerked her knee away from his hand. Martin sat back, and after a long stretch of silence, he stood and walked into their adjoining gym to begin a workout, taking his warmth and comfort with him.

FOUR

RAVENO SLOUCHED AT THE CONTROL PANEL IN HIS PRIVATE office, worrying the seam between his calf and prosthetic foot. According to the security footage he'd just spent a mind-numbing shift sifting through, Kinsley "Switch" Morales had been escaping her room and exploring *Sa Vivsheth* through the heating ducts for nearly their entire journey from Earth.

Apparently, not one of his crew—neither the guards in person nor the ones monitoring the security footage—had noticed.

Raveno flexed his vresls to keep them from rattling even as the irony of it nearly made him laugh aloud: the very modification Josairo had made on *Sa Vivsheth* to maintain control of its unwilling passengers was the instrument of her escape.

Raveno curled his middle finger toward his wrist, slipping a long claw between his scales to activate his glowing *anku*. "Vri Cilvril Raveno Hoviir to Fyvril Zethus Rysheer," he muttered. Svik, even his voice sounded unnerved. "Do you receive?"

A moment passed, then Zethus's voice echoed from the implant in his ear: "Fyvril Zethus Rysheer here. Signal received. Proceed."

39

"How are the humans' missing persons investigations proceeding on Earth?"

"Not well," Zethus said cheerily. "Without any new leads, their law enforcement is prioritizing other cases over ours. Some of their relatives are upset. One sister in particular is more vocal than the others, but despite her efforts, I believe they will cease investigating soon."

Raveno straightened. "Truly? Without even a chance of retaliation?"

"Correct. They suspect 'foul play,' as they call it, but believe one of their own is responsible. The possibility of an animal attack has been mentioned. Should they eventually suspect us, which is unlikely, the humans lack the technology necessary to pursue *Sa Vivsheth* through deep space."

"Good. I require intelligence on one of our female passengers, but I didn't want to risk attracting attention to your presence."

"Risk is minimal. Their technology is ancient, but I've managed to breach their cyber defense systems. Her name and description?"

"Kinsley Morales. Choppy, wild brown hair. Intense eyes. Dark, like..." He shook his head. "Short in height. Although for a human, she's rather tall, I suppose."

"What information do you need on her? Anything specific?"

"Her occupation, skill sets, connections, and off-world communications, if any. Family and friends, and their potential off-world communications." He hesitated, then added, "Children and their ages." *Svik, how she must miss them.*

Like a losing a limb, he imagined.

"And their potential off-world communications?"

His heart throbbed. "Yes."

"Your will by my hands. Anything else?"

Raveno rubbed a little deeper at his calf. "Research the details of human reproduction, both their biology and their...customs."

Silence.

"We don't want them breeding, do we?" Raveno added, then

cringed. He was Vri Cilvril. He didn't need to justify anything he did or ordered.

"What is the nature of your acquaintance with this Kinsley Morales?" Zethus asked. "Are you—"

"Just—" Something stung his residual limb, and Raveno realized it was his own claw. He removed his hand from the proximity of his calf and gripped the chair's arm before he did something impulsive and regrettable. Again. "Do you receive or not?"

A beat of silence. Then: "Yes. Orders received, but—"

"Good. Signal terminated." Raveno removed his claw from his anku, cutting the connection.

"What's with your sudden obsession with my old cellmate?" The human—Riley, Raveno reminded himself—asked from within his room. "Gonna add stalking next to human trafficking and attempted murder to your rap sheet?"

"I can remove the *attempted* from that last one, if you'd like," Raveno said over his shoulder, but the jab was halfhearted at best. "Silence yourself, or I will mute your room."

"Cage," Riley spat.

Raveno ignored him, and as he rewatched the footage in fast-forward, he was once again distracted by his crew's utter incompetence.

By will or wrath, how difficult was it to guard people in locked rooms with floor-to-ceiling viewing walls! Apparently impossible, because Kinsley managed to escape time and time again undetected. In the beginning, she'd escaped from her room during second shift. She'd switched to third shift after several *shaoz*, then to first for a while, and eventually, she'd resumed escaping during second shift.

Why change what worked? To remain unpredictable? But even her changes were predictable. Every five shaoz, she adjusted the time of her escape.

Every five shaoz.

Raveno hissed between his teeth. She was changing her escape pattern in sync with his guard schedule.

The glowing anku within his wrist vibrated. "T-T-Tironan to Vri C-C-Cilvril. Do you receive?"

His brother's voice echoed from the audio implant this time. Wonderful.

Raveno curled his middle claw down into the receiver. "Signal received. Proceed," he said, skimming through the footage *again*, but this time, cross-checking Kinsley's movements with the guard log.

"I s-s-sent you an updated pharmacy report. Did you r-r-review it?"

Thev sa shek! Raveno rechecked the time stamps against the shift schedule, but even with as much power as he'd amassed as Vri Cilvril, he couldn't change reality. All of Kinsley's escapes without fail coincided with Jhoni Nassio's guard shifts in the *shols* wing.

Raveno let his head fall limp against the chair back. Of his entire crew, he never would have suspected Jhoni as his betrayer. Not young, naïve, hero-worshipping Jhoni.

The best quality of a betrayer, he supposed: guilelessness.

"Vri C-C-Cilvril? Do you receive?"

Raveno startled. Ah, Tironan. "I will review whatever you have to report during our next scheduled meeting," he told the ceiling. "Did you save it in the appropriate log this time?"

"I sent it to you directly. It's u-u-urgent."

"Save it appropriately, and I will review it during our next meeting. Signal terminated."

"B-b-but—"

Raveno removed his claw from his anku, lifted both hands over his face, and dug the heels of his palms into his eyes, keeping his claws well out of range.

"It's the hard-knock life, being king of your kingdom, isn't it?" Riley taunted between his endless sitting-ups. "The stress of running an intergalactic crime organization must be overwhelming."

Raveno choked back a laugh. He imagined that in different circumstances, in another life, in a parallel reality, he and Riley would be friends.

A life in which Raveno could enjoy the luxury of friendship.

Raveno considered the possibility that Jhoni had truly turned against him. However unlikely his betrayal seemed, security footage didn't lie. Jhoni was abandoning his guard shift, affording Kinsley the opportunity to escape. She returned just before Jhoni, and he returned just before his relief arrived. The two of them, working together like synchronized clockwork.

But even if Jhoni was his traitor, why risk discovery by physically leaving his post? Where did he go while Kinsley was crawling through the heating ducts?

Raveno sat up and glared at the security footage with the full force of his disapproval.

To compound question upon question, as much as he searched through the footage, he couldn't find a moment—not *one*—in which Kinsley conversed with any of his guards, not even Jhoni. She only ever spoke to her fellow humans, and even to them, she listened more than she spoke. What he wouldn't give for a security system with audio transmission! Of all the times for Josairo to show frugality while modifying *Sa Vivsheth*. Nevertheless, even with only the visual footage, he should have been able to spot Kinsley making her deal as well as reporting back to him, accepting new assignments, and providing mission updates.

The footage must have been tampered with.

Or Kinsley was lying. She'd been recruited for this mission while still on Earth and deliberately abducted by the Lorien to infiltrate his ship via the trade that Tironan had commissioned. And now she was implementing the orders she'd been given long before boarding *Sa Vivsheth*.

Raveno leaned his elbows on the desk and cradled his head in his hands. If the Lorien, Tironan, Kinsley, and Jhoni were *all* against him, he'd have to take swift and drastic action to stop this coup before it endangered his position to overthrow Josairo.

When did I so thoroughly lose control of this mission?

A shuffle. A slide. A small grunt followed by two more slides.

Raveno glared through the bars of his fingers at the ceiling.

Of course Kinsley was currently crawling through the heating duct above him. He skimmed the guard log. Right on schedule.

His vresls quivered.

Raveno cut the security footage, stood, and strode toward the exit.

"Off to incinerate more innocent captives?" Riley asked. He'd stood and was leaning, arms crossed, against the clear viewing pane of his room. His upper lip was curled back—his usual expression—but his fists were trembling.

"Off to do what I do best." Raveno left the confines of his private office. Even as the door slid and sealed shut behind him, he could hear Riley's fist striking the viewing wall.

In different circumstances, in another life, in a parallel reality...

Raveno slipped from the hidden passage, closed and locked the closet behind him, and exited his cabin at a brisk clip.

With his first step into the hallway, Raveno physically plowed into Tironan, hovering outside his door.

His brother grunted, falling back a step.

Raveno straightened his uniform with an impatient tug. "Tironan."

"My apologies, R-R-R—" Tironan shook his head. "Vri C-C-Cilvril." He clicked his heels together in formal greeting. "I was j-j-j—" He took a deep breath. "This couldn't w-wait for our next meeting."

Raveno forced a glare, and the tips of Tironan's ears flashed a bright blue.

Their mother had always blushed easily as well. Raveno used to have the same tell, but he'd worked diligently to break it. Tironan, on the other hand, could work as diligently as he wanted. His efforts were wasted. The only personal attribute that Tironan seemed capable of strengthening was his brain. No matter how intensely Raveno trained him, Tironan's muscles remained all slim sinew. No matter how persistently Raveno drilled him on calming techniques, Tironan still blushed and stuttered and, in extreme circumstances, suffered from air deficiency. And no matter how fervently Raveno insisted he care more precisely for his hair and appearance... Raveno fisted his hand against the urge to straighten Tironan's circlet.

Raveno had come to terms with his mother's sage advice a long time ago: He'd need to be brute enough for both of them to survive their father. Which was just as well since Tironan had brains enough for both of them.

Just no common sense.

"D-d-d-d—" Tironan blew out a harsh breath and tucked a lock of russet hair behind his ear, inadvertently showcasing his blush to better advantage.

Raveno didn't roll his eyes, but it was a near thing.

"Did you review the reports I s-s-s-sent you?"

Shuffle. Slide. Slide. Shuffle.

Raveno scowled up at the heating ducts. Considering the direction of her crawl, Kinsley was headed toward the control room. Again.

"I've had other matters to attend to." Raveno sidestepped past Tironan.

Tironan pivoted to meet him stride for stride. "It's r-r-rather urgent. The pharmacy—"

"Last shift alone, I received reports from you, Avier, all four of Josairo's Vri Shavrili, and three from Veilon—you know how helpfully thorough our sister's reports are compared to Josairo's other advisors." Raveno reminded him. "Everything sent to me is considered rather urgent."

"Of c-c-course," Tironan said, and how he managed to sound simultaneously respectful and snotty was a skill unto itself. "However—"

"Jhoni is consistently abandoning his guard shift in the shols wing." Raveno kept his tone even, watching for Tironan's reaction in his peripheral vision.

Tironan's eyes widened. "J-J-Jhoni is ab-b—"

"*Abandoning* his guard shift. Yes."

"You're s-s-sure?"

Raveno met Tironan's gaze. "One can't argue with video evidence."

"Hmmm," Tironan murmured, managing to argue without words. "If I have p-p-permission to speak freely without c-causing offense?"

Again, that respectful snottiness. Raveno felt his lips twitch and forced a deeper frown before Tironan could notice. He flicked his claws with impatient permission.

"You've d-d-disciplined more guards than usual on this m-mission."

"The guards are more incompetent than usual on this mission."

"Yes," Tironan immediately agreed. "They earned their p-p-punishments, but now the crew is more f-f-fatigued, earlier than usual. Many are pulling d-d-double shifts to cover for those still in the infirmary, and those recovered are wary. B-b-beaten down."

Yes, they certainly were. "Are you telling me that the crew deserves leniency because they're overworked and tired?"

Tironan opened his mouth.

"Are you telling me that skipping shifts and *falling asleep* on duty are actions that *don't* warrant discipline?"

"I—I—I—" Deep breath and an even deeper blush. "Can't speak for Jhoni. I would s-s-suggest you talk to him. I would advise leniency depending on the c-c-circumstance."

"Oh, is that what you would advise?"

Tironan nodded, deaf to Raveno's sarcasm. "As for my recent b-b-bout of narcolepsy, I found something of n-note in the pharmacy report. That you have yet to r-r-review."

Raveno waited a beat, but Tironan didn't seem inclined to continue. In the silence between footfalls, Kinsley's *shuffle-slide-shuffle* grated on his last nerve.

She was about to beat him to the control room.

Raveno narrowed his eyes at Tironan, but his demeanor was earnest and open, completely focused on the conversation at hand.

Apparently unaware of the escaped human navigating the heating ducts above their heads.

"Summarize the report," Raveno snapped.

"The logged amount of *svirros* in our r-records is more than the physical amount we have in s-s-stock."

"Svirros?"

"The sedative we s-s-stock for major procedures, so that patients may receive t-treatment without the agony of healing." A beat, and then, "It puts people to s-s-sleep."

Raveno stopped walking.

Tironan faltered a step. He paused, then pivoted to face Raveno directly. "I'm s-s-still waiting on the results of our blood test, but I have no d-d-doubt that Dellao and I didn't fall asleep naturally while on duty. We were d-drugged."

Raveno crossed his arms. "Even if your blood tests return positive, both of you have recently visited the infirmary. You probably received a dose of svirros during your healing sessions."

Tironan shook his head. "You have a s-s-s-strict policy against using sedatives to heal d-disciplinary injuries."

Of course he did. Raveno tried to spy the evidence of Tironan's discipline, but his brother clasped his hands behind his back. "What is the discrepancy between the quantity of svirros we have logged and the amount we have in stock?"

"Substantial." Something suspiciously like aggravation lit Tironan's eyes. "I listed the exact n-n-numbers in the report."

Finally, progress on *some* front! "Whose code was used to access the medicine dispensary during these discrepancies?"

"Mine."

All that lovely excitement curdled. "I appreciate you admitting your guilt directly."

"It wasn't m-m-me. Obviously." Tironan had the gall to roll his eyes. "Why would I b-b-bring it to your attention? Why would I dose m-myself?"

The better to deflect suspicion.

"There must b-b-be an investigation, and—"

"No investigation." *Cry mercy, he proposes an investigation!* Everyone's eye would be upon him, their father's most seeing, anticipating that Raveno would, as usual, do whatever must be done.

Tironan stilled, his ears nearly glowing with anxiety. "The c-c-culprit must be found. One guard is to blame. Only one should r-receive discipline."

Yes, and I don't want that guard to be you. "I will handle this investigation and the discipline of one or all of my crew as I see fit."

Tironan's eyes widened. "Y-y-your will by my hands, Vri C-C-Cilvril. Or in this case, not in my hand, I suppose. But I—I—I—"

"You are dismissed."

The blue at the tips of Tironan's ears spread down the sides of his neck. "Our c-c-crew needs to be built back up. You're hurting m-m-more than disciplining."

"Is that something new?" Raveno shouldn't express such contempt for himself, not while undercover, but thev sa shek! Missing drugs. Guards abandoning their shifts. Captives escaping through the heating ducts. What more could catch fire?

Tironan chewed on his lower lip.

Raveno leaned down and growled. "Must I dismiss you a second time?"

Tironan didn't flinch. He didn't cower or blush, and Raveno realized his little brother was seriously considering the question, weighing the risk versus the reward of pushing this conversation into what would obviously become a confrontation.

Raveno held his breath.

Tironan clenched the few claws he still had into fists, but he clicked his heels respectfully, even as his expression twisted with disgust, and left. The clip of his retreat echoed down the hall long after he'd turned the corner, out of sight.

Raveno flexed his vresls, attempting to release some of the tension straining his neck.

Slide. Shift. Slide.

Raveno glared up at the heating ducts. Grimacing, he strode down the remaining hallway and entered the control room.

The guards on duty, Syish and Bvet, both leapt to their feet and clicked their heels at his sudden presence.

Raveno nodded. "You're dismissed. I'll finish your shift."

Both guards, without question or hesitation, fled the control room.

The door slid shut behind them. Raveno engaged the lock, leaned against the doorjamb, and waited, his eyes locked on the heating vent.

Minutes passed, and he continued waiting.

Shift. Slide. Shift.

She was leaving.

Raveno straightened, unsure if he was more surprised or annoyed. Kinsley "Switch" Morales might be accustomed to running her missions without reporting back to his traitor, but she was sorely mistaken if she thought to avoid reporting back to him.

Raveno reached into the heating vent, took hold of whatever he could find—an ankle, he thought—and tugged her from the heating duct.

Kinsley yelped. She slid out through the heating vent, and Raveno watched, reluctantly impressed, as she twisted and caught its lip by her tiny fingertips. She hung from the ceiling by one hand, face-to-face with him, swaying midair.

Raveno crossed his arms. A member of his crew, faced with that look, might wet their groin strap.

Kinsley wiggled the fingers of her free hand at him. "Fancy meeting you here."

She appeared calm, flirtatious even, assuming he was interpreting her tone and expression correctly, even as the rhythm of her heart skipped a beat and then spiked. Its acceleration heightened his awareness of her—the rough scrape of her throaty voice, her impressive tenacity, the spark in her dark eyes—and before he could think to seal his nostrils, he breathed in her scent.

Sweet musk and smooth smoke shot with a bite of spice.

Inexplicably, her scent was familiar. It reminded him of the folly of his youth, when he'd been prone to acting on feelings rather than logic. A time before needing a prosthetic leg, when he'd still harbored hope for swaying his father's heart. When he'd naively believed Josairo had a heart to sway.

"Where are you going?" Raveno growled.

"Back to my cell."

He cocked his head. "Without deactivating the autopilot or rerouting our flight path or arming the lir s'flis?"

"Arming the what?"

Raveno chopped his palm at her. "What about your orders?"

She raised the tufts of hair over her eyes—eyebrows, according to Zethus, he reminded himself. "What about them?"

"You are *my* killing hand now, remember? In exchange for your life, you now report to me." He crossed his arms. "So. Report."

Kinsley took a deep breath, the veins in her neck straining from the effort of dangling one-handed. Perspiration had plastered a lock of feathered hair to her flushed skin. She tried ineffectively to blow it away from where it lay, obstructing her vision.

An unbidden force took control of Raveno's arm, and before logic could stop his reaction, his hand was touching her cheek.

She ceased blowing. She ceased breathing entirely.

Careful of his claws in such close proximity to that delicate skin, Raveno brushed those stubborn hairs back from her face and behind her ear, out of her eyes.

Her throat swelled and contracted as she swallowed.

"Are you figuratively stabbing my back?" he asked.

"No," she whispered.

"Then speak. I cannot imagine you earning your freedom by spying on an empty room."

"The room wouldn't have been empty had you not dismissed the guards."

"Are you telling me that your orders have changed? Are you now to observe and not cause chaos?" Raveno cracked his knuckles in subtle warning. "When did you meet with him for this mission update?"

Her eyes flicked to his claws. "Are you implying that you'll pound the truth out of me if I don't answer you?"

Perhaps not so subtle. He grinned, flashing every tooth to lethal advantage. In his experience, people without such teeth found them intimidating.

She sniffed. "Before you commence the pounding, may I at least have the dignity of standing on my own two feet?"

Raveno retreated a step and swept his hand out generously. "By all means."

Kinsley released the lip of the heating vent and landed on said two feet. She straightened, slow and cautious, as if braced to run.

As if she'd get very far if she tried.

Try.

He shook his head. What kind of thought was that? "I will ask for the final time. By will or wrath, what are your orders?"

"By will or what?"

He held up a hand. "Do not attempt to change the subject."

"I wasn't—"

"You drugged my guards."

"I didn't—"

"For nearly one hundred shaoz, you've been drugging them!"

She reared back at that. "One hundred *shoes*?"

"Shaoz. A measurement of time. You have this on Earth, but you base it on the sun instead of shifts. It is..." Raveno rubbed his brow, calculating. "The equivalent of our three shifts."

She stared at him, uncomprehending.

"On Earth, it's the time between sunrises."

Her face lit. "Ah! A shoe is a day?"

"Shaoz," he corrected her. Again. "But a shaoz is a measurement of time independent from light and darkness."

"Interesting. Then how is a shoe measured if not by the sun?"

"By shifts. We—" Raveno raised a hand, interrupting himself. "I will not allow you to distract me! After over a hundred *days* of escaping your room and drugging my crew, the benefit of my doubts has run dry. When do you report to your superior?"

"Who?"

"My traitor! The next time you meet with him, I want to be there. I will finally know his face and whether my loss is Tironan or Jhoni."

"We need to be more subtle than that!" Her eyes scanned their surroundings, as if his traitor might be right here in this very room. "If my *superior* discovers that I've flipped sides, he'll take me out."

"We're in deep space. No one can go out, except in a solo cruiser if I permit it."

"That's not—" But she interrupted herself with a sharp head shake. "What's a solo cruiser?"

"A single-occupant spaceship." Raveno flicked an unconcerned claw. "During your next rendezvous, I will observe your meeting covertly."

"What, you'd hide around the corner? Behind a fern? We're not exactly making it difficult for him as it is. He could know already!"

Raveno snorted.

"I'm serious! What if he's spying on me from this room's security footage, hmm?" She traced a line across her neck. "I'm dead."

"No one can spy on you here," Raveno said, exasperated by her temerity. Why was his own crew not as competent? "We only have surveillance set up in the *shols* wing."

"In the what?"

"The hallway and rooms where you and your humans...reside."

"Ah. The brig."

Raveno blinked. "The what?"

"A brig is the prison on a ship. It's where we *reside*."

That was exactly what this ship had become, wasn't it? After a lifetime being caged by his father's rule and society's expectations and thinking himself so clever and above all that nonsense, he'd gone and become someone else's warden.

"What did you call it? A 'sholzwing'?" Kinsley attempted to mimic his accent and coughed from the strain on her throat.

"It's two words." Raveno held up one thumb. "Shols." And then the other. "Wing. A hallway or extension of a—"

"I don't need you to define the English word," she said, rolling her eyes. "What is 'shols'?"

Thev sa shek. Raveno could happily bite off his own tongue. "I have a more pressing question." He stepped closer, bridging the distance between them in one stride. "I studied the surveillance of your cell, at length, and you never converse with any of my crew. Ever."

Kinsley sidestepped, sliding the pilot's chair between them. "So? I doubt the other humans converse with your crew."

"The other humans are not my killing hand." Raveno wrestled the chair from her grip and pushed it aside. It swung in a wide arc on its bolted hinge and slammed into the console. "Even if your plan is already set and you do not receive regular orders from your superior, which I find highly unlikely, you must have spoken with him at least once. Otherwise, how did you strike your deal?"

FIVE

IF NOT FOR A DEEP SENSE OF SELF-PRESERVATION, KINSLEY might have laughed in Raveno's face at the irony of his question. Hmmm, how would a human captive strike a deal with her alien captor, Raveno? Maybe exploit his worst fear and lie lie lie until he believed she was useful enough not to kill?

Kinsley bit back her sarcasm. How might a human captive *legitimately* strike a deal with her alien captor on this prison spaceship from hell, indeed.

Not in the brig, apparently, since it was bugged.

I've studied the surveillance footage of your cell. At length.

Kinsley's face flamed, recalling everything he'd have surveilled. Were their sad attempts at speaking in code too little too late?

Raveno raised a hand.

Kinsley braced herself, but he touched his own face this time. Where her skin would have split under such pressure, his scales retained their shape even as he scraped all four claws down the concave of his cheek to his chiseled jawline. He rubbed at his mouth, considering her.

She did *not* see a tired, depressed sort of frustration on that alien face. She did *not* recognize the pinch at the corners of his lips as uncertainty, and she certainly did *not* suspect that fear was making his bony frill quiver at his collarbone.

After all, he had every advantage at his disposal: guards, weapons, technology, knowledge, power. Freedom. What could *he* possibly have to fear?

"How did you strike your deal, little *lilssna?*" His voice was more hiss and rattle than actual words.

Lilssna? Kinsley bit her lip. Best to stick with the truth as much as possible. "He found me in the incineration shaft."

"What were you doing outside your cell?"

"I was feeling trapped and needed a stroll to clear my thoughts."

Raveno's scowl was molten.

Kinsley rolled her eyes. "What else is there to do but rot in my cell or explore the ship?"

"To what purpose?"

"Are you experiencing déjà vu? Because I—"

"You claimed to be navigating through the heating ducts on undercover missions to cause chaos for a traitor on this ship." His grip on his own chin tightened. "So why were you escaping through the heating ducts *before* making your deal?"

"To map the ship's layout and understand the location of the brig in relation to the rest of the ship. To count the crew and memorize their shifts and patterns. To—"

The bony protrusions of his frill flexed out rigid, then slapped flat against his chest. "You took it upon yourself to spy on my crew *before* striking your deal?"

"Yes."

"Why?"

"What would *you* do if you were abducted and imprisoned by unknown hostiles, hmm? Stay in your cell, quiet and compliant, like a good little prisoner should? Ha! I'd rather die today trying to survive than five years from now, still caged, hoping to live."

Raveno stared at her for a long moment, and Kinsley suddenly realized that in her fervor, she'd prodded him in the chest with her pointer finger. She dropped her arm and held her breath.

His inner eyelid swiped horizontally across one eye, then the other. His tongue, long and bifurcated, flicked out and danced on the air. His chest flap pulsed open and closed in rhythm with his slow breaths.

The six talon-tipped spines around his collar were connected by a thin, scaled webbing. When relaxed, the spines lay flush against his opaline chest, but when flexed, the spines hinged up at the base of his neck and trembled. The movement was as fascinating as it was disturbing.

By stubborn grit alone, Kinsley maintained eye contact.

Eventually, he released his chin and flicked his claws. "So my betrayer found you outside your room?"

She nodded. "Same as you, he found me in the cockpit."

Raveno's eyes bugged. "The *what*?"

Kinsley spread her arms wide. "Here, in this room."

Raveno pointed a claw at the floor. "This is the control room."

"Yes."

"You called it a *cock pit*."

She waved away his confusion. "*Cockpit* is a synonym for *control room*. A word that means nearly the same thing as another word."

"How is this room nearly the same thing as a...a..."

She tilted her head and waited, perversely enjoying his struggle.

He coughed. "A male reproductive organ?"

Kinsley didn't laugh—she had *some* self-preservation instincts, after all—but it was a near thing. "That's one meaning of the word. It's also a male chicken, and when used as a verb, it means to tilt something. And a pit is a hole in the ground or the hard, center seed of a fruit, depending on the context, but when the words are spoken together, *cockpit* is the control room of an airplane." At his blank expression, she continued. "An airplane is a machine that flies. It—"

"I know what an airplane is." He narrowed his eyes on her, his blood-orange irises eerily penetrating. "I have resources to improve my fluency and confirm this definition."

She crossed her heart and raised her palm. "I swear on your life, everything I'm saying is true."

"On *my* life," he snorted, seeming to like that bit. His expression softened. "English is a strange language. So many of its words have multiple meanings that have nothing to do with one another." He shook his head. "Cockpit."

"I'm sure your language has its quirks too." She lowered her hand and narrowed her own eyes. "Nothing as strange, however, as an alien speaking English."

His lip quirked. "To me, *you* are the alien, and you are speaking it."

Was he teasing her? "English is my native language, so there's nothing strange about *me* speaking it."

"Something is strange about someone speaking multiple languages?"

"When the language isn't native to their planet, yes."

"You only think that because humans have not connected with life beyond Earth. For modern civilizations, knowing off-world languages is common. How else would we communicate with other planets?"

"You've met other humans before this abduction? Enough to become fluent in English?" Breathe. Just breathe. "How many humans have you trafficked across this galaxy?"

"Enough to suspect that my traitor finding you in the same room *I* found you is a bit of a coincidence." Raveno crossed his arms. "Best not to make him suspicious as well. You should complete your mission while you're here. And quickly. Jhoni will return for the end of his shift."

"Who?" Kinsley asked, genuinely confused this time.

Raveno leaned forward. "As if you're not timing your escapes with the guard who abandons his shift every shaoz."

"Ah, well—" Kinsley thought fast even as her heart spiked into her throat. If Raveno thought he'd found his traitor, he wouldn't have any purpose for her. And without a purpose… "I'd ask you to pass along my thanks, but if this negligent guard were aware of my escapes, he would stop abandoning his shift. And we can't have that, now, can we? If you blow my secret, you won't find your traitor."

"You must do your part as well." Raveno spread out his arms magnanimously. "Do not let my presence hinder your mission. Cause chaos before you depart. I insist."

Oh, well, if you insist. Kinsley kept a wary eye on Raveno and his sudden smugness as she turned toward the control panel, but he merely crossed his arms again, a spectator to her mission.

Just what she'd always wanted: an audience.

Even under Raveno's scrutiny, the orange button called to her. *Press me*, it taunted with each glowing pulse, and now that she knew it would begin a countdown, her body sang with longing. She might be in space over four months from Earth with the captain of an alien criminal enterprise watching her, but she could still press a button and watch the sparks fly.

Kinsley resisted her natural impulse to blow everything up and instead reached to press the blue buttons on the bottom quadrant of the control panel. She'd already successfully steered the ship left and right utilizing those directional blue buttons. Might as well experiment with driving this bad boy in reverse.

Raveno choked back what sounded like a protest.

Kinsley peered over her shoulder, hand hovering. "Is there a problem?"

"No," he said quickly. Too quickly.

She raised her eyebrows. "Then what was that noise?"

"Nothing."

"Sounded like something."

He shook his head, but the spines around his neck separated from his collar, rubbed together like sandpaper, *tsh tsh*, then slapped flat against his neck.

Definitely something. Kinsley refocused on the control panel—

the only way to learn was to do—and moved to press the buttons anyway.

Raveno lunged forward and grabbed her wrist, her fingertips inches from the blue buttons. "You cannot engage the forward thrusters. The stern thrusters are still on."

Kinsley grinned. "So, there *was* a problem."

Raveno glared down at her.

"What happens if I don't disable the stern thrusters before engaging the forward thrusters?"

"The redundancy alarm will sound, warning the pilot, *you*, that fuel and energy are being wasted. Some of my crew might come to help, so we should avoid that kind of attention."

"Okay, fine, I'll disable the stern thrusters first."

Raveno released her wrist.

Kinsley reached up to press the blue buttons on the top quadrant of the control panel.

"Ah!" He snatched at her wrist again. "Not at random."

She rolled her eyes up at him. "I've done it before without an alarm sounding."

"Correct, but you need to disengage the thrusters with parallel equality to maintain our trajectory. Otherwise, we will veer off course."

That's the point. Chaos, remember? Kinsley thought, but when she opened her mouth to say as much, she found herself saying, "Show me," instead.

He released her arm and pointed to the blue buttons in the top quadrant in pairs. "Starboard and port forward thrusters, mid-forward thrusters, mid-stern thrusters and stern thrusters. Press them in pairs, forward to stern."

She did. "And to fly in reverse, I do the same, but opposite, to the bottom quadrant of blue buttons? Stern to forward in pairs?"

"You are quick to learn," he murmured.

She pressed the bottom quadrant's blue buttons in pairs, as directed. Then, while Raveno was still nodding his encouragement, she entered the combination to cancel autopilot and flipped the switch for manual override.

Raveno tensed. "Wait, what are you—"

Using the joystick, she set the medial movement of the ship into a counterclockwise tail spin. "Just having a little fun." She jerked her head at the wide-open space of, well, *space* featured in the backup camera. "We've got room for it."

"Careful. The blue buttons. You see how that one turned yellow? You need to—"

"I have it." She pressed the yellow button, turning it blue again, but the one next to it flashed yellow. "I just need to—"

An alarm sounded. Shit.

She peeked back at Raveno guiltily, but he didn't seem angry. He'd covered his mouth with his palm, and his shoulders were bouncing.

He was laughing!

"Well, how do I fix it?" she asked.

"Do you not, as you say, 'have it'?"

Kinsley released the joystick and pressed all the yellow buttons, five now, but the more buttons she pressed, the more turned yellow.

One of them flashed red.

"Eventually, someone is gonna care about these damn alarms and come investigate," she warned. "What happened to avoiding this kind of attention?"

"I am finding your panic more enjoyable than anticipated."

Men—whether they had skin or scales, they were all the same. Impossible!

She'd maneuvered all the yellow buttons back to blue, but another three bypassed yellow, flashing red.

Raveno eyed the instrument panel. "Cease fiddling with the thrusters. Take the yoke in both hands and reestablish control of your rotation."

The joystick, yoke, whatever, was what had gotten her in this jam to begin with! She ignored him and flipped three of the silver switches instead.

Raveno lunged forward and flipped the switches off. "*What are you doing?*"

"Isn't it obvious?" Kinsley snapped. "I don't know!"

"Releasing three of our solo cruisers will not help you regain control of the ship," he said dryly.

All the buttons suddenly flashed red.

"Fuck. There's no time." She shot a look at the doorway and then up at the incineration shaft. "I'd better beat it now while I still can."

She tensed to run.

"The door is locked. There is time." He snatched both her hands in his and slapped them to sandwich the joystick. "Like this. Now, ease up and out of the spin. *Slowly.*" He encouraged softly, guiding her pressure on the controls. One of the buttons flashed back to blue. "There. Now increase the backward throttle, so we're not just spinning in place. That's why those two are still red. They're working against each other. Good."

He loosened his grip, so she was the one in control. Although his hands still hovered, ready to swoop in again if necessary.

"Keep it up. A little looser now. Let the ship steer itself. There." The last button turned blue, and the alarm cut to silence.

Kinsley grinned, feeling the rush of success and adrenaline ignite her blood. "We did it!"

"*You* did it."

"Yes, I did. Ha! That was awesome!" She glanced back at him, and suddenly, his face was inches from hers. His arms were still wrapped around her, had been ever since he'd forced her to grip the yoke in both hands, but she hadn't noticed until now. His hard front flush against her back. His muscular arms surrounding her arms. The glowing dot in his right wrist illuminating his steady hands over her hands.

His nostrils flared wide.

Yes, something did smell rather good. Fresh and clean, nearly like eucalyptus, but bright. It made her mouth water.

Without thought, her eyes dropped to his lips.

Raveno's bifurcated tongue slipped out and flicked between them.

She could pull away if she wanted to. His grip was loose as he stroked a knuckle across the inside of her wrist. The way his finger was bent, he was being very careful of his claws in such close proximity to her veins. His touch was light. It should have been barely imperceptible, except the texture of his scales was foreign and unfamiliar. They looked cold, but felt warm. How could something so warm raise goose bumps across her skin? A shiver shot up her arm, across her collarbone, and her unmentionables clenched.

His eyes closed for a moment on a shuddering inhale.

Citrus. That was the smell. Somehow, his scales smelled like eucalyptus and citrus. Oranges, specifically.

To match his blood-orange irises, she thought as they opened to meet her gaze.

He swayed toward her.

Was that longing in the strain of his expression?

Worse, was *she* swaying toward *him*?

Oh, this was not happening.

Kinsley jerked away. He stepped back, and when Kinsley glared up at him through the curtain of her bangs, his ears blazed a deep, bright blue.

"Thank you," Kinsley murmured hastily. "I appreciate the impromptu piloting lesson."

Raveno found the ceiling suddenly fascinating. "Perhaps during future missions, you can manage to cause chaos without shorting out my redundancy alarms."

"Is that why you helped me?" Kinsley crossed her arms. She should retreat—mission complete and still in the clear—but those lingering tingles from his touch must have shorted out her common sense. She licked her lips. "In concern for your alarm system?"

His nostrils flared before sealing shut.

Interesting. Very interesting. "I should go. That guard who leaves his shift—"

"Jhoni."

"Yes, Jhoni. He'll be back soon. I need to beat him there before—"

"Before you are found." Raveno practically shoved her toward the incineration shaft. "Go. Now."

Kinsley let him push her along, but the relief she should have felt at having survived another close encounter of the third kind was tempered by terror.

One hundred and sixteen days of celibacy, she thought, trying to justify her body's reaction, but even Martin, who was just her type had they not been imprisoned, hadn't sparked anything so embarrassingly undeniable.

Raveno wasn't human, she reminded herself.

The fact that she needed reminding was disturbing enough.

Who was she becoming if *Raveno* was her type?

The orange pulse of the rocket launcher drew her eye as she passed, and a familiar longing rose in her chest. Now *that* was a desire that made sense. It had never made sense to anyone else, but for her, it was as normal and constant and recognizable as her own reflection.

Seizing the moment and that bare scrap of normalcy, she lunged out and pressed the button for the rocket launcher.

Raveno sprang forward, snagging her wrist in his grasp, but the alarm was already whooping overhead. "Why would you—"

"Why not? I'm causing confusion and chaos, remember? Let me go."

His grip tightened painfully.

"You promised to let me live." She pointed a finger at him. "If he finds me now, I'm dead. On Earth, a promise is a bond of truth. Is it not the same on Havar?"

His jaw clamped shut, but he released her. "Go!"

Kinsley jumped up onto the pilot's swivel chair and lunged for the incineration shaft. She caught the lip of its vent with just the bare

63

tips of her fingers—what was it about his presence that made her nearly miss?—and strong-armed her torso inside. She was about to worm up her bottom half when something grasped her thighs, lifted, and shoved her all the way in.

The crown of her head hit the roof of the shaft. "Ouch! I had it!"

"Yes, just like you had the manual steering."

Kinsley whipped back to snap at him through the fire vent, but her breath caught at the sight of the pulsing symbols on the monitor behind him.

The countdown had begun.

"You'd better leave too," Kinsley warned. "Unless you want your crew to think *you're* the one causing chaos."

Raveno made a choked noise in the back of his throat. With a final burning glare at the control panel, then her, he exited the room.

Kinsley watched the alien symbols flash on the monitor. *Come on. Count down faster!*

The faint rumble of an approaching stampede echoed from the hall.

She held her breath, waiting.

The door slid open, and the two guards that Raveno had dismissed from their shift tripped over themselves into the cockpit. Claws click-clacked over the keys in a frenzy of panic and purpose. They shouted over the intercom as they worked, hissing at each other in their slippery language.

Maybe they wouldn't be fast enough. Maybe the countdown would make it to its end, and maybe the rocket would—

The intercom cut, the monitor froze mid-count, and the pilot recorrected the ship's course back on route. As usual.

Fun for another day, she tried to comfort herself, but the unwarranted bitterness at having her fun for today snatched away stayed with her during the entire thirty-minute crawl back to her cell. Back to captivity. Back to Martin's gruff hope and Benjamin's embarrassing attempts to woo Leanne.

And Leanne just being Leanne.

Eventually, Kinsley would blow something up. She had to, or at the very least she had to convince herself she would get the opportunity. Because if she didn't have the pleasure of that one little lie as motivation to keep her sanity, she'd lose it.

She thought of Raveno's knuckle sliding, delicious, across her wrist and shuddered.

Assuming her sanity wasn't already lost.

SIX

Raveno was painfully aware of Vri Zyvril Avier Risan standing at attention in his cabin. He'd entered, clicked his heels together, and announced himself, per protocol, and now he was gnashing his teeth, per usual, as he waited. Raveno had known Avier his entire life, and as much as he trusted him and his healing hands—with his life—Avier was not a patient man. One of the many things they had in common. He would continue gnashing for however long it took for Raveno to finish reviewing Tironan's pharmaceutical report, as if the numbers glowing from his *yensha* would change with repetition.

Raveno pressed his palm against his forehead. They hadn't even begun this conversation, and his brain was already aching.

Avier's brown hair was woven away from his face at his temples, as was custom for all havarian soldiers, but where Tironan's hair always seemed on the verge of unraveling, Avier's was tight and precise against his scalp. His uniform straps were flush against his scales, snug enough to accommodate but not constrict his muscles. His weapons were polished, his boots buffed, and his bearing confident, if not completely composed. His impatience made his jaw tic, but otherwise, Avier was the epitome of the dutiful, loyal brother-in-arms Raveno knew him to be.

How much of his burden would be relieved if Avier, not Tironan, had been his brother in blood?

Raveno knuckled his left eye at that betraying thought, but the pressure behind it only increased.

Avier's gaze flicked to the report. He took a deep breath, then resumed his gnashing in silence. For Avier, such a display was practically a temper tantrum.

Raveno waved his hand at the chair in front of his desk, putting them both out of their misery. "How is Dellao recovering?"

Avier perched on the chair's edge. "Dellao is well, taking his punishment in stride. Tironan, however..." He grimaced.

Raveno straightened. "I just spoke with Tironan. He seemed fine."

"Seeming is not being. How would you *be* with only two claws on your right hand?"

The twinge behind Raveno's left eye spread to his temple and throbbed. "His stutter is worsening," he confided.

"Yes, well. He's stressed."

"Aren't we all?" Raveno grumbled. "Find a reason to reward him —any reason, I don't care—and heal him."

"All four claws?"

"I was recently informed that our crew is feeling beaten down."

Avier, wisely, remained silent.

"Don't say the order came from me," Raveno added. "You take the credit. Risked your life to convince me on his behalf. You're impressed by his skills. See his potential." He circled his hand midair. "Make something up."

"Tironan will see through that."

"Just make it so he *earned* back his claws."

"That'll be a stretch."

Raveno scowled.

Avier grinned. "Your will..." He circled *his* hand midair in lofty imitation.

Raveno tugged his second thumb at his mocking. Anyone else would take extreme offense, but Avier just chortled at having earned the gesture.

"Are Dellao and Tironan suffering any side effects following their impromptu nap on duty?" Raveno asked.

"Other than the inability to properly grasp and wield their weapons?"

"I may have confirmation that neither Tironan nor Dellao fell asleep of their own accord." Raveno swiveled his yensha to face Avier. "They were drugged."

Avier leaned forward. "They tested positive for svirros? We don't use sedatives for disciplinary offenses."

"I'm aware. They—"

An alarm whooped over the intercom. Raveno listened a moment and nearly laughed. Again? What was Kinsley's obsession with the lir s'flis?

He should be annoyed. She was running his guards in circles, outmaneuvering their protocols, and keeping one jump ahead of their watches, and it was no wonder. According to his most recent update from Zethus, she'd been employed and trained by one of her planet's elite defense organizations. Granted, his traitor was undoubtedly aiding her, and Raveno himself certainly was, enhancing her already impressive piloting knowledge, but he couldn't help himself because despite what he *should* feel, he wasn't annoyed in the slightest. How could he be when he was so thoroughly impressed?

Kinsley, now *she* was a soldier with skill and potential.

He'd nearly taken a knee to breathe her in.

She'd twisted toward him after having corrected the ship's operational errors, her expression thrilled, her heart jubilant, and the scent of her excitement had throbbed from her chest and inexplicably straight to his groin. And thev sa shek, he'd nearly *dropped to his knees* right then and there.

Never mind that she wouldn't understand the gesture. Never mind that she'd been staring at his mouth, and the only reason he hadn't made a move was the hesitation—bah, the hope—that she was poised on the cusp of her own gesture of affection.

Insanity.

According to Zethus, their customs differed slightly, but the mechanics of their biology were very much the same.

His vresls quivered at the thought before he reined in the reaction.

Luckily, Avier was glaring at the intercom and didn't notice. "If I hear one more alarm trip, I'm stealing a solo cruiser and jumping ship."

"Can I come with you?"

"They enjoy punishment," Avier insisted. "They must. It's the only explanation for how terrible this crew has become."

"There's another explanation. It's why I called you here." Raveno realized he was digging at his eyes again and clasped both hands on his desk. "The female human you recently healed has been escaping her room nearly every shaoz since boarding this ship."

"That's impossible. How—"

"In exchange for her freedom, she's been working with one of our guards to cause chaos on this ship and undermine my authority: drugging our pilots, rerouting our flight paths, experimenting with our systems, so on and beyond." Raveno paused, allowing the obvious to sink in.

"So why didn't we fake her death and bunk her with the other one?" Avier asked.

Raveno waved that away. "His name's Riley. And your point is moot. I flipped Kinsley to our side."

Avier pointed at the alarm whooping from the intercom. "Clearly."

"You're missing the point. One of our crew is working for Josairo against me. With Kinsley's intel, I can sniff out who."

Avier slouched back in his chair on a groan. "Not this again," he lamented to the ceiling. "We *all* work for Josairo."

"But not *against* me. Someone is betraying me. Read the report."

"No one is betraying you. They might want to at times. They're certainly beginning to resent you. But you're a legend. As untouchable as Josairo."

Raveno shot him an arch look. "And we're betraying him."

Avier flicked an unconcerned claw. "They fear you. No one would dare stand against you."

"Fear and resentment sparked my own betrayal."

"No. Grief did that."

Raveno felt his vresls about to bristle and forced them flat.

Avier straightened. "Seela loved you, but she asked the impossible."

"My mother wouldn't have asked what she didn't believe me capable of."

"She believed you capable of anything."

"Read," Raveno gritted out, "the report."

Avier heaved a sigh even as his eyes scanned through the numbers. His jaw tightened as he read. "Whose code was used to access the medicine dispensary?"

"Tironan's."

Avier stiffened. "Who submitted this report?"

Raveno clicked a claw on the desk. "Tironan."

Avier relaxed, but even so, he closed his eyes, pained. "You need to confide in him."

"We have discussed this many times."

"His ignorance will get him killed." Avier pointed a claw at Raveno's chest. "And since you're the one keeping him ignorant, you'll blame yourself."

"He could be my traitor," Raveno whispered.

"In the unlikely event that someone on this ship is a traitor," Avier hissed. "That someone is not Tironan."

"And if he's not, he still can't know."

"You—"

Raveno slammed his fist on the desk. "By will or wrath, I will not drag him down with me should I fail!"

Avier's vresls throbbed in rhythm with his breaths. "You *will* fail if you don't confide in him. You need his support. You need clarity of mind. He's your brother."

"Precisely. He's my brother, and I *will* shield him from Josairo's wrath." Raveno pressed his palm flat on his desk before he punched it again. "I won't have him pay for my betrayal."

"Don't you think that should be his choice?"

"No."

Avier narrowed his eyes. "If the situation were reversed, wouldn't you want the opportunity to stand beside Tironan against your father?"

"Tironan would never betray Josairo."

"To stand beside you, he would. I did."

Raveno shook his head. "Just the thought of Tironan matching ezili with Josairo makes me sick."

"It would never come to that because you—"

"Because *I* won't burden Tironan with this."

Avier didn't reply, but he didn't need to for Raveno to know he had more on his mind.

"Just say it," Raveno muttered.

"Tironan isn't the only person on this ship you should confide in."

"Oh?"

"Our crew remains loyal to you because, unlike the shols on other carrier vessels, the Bazaili, Iroanio and Frayans we've 'escorted' to Havar have always wanted to compete in the Intergalactic Frisaes."

Raveno grunted. "Yes. So, it would seem."

"At the very least, they were your allies in our efforts against Josairo, so we never needed to lock them in their rooms to maintain order. They were here of their own will." Avier met Raveno's eyes meaningfully. "The crew know that the humans are not."

"Our orders from Josairo are clear, and unless we want to include the entire crew in our plot to overthrow Josairo, we must follow those orders. Which means the humans remain locked in their rooms as we transport them to Havar."

Avier didn't even blink. "We should include the entire crew in our plot to overthrow Josairo."

"Absolutely not."

"If we gain the crew's allegiance, we can return the humans to Earth and have that many more warriors behind us when we confront Josairo."

"You don't know the crew will remain loyal."

"I remained loyal."

"There's at least one traitor on board!"

"There isn't—"

"We can't risk our entire mission now. Not when we're so close. As repugnant as this is, as much as it's killing me to do so, we must remain under cover to the bitter end."

"But the humans—"

"Will be returned to Earth. *After* we kill Josairo."

"But our crew—"

"Will follow my orders as given by Josairo, as they always do." Raveno chopped his hand at Avier. "You will conduct a private investigation and determine who is stealing svirros from the dispensary. Proving Tironan innocent will be your focus."

Avier resumed gnashing his teeth. "What have you told Josairo regarding our missing one hundred and sixty shols?"

"The truth." Raveno's grin was all fangs. "The number of shols for sale was an unwelcome surprise, so we blew up Lorien's carrier vessel in retribution for their betrayal."

Avier groaned. "And he accepted that excuse?"

"Difficult to tell via anku. Josairo refused to speak over live projection," Raveno confessed to the ceiling. "Too busy hosting the fifty-third Intergalactic Frisaes."

"Ah." Avier slouched back in his chair. "I didn't know *Sa Tashis* had returned to Havar already."

"Yes."

Avier knew where *Sa Tashis* had been ordered, so he didn't bother asking how many people had been bought or if any had survived.

Raveno was sure they hadn't. They rarely did.

"Josairo didn't host the event in person," Raveno added, knowing such intel would amuse.

Avier's vresles expanded. "How did he host?"

Raveno shimmied his hands around his head. "An enlarged, six-tier-tall live projection."

"No!"

"Yes."

"*Why?*"

"Something about sensationalism. According to their latest report, the Vri Shavrili are attempting to improve viewership."

"Josairo needs new advisors," Avier said dryly. "Viewership is required."

"*Willing* viewership, then."

"Hmmm." Avier was silent for a long moment. "I don't want the crew of *Sa Vivsheth* to suffer the same fate as the crew of *Sa Riluuz*."

"I will not allow that to happen," Raveno said, pained even by the thought of such a disaster: his entire crew being executed—instead of just himself—for his mistakes.

"Then what of the escaped human?"

Despite the grimness of their conversation, Raveno felt his chest lighten. "I'll deal with our little firework."

Avier blinked, the movement painfully slow.

Raveno cleared his throat. "Kinsley, I mean."

"I can see why you like her, but—"

Raveno jerked at that and laughed. "I *like* her? What does that even mean? I *like* her," he repeated on a snort. "I like *losths*. Might that be a problem too? Enjoying some dessert after dinner?"

"Depends on the quantity and regularity. If you enjoyed it now as much as you did in our youth, you could lose your intimidating physique."

Raveno snorted a second time.

"You admire her strength. You appreciate the risks she's taken on behalf of her people." Avier eyed him meaningfully. "I think you see a little of yourself in her, backed into a corner and doing what needs to be done to survive. But admiring her, getting too close to her, *liking* her... It's an unnecessary risk to this mission, a mission that's risky enough."

Raveno strained to keep his vresls from rattling. "If I want to discover my traitor, I need to keep her close."

"Isn't that why I'm investigating the stolen svirros?"

"Whoever is stealing svirros may or may not be my only traitor. While you're investigating the missing medication, Zethus is investigating Kinsley. According to him, humans don't have the technology for intergalactic communication, so whatever deal she made with my traitor occurred either with the lorienok or on this ship."

Avier lifted a knuckle and rubbed his forehead. Raveno's headache was apparently catching. "Soon you'll suspect the entire ship is against you."

"It's not out of the realm of possibility."

"You need to overcome this paranoia."

"It's caution, not paranoia," Raveno insisted. "If I were a member of my crew, I'd turn against me."

Avier leaned forward, both elbows on his desk. "If you gave them the chance to stand beside you, it wouldn't be you alone protecting the world. Given the opportunity, the world can protect itself."

Raveno inhaled deeply. "I disagree."

"Shocking." Avier slumped back. "Would you like to point your claw at anyone in particular, besides Tironan, or are we all suspects?"

Raveno nodded sadly. "Jhoni."

Avier shaded his eyes. "I'm done asking questions," he muttered. "Your answers only become more and more ridiculous."

"He's the reason Kinsley is able to escape from her room unde-tected," Raveno explained. "He consistently abandons his guard shift, and I want to know why."

"Your will by my hands."

"Avier," Raveno warned.

"I'll handle it. You know I will, but I wouldn't be surprised to find collector cards of you in Jhoni's cabin. He's thrilled to breathe the same air as you, let alone serve under your command." Avier shook his head. "He's not betraying you."

"I'm sure finally meeting me in person has disabused him of any lingering hero worship inspired by Josairo's propaganda."

"It won't be propaganda when you successfully unseat him. Then you'll be 'the savior of Havar' in truth."

"Avier," Raveno snapped. "Just find my traitors, even if that means outing Tironan."

"It won't."

"And I'll deal with Kinsley."

Avier swiped a hand down his face. "And you think Tironan will be your undoing."

"She will be *my* savior if she can identify my traitor, as she claims."

"*Claims* being the operative word."

"If she can recognize the guard betraying me and you can iden-tify the guard stealing svirros, then—"

"Then I will *shek* your sister."

Raveno sniffed. "Veilon would eviscerate you."

"I'm serious."

"So am I." Raveno pointed his claw. "You—"

The door buzzed.

"—are saved from my wrath at the moment."

"Don't. We're not—"

Raveno pressed the button to unlock the door, and it slid open.

Avier clamped his mouth shut with an audible clack, his vresls bristling.

Jhoni entered the cabin, looking newly returned from a losing battle. His braids were pulled lopsided. The scales around his left eye were flushed a deep shade of blue. He'd lost his breath and was failing to catch it.

He clicked his heels together. "Vri Cilvril Raveno Hoviir," he managed between gasps.

"Report," Raveno intoned.

Jhoni met Raveno's eyes. "One of the shols," he breathed, "was found outside her room."

SEVEN

Kinsley was screwed—massively, royally, life-flashing-before-her-eyes-level screwed.

The mission had started out like all her other hundred-some escapes. She'd incapacitated the pilot and copilot, swiveled their chairs out of her way, and approached the control panel. Steadfastly ignoring the pulsing lure of the rocket launcher, Kinsley had entered the manual override access code. She'd gripped the yoke in both hands, as Raveno had taught her, steered the ship off course, and spun them in a forward somersault with a clockwise spiral—with minimal button flashing and a bit of flair, if she did say so herself.

After everything Raveno had divulged over the past week, she didn't need to experiment anymore. She could interpret the many status reports on the monitors. She knew the function of nearly every switch on the instrument panel. She could anticipate the flashing buttons and their various colors and correct her trajectory without panicking. The only systems she still needed access codes for were the heating ducts and cell locks.

It was only a matter of time, and for once, that ticking clock felt more like a countdown than a measurement of days lost.

As she stared out the viewing panels into the speckled void of unending space, the ship spinning off course from a beautiful maneuver she'd learned and perfected from the aliens' own uncompromising captain, it seemed like anything was possible. Maybe in another hundred days, she'd have pulled off *the* impossible, and she'd be steering the ship in earnest, programming its autopilot for Earth. Completing her mission. Rocketing them home.

Unbidden, something warm and tight bloomed within Kinsley's chest. Dare she allow the dream of returning home twist into hope?

The cockpit door slid open.

Kinsley wiped her eyes, pivoted to snap something scathing at Raveno, and gaped. The guard standing at the threshold, gaping back at her, was decidedly *not* Raveno.

He was shorter and leaner than Raveno. His hair was long and straight, like Raveno's, but strawberry blond, not platinum, and the messy braids at his temples held only a thin cord around his forehead, not the bone-studded Conan crown adorning Raveno's big head. His black eyes were round with shock, and his entire face, not just the tips of his ears, flashed a deep, bright blue.

He still hadn't moved except to swipe his inner eyelids.

Kinsley tried smiling. "Hi. My name is Kinsley. What's y—"

Not-Raveno whirled around and shouted at the top of his lungs in Haveo.

Fuck.

Kinsley scanned the room: viewing panels, dashboard, monitors, yoke, glowing buttons, pulsing orange rocket launcher, unconscious guards. She snatched one of the ice picks from the pilot's hip holster just as Not-Raveno lunged for her.

Kinsley jumped sideways onto the dashboard, brandishing the ice pick like a knife, and stomped on the rocket launcher's orange button along with at least a dozen other buttons.

The overhead alarm whooped.

Not-Raveno shrieked, and the scaly frill around his neck snapped open like a popped umbrella.

He dove for the control panel.

Kinsley leapt out of reach, but she was obviously no longer his top priority. Not-Raveno was frantic, eyes darting over the countdown monitor and fingers dancing a mile a minute across all the wrong keys. It didn't help that he was missing nearly all the fingers on his right hand. Every button on the dash, including the pulsing rocket launcher, flashed red.

Kinsley considered the back of the alien's head, hefting the ice pick in her hand. The weapon was perfectly balanced, about twelve inches long, and lethally sharp. One deft stab to the neck between the scales would be enough to reach his spinal cord.

And more than enough, no doubt, to seal her own fate with Raveno.

I could claim this alien as his traitor.

But even as that horrible thought surfaced, Kinsley lowered her weapon and climbed back into the incineration shaft.

Not-Raveno—still spitting curses and panic—mistyped access code after access code. Kinsley should leave and return to her cell before another alien tried to negotiate a deal with her, but as she watched from the relative safety of the shaft, anticipation ripened.

Maybe he wouldn't type the correct access code in time. Maybe the rocket would complete its countdown and launch.

Not-Raveno must have had a similar thought, because he abandoned the control panel and dashed into the hallway, snapping his head left then right. His neck frill flapped open on another shout before he sprinted back into the room and commenced pressing all the incorrect buttons in desperate haste. Again.

Kinsley squinted at the monitor. He was accessing *something* with his combination, just not the weapons system. His combination was giving him access to... Kinsley's brain finally made sense of the block layout on screen, and she froze. This idiot, who couldn't even disarm a rocket with a simple combination code, had access to the brig's cell lock system!

She studied and memorized the combination he was using.

Not-Raveno spat something in his hissing language and raked a hand through his hair, further mussing the wreckage of his braids. Was he on the verge of tears? If the terror tightening his expression was any indication, the rocket was going to launch, and when it did, he was dead.

Knowing Raveno, literally.

First the humans, now this alien. What was she, a bleeding sheep magnet? She sighed, knowing what she was about to do and already regretting it. Really, who was the idiot?

"Hey!" she shouted. "Hey you!"

Not-Raveno yanked out an entire braid in his frustration, then continued typing.

Kinsley gripped the ice pick and lobbed it at his shoulder, butt first.

He whipped around on another shriek—had he forgotten she was there?—and stared at her, all six points of his bony frill trembling.

Kinsley pointed at the first button in the deactivation code. "Fsd," she said, attempting to break the language barrier. She pointed at the second button in the sequence. "Ksp." And then she pointed at and enunciated the third, fourth, fifth, and all the rest of the buttons she'd witnessed Raveno press to deactivate the rocket.

But Not-Raveno did what sheep did best. Nothing.

Well, maybe not technically nothing. His frill was still trembling.

The countdown droned on.

Kinsley groaned. If attempting to trill and hiss in their slippery language wouldn't work, there was no help for it. Kinsley swung down from the incineration shaft and landed on her feet in front of him.

Not-Raveno's already round eyes widened to near perfect circles.

"You." She pointed at him.

He jumped back, staring at her finger inches from his chest.

She pointed at her eyes with two fingers, then at the control panel. "Watch this closely."

The alien stared at her the way one might a feral cat offering to teach her algebra.

She pressed the first button and did her best to pronounce the sequence properly. Again. "Fsd." She pressed the second button. "Ksp." She pressed the third and fourth and so on through the entire sequence.

The countdown ceased. The monitors froze, and the air was strangely empty in the intercom's absence.

Kinsley gestured to the control panel like a bedraggled Vanna White. "You're welcome."

Not-Raveno gaped at the monitor.

Footsteps pounded down the hallway.

"Hope you were paying attention." And at the risk of becoming predictable, Kinsley pressed the orange button.

Not-Raveno's frill sprang out. He reached for her instead of the control panel, but Kinsley dodged his grabby hands. She vaulted back into the incineration shaft, and without hesitation this time, she crawled as quickly as her knees and elbows could slide her to the brig. Dude was on his own. If he couldn't remember the access code combination after that demonstration, he was too stupid to live.

Thirty minutes later, Kinsley reached the fire vent over her holding cell, a little surprised that she'd made it without being caught or incinerated. She tapped the vent three times, alerting her cellmates to her presence. If the coast was clear, Martin would *clear* his throat, per their new code. And if it wasn't—

"One thing I *do not* miss is grocery shopping," Martin said.

Damned it. Kinsley inhaled long and deep to curb the hitch in her breath. She was more likely to fry like Riley than suffocate like Brandon, she reminded herself. The walls only *felt* like they were closing in. Her body wasn't *actually* being crushed. She wasn't *really* trapped. She just couldn't exit the incineration shaft *yet*.

"Seriously?" Leanne asked. "The food here is great."

"No, he—" Benjamin sighed. "Never mind."

Martin grunted, annoyed but tolerant. Riley would have set her straight.

As if in defiance of her efforts to remain calm, her mind flashed to her last memory of Riley—his screams and charred flesh—then immediately to Brandon and his screams and mangled limbs. Both entombed in their respective final resting places before finally dying. And they'd died in agony.

Breathe.

Air was still entering her lungs. It ached when she held her breath and burned when she finally exhaled because she was still alive. And if she wanted to stay that way, she needed to calm down and do the most difficult thing of all: wait.

She rested her forehead on the chrome shaft. She breathed. She determinedly did not think about Riley or Brandon, even if by deliberately not thinking about them, she was, in fact, thinking about them.

She waited.

An eternity later, a metal flap squeaked open and slapped shut. The food platter.

Kinsley tapped three times on the panel.

"Nope," Martin called out. "No grocery shopping for me anymore. Yum."

"What is he going on about?" Leanne whispered.

Benjamin murmured assurances.

Kinsley covered her mouth to hold in a self-deprecating snort. Why couldn't she just stay in her cell in oblivious self-absorption and make friends and play nice like all the other captives? That was all anyone had ever wanted to know—Why, Kinsley? *Why?*—and for the first time in her entire life, she didn't understand her either.

She waited longer this time. Much longer. She waited until the guard returned for the empty platter, for Benjamin to announce the time, and then she dozed off until his second announcement the next day, when she would normally be *leaving* for her mission.

Her stomach growled.

Kinsley gritted her teeth and tap-tap-tapped on the fire vent.

"No," Martin said flatly.

Damn it. The only thing more pressing than her empty stomach was her full bladder.

Leanne hiccupped. Was she crying? Someone must have finally explained to her what was happening.

"It's okay," Benjamin said. "She'll be fine."

This might be my last mission.

Kinsley wiped the sweat from her eyes. "Leanne, move your mouth like you're talking, but don't say anything. Just lip-sync my words."

"What? Why—"

"Because the cell is bugged, remember?" Martin whispered. "She wants whoever is watching the security feed to think we're talking to you."

Kinsley felt her throat constrict. *This might be the last time Martin and I share a brain.*

"Go ahead," Martin called up to her.

Kinsley swallowed. "Even if I could pay for my groceries, I can't leave the store."

"What happened?" Martin asked. "Did they catch you stealing?"

"Yes."

"Only move your lips when Switch is speaking," Benjamin whispered.

"I get it," Leanne whispered back. "I just think it's pointless."

"They'll leave if you wait long enough," Martin said, ignoring Tweedledee and Tweedledum. "Then you can—"

"No," Kinsley sighed. "Big Brother is watching, remember? If they're searching for me, they'll find me even if they're not physically there. And then we're all screwed."

"I'll find the bug."

"We've already looked everywhere. I'll dehydrate before you find it, and even if you do—"

"I'll find it," Martin insisted.

"Fine. *When* you find it, you need to spread the word. If everyone can find their bugs—"

Leanne gasped. "Martin can't escape—"

"Go grocery shopping," Benjamin cut in.

"Martin will do what needs to be done," Kinsley said. "Right, Martin?"

Silence.

"Martin?"

Something rumbled. The incineration shaft vibrated under her palms.

She knew that sound. She was intimately familiar with the rush and crackle of a backdraft. Under different circumstances, she loved that sound. She still sort of did even as her heart wedged into her throat.

"Do you hear that?" asked Benjamin.

"That sounds like—"

"Switch, get out of there," Martin snapped. "Now."

"Find the bug," Kinsley demanded. "Tell everyone when you do, and use the technology to your advantage. Play it safer than I did, Martin. Lead them home."

Martin was suddenly directly under the vent, staring straight up at her. "Shut up, and get down here! Now!"

Kinsley didn't even realize she was biting her lip until she tasted the tang of her own blood. "Promise me."

"Don't just sit there!" Martin shouted at Benjamin. "Give me a hand!"

Whispered muttering.

"So I can reach up and drag her out!"

"I'm not putting you three in harm's way when they only want me. I'm sorry, I—" Kinsley shook her head. "You can survive this, Martin. I know you can."

But Martin was ignoring her now in favor of arguing with Benjamin and Leanne. "She does *not* have a point!" he shouted. "Imagine it was *you* up there!"

Kinsley didn't stay to hear the rest. Let them argue. She knew what she had to do. Kinsley wedged herself around and began back-tracking away from their cell.

In her professional estimation—based on a perilous career in which she'd narrowly survived countless missions and been the sole survivor of her last—she was screwed. She could return to the cockpit, but if they were monitoring the brig, they were most certainly monitoring the room where she'd been discovered. Plus, she needed water. And a toilet. And—

One need at a time. Water. The galley was straight ahead and her best option for that. She could sneak in through the adjacent bathroom, killing two birds with one—

Kinsley halted, blinking at the wall in front of her. The galley was ahead, straight ahead, she was certain, but the shaft was blocked. Her only options were to turn right toward the cockpit or to double back toward the brig.

Either she was becoming disoriented in her dehydration—possible, but not likely (Not yet, anyway)—or the aliens were blocking her path, herding her right where they wanted her.

She'd become the sheep.

The backdraft was rumbling louder, like thunder. The shaft was growing hotter. Blisteringly, hot. Logically, she knew the walls we not getting smaller, but she could feel them pressing in on her. Trapping her.

Entombing her.

The panel to her right lifted with a sliding *zip*.

Kinsley snapped her attention to the open shaft. Not one foot away was a vent.

She tensed to dive through it.

A scaly arm reached up from the room below.

Kinsley slipped on the slick of her own sweat trying to dodge that grasping hand, but its claws banded around her wrist, its grip unyielding. Before she could find any traction, it yanked her through the vent and out of the incineration shaft.

She was falling. Her gut jumped. Her heart skipped a beat, and then the floor knocked the wind from her lungs, and her heart forgot to beat entirely.

Flames blasted from the vent directly above her, just suddenly there, exactly where she'd been crawling a moment before. The heat fried her face before the fire even touched her.

She'd been right: more likely to fry like Riley than suffocate like Brandon.

Someone rolled over her, shielding her from the hit.

Kinsley squinted through the heat.

Not-Raveno.

He was using his own body to deflect the column of fire. The flames billowed out on either side of his back like wings. With his chest heaving, his frown thunderous, the tangled mess of his straw-berry-blond head haloed by light, he was a furious, avenging archangel.

Not such a sheep after all.

He didn't ignite or scream or burst into ash like he should have. His grimace seemed distinctly more annoyed than agonized.

Another manner in which their alien scales were apparently different from human skin: They were flame-resistant.

So much for her plan to take out Raveno and his entire crew in a fiery explosion.

The flames cut off.

Not-Raveno rolled his shoulders. A little of the tension compressing his lips eased.

Kinsley opened her mouth—would he understand if she thanked him? Certainly, some sentiments were beyond language—but before she could say anything, he startled upright. His frill sprang out around his head.

What could possibly be worse than a raging column of fire? Kinsley followed his gaze and stilled.

They had an audience. Six other guards had entered the room, weapons drawn. Their attention darted from her to Not-Raveno and back to her, uncertain.

Not-Raveno hissed out a curse. The consonants were familiar—something Raveno had said to her on several occasions—but even without the familiarity, she would have recognized the word as something foul by the way he spat it.

That sentiment was definitely beyond language. They were both massively screwed.

The shift in his expression was her only warning. Not-Raveno's lip curled with apology and self-disgust as his arm cocked back, and the hard knuckles of his scaly fist slammed into her face.

EIGHT

RAVENO DIDN'T BETRAY HIS EMOTIONS, NOT THE BITTER disappointment that Kinsley had been discovered, not the gnawing anxiety that Tironan had apparently been the one to find her, and certainly not the dread that without some quick thinking, everyone would expect him to deliver her punishment. Vri Cilvril Raveno Hoviir wasn't even supposed to have emotions, least of all the icy terror that spread through his veins and stopped his heart cold at the sight of her and the blood spattered throughout the room: saturating the thick vespirs rug beneath her, staining the cream cushions of the lounger behind her, sprayed across the inlaid detailing of the carved illuminators surrounding her.

This room was one of dozens that had once transported excited families across space to exotic destinations in style and luxury.

Now...

Svik, now he had another reason to feel vindicated when he finally impaled his ezil through Josairo's heart.

She was still breathing. Her limbs might appear limp and lifeless, her mouth slack with unconsciousness, her skin a ruin of burns and bruises, but she was alive. Raveno tried to find some scrap of comfort as Kinsley's back expanded with each inhale, but her breaths were shallow and wet, the terrible struggles of someone suffering—from a speared lung, perhaps? Avier would know.

Struggling to breathe was better than not breathing at all. He forced his fingers to uncurl from their fists.

Avier joined him in the room, took one look at Kinsley, and hissed out a curse, confirming Raveno's fears.

Not good. Not good at all.

In perfect, practiced synchrony, Dellao, Kual, Jhoni, and Tironan snapped up straight and clicked their heels together when Raveno entered the room.

"Vri Cilvril Raveno Hoviir," they belted as one voice.

As the highest-ranking officer among the guards, his brother stepped forward. "W-w-we found and detained the escaped shols in a p-p-private room, as ordered."

"Jhoni reported that you were waiting on my next command," Raveno said.

"That's c-c-correct, Vri Cilvril."

Such a formal address from his brother's tongue always chafed, but with Kinsley half dead between them, it stabbed. Raveno forced his voice to remain as controlled and calm as his expression. "Interesting, then, that I don't recall commanding you to kill her."

The tips of Tironan's ears burned a bright blue. "Y-y-you didn't."

Raveno swept a hand at Kinsley. "Then why does she look dead?"

Tironan glanced down.

Kinsley's labored breaths filled the silence, and Tironan's embarrassment lit his entire face.

Pull it together, little brother, Raveno willed. "That was not a rhetorical question."

Tironan's expression pinched. He nudged Kinsley's hip with his boot. "L-l-look alive."

Kinsley released a low, guttural groan, but she didn't even wince. Her body lifted with Tironan's boot and returned limply to her side when he stepped back.

"Didn't you hear him?" Kual drew back his foot. "Look alive!"

Thev sa shek. Raveno lunged between them. "Halt!"

Kual froze, his leg poised midair. "Vri Cilvril?"

Avier scratched at his neck.

Yes, he knew how this looked. "How will I interrogate her if she isn't conscious to speak?"

Kual lowered his foot, suddenly unsure of himself.

Raveno crossed his arms. "My orders were to detain her. Did I say anything about harming her?"

"Shols are great warriors," Kual began. "We feared she'd fight—"

"You *feared*?" Raveno asked, more warning than question.

Kual clamped his mouth shut.

Jhoni shifted from foot to foot. "We *thought* she'd fight back. That if we didn't—"

"You *thought*?"

Dellao braced himself. "—if we didn't gain the immediate advantage, we might not have been able to detain her."

"Are these the soldiers *I've* trained? Soldiers who fear and make decisions and assumptions?" Raveno cocked his head. "You do not think. I order, and you do!"

Dellao, Kual, and Jhoni stared straight ahead, absorbing Raveno's wrath in grim resignation.

Tironan's expression was just as grim, but he met Raveno's eyes. "W-w-we acted as we deemed fit to complete your orders. You w-wanted her detained. Here she is. D-d-detained."

"She's not going to rank well in the Intergalactic Frisaes," Kual muttered to Jhoni.

"Have you looked at the humans? *Really* looked at them?" Jhoni murmured back. "None of them will."

"As if you could do better."

"I didn't sign up to fight in the frisaes."

Neither did they.

Svik, these were the masterminds who Avier wanted to entrust with his life's mission to overthrow Josairo and save Havar?

Were they so accustomed to blindly following orders and oblivious to the humans' plight that they truly thought Kinsley would fight with the strength and skill of a real shols?

Or was the traitor presently among them? Having discovered Kinsley's switch in loyalties, had he used this opportunity to "take her out," as she so feared?

Raveno prepared to lay into Jhoni and Kual.

Kinsley stirred.

Raveno froze, watching as she braced her unsteady arms to lift her meager weight. Just last shaoz, he'd witnessed her pull her entire body up into the heating duct by her fingertips. Now, she struggled to simply sit up. She raised her head and peered at him through the fall of her blood-matted hair.

A head wound. No wonder so much blood was spattered everywhere.

Raveno forced himself not to flinch under the weight of her regard. If she could find the strength to meet his gaze, he could find the courage to hold it.

Her soft, delicate skin was split from forehead to cheekbone on the left side of her face. The opposite side was puffy and purple. A matching wound sliced through her bottom lip, and the blood streaming from her nose merged into that wound, flowing over her chin and down her throat in one river. One of her dark, too-seeing eyes was forced shut by its swelling.

Raveno pressed his vresls flat before they bristled.

"I'll tell you what I've already told them," she whispered in English. "I escaped my cell searching for medicine. I'm sorry. Let me go back. Please. I won't escape again."

Something was wrong with her jaw. She was enunciating the words from between gritted teeth.

And then the meaning behind her words struck him like a *pivz* between his scales: she was upholding their deal.

She was half dead, without recourse or resources, and she was maintaining her cover.

He'd seen her skill and potential from the beginning, but cry mercy, this...this...

This was the crew he needed. Her.

Raveno refocused on the crew he was saddled with. "Has she been babbling like this the entire time?"

The men glanced at each other, as if they could glean the correct answer from the nervous shift of each other's eyes.

"My question is still not rhetorical."

"Yes, Vri Cilvril," Dellao calmly told the wall behind him. "She has been attempting to communicate with us in her language since we detained her."

Kinsley couldn't have understood their words, but her eyes jumped from person to person, tracking their conversation. She compressed her lips into a thin, bracing line. Another rivulet of blood oozed down her chin.

"What could she be saying, I wonder?" Raveno mused.

"What does anyone say when scared and in pain?" Jhoni fixated on Kinsley's chin. "Whatever she thinks we want to hear."

Raveno rounded on Jhoni. "What is it you think I want to hear?"

"I. Um." Jhoni's eyes darted about for help, but Kual and Dellao stared stoically straight ahead. "I don't understand the question, Vri Cilvril?"

Tironan closed his eyes on a low groan.

Raveno nearly grinned. "Hmmm." He clasped his hands behind his back and paced around the guards in a slow circle. "You allowed a shols to escape." He locked eyes with Dellao. "You allowed her to engage the lir s'flis. Twice."

Interestingly, Tironan flinched at that.

Raveno locked eyes with Jhoni. "You failed to capture her for three shifts, and when you *did*, you attempted to kill her."

Dellao opened his mouth, about to speak out of turn.

Raveno stopped pacing and faced him squarely, waiting on him to light his own pyre.

But after a long career serving under his command, Dellao knew better. He shut his mouth and composed his expression.

Raveno continued circling. "Did I hear the heater engage while she was still inside the ducts?"

Silence.

Raveno pivoted on his heel to face Jhoni. "None of my questions are rhetorical!"

Jhoni jolted like a live wire. "Yes, Vri Cilvril! We engaged the heater to drive her out of hiding."

"And what about engaging the heater, the very system we use to *execute* people, made you think that was the appropriate means to capture her *without* killing her?"

His ears bled to midnight. "I. Um. Well—"

"Unacceptable!"

The wet, wheezing gasps of Kinsley's breathing filled the silence, but if he wasn't mistaken, a smirk quirked her bloodied lips.

"But we captured her," Dellao said, unable to hold on to his good sense any longer. "Our methods were rash, but our results, thanks to Tironan, were worth the risk. She's here, and she's alive, per your orders. Vri Cilvril." He tacked on the title nearly as an afterthought.

Raveno sidestepped to shout into Dellao's face, "She never should have escaped to begin with! And having escaped, she never should have remained free for so long! And having been captured, she never should have been this injured!"

Dellao's mouth pinched, but he clicked his heels together. "Yes, Vri Cilvril."

Raveno straightened. "She was a test, and all of you failed abominably."

Kual frowned, his scales creased with confusion.

Tironan looked about to interrupt—again, cry mercy!—but before his tongue could form the words, Jhoni burst out with, "A test?"

Dellao rolled his eyes.

Raveno knew the feeling.

He took mercy on Dellao and rounded on Jhoni. "Yes, a test. I asked her to effect an escape to test your skills against hers."

Jhoni startled. "You've *talked* to her?"

Avier leaned in. "What are you—"

Raveno raised a silencing hand. "She's my *Vri Sa Shols*."

Avier stiffened beside him.

Tironan openly gaped.

"Your Vri Sa Shols? We haven't even had Selections yet." Jhoni tilted his head. "Have we?"

Dellao honed his stare on the ceiling.

"A formality that I'll resolve once we land on Havar," Raveno said.

Kual's frown increased with deeper confusion.

"Is her *ankesh* even activated?" Jhoni asked, glancing down at her wrist. "How could we have known she was yours?"

"That was the point. Do better next time." He eyed each one of them in turn. "Or there may not be a next time."

Dellao nodded. "Your will by my hands."

"Your will by my hands," Kual said, obviously still trying to wrestle through what that will was.

"Y-y-your will b-b-b—"

"Your will by my hands," Jhoni muttered.

"Dismissed!"

All four clicked their heels and marched from the cell.

Well, "marched" was a loose description. They poured from the cell like organs spilled from a gutting.

Raveno waited until the brig door locked shut behind them before crouching beside Kinsley. "What happened?" he asked in English.

Kinsley eyed Avier behind him.

"Speak freely," Raveno assured her. "He is my Vri Zyvril. My healing hand. How would you say it?" He rubbed his mouth, thinking. "My medical doctor and brother in all ways except blood. We have no secrets."

94

She eyed the room around them.

Raveno felt an uncommon, unwanted bloom of respect unfurl within his chest. "Our surveillance technology on this ship is only visual. No audio. Unfortunately," he added warily.

She met his gaze at that. "Thanks for the performance."

Raveno cocked his head. "Learned to speak Haveo, have you?"

"After eight years in the army, I know a proper dressing-down when I hear one, no matter the language."

Raveno grunted at that. "You were caught."

"Can't get anything past you."

Avier coughed to smother a chuckle.

Patience, Raveno reminded himself. She'd suffered a head wound.

Although Avier didn't have an excuse.

"What happened?" Raveno asked. Again.

She released a long breath. "I let compassion get the better of me. Instead of running when I had the chance, I helped one of your guards. He was panicking over the rocket countdown. Pressing all the wrong buttons and freaking out and—" She swayed to the left, shook her head, and braced an arm to steady herself. "I felt bad for him."

Raveno stared, incredulous. "Causing chaos among my crew is the main objective of your mission, is it not?"

"Yes, but this guard in particular... His panic was so sharp and real, and his... I..." She blinked, and her eyes stayed closed a fraction too long. "I'm an idiot."

Raveno snorted. "I do not think a lack of intelligence is your greatest flaw."

"You're right. That would that be my lack of self-preservation instincts."

Avier grunted.

Raveno frowned. "You—"

"Or my compassion, since that's what got me into this mess. I should've just let him pull *all* his braids out of his scaly head."

"You, my little lilssna, cannot grasp the concept of defeat. *That* is your greatest flaw." And then Raveno realized what she'd just said about braids. "The panicking guard was Tironan?"

Her deep, dark eyes lost their focus. Her swaying was becoming dangerous. "Who?"

"Describe the panicking guard," Raveno hissed.

Her eyes narrowed on him, even through the pain. "Why?"

"'Why' does not concern you."

"I'm concerning myself."

"Were any of the guards in this room my traitor? Is one of them giving you svirros?" Raveno took hold of her shoulders before she fell over.

She released a low, guttural groan.

He loosened his grip, frowning. His palms were wet. He examined his hands and then Kinsley. Her shoulders were weeping from the severity of her burns.

His vresls bristled.

"He saved me," she murmured. "And then he did what he had to do to save face. I'd have done the same."

He grabbed her by the lower arms, more careful of her wounds this time, and shook her. "*Who?*"

Her eyes rolled back, and she fell limp, unconsciousness, into his arms.

NINE

THE FIRST THING KINSLEY NOTICED WAS THE SILENCE. SWEET, blessed, unattainable silence. Leanne wasn't asking migraine-inducing questions. Benjamin wasn't announcing the time. Martin wasn't inquiring about her health. No one was whining or crying or bleating at her. No one, besides herself, was even breathing.

The second thing Kinsley noticed was the smell. Instead of the sickly combination of all seven scented shower gels competing for dominance because no one could agree on a single scent for the day—Leanne alone rarely committed to a matching scent for her hair, face, and body—the air was fresh and clean, nearly like eucalyptus, but bright. Citrus?

The third thing she noticed was her body's comfort. Her hip didn't ache. Her shoulder wasn't numb. Her back wasn't knotted in kinks and aches and misaligned disks. The wonders of sleeping on a mattress instead of being huddled on the cold, unforgiving cell floor.

But she preferred the cell floor over the comforts of freshly laundered sheets while in captivity.

Maybe she was back on Earth.

Better yet, maybe the entire abduction had been a nightmare. Or, more likely, she'd been caught in an IED blast after all, and she was just now waking up from being in a coma. She could be lying in a hospital bed, except in her experience, the silence of a hospital room was always punctuated by the steady beep of a heart monitor.

Maybe her heart wasn't beating. She was dead, and the abduction had been her purgatory. After all she'd suffered, her penance was finally complete. And this was—what, heaven? Even for her spiraling imagination that was a stretch, but crazier things had happened. She'd been abducted by aliens, after all. Anything, absolutely anything, was possible.

Kinsley opened her eyes, then closed them and tried again for good measure.

She wasn't dead. She wasn't waking from a coma. And being abducted by aliens might be a nightmare, but she was still living it.

But she wasn't in her cell.

By the glow of a palm-sized, digital time-keeping device—oh, hell, a tablet. She was on an alien spaceship, who knew how far from Earth, and the glow of a tablet alarm clock on a nearby desk lit her surroundings. The room was small, spartan compared to the luxury of her cell, barely large enough to accommodate the extra-long bed she was currently snuggled in. A floor-to-ceiling window—like the viewing panel in the cockpit—showcased the beautiful magnitude of the universe just inches away on the other side of the wall. Except for the bed, the furnishings were cold and chrome, in theme with the rest of the ship: built-in shelves on either side of the bed and a mini cockpit arrangement complete with an instrument panel, a single monitor, and a swivel chair.

An alien office space to match the alien alarm clock.

Kinsley inhaled that clean, citrus air until she thought her lungs might burst. She was in someone's bedroom. An alien's bedroom on a spaceship hurtling through the Milky Way. In said alien's bed.

What did it say about her life lately that this wasn't the worst circumstance she'd woken up in?

She wiggled her toes, and the sheets at the end of the bed shifted with her movement. And, oh, those sheets! No wonder she'd nearly mistaken this bed for heaven. She didn't recognize the fabric, but she'd hazard a guess that whatever the material, it didn't originate on Earth. It was fuzzy but smooth, warm yet wicking, and it felt amazing against her skin.

Against her skin.

She felt herself under the sheets and groaned.

They'd removed her clothes. She was *naked* in an alien bed.

And *still* not the worst circumstance.

She felt pretty good for someone who had nearly been broiled alive and beaten to death after not eating or drinking for twenty-four hours. Her face wasn't throbbing. Her shoulders weren't burning. Her side wasn't cramping.

They must have treated her to another round in the healing tube.

Was she very lucky that their alien leader was willing to treat her injuries or very unlucky that she had so many injuries to treat?

Kinsley lifted her arm to rub her eyes and froze.

Something besides the instrument panel was glowing in the darkness. Something was glowing beneath her skin.

A blue dot the size of a dime—similar if not identical to the blue dots that pulsed under *their* scales—was pulsing on the inside of *her* right wrist.

Beneath my skin.

Her stomach dropped at the sight, and the glowing pulse accelerated in time with her heartbeat. She swiped her thumb over the dot, then scratched at it, then dug at it with her nail, but she couldn't feel it, whatever *it* was.

It faded, then reappeared as a symbol: a swirling horseshoe with a dot in the belly of its U.

Just because she couldn't feel it didn't mean it couldn't be removed.

She was scanning the room for something sharp when a metallic whir sounded from one of the closed doors. Kinsley whipped her head up. There were four doors, three of which were closed. The open door on the middle left revealed a full bath—again, similar to the contents of her cell, but downgraded. Simple instead of opulent.

The orange locking mechanism on the far-right door flashed to blue.

Kinsley tossed the sheet aside, sat up, and swung her feet over the side of the bed. Immediately, the room somersaulted. Kinsley blinked, and when she opened her eyes, she was flat on the floor, half the sheet under her body, her elbow throbbing.

Shit, no time to run. Just as she rolled under the bed, burritoing herself in the soft linens to hide the path of her escape, the door slid open.

A pair of boots appeared in the doorway. They entered the room in two strides and stopped.

The door slid shut.

"Kinsley?"

Raveno. Besides the fact that he was the only alien who knew her name, she was annoyed to realize that she recognized his voice. Deep and rumbling. He lingered a second too long on the slurring *sl* of her name, vibrating his bifurcated tongue unnecessarily. The accented consonants pricked both her temper and the hairs on the back of her neck.

She bit her lip.

Raveno pounded across the room. Something clattered onto the instrument panel. He grabbed the chair as he passed and swiveled it across the floor. First one and then both feet disappeared as he stepped up onto the chair.

Kinsley craned her neck for a better angle. Yep—Raveno. The long, thick fall of his platinum hair hung down to mid-back, and what a back it was. The leather straps of his weapons holders didn't leave much to the imagination. His muscles flexed under his scales as he lifted himself neck-deep into the incineration shaft. His shoulders were broad—too broad for the vent's opening—his waist trim, his ass—

Kinsley tore her eyes away from that studded gladiator skirt, her cheeks on fire. It had been a very long time, but certainly not *that* long.

"Kinsley!" he called. "You can't return to your room!" He waited a moment—listening?—then pounded the shaft with the flat of his fist. "Svik!"

He jumped from the chair and rushed to the door, muttering obscenities, no doubt. Just as he reached the hallway, he halted midstride.

Kinsley held her breath.

Raveno pivoted slowly, the toe of his boot rotating to face the bed.

Damn it.

Raveno dropped to his hands and knees. His claws clicked on the floor as he braced himself into a push-up, and his face appeared sideways under the bed, inches from hers.

Their eyes locked.

Kinsley forced a smile. "Fancy meeting you here."

A single fang—the left front incisor—slipped from behind his lips, and Kinsley had the distinct impression that Raveno didn't realize he was sneering.

Or, perhaps, he was trying very hard not to.

"What gave me away?" she asked.

The slits of his nostrils flexed wide, then sealed shut.

"You smelled me?" Kinsley sighed. "Figures."

"What," he began, his voice a low, rasping rumble, "are you doing here?"

"Your guess is as good as mine. I woke up in this room with no recollection of how I got here. Honestly, I was hoping you could fill me in."

"What are you doing *under* my bed?" he enunciated, barely moving his lips.

"*Your* bed, hmm? I can do you one better: Why am I naked?" She wriggled one arm from the sheets and held out her wrist. "And what the hell is *under my skin?*"

Raveno massaged the frown between his eyes. "I'll answer your questions after you've answered mine."

"*What did you do to me?*" Kinsley shrieked, shaking her wrist at him. If she'd been wrong and they *were* androids, did that make her an android now too?

She didn't feel like an android.

How would an android that didn't know it was an android feel?

She shook her wrist at him a second time when he didn't immediately answer.

Raveno flinched back as if *he'd* been the one violated. "It is called an ankesh. Come out from under the bed, and I will explain."

She studied *his* glowing wrist braced on the mattress. "It's like yours."

He sighed. "Similar in appearance, but not in function. Mine is called an anku."

"What does—"

"I will answer your questions, I promise, but not like this. Please." He chopped his palm between them, then aside. "Let's discuss this face-to-face."

"What is the purpose of this...this..." She poked at her wrist, unable to cough up the syllables of the glowing alien technology inside her.

"Ankesh," he repeated helpfully. Calmly. Infuriatingly. "A perk of having one is this cabin." He swept an offering hand behind him.

"*Your* cabin. How is that a perk?"

"You will have one roommate instead of three. Your own bed—we will swap sleeping shifts—and more privacy."

"Not much privacy with you here, is there?" She narrowed her eyes. "Why can't I return to the brig?"

Raveno's frill pressed so flat against his chest, its spines were nearly concave. "I know the bathing room is a bit more primitive than the one in your cell, but for cleaning and defecating, it should serve your needs well."

"I'm sure the *bathing room* is perfectly fine, like everything else on this ship—besides the fact that I don't want to be here. I—"

"And the bed is soft, yet supportive, which is great for spine health."

"The bed is great, but—"

"I know 'square footage' is appealing to humans. Although my cabin is much smaller than your previous accommodations, and it does not boast a private workout suite, it does—"

"You don't need to sell me the room, Raveno. I'm not buying." She met his gaze squarely. "Why. *Can't*. I. Return. To the brig?"

His thin, bifurcated tongue flicked the air.

Her stomach rumbled.

"Are you hungry?"

No, she was starving. She opened her mouth to continue pressing him about the brig, but he leaned to the side and hitched a thumb at the instrument panel.

He'd brought a food platter. Some sort of sliced roasted meat, white gravy over a pile of her favorite blue beans, a leafy side with a sliced juicy red something on top of it, and a flaky puff. Too much, as usual, and so fresh from the galley, it was still steaming.

"Considering your weakened condition, I do not want to tax your sensitive stomach. You vomited twice while healing," he said, wincing. "But if you feel ready...please, help yourself."

Oh, now that she knew the food was there, she could smell it! The cooked meat, especially. She swallowed before her betraying tongue choked on the burst of saliva flooding her mouth. "Some food would be great."

He nodded. "Then come out from under the bed, and as you eat, we will have a true conversation."

As bribes went, it was a pretty good one. And as deals went, it wasn't bad either, considering the circumstances.

Kinsley moved to crawl out from under the bed and nearly strangled herself. The sheet snagged on something—the bedframe, maybe—and she was too tightly wrapped in it to wriggle her second arm free. If she rolled onto her stomach, maybe she could inchworm her way—

"What," Raveno hissed, "are you doing *now*?"

"Trying to crawl out." She blew an overly long bang out of her right eye. What she wouldn't give for a haircut! "The sheet is stuck on something, and I—"

Raveno grabbed a fistful of sheet, and with a loud, long rip, dragged her across the floor and out from under the bed. He snatched her up by the waist and propped her on her own two feet. "There! Now, we—"

The room dipped sideways.

Here we go again, she thought and braced for the hit.

Raveno caught her inches before the floor would have slammed into her face.

"That was a close one," she murmured.

Raveno swung her up into his arms. His body was surprisingly warm, even through the layers of blanket. She wasn't sure why that was so jolting, why she always assumed his scales would be as cold as they were hard, but they weren't. She didn't want to enjoy that warmth or the feeling of his arms around her. His proximity while she was this weak should have been terrifying, but it wasn't. He seemed more inclined to make deals than deliver punishments lately.

He murdered Riley, she reminded herself before she could spiral into full-on Stockholm syndrome. *He's the captain of this ship, leading a mission to abduct and traffic dozens of people across the galaxy. He's the enemy.*

He smelled like eucalyptus and citrus.

Raveno sat her on the bed, and with a quick, efficient tug, loosened the wrap of the sheet so she could free her left arm and hold the sheet in place under her pits.

"Thank you," she murmured grudgingly.

Raveno stepped back. "Were you this weak following your last visit to the infirmary?"

She raised her eyebrows. "You didn't spy on my recovery from the security footage of my cell?"

He crossed his arms, waiting.

"Not quite this severe, but yes, I was drained," Kinsley admitted. "Of all the technology on this ship, those healing tubes are pretty impressive."

"Healing tubes?"

"Pods?" Kinsley waved a hand. "Whatever you call them, they're magic."

"I believe you're referring to the—what would it be in English? The RRC. Each symbol—in your case, letter—represents the first letter of its full name: rapid repair chamber."

Kinsley snorted. "I'm familiar with the concept. Medical technology on Earth is abbreviated like that too. They fixed my broken bones, torn ligaments, bruises, burns, and lacerations so far. Is there anything they can't treat?"

The frill around his neck flexed. "They can't treat death."

"Good thing I only ever *tempt* death, then, huh?" She shook her head on a dark chuckle. "How does the RRC work?"

Raveno flicked his claws dismissively. "You couldn't comprehend the science behind such technology."

Kinsley grinned. "You don't know how they work, do you?" She held up a placating hand. "I used technology on Earth all the time without knowing exactly how it worked."

"Avier knows the science behind it, so I don't have to."

"Does he really, though? Even on humans?"

His frill flattened.

"That's what I thought. Maybe healing me the first time was fine, but using it on me a second time? Who knows? Maybe I drop dead tomorrow from rapid repair syndrome."

His eyes narrowed. "I have never heard of such a syndrome."

"How would you? Have you ever healed a human before?"

He cocked his head menacingly. "Maybe when you need healing a third time, I shouldn't take the risk."

"Will I need healing a third time?"

"If your habit of 'tempting death,' continues, yes."

Kinsley tested the lateral movement of her recently bruised jaw. Not even a twinge. "Well, besides the lingering muscle weakness, it feels like the RRC worked a miracle. Again."

Raveno stepped forward, cupped her chin in his hand, and tilted her cheek toward him. The thin webbing between his fingers, like gossamer, tickled her jawline. "Yes, Avier was able to successfully heal your injuries," he murmured. His scrutiny, nearly as intimate as his touch, swept over the planes of her face.

Kinsley stilled. "Then why am I so weak?"

"Healing is hard work." He released her chin, twisted to grab the flaky puff from the food tray, and offered it to her. "Here. I recommend starting with a *rhef*."

"Rhef?" she asked, refusing to feel the lack of his touch.

"You might call it a pastry, I think. But not quite as humans do not eat pastries to refuel after exercise."

"Speak for yourself." She took the pastry but eyed the beans. "I'd prefer—"

"I recommend you eat slowly," he interrupted, following the line of her gaze. "And begin with something light. Like the rhef."

She inhaled for patience, and the savory sweet aroma from the rhef distracted her. Giving in didn't feel quite like defeat with a pastry in hand, so she took a bite.

Oh, sweet baby Jesus! She moaned.

"I knew it was too much too soon."

Raveno tried to swipe the rhef from her, but Kinsley snatched it to her chest. "Get your own exercise pastry."

"You sounded in pain."

"That was the sound of intense appreciation. It's delicious."

Raveno's frill flared slightly, then relaxed. "Bvet is an excellent cook."

Bvet, whoever he was, certainly could bake a mean pastry. The rhef was flaky but moist, sweet but not too sweet, and somehow almost floral as well as buttery in its aroma. Kinsley breathed it in as she chewed, savoring its warmth in her hands and the solid bite of it in her full mouth. Heaven—if she ignored the alien in front of her and his ship around her and his mystery blue dot inside her.

"Not that I'm complaining—the opposite, in fact—but why are you feeding us like this?" Kinsley asked.

Raveno tilted his head. "Feeding you like what?"

"Like we're friends instead of captives."

"How else should I be feeding you?"

Kinsley shrugged. "I can't imagine that human trafficking victims typically *gain* weight after being kidnapped. Unless..." She bit her lip. "Are you fattening us up deliberately?"

"This I must hear explained," he muttered. "What could possibly be my purpose in deliberately over feeding you?"

"Well, not to give you any ideas, but...to eat us."

Raveno reared back. "Eat you? You think I intend to *eat you*?"

Why was everyone always so shocked by the notion? "Not you specifically, but if we are being trafficked for sale, like cattle—"

"The havari will not eat you. Despite the tangled mess I have made of my life, that is the one thing I can absolutely guarantee." Raveno shook his head. "Eat you."

"Then why are you feeding us so well?" Kinsley snapped.

"My mission is to return with a ship full of healthy, *living* humans. Why would I risk that mission with something as preventable as starvation?"

"There's certainly no risk of that," she muttered.

"How did my crew catch you? You mentioned—"

Kinsley shook her finger at him. "Nope, we're continuing with *my* questions. Why am I here in your room, why can't I return to the brig, what is an ankesh, and what is it doing under my skin?"

The tips of Raveno's pointed ears bled a deep blue. "I promise to answer all those questions, but I fear if we discuss your questions first, you will lose your appetite. You need to regain your strength with nourishment."

Kinsley pouted. "Oh, you're worried your evil master plan will upset my little stomach?"

Raveno nodded, completely missing her sarcasm. "My answers upset *my* stomach. They are sure to upset yours."

Kinsley nibbled on her rhef, considering. "What happened to the man who once ripped my arm out of its socket to extract the information he wanted? Again, not that I'm complaining."

"I didn't mean—" he began, but shut his mouth and hissed, "When you were caught by my guards, you could have revealed our acquaintance. Knowing the traitor among them, you could have attempted to turn them against me." He jabbed his pointer claw at her. "You would have failed," he warned. "But you could have tried. *Should* have tried, really, but you did not. You remained loyal to me, and I treat those who are loyal very differently than those I distrust."

By God, how was it possible that his fictitious traitor was still managing to bail her out of trouble? How long could she possibly play this game?

As long as it takes. "You promise to answer my questions after I answer yours? You pinky promise?"

He hesitated. "How does a pinky promise?"

Kinsley waved away his question. "If you break your word, our entire deal is off. I don't make deals with people I can't trust."

"If I *break* my word?" Raveno asked. "That is an idiom, yes?"

"Yes. To break your word is to say one thing and do the opposite. It's not fulfilling a promise."

"Ah."

"I will answer your questions first on your promise that my questions will be answered next."

Raveno nodded. "Yes, I promise that."

Kinsley spread out her arms and met the fire of his blood-orange eyes. "What do you want to know?"

"You mentioned that your compassion got you caught. That you took pity on one of my guards because he was pulling his braids out in panic."

Kinsley froze. Maybe she couldn't play this game after all. "Yes," she said carefully.

"Describe him."

"I, well..." Kinsley bit into her rhef and took her time chewing through her options. "I'd prefer not to."

Raveno leaned forward. His tongue lashed the air. "You feel some loyalty toward *another* one of my guards?"

Kinsley compressed her lips.

"Careful, little lilssna," Raveno murmured. "Too many loyalties, and you won't have a side to stand on. Not even your own."

"He saved me, okay? Right before beating me to a pulp, he pulled me from the heating duct seconds before I would have been deep fried. Literally. He was grateful, I think, for my help disarming the rocket, but when the other guards caught us, the beating was for their benefit, to disguise his gratitude."

"That's touching. *Describe him.*"

She shook her head.

Raveno narrowed his eyes. "Was he one of the guards in the cell when I disciplined them?"

Kinsley shrugged, nibbling on the rhef.

"What is this?" He hiked his shoulders to his ears in exaggerated imitation. "Shoulders do not speak. Use your voice."

Kinsley rolled her eyes. "It means that it doesn't matter which guard saved me. Whoever he is, he's not your traitor, so I'd prefer not to get him in trouble over nothing. You don't need to concern yourself with him."

Raveno stared at her as if by simply wanting the truth hard enough he could peel it from her mind. "The guard who saved you is *not* my traitor?"

"Correct."

Raveno tilted his head menacingly. "You are telling me that one guard made a deal with you against me to return you home, and a second guard saved your life after you helped him disarm the lir s'flis. All while you are reporting to me?"

"What's the lers fliz?"

"Lir s'flis," he repeated, correcting her pronunciation. "The weapon you engage every time you are caught in the control room."

"Ah, the rocket launcher? Learz fleez," she repeated, attempting to mimic his accent.

His frill flexed. "Lir s'flis."

"Lees flees."

"No. *Lir—*" His frill snapped shut. "Cease this insanity! You claim that the guard who saved you is *not* my traitor?"

"I'm not claiming it. I *know* it."

"Which guard?"

"I don't know their names."

"*Describe him.*"

Kinsley clamped her mouth shut.

Raveno heaved a frustrated breath. "I do not intend to further discipline this guard. My *pinky* promises, if such a thing makes it more true. Of the four guards who found you, two of them are my top —how would you say it?" He crossed his arms and tapped his armband in thought. "Suspects. I would like to know which suspect I can cross off my list."

Kinsley inhaled, weighing her decision. Hers wasn't the only life balanced on her silence or cooperation.

Raveno waited.

"He's petite, compared to the rest of you," Kinsley admitted. "Muscled, but lean. Dark eyes. Sculpted features. Reddish-blond hair, straight and long like yours, the braids at his temples keeping his mini headband in place."

Raveno's nostril slits flared, then sealed shut. "Mini headband?"

"Like yours," she said again, pointing at the bone-studded monstrosity on his forehead. "But with less gravitas. No bone studs. Just a thin cord across his forehead."

"And this guard who saved you, the one with the 'mini headband,' he is *not* the guard who made the deal with you? He is *not* the guard trying to undermine my power?"

"No. He's not."

Raveno didn't move. He didn't rattle or sneer or taste the air with that reptilian bifurcated tongue. He didn't even blink, not with his inner or regular eyelids. "Give me your word," he whispered. "Your promise."

"I—" Kinsley frowned. Was Raveno trembling? "I give you my word. The guard with the mini headband who saved me is not your traitor."

He still didn't react, and then, from one heartbeat to the next, like a marionette whose strings had been snipped, Raveno crumbled to his knees. He caught himself by his elbows on the edge of the bed and covered his eyes with the sharp blades of his claws, his shoulders heaving.

TEN

When Raveno was younger, before he'd lost hope in the possibility of his father's redemption, he'd fought to prove himself, his strength and worth to Josairo. If only he ran faster, tried harder, aimed tighter, battled fiercer, his father would not just accept his infirmity, but be proud of him. And in that pride, Josairo might listen to his council, consider new policies, adopt a more lenient rule: change.

As Raveno grew older, wiser, and more realistic, he knew that earning such pride from Josairo was impossible without literally losing his leg and figuratively losing his soul, and once earned, that pride didn't have the power to change anything.

Raveno's future and that of Havar could only thrive without Josairo in it.

When the time came, maybe his people would back him. Maybe they wouldn't. Maybe the alliances he'd carefully cultivated would follow through on their pacts. Maybe they wouldn't. Maybe he'd survive to taste the sweet fruit of his labor and maybe he'd die trying, but no matter the uncertainty of the future, he intended to fight for it. Righting Josairo's wrongs—and by extension, his own—was worth every sacrifice he'd ever made: his ideals, his leg, his soul. All except one.

He couldn't sacrifice his brother. Not Tironan.

But according to Kinsley, he didn't have to.

Tironan isn't the traitor.

He'd been so certain of his brother's betrayal that the sudden knowledge that the traitor *wasn't* Tironan had punched the wind from his chest. Raveno gasped in a ragged breath

A hand gripped his shoulder and squeezed.

Raveno startled. He wasn't alone, obviously, but the relief had been so all-consuming that he'd forgotten everything else, even the room he was in and with whom he shared it.

Kinsley was touching his shoulder. Her eyes had widened to show the whites all around her dark irises. Her pink lips were parted in surprise, and the wings of her brows puckered at their center—a look of concern, same as an havarian, just with hair.

"Are you all right?"

She was half starved and newly recovered from multiple injuries after being captured and caged *by him*, yet she was inquiring about *his* well-being?

His chest ached.

No one had inquired after his well-being in—well, he couldn't remember how long. Maybe since before his mother had been murdered. Certainly before he'd risen to Vri Cilvril. Everyone was too terrified of him now to inquire. They answered direct questions and provided the requested reports, but caring wasn't required. In fact, it was discouraged. By him.

"Raveno?"

If he attempted to speak, more than words would spill out.

"Does the guard who saved me mean something to you? A best friend or brother, maybe? Your Tiro-man," she hedged softly.

"Tironan," he corrected her, just as softly.

"Was he one of the two people on your suspect list?"

Raveno inhaled deeply, attempting to piece together his shattered composure, but she was so close—her hand on his shoulder, her lips only inches from his forehead, her knees beside his elbows—all he smelled was her. The sweet musk of her scent drowned his senses and all reason. Without conscious thought, he leaned into her touch and brushed his cheek against her forearm. His vresls quivered. The soft warmth of her skin was strangely overwhelming. The constriction in his throat relaxed even as baser parts of him stiffened.

Thev sa shek, but Avier was wrong. He didn't see himself in her. She was everything he could only hope to be: strong when physically weaker, courageous against the odds, persistent despite fear.

Her pulse sprinted.

Raveno's breath hitched. Could Kinsley feel the same way?

He peeked up and stilled.

She was staring at him with wide, shocked eyes, her body frozen.

He forced himself to pull away, self-disgust rising like bile in his throat. Why would she feel the same? Her accelerated heartrate was fear. Considering her circumstances and what he'd allowed her to believe of him, it could be nothing else.

He stood, retrieved the food tray, and sat on the edge of the bed beside her, careful to keep a respectful distance.

Kinsley tracked his movements with a cautious flick of her eyes.

He snagged an *eussh* from the tray, fitted his claws into the grasping sheaths, speared a meaty hunk of a *vespirs* breast, and held it aloft for her to bite. "The rhef settled well?"

"It did." Kinsley's gaze darted from Raveno to the food to the utensil in his hand and back to Raveno. Her stomach groaned in protest of her hesitation.

His lips twitched. "Care to try more?"

"I don't suppose you have a fork?" she asked warily.

"I do not."

"Hmmm." She picked up the second eussh from the tray, but as small as her fingers were, they didn't fit inside the grasping sheaths properly without claws. The eussh fell from her fingertips and back onto the tray when she attempted to scoop a helping of *shetn*.

Raveno waited. He could be patient.

Grabbing one of the claw sheaths by its rim, she attempted to spear a single shetn with its pointed tip.

Raveno winced. "Careful. All sides of the eussh are—"

"Damn it." She dropped the eussh with a clatter and sucked on her finger.

"—sharp."

She glared askance at him.

Raveno lifted the meat on his eussh a little closer to her mouth.

She parted her lips on a long-suffering eye roll, and seemed, strangely, to brace herself.

He fed the vespirs to her, suppressing a grin.

The moment her mouth closed on the meat, however, all obstinate, stubborn pride melted from her expression, replaced by pure bliss.

She moaned.

Raveno did grin then, while she still wasn't looking. He hadn't heard a moan quite that enthusiastic in seven thesh, not since separating from Cresha.

"The guard you described, the one who saved you, *is* Tironan. My brother," he admitted.

She opened her eyes and finished chewing. "And you suspected him, your own brother, of betraying you?"

He scooped a clawful of shetn for her and held it up to her lips. "If I were him, I would betray me."

Miraculously, she ate the shetn without finding something to protest. "If you feel that way about yourself, it's not too late to turn over a new leaf. To change, I mean. Self-awareness is, after all, the first step."

"It's a bit more complicated than that."

"With sibling betrayal, it always is," she murmured.

"Sounds as if you are familiar with the subject?"

A muscle in Kinsley's jaw tightened. "What would you do if Tironan *had* betrayed you?"

Raveno sliced his eussh through the shetn, carving lines in its viscosity. "No need to dwell on that horror now."

She considered him a moment. "You would execute your own brother?"

"If he betrayed me, I...I would do what must be done."

"Hmmm."

"What, 'hmmm'?"

She raised her shoulders and let them drop. "Who determines what must be done?"

"Someone higher in command than me."

"Ain't that the truth?" She pointed to the food tray. "More of the blue beans, please, before you smush them into paste."

They weren't beans, but Raveno scooped up the only blue thing on the food tray, the shetn, and obliged. "You do not like the vespirs?"

"The what?" she mumbled around a mouthful.

He pointed at it.

"Mmmm." She swallowed. "I do, but I shouldn't."

He felt his vresls rise slightly. "Why *shouldn't* you?"

"If there was something higher on the food chain that could choose to either eat me or plants for their protein, I'd want them to choose the plant."

Raveno tilted his head. "In this scenario, you are the vresls?"

Kinsley nodded.

"What if you were the plant? Then what would you want?"

"Why would I be the plant?" she asked. "I'm a thinking, feeling being with a brain."

"You think plants do not feel without a brain?"

"I'm just uncomfortable with the idea of killing a living thing."

"Are plants not living?"

Kinsley narrowed her eyes. "You're being deliberately obtuse."

"Where I'm from, on the planet Havar, plants eat animals without discomfort. Why shouldn't I do the same?"

"Plants eat animals," she said deadpan, and then something lit in her expression. "You mean they eat insects? Like a Venus flytrap?"

"Like that, yes, but our native vegetation cannot sustain themselves on insects. They consume larger prey. People even."

She tapped her temple. "They might not if they had brains." And then she froze. "Wait, did you just say people? The plants on your planet eat *people?*"

"Well, they consume dead people," he clarified. "It has been somewhat beneficial, actually, considering Havar's...limitations on the disposal of our departed. Our soil composition does not—"

Kinsley held up a staying hand. "I believe you without the details of Havar's soil composition. Plants eating people. Jesus."

Raveno laughed. "So do not mind me enjoying the few plants and animals that do not eat me." Slowly, very deliberately, he speared a slice of vespirs and chomped it down whole.

Kinsley shook her head. Her eyes weren't amused, but the pull to her lips said otherwise.

"What about Jhoni, Dellao, and Kual?" he asked. "The other three guards who captured you."

"How should I know their dietary preferences?"

"Now who is being obtuse?"

She had the nerve to grin, and his vresls had the gall to quiver.

"Were any of the other guards who captured you the guard who is betraying me?" he asked.

She opened her mouth for more food, and Raveno accommodated with another scoop of shetn.

She chewed for much longer than the soft shetn could possibly require. "I'm not sure."

"You saw their faces."

She lifted her hands, seemingly helpless. "After your brother punched me, everything sort of blurred together. Between my eye swelling shut and the pain and what I'm assuming was a concussion..."

Raveno nodded grudgingly.

"I can't recall their facial features with any real accuracy."

Raveno clinked his eussh against the food tray in thought. "The way you spoke to me in that cell, the way you maintained your cover...one of them was my traitor. I'm sure of it."

Her shoulders bobbed.

"You think this does not matter?" he growled.

"It does, but I can't tell you what I don't know. I'm sorry."

Raveno heaved a sigh. "At least you eliminated Tironan as a suspect. That is more than Avier has accomplished."

"What's Avier trying to accomplish?" She nodded at the tray. "More of the blue beans, please."

"Shetn," he corrected and scooped up another helping. "While you know my traitor's face, Avier may be able to track his movements."

"Oh?" she mumbled, still chewing.

"If Avier can determine who is stealing the drugs from the pharmacy, then you can confirm his identity, and I..." Raveno massaged his pounding temple at the thought. "I can deliver punishment and have one less problem to worry about."

Kinsley swallowed, nodding.

He scooped another helping of shetn into her mouth. "What is your fascination with the lir s'flis?"

She covered her mouth with her hand as she chewed this time—it had been a rather large scoop. "Fascination?"

"Of all your many attempts to incite chaos, you take strange enjoyment from pressing that button. It is certainly your preference for exiting a jam."

"*Getting out of* a jam," she corrected. "It's not specifically the lersh fleesh. And it's not strange."

"Lir s'flis. And I think it *is* strange. You have engaged it four times now, and even when you do not engage it, your eye is always upon it."

She snorted. "My eye is not *always upon it.*"

"I have witnessed you caressing it."

She tucked her arms across her chest. "I'm just a hands-on learner, is all."

"Hands-on learner?"

"I need to hold a thing, break it down, and rebuild it myself to understand how it functions. Like, you couldn't just show me a diagram of a radio-controlled IED, for example, and expect me to understand the steps to disarm it. I need the device in person. I need to hold it and touch it and disarm it myself to understand how it functions, even if that means singeing my eyebrows a few times before I get it right."

He stared at her, deciding which of his many questions from all that was most pertinent. "What is a radio-controlled i-ee-dee?"

"I-E-D. It's an acronym like your RRC. Which is—you know what? It doesn't matter. My point is that touching the lerch flees—"

"Lir s'flis."

"It's just part of my process."

"Process for what?"

"For learning."

Raveno studied her flushed, embarrassed expression. Learning from experience was a skill many people struggled to master. He thought of Tironan and how she'd described his panic while trying and failing to deactivate the lir s'flis. Tironan was the opposite of Kinsley's hands-on learning. He could read something and thoroughly understand the complexities of that subject, yet still manage to bungle it the moment he was in the field, attempting to put that concept to practical use.

"Thank you," he murmured.

The wings of her eyebrows pinched in their center. "For what?"

"For acting on your compassion for Tironan. In saving him, you inadvertently saved me from having to discipline him. Had he allowed the lir s'flis to launch..." His vresls flattened, and he shook his head. "I thank you."

Kinsley studied him for a long moment. "Who is this person higher in command, forcing you to deliver such punishments? I thought you were captain of this ship."

"I am. But the punishments are expected."

"Expectations that you've cultivated." Her eyes narrowed. "Why?"

Raveno felt a betraying muscle in his cheek twitch.

Kinsley reached out, and before he realized her intention, her hand landed on the nape of his neck, over one of the sensitive spines of his vresls. Soft and light and smooth, so smooth, her thumb caressed his scales.

He stilled. He didn't even breathe.

No one had touched him, not willingly and not gently, not since... Svik, it *had* been since his mother had died. Had it really been ten thesh?

And here Kinsley was again, for the second time in the span of a single conversation, reaching out. She'd reacted from instinct—her compassion—before, but this time, her movement felt deliberate. Cautious, but no less disarming.

"Sometimes the most constricting cage is the one we build ourselves," she murmured, the continued caress of her thumb nearly hypnotic in its gentleness.

An unfamiliar, achy pressure banded his chest.

His hand reached out of its own accord and swiped a knuckle across her jawline.

Her pupils dilated. Her skin puckered in pebbles down her neck, over her collarbone and under the sheet. Her heart contracted in a burst, and she didn't smell only of fear.

Her tongue darted out and licked her lips.

His vresls leapt from his neck at the sight and quivered.

Raveno shut his eyes. He couldn't want her. He absolutely *could not*—not even in his thoughts—because to have wants and hopes beyond his mission was to have weaknesses.

"Raveno?"

Warily, he met her gaze, his ears scorching.

She should despise him for kidnapping her and leading this mission against her people, but her parted lips didn't look like hate. She should fear him after watching him execute her cellmate, but the heightened spice of her smoky smooth scent didn't smell like fear. She should resent his bullying and recoil from his person, but the catch in her breath sounded more like anticipation than revulsion.

And worst of all, as much as he was perplexed by her touch in this moment, he was painfully clear on his own feelings. From the first moment he'd caught her in the control room through every frustrating, impressive, confounding encounter since, she riveted him. She'd only ever done the unexpected, so he shouldn't be surprised by anything she did anymore, but he was. Shocked, actually. She regularly defied her circumstances and him, but this was impossible. Wanting her was impossible. But inexplicably, with her cunning, courage, and heart, *she'd* managed to enslave *him*.

What other explanation could he have for sliding his hand from her jaw to the dip in her cheek and across those plump lips? He stared into the dark depths of her eyes and wished for more. Maybe in the future, assuming he accomplished the future he was working so hard to achieve, he could act on his feelings.

Until then, the only way to ensure that future came to fruition was to not have feelings at all.

He stood, and Kinsley's hand fell to her lap.

"You must be full. And you answered all my questions, for which I thank you. Again. I will uphold my end of our deal. As promised." He turned on his heel, strode to his closet, opened the door, and unlocked the passage to his private office. He swept his hand forward. "After you."

ELEVEN

KINSLEY STARED AT THE PITCH-BLACK SECRET TUNNEL THAT Raveno had revealed in his closet and thought, *Sure, I'll follow the murderous kidnapping alien into his hidden bunker. What's the worst that could happen?*

There was zero chance she could enter that tunnel without hyperventilating.

Not to mention that every time she thought her circumstances couldn't possibly get any worse, he proved her wrong.

Not to mention that under the sheets, she was still naked.

Sometimes the most constricting cage is the one we build ourselves. Ha! The most constricting cage was the physical one he'd locked her inside! But he'd been so affected by her touch, she would have said anything to exploit that unexpected reaction. This was her chance to establish a connection beyond her role as his informant, to gain *his* compassion.

What she hadn't anticipated was that connection affecting *her*.

Heart racing, fingertips tingling, stomach clenching, she reminded herself that he was evil. He'd kidnapped her along with dozens of people, was trafficking them across the universe for who knew what purpose—an *evil* purpose—and he'd murdered Riley. That tender moment of vulnerability was an opportunity to *feign* empathy for him and gain some leverage in her ultimate goal to commandeer the ship. Not to feel empathy for said kidnapping murderer.

If only her traitorous body could get on board with the logic of her mind.

She'd always been inexplicably drawn to dangerous, complicated things that had the potential to kill her.

But she wasn't the only one rattled by their chemistry.

Even having put several feet between them, Raveno's ears still glowed a bright blue, and there went his frill. It separated from his chest and rattled. His breathing was ragged, and, she noted, his nostrils were sealed shut.

Kinsley chewed on his reaction a moment, ignoring her own. "Should I stay wrapped in your sheet as we journey down the rabbit hole? Or were you intending to have this conversation with me naked?"

He dropped his beckoning hand to his side. "Neither. You may open the top bedside drawer, the one to your right."

"Oh, may I?" she quipped, but she opened the drawer, too curious to battle him in earnest.

Inside was one of Raveno's uniforms.

She lifted the garment from the drawer and revised her assessment. It *appeared* to be one of his uniforms in that it was strappy and leatherlike, with multiple holsters and a gladiator skirt, but this uniform had been professionally tailored with a few specific accommodations.

The flat band across the chest was now wide, molded cups, and instead of joining at the sides with buckles, the entire front, from waist to breast, was a front-laced corset.

"I haven't seen any female guards on board."

"Of course not," Raveno said, taken aback. "And until we have proper plumbing installed, you never will, not on my ship."

Kinsley opened her mouth, her inherent offense at "and you never will, not on my ship" tempered by confusion. What did "proper plumbing" have to do with anything? "Then where did you get this uniform?"

"I altered one of mine based on your measurements."

"*You* altered it?"

He nodded. "Your body is..." He made a suggestive, cupping motion with both his hands.

Kinsley tilted her head and let him struggle.

"Lush from motherhood," he coughed out. "So, I decided upon ties rather than buckles to accommodate your figure."

"My body is *what*?"

His ears glowed brighter. "Lush from motherhood."

Kinsley patted her flat stomach. "I look pregnant to you?"

"Not currently."

"Then why would you even say such a thing?"

He made that suggestive, cupping motion with both his hands. Again.

She smacked his hands down. "They're called breasts."

"I know what they're called." He pursed his lips, his expression suddenly grave. "You must miss them terribly."

"Miss them?" Kinsley glanced down to confirm. "They're still right here. On my chest."

"I meant your children. Unless..." His frill flapped out. "Are they adult children? Here aboard *Sa Vivsheth*?"

"How old do you think I am? I don't have any children, let alone adult children." Kinsley said, baffled. "Why would you assume I have children?"

His hands crept back up into cupping position, but at her glare, he dropped them to his lap. "Your breasts."

"What about them?"

"Breasts form during pregnancy, therefore—"

Kinsley raised a staying hand. "Let me stop you right there. Women develop breasts during puberty, not pregnancy."

He hesitated. "To what purpose?"

"Purpose?"

"Breasts lactate to feed your children, yes? Same as havari women?"

"Yes."

"Then to what purpose would you develop them during puberty?"

Kinsley chortled at his logic. "To lure a man into making a baby, I suppose."

"Human men need such lures?"

"As if you don't have 'such lures.' What attracts you to a woman?"

"Fierce resolve and a spirit of fire." Raveno managed to keep a straight face as he said that, but even as the words left his mouth, his eyes dropped to her chest.

Kinsley shook her head. Men! "You just whipped this uniform together last night, did you?"

"I did not whip anything at night. I used a machine that threads material together and hand-stitched the rest during third shift."

"*Whipped together* is just a phrase. I was being—" she began, then caught his grin.

"Snarky," he finished for her.

She compressed her lips, refusing to feel amused.

"And I had more than one *night*. I had several, waiting as you healed, to plan how to proceed with our deal." He gestured to the uniform. "This is one way I plan to proceed: proper clothes."

Kinsley studied the uniform—those careful stitches and cups and corset—with new eyes. "Where are my clothes?"

He flicked a claw. "In the bottom drawer. I only removed them from your person for the RRC, and then I cleaned them as well." He frowned. "You may wear them if you prefer, but the material is thin. They will not protect your skin as well as my uniform will."

She bit her lip. "Thank you."

Raveno, still frowning, inclined his head in that deep, stiff way of his. He pivoted on his heel in an about-face. "Let me know when you are ready, and we will proceed."

She considered his very broad, suddenly chivalrous back. This was the same man who had dislocated her shoulder during interrogation? Who inspired such fear in his own guards? Whatever he was about to tell her must *really* be bad if he was trying this hard to assuage his guilt.

And why would a murderous human trafficker even feel guilt over delivering bad news to one of his captives?

Well, she wouldn't get any answers sitting on this bed. Kinsley stood on shaky legs and slipped into the uniform. Tightening the corset was easy since it laced up the front, achieving an impressive cleavage even more easily. She pressed the girls flat and out to reduce such unnecessaries, finished lacing the top loops, and scrutinized herself, impressed. It fit perfectly.

How annoying.

She peeked over her shoulder.

Raveno's ears and neck were still glowing.

Hmmm. "I think I need your help."

"Help?" He coughed in a rattling *ahem*. "With what?"

"I'm not sure how to tie this after lacing it up."

"You just—" He made a swirling motion in the air with his left hand. "Tie it with two loops. Like you would a boot."

"Human boots have zippers."

"Some have ties."

"I'm just not sure how I'm supposed to—"

He spun around. "You—" He locked eyes on her, and his frill lifted, rattled, then pressed flat against his chest. His nostril slits sealed shut

She waved the loose laces at him. "I what?"

A muscle ticked in his jaw. He stepped forward, took the laces in hand, and, with a swift loop-loop-knot-knot, deftly and efficiently achieved a double knot.

The moment the laces were tied and tucked, he dropped his

hands to his sides and stepped back, the crevice between his brows fierce and deep.

Kinsley peered down at herself, then spread out her arms. "Well? How do I look?"

"Good," he said, still frowning. "Very good."

"If being a maniacal overlord doesn't work out, you could become a seamstress."

He scoffed, taken aback.

"It's always good to have career options." She caressed her hands over her hips, genuinely admiring the fit. "When I return to Earth, I'll have to put this thing to good use. Be a gladiator for Halloween or something."

If possible, his frown deepened. "What is a gladiator?"

She released a mock gasp. "I thought you knew everything about Earth!"

"I do not know everything about *everything*."

She raised a hand and cupped her ear. "I'm sorry, what was that?"

He leaned in. "I said, I do not know everything."

She let her hand drop, grinning. "Between the development of human breasts and the existence of gladiators, you don't seem to know much of anything."

Raveno snorted. "Please, enlighten me."

"Way back when on Earth, in one of our cities called Rome," Kinsley began, "gladiators were prisoners forced to fight to the death in a public arena for entertainment. It was bloody and barbaric, but that's how they got their jollies back then." She shrugged. "According to the movie, anyway."

Raveno's frill separated from his collar and its spines bristled, rubbing together with a rhythmic *tsh tsh* that, for once, he allowed to go unchecked.

Kinsley eyed that frill uncertainly. "What's wrong?"

His mouth opened and closed, and his tongue flicked out to taste the air.

Kinsley took a step back. "Did you, um, not like the movie?"

"I did not see the movie, but I can envision this Rome and their gladiators very well. Come. I must answer your questions now." He whirled around on his heel. "Before I lose all sense of nerve and purpose," he added on a mutter.

"Just tell me here," Kinsley said, eyeing that closet bunker with dread.

"There is something you must see in order to believe."

"Aliens exist. I'll believe anything now, trust me."

He stopped walking. "You will not believe what I have to say, not after I tell you what I have done," he ground out. "But you will be more inclined to believe me after you see what I have *not* done."

"What you're not doing is making any sense," Kinsley said. "What have you done?"

"Something unforgivable." He turned around to face her, his expression tight. "You were unconscious and could not be consulted at the time, but it saved your life."

The pulse of her blue dot glowed between them. "Saved me from what?" she whispered.

"Not what. Who." Raveno heaved an aggrieved sigh. "Me."

"You brought me to your private room to save me from yourself?" She raised her eyebrows.

"I had two options." He raised his hand and lifted a thumb. "One was to continue the pretense of not knowing you, in which case I would be forced to sentence you to a public execution to demonstrate what happens to humans who escape."

Kinsley waited for more, but Raveno only ground his teeth.

"Obviously, you chose option two, which was...?" She circled her hand in the air.

His frill flexed rigid against his chest. He lifted his second thumb. "To tell the truth."

"Oh? And what truth is that?"

Raveno gestured to the hidden hallway of death in his closet. "I would prefer we have this conversation in—"

"Tell me now, Raveno." Kinsley lifted her wrist to beam her blue dot at him. "What is this blue dot? Why am I in your room, eating your food, dressed in your clothes, and unable to return to the brig?" She bridged the distance between them, and Raveno flinched back. "What unforgivable thing did you do? What *truth* did you tell them?"

"I told them that you were acting under my orders!" He burst out, chest heaving. "I told them that your escape from the brig was planned. That it was a test sanctioned by me. A test that they failed."

"Okay, so not the full truth then," Kinsley said, nodding in what she hoped was calm encouragement as she waited for the anvil to drop. "So, your guards think my escape was a test. What does that have to do with why I'm here and not in the brig?"

"No one came to your defense in the moment you needed it most," he rasped. "The guard who made that deal with you, my traitor, he would have let you die. He has no sense of loyalty, not to me nor to you, but I did what was necessary to ensure you lived."

"What exactly did you *do*?" Kinsley snapped.

"The only way my crew would believe that a human was acting under my orders would be if I claimed you as my vri sa shols," he confessed.

Kinsley stilled. There was that word again...showlz? "Claimed me as your what?"

Raveno released a long, tired breath. His voice was calm this time, nearly resigned, when he repeated, "My vri sa shols. Once we get to Havar, there will be a Selection Ceremony in which our greatest warriors bid on the humans. I have bid on you now, in advance of that ceremony. It means that you are mine, to order, to spar with, to..." He sighed, shaking his head. "I'm getting ahead of myself."

Her heart jumped into her throat, then plummeted in a sickening drop back into her stomach at his words: *it means that you are mine.* "What does the blue dot on my wrist mean?"

"It is called an ankesh."

"You already told me what it's *called*," Kinsley spat. "What does it *mean*?"

"It displays an *ouk,* the symbol of my family. Anyone who sees you knows who won your bid."

"You..." She scratched at the blue dot, and there it went again, pulsing into the swirly U. An *ouk,* apparently. "You *branded* me?"

"It is also a tracking device," he added on a whisper.

She could hear herself breathing—the scraping inhale and trembling exhale—but somehow, her lungs still felt deflated.

"Stop that." He grabbed and separated her hands, and she realized that she'd been digging at her wrist, making it bleed. "The ankesh will convince everyone I own you, but we know better. It is a ruse. We will need to pretend in public, but—"

"Who owns you?" she asked, pointing to his wrist.

"Mine is called an anku. Its purpose is not for identification or tracking. Although Josairo could certainly make it such," he mused. "The tech would support it."

"Then what does—"

"It is a communication device. Wherever I am, I can speak to my crew and they to me, no matter the distance."

Something foul coated the back of her throat. "You're *evil*," she spat, every clever plan she'd had to woo him into complacency sucked out into deep space on the vacuum of her rage. "You're a kidnapping, human-trafficking tyrant. You're a *murderer,* and you can go f—"

"I am not a murderer."

"You killed Riley!"

"That's why I wanted to have this conversation in my private office," he said. "I did not—"

"This isn't a conversation. It's a revelation, and one I shouldn't have needed." Kinsley could hear the rising hysteria in her voice, but even hearing it, she couldn't stop it. "I knew who you were the moment we met. I made that deal with you to buy myself time, but somehow, I managed to forget that you're the *devil.* And people can't make deals with the devil. They only get burned by him! Or branded, in my case."

"I told you that this news would turn your stomach and make you doubt my sincerity. But I also told you that I can prove I am not the person you think I am." He grabbed her hand. "Let me show you. I—"

Instead of struggling against him, Kinsley tugged him closer, knocking him off balance. His hold didn't loosen, but she was able to land a solid knee strike to his inner thigh.

He doubled over.

"That was for kidnapping me in the first place!" Another kick, to his outer thigh this time. "That's for killing Riley. And this—"

He released her wrist, and suddenly, his shoulder rammed into her stomach, punching out her wind along with the words from her lungs as her feet left the ground.

He carried her, kicking and cursing, into the pitch-black hidden tunnel in his closet.

TWELVE

Even with his nostril slits sealed, Raveno was overwhelmed by Kinsley's scent. Even with the thick material of their uniforms between them, even with her struggling against his hold, even against his will, every part of her infused into every part of him: her soft skin against his scales, her hot breath filling his lungs, her throbbing heart heavy on his shoulder.

He snorted, attempting to clear his head—now was not the time for this!—but his senses were already swimming in her. He could only attempt not to drown.

She reared back, hitting her head on the ceiling.

"Careful," he chided, clamping his arm tight across her thighs. The sweat between them was more honeyed than the sweat rolling between her shoulder blades.

He shook his head. *Focus!* "Avier will be cross if I bring you to him with *another* concussion, so calm yourself."

Her only response was to pummel his lower back with her fists.

"We are nearly there, and then you will see that I—"

She managed a right hook under his groin, inches from unmanning him.

"Svik! Cease this tantrum!"

She bucked back, hitting her head a second time, but the pain didn't slow her struggles. If anything, she struggled more desperately, kicking and twisting against his hold. If he didn't know her better—if she hadn't already proven herself to be the most composed soldier he knew under pressure—he'd think she was panicking.

Her throbbing heart wasn't just beating; it hammered frantically against her sternum. The last time he'd heard a human heart beat that fast, the man had been facing the inferno of his own execution.

And, strangely, she was holding her breath.

Raveno stopped walking, concerned. "What is wrong? Why are you not breathing?"

She jabbed a bony elbow into his shoulder blade.

"Kinsley," he hissed.

She bashed her head against the ceiling a third time.

The tang of blood soured the air.

Cry mercy, could nothing be easy with her?

He set Kinsley on her feet, and she lunged sideways, nearly dodging his grasp. He gripped her shoulders and shook her. "Kinsley!"

"What?" she gasped, chest heaving.

At least she was breathing again. "Do you have a coronary medical condition I should be aware of?"

"Not that *I'm* aware of," she bit out.

"Then what is wrong with your heart?"

"Nothing"—wheezing inhale— "is wrong"—harsh exhale—"with anything."

Raveno narrowed his eyes. "This is more than just anger from our argument. This is panic. This is..." *Thev sa shek*, her eyes were glazed. He released her left shoulder and grasped her chin, forcing her gaze to his. "*What is this?*"

Kinsley flinched back, hitting her head—for the fifth time?— on the wall behind her.

Terror. That's what this was.

She was terrified.

He wouldn't have thought her prone to panic, but he recognized those wheezing gasps all too well from when Tironan suffered from air deficiency.

He plucked her off her feet, and before she could land any more blows to herself or his person, Raveno sprinted down the remaining passageway to his private office. He locked the door behind him, deposited her on a chair, grabbed the nape of her neck, and shoved her head between her legs.

"Inhale deeply and slowly. You need to regulate your breathing."

Her eyes sliced up to glare at him. "I know...what...I need," she wheezed.

"Then stop talking and just breathe. That's it. Close your eyes. Envision yourself somewhere peaceful. Somewhere not here," he muttered. "And *breathe*."

He inhaled along with her, the cloying scent of her blood sabotaging his efforts to find a measure of calm. Unsurprisingly, the back of her stubborn head was split.

Could she manage to pass a single shaoz without injury?

Raveno gritted his teeth. "What peaceful location are you envisioning? Describe it to me."

"I'm fine," Kinsley gasped out. "Are you okay?"

"Me?"

"Yes. I wasn't thinking when...I attacked you."

He rubbed his thigh where that last strike did admittedly still sting. "Impressive self-defense, but only because it was so unexpected. Still, I admit it was effective."

She laughed, or tried to, while still gasping. It came out sounding a bit hysterical. "Of course, it's effective. That's the point."

"Where did you learn such skill?" he asked. If she refused to envision her distraction, he would need to distract her himself.

"I was trained to defend myself." Deep inhale. "For my job to"—quaking exhale—"protect my country." She frowned up at him. "Why don't you look surprised?"

"I am familiar with your United States Army."

"Naturally. You live across the friggin' galaxy, but you speak our language, know what we eat and drink, and understand our culture. Why am I not surprised that you're familiar with our military defenses?" Kinsley narrowed her eyes. "Where did you learn to treat a panic attack?"

He kneaded the back of her neck. "Is that what you call this?"

Her breathing had finally begun to ease, and her heart, though still racing, didn't sound quite as if it was about to burst from her chest.

She sat up. "What do you call it?"

"Air deficiency." Raveno let his hand fall to his side. "I have witnessed this before."

"Under the terror of your leadership, I imagine air deficiency is a common occurrence."

He allowed himself a brief grin; her wit was as delicious as it was cutting. "What caused your panic to attack?" he asked.

"You."

"Me?" Raveno crossed his arms and sat on the edge of his desk. "This I must hear explained."

"I told you how many times that I didn't want to go into the creepy, dark secret tunnel in your closet, but you dragged me in anyway. I might have been able to suffer the walk of my own volition, but being dragged in against my will, trapped against your body, unable to move or escape..." She shuddered. "You triggered a panic attack."

He mulled that over a moment. "What is 'triggered' in this context?" he asked. "I only know it as the firing mechanism of a weapon."

"A trigger is like a sudden reminder of something traumatic that happened from years ago. The trigger makes the trauma feel like it's happening in the present."

He pondered that a moment. "And for you, that trigger is being forced into hidden closet hallways?"

"It's not so specific as that," she said on a chuckle. "Just darkness and cramped spaces."

He scowled. "The entire ship is dark to you."

"Yes, it is."

"And the heating ducts—"

"Are cramped, I know. They're my own personal brand of hell, but I go into them of my own free will." Kinsley rubbed her chest, over her heart. Her hand was trembling. "I grin and bear it, and I'm fine."

Raveno heard a crack and realized he was squeezing the edge of his desk. He forced his grip to loosen. "What trauma does darkness and tight spaces bring to the present for you?"

She shook her head in a jerky, lateral movement.

He breathed her—the sourness of her lingering terror, the bitterness of her embarrassment, the overripe tartness of what he thought might be grief—into himself, and before he realized what he was doing, he knelt beside her and met her eyes. "I have witnessed panic attack my brother. I misunderstood what was happening to you at first because he has a different trigger."

She stared at him in silence. Raveno wasn't certain if he was forging a bond or forcing a wider wedge between them by pushing this conversation, but considering who he was and everything he'd done, he couldn't possibly worsen their rapport.

"Tironan is not a warrior in the way our father would have wanted. His mind is his blade, but physical strength, pain tolerance, athleticism, performance under pressure, all the attributes that matter to our father, they are Tironan's weaknesses. One of the many skills that Tironan failed to master is swimming." Raveno shook his head. "Our father threw him in the water to improve his skill."

Kinsley winced. "Did he drown? Was no one there to help him?"

"Oh, we were all there," Raveno said, and even after all this time, rage gripped him by the throat. "All the vrili in training, Mother, myself, and our father."

"Everyone *let* him drown?"

"According to our father, he wasn't drowning. He was learning to swim."

Kinsley placed her hand on his.

Raveno startled, not having realized he'd placed his hand on her knee. "Let me guess: you defied your father to save your brother?"

He nodded. "But according to Father, I had interrupted a crucial lesson in survival, making Tironan's many future shortcomings *my* fault." Raveno rolled his eyes. "From then on, whenever Tironan so much as looked at a body of water, he suddenly had difficulty breathing, as if he were drowning all over again."

"And you would save him all over again."

"I would try to convince him that he did not need my saving."

"You forget that I've seen Tironan in action," she said, wincing. "Believe me, he needs saving."

Raveno's heart squeezed at that truth. "When Tironan believes that he does not need saving, he will be capable of saving himself."

Kinsley raised her eyebrows. "Are all maniacal overlords this philosophical?"

"You may think me a maniacal overlord, and we may be from different planets, speak different native languages, and have an imbalance of power on this ship, but I tell you this about my father to demonstrate that we have more in common than you might think. I understand."

"You? *Understand?*"

Raveno squeezed her knee. "The past isn't a burden that your present must carry. It *is* your present. People say that in order to have a future, one must release the past. 'Forgiveness is a gift you give yourself,' they say. Or my favorite: 'Living in the past prevents you from realizing your future.'" He released a guttural scoff.

Her eyes widened.

"But those people don't understand that the past isn't something you can choose to keep or release any more than you could choose to inhabit another person's body. The past *is* who we are in the present. My father's upbringing molded Tironan into...what you call a nervous wreck, and he must learn to live in that mold, make accommodations for it, and unapologetically be it."

Kinsley stared into Raveno's eyes, and he braced himself for the lash of her wit. She would say something about him using that philosophy to justify his becoming an unapologetic maniacal overlord. He swore she was thinking it so loudly that he could hear the words without her even speaking them.

"There was an unexpected incident in Yemen. My team's last mission," she whispered instead.

Raveno stilled.

"We were supposed to be long gone by the time my bomb sequence detonated. Instead, we were ambushed, and my superior officer and I were captured. We were underground with our targets when the bombs were set to explode."

My bomb sequence. Fascinating. "You were forced to stop the bombs? You failed the mission and disappointed your superior?"

"No, I didn't stop the bombs." Her breath hitched. "We completed the mission."

Raveno's heart lurched. "How did you escape your captivity before the bombs exploded?"

"We didn't. I detonated them while we were still underground, as ordered. Brandon—my superior officer—he...he died along with our targets."

Ah, my little lilssna.

"With their guns in our faces, I thought he was right—we were dead anyway—so I followed his order and blew everyone to pieces." She bit her bottom lip, but the top one still quivered. "Everyone but me."

Raveno waited in silence.

"Somehow, I survived the blast. I was buried under the rubble for two days."

"Trapped in the darkness."

"It was a difficult time. But worse was coming home. Facing

Reece." She looked away. "Brandon wasn't just my superior officer. He was my sister's fiancé." She cleared her throat. "A fiancé is—"

"I know what a fiancé is." Raveno caressed her knee with his twin thumbs. "Kinsley, I—"

"Well, aren't you two just the coziest pair of killers I've ever seen."

Kinsley startled upright, whipped around, and squinted at the cell on the far side of his office. Her face blanched. Her jaw dropped. Her eyes blinked several times and then widened to show the whites all around her irises, not blinking at all, and Raveno braced himself to catch her should she collapse again.

"*Riley?*"

THIRTEEN

KINSLEY MUST HAVE STOOD, BECAUSE SHE'D BEEN SITTING THE moment before and now she was walking, but she wasn't exactly sure when that had happened. Her brain couldn't comprehend anything beyond the miracle in front of her.

Riley was alive.

He was standing too, his arms crossed as he glared at her through the clear viewing pane of his cell.

Kinsley struggled to see him through the darkness, but she didn't think her eyes were deceiving her. He was here. He looked fantastic, and not just because the last time she'd seen him, his skin had been melting. His cheeks were smoothly shaved. His black hair was brushed. His olive skin was clean. Glowing, even. The biceps of his folded arms were thick and flexed. He'd been fit before, but now—Kinsley shook her head in stunned appreciation at those washboard abs—now he was jacked.

She hadn't noticed Riley or his cell or, honestly, anything about the room when Raveno had carried her here, distracted at first by just struggling to breathe and then by her efforts to study the security feeds on Raveno's desk with her peripheral vision. Yes, discussing

Brandon still felt like debriding an open wound, but he was dead. The dozens of people in the brig, featured on that security footage, were still alive. A little emotional debriding was nothing if it meant keeping them that way.

Martin was on that security footage somewhere, if only she could *see it.*

Now, however, she didn't even have peripheral vision. From one second to the next, her world had narrowed to one crazy impossibility.

"He—" Kinsley covered her mouth before more than words spilled from her lips. As it was, the backs of her eyes were beginning to burn. "But he *died,*" she choked out.

Riley's lip curled up on one side. "It certainly felt like I had."

Kinsley did a double take, settling her disbelief on Raveno. "He can hear us?"

Raveno nodded. "I haven't muted his room." His eyes warily flicked up to Riley. "To my persistent regret."

"I..." Kinsley faced Riley, shaking her head. "I saw you burn. I watched as, as—" *As your hair incinerated and your skin boiled and your eyes burst and—* Tears dripped from her jaw. When had they spilled down her cheeks? "I still see you screaming."

"I'm sure the memory keeps you up at night," Riley murmured.

"How is this possible? Have you been here all this time?"

"Does it matter?"

She couldn't seem to stop shaking her head. "Does what matter?"

"Whether I'm out there with Martin and Benjamin and everyone else—except you, apparently—or back here, alone in my bed," Riley sneered. "A cage is still a cage, no matter how well you're treated."

"I can remove the bed, if you prefer," Raveno offered.

"You're *alive.* That's what matters." Kinsley tried to step forward, but Raveno tightened his grip. When had he placed his hand on her shoulder? "How was it faked?"

"How was what faked?"

"You burning to death."

The noise that erupted from his mouth might have been a laugh, but he wasn't smiling. "That wasn't fake. You witnessed it with your own eyes: he turned me into a human candle wick."

"I witnessed you die, but—"

"Yeah, and you're obviously real broken up about it." Riley's gaze swept down her body. "Betrayal looks great on you. Especially love the corset."

"It's called surviving." *It's called spying, asshole.*

She couldn't say what she was thinking with Raveno in the room, but if Riley's expression was anything to judge by, he'd give her the opportunity to at least work the "asshole" part into the conversation.

Kinsley turned away from Riley to address Raveno. "Maybe *you'd* better explain."

"This is what I needed to show you." He swept a hand at Riley. "I am not a murderer."

She raised her eyebrows. "You *didn't* burn him alive?"

"I needed to put on a show. He was becoming vocal, well..." He huffed. "*More* vocal than usual. I had enough to worry about without him stirring up trouble."

"Guess your plan worked perfectly," Riley said, his tone scathing. "*No one's* stirring up trouble anymore."

Kinsley felt her face flame.

"I did what was required of me to maintain order on this ship and demonstrate what happens when humans defy me," Raveno continued, ignoring Riley. "And then, to my everlasting regret, I had Avier heal him."

"That's the confusing part. Why heal him?" Kinsley crossed her arms. "What game are you playing?"

"Like you, I am surviving. I did not really want him dead. I do not want *anyone* dead, but my life, and that of my crew, depends on me leading this ship in a manner that is expected of me."

"Expectations that *you* cultivated, as I recall."

"To *survive.*" He took her by the shoulders to face him, and it wasn't just the force of his physical grip that suddenly snared her.

"There is more at stake than just you or me or even the lives of your three dozen humans. The fate of an *entire planet* is on the line if I don't complete my mission."

"How many other people have you kidnapped and trafficked across the galaxy for your mission?" she whispered.

"None. Before this mission, before saving you and your humans from the Lorien—the people who originally kidnapped you—I *never* trafficked anyone before."

"Saving us from the *Lorien?* The cells in the brig—*your* brig—have locks, Raveno. *On the outside!*"

"One of the many modifications that Josairo made to our fleet of luxury destination ships so he could order us to traffic people across the galaxy. But instead of carrying out his orders, I used my missions to meet with potential allies. They sent people with me willingly, as spies, to confirm if everything I claimed about Josairo was true. I have never, *never*, kidnapped another species before. Ever. I only do so now because the Lorien were not the allies I'd hope for. I was forced to kidnap you to maintain my cover as Josairo's loyal killing hand, but when we return to Havar, I will overthrow him and return you home to Earth."

Kinsley froze. "You intend to return us to Earth?"

"Yes. I would have done so immediately upon saving you from the Lorien, but I couldn't risk my mission." Raveno's blood-orange eyes blazed. "I'm so close, Kinsley. After ten thesh, er, for you that would be years, *many* years, I will finally save my people from Josairo's rule."

She bit her lip.

"I am not a murderer. Riley is proof of that."

Riley cracked up. "Wow, what a rousing endorsement!"

Kinsley glanced at him. "You're still breathing, aren't you?"

"*He burned me alive!*" Riley spat. "I should have let you starve."

"I wasn't starving! I didn't need more food!"

"Yes, you did! All you did for two days straight was run missions.

You barely even slept, and Leanne was all too happy for the extra rations."

"I didn't ask for your help."

"You didn't need to ask!" He shook his head, disgusted. "All your talk of escaping and returning to Earth, and now you're his lap dog."

Kinsley clenched her fists. "Circumstances change. To survive, sometimes your plans must change with them."

Raveno squeezed her shoulder, in comfort this time rather than in urgency, and inexplicably, tears sprang to her eyes. Differences aside, perhaps he *did* understand, or at least, he understood more and better than Riley. How pathetic was that? Only slightly less pathetic than how deeply that understanding seemed to cut. Kinsley rubbed her chest, but the pang persisted.

"Left to my own devices, I would not kidnap anyone," Raveno murmured. The fervor and determination in his blood-orange eyes was scalding—like looking into a mirror. "I would not hold anyone prisoner. You would not bear my *ouk*. But I am not left to my own devices. I have a master that *I* serve, and until the time comes that I am my own master, I do his bidding the best I can." He eyed Riley. "Sparing people when I can." He turned to Kinsley. "Saving people if I can."

"I believe you." *Not that it changes anything,* she thought, wishing that it did.

Riley laughed bitterly. "Of course you do."

She rotated away from him, and Raveno followed her movement until his back was to the security feeds. "But I don't understand," she murmured. "What could possibly justify abducting and enslaving people from another planet?"

"Nothing justifies such a thing," Raveno said hoarsely. "As I told you, your position as my vri sa shols is a ruse and only temporary."

"But for how long? And to what purpose?" The entire brig was bugged, but as he'd previously confided, the cameras were positioned only in the brig and only capturing visual. No audio.

"Only until we land on Havar and I overthrow Josairo. In the meantime, we will spar, as everyone will expect, but we can use that time to train you in combat. Your self-defense shows promise. We will expand on that."

Ah, there! Her cell was third to the right on the security feed screen. Leanne and Ben were spooning.

Ah, take that back. Leanne and Benjamin were progressing well beyond spooning. They were alone in the cell.

Martin wasn't there.

Her heart leapt into her throat.

"Kinsley?"

She jumped and jerked her eyes as well as her attention back to Raveno. Shit, she'd been staring! "Sorry. Just..."

Raveno pivoted, following her gaze to the security feeds. When he turned back to face her, he was, of all things, rolling his eyes. "Those two have an abundance of affection to demonstrate." He shook his head. "I find it distracting as well."

"Do they, um, demonstrate such affection often?"

"Constantly. Not that I..." The tips of Raveno's ears bled a bright blue. "While the mechanics of human procreation are fundamentally similar to havari procreation, the differences are, well..." Raveno's eyes drifted sideways, as if he was about to look again, before catching himself. "Different."

She refused to ask—what did she care about havari procreation?—but independent from her thoughts or will, her eyebrows rose. "Differences?"

The blue in Raveno's ears swept down his neck. "What I mean to say is—"

"What he's trying to say,"—Riley interjected, and Kinsley and Raveno both jumped back from one another. When had they drifted so close?—"is that he's a pervy peeping Tom."

Raveno tugged his second thumb, then splayed his palm open at Riley.

Had Raveno just...

Yep, because Riley gave him the finger right back.

And then what Raveno had said earlier, before she'd been distracted by Leanne and Benjamin's *affection,* struck her. "Did you say you're going to train me in combat?"

He nodded. "And you will continue your previous assignment to identify my traitor. In that effort, you will need to methodically meet every guard on board. *That* will be your priority. As my vri sa shols, you won't be questioned because your orders come directly from me." He cocked his head consideringly. "Perhaps you can also organize the disaster Tironan has made of my systems reports and help Avier uncover who is stealing from the pharmacy. He isn't making much progress on that front."

She managed to bite back her laughter, but just barely. "So I'm an unpaid personal assistant who needs combat training."

"Unfortunately, we cannot continue as we were. My traitor may assume you've flipped sides. Unless you have a scheduled meeting to regroup and assure him of your loyalty?"

"We don't."

"Then your cover is compromised." Raveno swiped a hand down his tired face. "Although I cannot pay you in currency, in exchange for your time and services, I will train you."

"Right, but *why* do I need combat training? You witnessed my self-defense skills firsthand."

"Will it hurt to improve those skills?"

"Are you foreseeing me needing improved combat skills?"

He found the underside of his claws suddenly fascinating.

"Raveno...why will I need improved combat skills? *What the hell does Josairo want with us?*"

He muttered a string of hissing syllables in his native language. "Cry mercy, let us leave the remainder of this conversation for later." His eyes darted to Riley. "We have endured enough revelations for the moment."

"You expect me to have your back when you're being less than completely honest with me?" Kinsley shook her head. "You're still hiding something, and I'm not in the habit of blindly following orders. Not anymore."

"'Have my back'? I assume you do not mean literally."

"Uh. Sort of. It means to cover your blind spot, to be your backup, or to, like, come through for you in a difficult situation. But you're expecting my loyalty when you haven't earned it." She crossed her arms. "You should've spared us both all this trouble and just made an example of me like you did Riley."

Raveno looked taken aback. "Are you saying I should have *burned you alive?*"

"Then you could've kept me locked up, out of sight. No ankesh. No training. No ruse." She stared at him, shocked, now that she considered it, that he hadn't done just that. "I'm glad you didn't, but frankly, it's the easier option."

"That is not the easier option."

"Why not?" she asked, incredulous. "You did it to Riley."

Raveno's nostrils flared and then sealed shut.

Riley laughed. "Must suck being gorgeous."

"I—" His frill quivered, just once, and then pressed flat against his neck. "I do not allow personal feelings to cloud my professional judgment. I need you to identify my traitor, and for that, I need you by my side, not hiding in a cage."

He had personal feelings? "I was working to identify your traitor while in a cage before."

"Yes. That was before. If I had faked your execution and you were caught again, then Avier would be held accountable for healing you, seemingly against my orders. Questions would be asked. An investigation into my orders and how they are or are not being carried out would ensue. And from there, it would be a sharp slide to being executed and failing my mission. Which I will not allow to happen."

Kinsley was glaring at Raveno, not even attempting to study the security feeds behind him, when it clicked: the angle from which the camera captured Leanne and Benjamin. Their entire bodies were being shot from an aerial view with their faces toward the camera, and knowing their preference for the chaise longue, which was on the right side of the cell, the security camera was in the ceiling near or behind the lip of the fire vent.

She skimmed over the other security feeds. The view of the cell was identical for each one.

Kinsley suppressed a grin. She'd finally found the location of Big Brother.

If she went along with Raveno's mission, she'd need to wait who knew how long for Raveno to overthrow Josairo before returning home to Earth, trusting that Raveno would keep his word and stay true to his mission. Her life, Martin's and Benjamin's lives—all their lives—would rely on the success of Raveno's undercover op.

But the success of Kinsley's mission would result in returning home before ever reaching Havar and facing whatever fate Josairo intended for them.

Fuck Raveno and his mission. Fuck Josairo and whatever he had planned for them.

Kinsley had her own mission planned.

And the one person she could always rely on was herself.

She reached out to caress Raveno's forearm. "I know what it's like to have a mission and to stay true to its course no matter the consequences." She let herself grin. "Different planets, different languages, and all that, but I understand."

Raveno's frill lifted and remained separate from his chest, unchecked as it quivered.

Riley spat at them, but his saliva only soiled the inside of his cell wall, his resentment just as caged as his person.

FOURTEEN

"Bend your knees more. *More*. Arms remain out—yes, like that, sort of—but your knees..."

"They're bent!" Kinsley yelled at the ceiling, inadvertently dropping her arms, and with them, the pivz in each hand.

Raveno deliberately deepened his scowl. It was either that or laugh, and laughing was unacceptable. She would think he was teasing her—which he was, to a point—but she honestly did need to bend her knees more.

They were nearing the end of their tenth training session, one per shaoz since they'd struck their new arrangement. She was flourishing under his instruction, and he couldn't help but feel a measure of pride in her improvement. What she lacked in physicality, she more than made up for in quick learning and sheer determination.

"Yes, your knees are bent," Raveno explained patiently. "That is why I said they should be bent *more*."

Her nose scrunched with horizontal wrinkles when she was frustrated, as she was now. He found the mannerism strangely satisfying, especially when the target of her frustration was him.

"Ready yourself," he barked. He would not allow those nose wrinkles to get the better of him.

She sighed noisily, but mirrored his stance, bent her knees more, and lifted her arms. Her grip on each pivz hilt was firm, but not clamped, its sharp "business end," as she referred to it, aimed at him. Her arms were positioned as he'd instructed: one straight out, the other bent at the elbow, prepared to strike or block as necessary.

"Acceptable. Now, this time, when I attack, do not remain on the defense. Use my momentum against me, and counterattack."

Kinsley's arms shook with fatigue as he spoke, but she nodded, ready in spirit if not in body.

He leapt forward, slashing down with the pivz in his right hand. Her army had not done wrong by her. She was already quite skilled, and the new skills he taught her, such as the efficient block-pivot-drop she'd just employed to avoid having her shoulder impaled, she learned and mastered faster than most guards under his command.

She rolled right and popped to her feet at his side, striking up hard and fast.

Raveno blocked her pivz before it could slip between his scales.

He frowned. Her aim was off. By the width of hairs, perhaps, but still off.

"You must set your sights beyond the location of your aim to your ultimate target." He jabbed at her heart or, rather, where it would have been had she not deftly dodged his blow. Well done. "You do not want to pierce my uniform. You want to pierce my kidney. Sight beyond my uniform, beyond my scales and flesh, and your aim will remain true." He swiped out to knock her from her feet, but she jumped over his leg, arms still up, still trembling, but still at the ready. "Do not punch me. Punch *through* me."

"I know," she panted.

"Anticipate my movements, if you can, and improvise around them." He snorted. "You and your lir s'flis launches. You love improvising."

"*I know.*"

"Then do it!"

He countered with a downward strike to her neck, which she avoided with another block-pivot-roll.

She was as agile as she was petite, determined as she was physically weaker, and quick-minded as she was slow-footed. Against her own kind, he imagined she would fiercely dominate. Against an havarian, well, for those who preferred an underdog, she'd be their best bet by far.

Josairo was going to love her.

Raveno shuddered at the thought.

Pain pierced his back.

Raveno twisted and delivered a hard chop to Kinsley's inner elbow, stopping the momentum of her blow before she compromised anything vital.

She released the pivz on a gasp.

The blade remained embedded in his side, perfectly aimed over his kidney.

Raveno grinned. "Well done."

"Sorry," she murmured.

He holstered both his weapons. Grimacing, he reached back, gripped the hilt, and yanked the pivz from his scales.

"I thought you would block me. You always block me."

"Do not apologize. I was distracted." He plucked a towel from the bin, wet it in the sink, and wiped the blade clean. "*That* strike was on target." He returned the pivz to her, hilt-first. "Very well done."

She accepted the weapon with her left hand, keeping her right arm cradled against her stomach.

Oh, cry mercy. "Are you hurt?"

"I'm fine."

"You have taught me that, counter to its literal meaning, *I am fine* in English means that you are not." He reached for her arm.

She twisted away, sheltering her elbow from him. "All you'll do is poke at it until it hurts more, then declare that Avier should examine it."

"If it hurts at all, Avier *should* examine it."

"The pain will pass."

"Pain does not indicate something is *fine*."

"When do I start training with *that* weapon?" she asked, shamelessly changing the subject without any tact whatsoever.

Raveno let it slide for the moment and followed her gaze to the weapons rack behind him and all the many pivz displayed, organized by their various lengths. "We've already gone through most of them. I maintain the three-blade is the perfect weight for you without compromising reach, but—"

"Not those." She waved a dismissive hand at the weapons rack. "The one strapped to your back."

"My ezil?" He crossed his arms. "Never."

"Never? Like, not ever?"

"Is there another type of never?"

Her nose wrinkled.

Since they were no longer sparring, Raveno gave in to the impulse and laughed.

"I thought you wanted me to improve my skills. Broaden my combat knowledge," Kinsley said, and how she made a weapon of words and truth was a skill unto itself. "Why are you limiting me now?"

"It is not I who limits you, but the weapon itself. The pivz is better suited to your strengths, anyway." Raveno racked his weapons and gestured for her to follow suit.

She crossed her arms instead. "What if I need to defend myself, and the only weapon at my disposal is an easel?"

"It's pronounced ezil."

"Easel."

"You're missing the hard trill in the middle."

She scoffed. "You know I don't have a bifurcated tongue to make that vibrating, hissing noise."

Raveno spread his palms. "It's how it's pronounced."

Her lips compressed. "If I need to defend myself, and the only weapon at my disposal is an *easel*, then—"

"Then you should run, not fight." He unsheathed his ezil and offered it out to her. "Let me demonstrate."

She took it and immediately nearly dropped it. "Shit, it's heavy!"

"Like this." He adjusted her grip. "Let the grooves for each finger guide your hold. Good. Now, feel the depression at your first—well, only—thumb?"

She nodded.

"Press it."

She peeked up uncertainly.

"I thought you liked pressing buttons."

She wrinkled her nose at him—would he ever tire of that expression?—then bent her knees, braced herself, and pressed the button. "Nothing happened."

"Exactly. Every ezil is made specifically for its havarian owner, so even if you were to wrest the ezil from your enemy's grasp, you could not fire it."

"I could beat him with it like a club."

"You could, but remember, considering our scales—"

"'Piercing, not bludgeoning, weapons are most effective.' I know." She groused. "What happens when *you* press the button?"

He took the ezil from her, aimed it at nothing, and squeezed the trigger.

A spear six times the length of the ezil's outer shell jutted from its end in a lethal jab.

Kinsley startled, then jumped, laughing, as the spear retracted back into its casing. "Do it again!"

Raveno grinned, happy to oblige.

"It reaches over twelve feet!"

"And..." He flipped the ezil, caught it, aimed its opposite end, and squeezed the trigger with his second thumb.

A second blade, just as long as the spear but with a hinged hook at its tip—perfect for slicing—jabbed in a lethal second strike.

Kinsley whistled. "That's definitely more effective than attempting to bludgeon someone to death, no matter their species."

Raveno eased his thumb from the trigger to show her how the depressed button glowed under his touch. "The ezil recognizes the unique pattern of my scales and fires from my fingers only. Our Vra Cilvril s'Hvri programs each ezil himself, not that Josairo ever bothers to attend the presentation ceremonies."

"Vrasil vrilsa what?"

"Josairo. His title is Vra Cilvril s'Hvri." Since she seemed unlikely to rack her weapons anytime soon, Raveno sheathed his ezil, plucked her pivz from their scabbards, and racked them himself.

"What does his title mean?"

He turned to face her and stiffened at her sudden proximity. "Well." He flexed his vresls flush against his chest to keep them from quivering. "Literally, it means 'killing hand of Havar.'"

She frowned. "I thought you were a killing hand."

"I enforce Josairo's laws as *his* killing hand. Josairo is *Havar's* killing hand."

"Killing hand of Havar." She blinked. "Like, he's the ruler of Havar? Of the *entire planet*?"

He inclined his head. "Yes." For now. "And then there's Avier, who is Vri Zyvril, translated as 'healing hand.'"

She just stared at him.

"Because he heals. My sister, Veilon, is one of four Vri Shavril, or 'advising hand,' to Josairo. And Tironan, my brother, is Fyvril, roughly translated as 'helping hand'—an officer. And our many Vrili, translated as just 'hands'—the rest of my crew."

"So many hands, so little time." Although her tone was flippant, amused, even, she was still cradling her right arm.

Raveno activated his anku. "Vri Cilvril to Avier."

Kinsley eyes widened. "Don't, I'm—"

"Report to training room one for an injury examination."

"—fine." Kinsley groaned. "It's probably just sprained!"

A second passed before his anku vibrated, and Avier's mocking voice echoed inside his ear. "Your will by my hands."

"He is coming," Raveno relayed.

Kinsley grimaced, but her disgust was aimed at her own hand now, instead of him.

Raveno startled at the blood coating her palm.

He snatched another towel from the bin and wet it at the sink. "Allow me."

"It's your blood."

"Hmm." He wiped the cloth over her palm, inspecting for injury himself.

"I can just wash my hands at the sink," she murmured.

"We should keep your elbow as immobile as possible until Avier examines it." Raveno cleaned the back of her hand, her palm, then each small finger. Svik, her bones were so delicate. Not for the first time, he marveled at her skill and ability.

"Your hands are so warm."

Raveno glanced up at her tone and inhaled sharply. She remained outwardly calm, still, and composed, but he hadn't misheard the tremor in her voice or the acceleration of her heart.

Her arousal sounded so much like anger, but in no way did it smell even remotely the same.

Raveno sealed his nostril slits against the scent, but he could still taste its peppery musk in the back of his throat from that one whiff.

"You sound surprised," he forced out, wiping a smear of blood from her cheek.

"I always am when it comes to you," she murmured.

The waft of her whispered words was warm against his scales, soft and delicious. He resealed his nostril slits, annoyed. When had they opened?

She leaned closer, the movement minute, but he could feel her skin nearing his scales the way one can feel the billowing warmth from a wildfire. Any closer, and he might ignite.

"Is blood smeared on my forehead too?" she asked, wriggling her eyebrows. "It feels sticky."

They shared the same soap, but somehow, her hair smelled sweeter than his ever had.

"Raveno?"

His head swam, his vision dimmed, and svik, he breathed in deep, giving up on restraint. He was drowning in her.

She met his gaze and stilled. Her heart was beating like a turbine now—fast, powerful, unstoppable—and he swore he could smell that too: the savory scent of that organ taking flight.

Could she truly reciprocate his feelings? Her body couldn't lie, but what about her mind? It wasn't possible that she could want him.

If she pressed her mouth to his, as strange and unsanitary as that gesture seemed, would he be able to taste the truth on her tongue as he could smell it wafting from her skin?

"Oh, this is not happening," she muttered so softly, he might have missed it if they weren't a hairsbreadth apart.

"Am I interrupting?"

Kinsley leapt back, then gasped on a pained flinch. She returned to cradling her arm.

Raveno sealed his nostrils, flexed his vresls flush against his chest, and composed his expression before slowly facing Avier.

Avier's eyes locked on Raveno, then flicked to Kinsley. His nostrils flared.

Raveno covered the possessive hiss that rattled from his throat with a cough. "Avier. Please attend to Kinsley. She is injured."

Avier approached Kinsley, eyeing Raveno's side as he passed. "She's not the only one," Avier said in Haveo.

"You may attend to me as well, but examine Kinsley's elbow first," Raveno said, deliberately answering in English.

Avier reluctantly reached out, but he paused just short of taking her arm in hand. "May I touch you?" he asked in English.

"As if either of us has a choice," she muttered.

Avier didn't smirk, but he wanted to. Raveno could tell by the flex of his cheek as he struggled against his own amusement.

Kinsley winced at Avier's "poking and prodding." He palpated her arm above and below the elbow. "Can you make a fist?"

She did.

"Straighten your fingers and press down on mine." He held out his hand. "I will provide some resistance."

She did that as well, still wincing.

"Good." Avier moved his hand above hers. "And do the same but press up. Very good. And can you move all your fingers for me?"

Kinsley wiggled her fingers in a coy wave. "See? I'm fine."

Avier unstrapped a portable scanner from his holster. "Hold your arm aloft and remain still as I search for internal injuries. This will not hurt."

"I know the drill," she said, managing with tone alone to twist fact into complaint, but she complied.

Avier scanned her arm, studied the results, then faced Raveno. "She is fine."

Kinsley stuck her tongue out at him.

Raveno pointed a claw at her. "By will or wrath, you will relax for the remaining shaoz."

Kinsley lifted her shoulders in that carefree way that was more defiance than acquiescence. "I need to finish organizing your files, anyway."

Avier stiffened. "I'd be remiss if I didn't express *again* how much I advise against allowing Kinsley near your files," he said, reverting to Haveo. "Tell me you didn't give her passcode access."

"If I expect her to trust me, I must offer my trust in return." Raveno countered, also in Haveo. "It's not as if she can read them."

"She reads well enough to organize them. She's clever and backed into a corner. By you. You can't trust her."

"There's a difference between trusting someone and wielding their talents to my purposes."

"A distinction I fear you're not capable of making concerning her.

I see how you look at her. You *want* to trust her. You *want* to confide in her." Avier sighed. "You want *her.*"

"She has information I need, and for now, this is the best way to obtain it, no matter what else I may want."

"You don't deny how you feel, then?"

"If I acted on feeling alone, would we have come so far? Would we have come this close?" Raveno fisted his hands at his sides. "I can handle her."

Avier scrutinized Raveno's waist, where his wound was still seeping. "I see how well you're handling her."

Svik, Raveno felt his ears instantly and furiously blaze.

"You're sharing a bed with her. You don't even trust Tironan enough to tell him the truth, but for her, you—"

Raveno took hold of Avier's shoulder and squeezed. Tight. "We sleep in the same bed during separate shifts. We do not share it."

Avier closed his mouth, but his tongue lashed the air.

"I want her, yes. But you're wrong if you think I would trust her not to carve out my heart should I give her the opportunity." He laughed. "She's fierce, and I plan to wield that fierceness to our advantage. With my heart remaining firmly within my chest."

Avier cocked his head. "So you didn't order Zethus to research the biological details and social ritual of human reproduction?"

Raveno glared at him.

The training room door slid open.

Raveno and Avier turned, startled to see Kinsley at the threshold, about to leave.

"Halt!" Raveno strode to her side. "Where are you going? We need to—"

"*We* are not doing anything. After you finish posturing with Avier, you have more training sessions with your crew while I salvage that wreck you call a filing system."

"Your elbow—"

"Is *fine.*"

"It doesn't hurt anymore?"

She rolled her eyes. "I can sit on my butt and press buttons on a digital screen without it hurting any worse, I promise."

"You will just work on filing?"

"Yes."

He narrowed his eyes doubtfully. "You are not meeting with any of my crew?"

"Not until tomorrow." She reached out of her own volition and touched his forearm. "I'll find your traitor eventually. I promise."

Raveno strained every muscle in his neck to prevent his vresls from moving. "Complete your filing, but before you begin any meetings tomorrow, Avier will perform a final evaluation to clear you for physical activity."

Kinsley smiled, and her cheeks indented. *Dimples*, he reminded himself, having consulted with Zethus about them. They were called dimples.

She glanced at Avier. "You want to swing by my room at first shift?"

"As if either of us has a choice," he murmured.

Kinsley released Raveno's arm as she laughed, and Raveno wasn't sure which loss he felt more keenly, the loss of her touch or the fact that her laugh was directed at Avier instead of him.

FIFTEEN

Hand over hand, Kinsley crawled through the dreaded incineration shaft. The experience was as suffocating and strenuous now, the hundred-somethingth time, as it had been the first, even with the flashing blue glow of her ankesh lighting her progress, but if she was successful today, she might never need suffer this crawl ever again. Because after she rallied with Martin, she was finally finishing what they'd started all those months ago: breaking everyone out of the brig, taking command of Raveno's spaceship, and flying home to Earth.

Kinsley imagined the cell doors opening and everyone inside escaping their imprisonment. Their faces would beam beside hers as she led the uprising against their captors. Martin, Benjamin, and Leanne would reunite with Riley and finally see a light at the end of this nightmare. Her throat tightened with something more, much more, than just the thrill of adrenaline and the longing for freedom.

This was it. She could do this. She *had* to do this. Now, before she lost all sense of purpose and reason and started spying for Raveno in truth.

Her heart contracted at the thought, and if it ached for something besides freedom, well, she'd just have to ignore that ridiculous feeling. She already had a mission, one of her own, and her people—dozens of humans kidnapped and being trafficked across the universe by *him*— were relying on her to remain focused and loyal. She would free them and, in doing so, free herself.

Kinsley reached the brig, specifically her old cell, and tapped on the fire vent three times.

An indrawn breath. Silence.

Someone cleared his throat, indicating the coast was clear.

Martin.

Kinsley grinned. Now all she needed was Benjamin telling her how long they'd been imprisoned down to the minute and Leanne complaining about something inconsequential, and she'd feel right at home.

"Who is it?" Leanne whispered shakily.

Kinsley nearly laughed. "So many people crawling through the incineration shafts now that you need them to identify themselves?"

"Switch!" Leanne squeaked.

"It's a miracle," Benjamin breathed.

"Jesus Christ descending from on high to finally deliver us from this hell would be a miracle," Martin muttered, but his voice cracked.

"Isn't it miracle enough that I'm still alive after getting caught?" She tried to contain the flutter unfurling in her chest. Why couldn't she stop grinning?

When I tell them about Riley, they're going to lose their minds, she thought and grinned harder.

"If I had my choice of miracle, I'd take Jesus."

She swore she could hear an answering smile through the snark in his voice. "I might not be the miracle you want, but I'm all you've got."

"Don't I know it?" Martin's face came into view directly beneath the vent. He *was* smiling.

Oh. Kinsley's heart flip-flopped. The miracle was seeing a familiar face.

"What are they going on about?" Leanne whispered. "Is this more code?"

Martin's grin widened.

Kinsley bit her lip. "Slide your eyes to the side, so it doesn't look like you're talking to me. The cell's bugged, remember?" she chided, but her tone missed its mark.

He let his eyes slide by, but his grin didn't lose any of its shine. "It's been a long grocery run. Did you finally find everything on your list?"

"Sure did. And their cameras only capture visual, no audio. We can speak freely."

"They can't hear what we're saying?" Benjamin asked. "You're sure?"

"I'm sure. I saw the security feeds myself. Besides, only two of the aliens on this ship would be able to understand us, anyway." Kinsley blew the bangs out of her eyes. "Granted, they're the two highest-ranking officers."

"*Two* of the aliens speak English?" Martin asked.

"Yes, although they have translators for those who don't speak the language. For interrogation purposes."

"That seems unlikely," Benjamin said.

Kinsley sighed. "Well, I didn't see the translators in person, so I suppose he could have been lying to intimidate me, but—"

"No, I mean it's unlikely that only two aliens speak English."

"Why is that unlikely?" Leanne asked. "Being abducted by aliens seemed unlikely too, but here we are."

"If it's common in their culture to abduct humans, why wouldn't they *all* speak English?" Benjamin asked. "Or if it's not important to their culture to communicate with their captives, then why would any of them speak English?"

"Maybe they only allow the highest-ranking officers to learn foreign languages," Martin speculated.

"Maybe this mission was personal, and those two deliberately learned the language," Benjamin offered. "Or maybe—"

"This is all speculation," Kinsley interrupted, but Benjamin was right. Raveno had deliberately pretended to not understand English in front of his crew. That coupled with his traitor paranoia and the fact that he was some sort of double agent against his planet's dictator, what did it all really mean? Did the details even matter if they didn't stick around to find out? "Listen, I don't have a lot of time. Raveno's distracted with training sessions at the moment, but I need to get back by the time he's done."

"Get back?" Martin's head whipped up. "You're not here to stay?"

"No, he still thinks I'm spying for him. But Martin, I did it. I have a workable plan to take control of the ship." Kinsley paused for effect. "This time tomorrow, we'll all be free!"

The entire cell, including Martin, remained silent.

"Don't stare," Kinsley reminded him.

Martin let his gaze slide passed, but he was no longer smiling.

"Tomorrow?" Leanne whispered.

"This is sudden," Benjamin added.

Kinsley reared back. "Sudden? It's been months in the making."

"One hundred and thirty-six days," Leanne corrected her.

"Exactly! What about that is sudden?"

"What's your plan?" Martin asked, but he didn't sound excited. He sounded like he was waiting for a reason not to like the plan.

Deep breath. They'd been imprisoned for one hundred and thirty-six days, after all. Everyone was bound to be cranky. "I'll access the cell lock system from the control room and open all the doors as well as the brig entrance."

"You can do that?" Benjamin asked.

"Yes," she said, but honesty made her add, "I think so."

"You *think* so?" Leanne squeaked.

Kinsley winced. The pitch of Leanne's voice was piercing. "It's not as if I can practice before our real jailbreak."

"You were able to practice with their other systems," Benjamin pointed out.

"That was before I was caught. Now Raveno thinks I'm on his side, and—"

"Who?" Martin asked.

"Raveno. You know, Captain Headband," Kinsley clarified. "The man I'm double-agenting for."

Leanne cringed. "The *man?*"

Benjamin scratched at his scruff. "You know his name?"

"Why wouldn't I? Now that all the aliens think that I'm his—" *Killing hand.* Kinsley grimaced. "That I *work* for him, I can't experiment with the systems anymore without breaking my cover."

"Why would they think that?" Benjamin asked.

Kinsley rubbed her forehead. Leanne wasn't the only one giving her a headache. "Why would they think what?"

"That you work for the captain of this ship."

"When his crew caught me, Raveno convinced them that my escape was a test for them designed by him."

"Why would he cover for you like that?" Leanne asked.

"He still believes I can identify his traitor."

"There is no traitor."

"But he doesn't know that!"

Silence.

"This is a *good* thing," Kinsley insisted. Why was she having to convince them? "I might not be able to experiment with their systems anymore, but I'm on the inside, which is even better. Raveno's been training me. I have access to his files and personal schedule. He trusts me now—as much as he's capable of trust—which is the whole point of going undercover."

"The point of your mission was to gather intelligence about the ship and the aliens, and then *come back*. Not leave indefinitely to go undercover," Martin said.

"Well, circumstances changed when I was caught. My plans had to change with them. It's called survival."

More silence mixed with a dark sense of déjà vu.

"Anyway," Kinsley said, forging ahead. "Once I unlock the brig, everyone—and I mean *everyone*—needs to cover up the cameras in their cells."

"I wasn't able to find the camera," Martin sighed. "I tried. I swear I did, but—"

"It's okay. I—"

"He risked crawling through the incineration shafts because you weren't here," Leanne cut in. "And his mission was for nothing. No one even knew what he was talking about. Maybe the cameras don't exist. Maybe—"

"They exist. I found them," Kinsley interjected before the conversation could completely derail. "They're somewhere on or near the fire vent."

"How could you possibly know that?" Leanne snapped. "You haven't even been here!"

Benjamin whispered something under his breath.

"Well, she hasn't. It's been weeks—"

"Ten days," Benjamin corrected her.

Had it really only been days? Somehow, it felt like years.

"And where was she that entire time?" Leanne asked. Suddenly her clueless pouting had a sharpness that was decidedly less clueless. "She just left us here to rot."

"I'm sure she had a good excuse for—"

"She was running for her life," Martin interrupted, his voice ice. "Having been caught in a dangerous, compromising position while on a mission to free and save us. Which is more than you've ever done."

Loud breathing filled the sudden silence.

"There's no reason to be rude," Benjamin whispered.

"There's every reason to be rude to harmful ignorance," Martin replied, calm as could be.

Someone inhaled sharply, but other than the whir of the air filtration system and the purr of the ship's engine, the cell succumbed to awkward stillness.

"Sooo... I saw the security feeds," Kinsley tried again. "From the view of the cell and the angle of the camera, they're hidden in the fire vent."

"I've searched every millimeter of this cell, including the fire vent," Martin said on a sigh. "There's nothing there."

"Maybe it's microscopic or camouflaged into the nozzle or something. But it's there," Kinsley insisted.

"What if she's lying," Leanne whispered.

"Annie, what would she have to gain by—"

"Her own freedom?"

"Then why would she come back to help us escape?" Martin asked, his voice nothing but gravel.

"I don't know." Leanne sighed, frustrated. "But she's acting like she knows so much when she hasn't even been here, and I—"

"You and Benjamin are lovers," Kinsley interrupted dryly.

Leanne's mouth clacked shut.

"You prefer it from behind, with Benjamin spooning you on the couch."

Silence.

Martin raised his eyebrows.

Benjamin gaped. "You've been spying on us?"

How was she not making any friends today when she had a plan to free them? "I told you. I found the camera feeds. I can't help what you were doing in the cell at the moment when I found them."

Martin coughed, but it had a decidedly suspicious hiccup to it. "So. The camera is somewhere on or near the fire vent?"

"Yes. You'll need to cover it the moment I open the cell door, so that Rav—so the aliens can't see what we're doing."

"How will we cover it if we can't see it?" Benjamin asked.

Did she need to think of everything? It's not as if they had much beyond food and excrement at their disposal.

"We'll smear something opaque over the entire vent," Martin said, echoing her thoughts.

Kinsley grinned. Some things never changed.

"Then what?" Benjamin asked.

"Then everyone exits their cells through the incineration shaft."

Crickets, and then:

"What?"

"The incineration shaft?"

"Why?"

"But the doors will be unlocked," Benjamin reasoned. "We could just walk out of the brig from the safety of the front door!"

"The front door will be unlocked, but it won't be safe, not with all the guards rushing into the brig to manually override the cell lock breach and contain you," Kinsley explained. "They'll assume you're escaping through the front door because, with your cameras covered, they won't know otherwise. Once they arrive, it'll be too late, and I'll lock them inside with you already having escaped through the incineration shafts."

"What's to stop them from following us into the incineration shaft?" Martin asked.

"They can't fit to follow you. Their shoulders are too broad." Kinsley grinned. "They'll be trapped in the brig."

"What about the guards who don't run into the brig?" Benjamin asked. "What's to stop them from incinerating us?"

"Or from waiting until we exit the incineration shaft and then throwing us right back in the brig?" Martin added.

Kinsley rolled her eyes. "As if I haven't thought of those scenarios. The guards who don't investigate the brig will already be unconscious."

"How will they be unconscious?" Benjamin asked.

"Because I'll have dosed them with svirros."

Another bout of silence.

"The sedative I use to knock them unconscious," she reminded them. "Nothing I haven't done before."

"I remember you dosing one or two guards at a time," Martin said. "How will you possibly dose all of them?"

"Easily, now that I control Raveno's schedule and meet with his guards regularly to find his traitor. I've already booked him with back-to-back training sessions tomorrow. He'll be too busy to notice what I'm doing."

Martin made a strange, creaking sound in the back of his throat. "Don't you think they've grown at least a little suspicious of the missing drugs by now?"

"Of course they have! Raveno even changed the pharmacy passcodes, but when he gave me access to organize his filing system, I found his passcode logs, including the passcodes for updating and managing passcodes."

"But won't they notice if more goes missing?" Benjamin asked.

"Not if I steal it *after* Tironan runs his daily report. Then—"

"Tironan?" Martin asked warily.

"Raveno's brother. *Then* during my regularly scheduled meetings with his guards, I'll drug them, one by one, and stash their bodies in Raveno's secret closet hallway. No one knows about it except for him and Avier."

"Who?" Benjamin squeaked.

"The ship's doctor. Raveno's BFF. By the time I'm through with them, it'll be safe for everyone to escape."

"Safe to crawl through the incineration shafts," Leanne said, deadpan.

Kinsley waited for someone else to chime in, but her patience was met only with more silence. "Martin?"

"There's a lot of moving pieces," Martin said hesitantly. "It wouldn't take much for the entire plan to unravel."

Benjamin and Leanne being nothing but doom and gloom and doubt was fine, but Martin too? Kinsley attempted to breathe in understanding and compassion along with oxygen, but it was pointless. They were unbelievable! "By will or wrath, are we sheep or are we survivors?" she spat. "I've been crawling through these incineration shafts for months! I've been caught *twice*! The first time, my shoulder was dislocated, and the second time, I was nearly beaten to death, *after* nearly being incinerated. You don't think I'm terrified too? You don't think I know what's at risk? But this is our chance to escape and go home!"

Silence.

"By will or wrath?" Martin asked.

Kinsley shrugged the sweat from her cheek. "If my plan works, this time tomorrow, we'll be free."

"And if it doesn't, this time tomorrow, we'll be dead," Leanne countered.

Kinsley dropped her forehead and rested it on the cold metal of the shaft.

"I agree, there are a lot of moving pieces," Benjamin said. "Accessing the cell lock system, covering the cameras, escaping through the incineration shafts, drugging the crew, trapping any remaining crew in the brig. If just one component doesn't go according to plan, Leanne is right. We might all die."

Kinsley shook her head, incredulous. "Did you think breaking out of an alien prison and commandeering their ship would be easy?"

"The plan was to burn them alive," Benjamin said. "'See how they like being flambéed,' I believe were your exact words."

"That was before I discovered that their scales are fire-resistant. We needed a new plan," Kinsley muttered. Their doubt and depression was catching.

"I liked it better when we were flambéing them," Leanne groused, as if she had ever really liked any of Kinsley's ideas.

"Trapping them is better than flambéing them anyway," Kinsley reasoned. "Even though I can reset the autopilot to Earth and manually steer, if necessary, we don't really have any experience operating and maintaining an alien spaceship long-term. If we keep Raveno alive, maybe we can use his expertise to survive."

Silence.

Kinsley sighed. "What's the problem *now*?"

Martin looked up, his expression pained. "You've gotten pretty close to him, haven't you?"

She frowned. "Him who?"

"Raveno."

"Getting close to him is literally the entire purpose of being undercover."

"You're in charge of his schedule. You file his reports. You've met his brother and best friend. By all accounts, he's taken you under his wing, training you to fly and fight." He raised his eyebrows. "Anything else he's training you to do?"

"Don't look directly at me," she hissed. "The cameras, remem—"

"Tell me I'm wrong."

"You're wrong!" Kinsley said, her heart racing. "You know, it's funny. I never thought you or Riley had much in common, but he basically said the same thing to me when I found him."

"What do you mean, when you found him?" Martin asked.

"Riley?" Leanne squeaked. "Our Riley?"

"Our Riley's dead," Benjamin whispered.

"No, he's not," Kinsley said. "One of the many perks of going undercover: I found Riley. He's alive. Raveno faked his death to scare us into behaving, but he healed Riley like he healed me. He's caged in Raveno's secret closet hallway."

"But we watched him burn!" Benjamin shouted.

"Now we *know* she's lying," Leanne said.

"Of all the things to lie about, why would she lie about Riley?" Benjamin asked.

Leanne said something ridiculous, Kinsley was sure, but suddenly, she couldn't concentrate on anything but Martin and his steady, suspicious stare.

"What?" Kinsley snapped.

"*That's* why you don't want to kill him," Martin murmured.

Kinsley frowned. "What do you mean?"

"That's why you want to keep Raveno alive, not to help you manage the ship, or, well..." He rubbed the back of his neck. "But because he spared Riley. You feel obligated to spare him in return."

Was that the ache in her chest every time she thought of Raveno? Obligation?

170

"You're a good person, Kinsley. You're smart and determined and brave, but..." Martin shook his head. "You need to face facts. This plan is a death sentence."

"There's a second option," Kinsley reluctantly admitted. "Raveno claims that he's working an undercover op to overthrow the big bad tyrant ruling his planet. He supposedly intends to return us to Earth after he completes his mission. That kidnapping us is just part of maintaining his cover."

Martin snorted. "Sure."

"I believe him. And before you claim that I believe him out of a misplaced sense of obligation concerning Riley," Kinsley added, "he had nothing to gain by reading me in. His own brother doesn't even know about his op to overthrow Josairo."

Martin rubbed the back of his neck. "Josairo?"

"The big bad tyrant."

Silence.

"We could just wait it out, then," Leanne suggested. "Keep a low profile while the aliens wage their civil war."

"We don't know how long that war will take," Kinsley said. "Are you willing to wait years? Decades? Return to Earth in your sixties with your entire youth spent in a cage?"

"At least I'd have a youth," Leanne reasoned. "I'd be alive."

"Assuming Raveno is telling the truth," Benjamin said doubtfully. "And assuming he wins the war. If he doesn't, and if this Josairo tyrant is the alien who ordered our kidnapping..."

"He is," Kinsley confirmed.

"We're toast," Martin finished.

"We're just as toast if Kinsley's plan fails," Leanne pointed out. "I'd prefer to bide our time and see what happens."

Martin raised his eyebrows at Benjamin.

Benjamin tightened his arms around Leanne. "Do we need to decide right now? Let's think on it."

"One hundred and thirty-six days in captivity," Kinsley laughed. "And you want more time to think."

"Raveno is treating you well," Martin observed.

She scowled. "Well enough, I suppose."

"You look fantastic, Kinsley. Clean, fit, healthy." Leanne and Benjamin were still arguing, but Martin spoke over them. "You should work for Raveno in earnest and just forget about us."

Kinsley jerked back, stunned.

"What did you just say?" Benjamin asked, abandoning his argument with Leanne.

"Forget about us?" Leanne parroted.

Martin held up a hand. "Kinsley's right. Her plan is the only plan we've got and the best plan we'll probably ever get. Even so, it's not likely to succeed."

"We'll succeed," Kinsley insisted.

"At least in the position you're in now, you're more than just surviving. You're living."

He couldn't be serious. Not Martin. "Don't you want to go home?"

"He wants to go home!" Leanne shrieked. "We all want to go home!"

"He's just scared," Benjamin said. "Don't listen to him. We need you."

Wow, that was a quick about-face for those two.

With his head cocked toward Kinsley, Martin winked.

Ah. Kinsley grinned. "Well, then. In that case, we're on for escaping tomorrow?"

"Yes," Benjamin said. "It's a risky plan, but it's better than no plan at all."

"When the cell doors open, you cover that camera and hightail it into the incineration shaft," Kinsley reminded them.

Leanne whimpered, but she nodded her agreement.

"I need to get back, but..." Kinsley scratched at her ankesh. "Someone needs to crawl cell to cell and tell everyone the plan."

"I will." Martin volunteered.

Kinsley inhaled an unsteady breath. "Martin..."

"I'll be careful. And tomorrow, I'll see you on the outside."

Harboring anything so unreasonable as hope could only jeopardize her focus, but Kinsley couldn't help herself. This challenge—spying on Raveno, learning his technology, commandeering his ship, and returning three dozen civilians home to Earth—had been the greatest mission of her life. So many times she'd thought it her *last* mission, but this time tomorrow, they would be outside their cells. Mission complete and in the clear.

And on their way home.

Kinsley smiled. "It's a date."

SIXTEEN

Raveno entered his cabin and hesitated midstride when he wasn't immediately set upon by Kinsley spouting his failings. Eleven shaoz into their new arrangement, and eleven shaoz straight, she'd cut into him before the cabin door had even fully slid shut behind him: What had taken him so long? She'd been twiddling her thumbs all morning! If she had the passcode to his hidden closet office, she could at least file while she waited.

Facing her fire with calm reason, he'd given her the passcode, endured another lecture from Avier regarding lust versus trust, and thought that would be that.

Yet the next morning: She was starving! If she had access to his calendar, she wouldn't need to guess at his schedule. How could he allow the files to become so mismanaged?

And thinking he'd settled those demands, he'd discovered the next morning—in high-decibel detail—that he'd once again thought wrong.

But not this morning.

This morning of all mornings, when they both had back-to-back and even double-booked meetings all shift, Kinsley was still sleeping.

He'd never witnessed her lying so still without having been knocked unconscious. She was sprawled on her back across his entire bed, which was quite a feat, considering it nearly doubled her in height. She wore her own clothes to sleep, which did nothing to shield her scent from his sheets. They were loose and soft, giving her fit body the appearance of a fluffed pillow. Her face in repose was peaceful, her brow smooth instead of furrowed, her lips plump instead of compressed, her jaw relaxed instead of clenched. Her cheeks were rosy with warmth. Her wild hair was in disarray, and he wondered, not for the first time, how the inconvenient length of the strands jabbing into her eyes wasn't a constant annoyance.

He crossed the room to her side, sat on the edge of the bed, and before he realized his own intentions, stroked those inconvenient locks away from her face.

Her eyes shifted beneath their lids.

Raveno snatched his hand away, feeling caught even with her eyes closed.

Kinsley arched her back, covered her mouth with her fists, and released a low moan.

Was she ill? "Kinsley?"

She froze. Then she snatched her hands from her face as if they'd been scorched and gaped at him wide-eyed.

What was the appropriate English greeting after waking? "Great morning?"

"Is it?" She blinked. "You're early."

"No. You're late."

Her eyes narrowed suspiciously.

He nodded toward the bedside table, where she'd once again moved his yensha. How she could sleep with its screen glowing at her was incredible, but then, her eyes weren't as sensitive to light as his.

She glanced aside at it, then bolted upright. "Crap!"

He'd never witnessed her move so quickly, nearly as fast as an havarian. One moment, she was boneless in bed, and the next, she was upright, on her feet, and sprinting for the bathing room.

He took a moment to suppress his amusement, allowing her to dress in privacy before following.

She glared at him in the mirror as she struggled to tame the undulating, frothy mass of her hair with water alone. "You should already be meeting with Tironan. He's the first of many training sessions on your calendar today."

Ah, would his failings never cease? He bobbed his shoulders in disregard of her concerns—as she so often did his—just to taste the anger spiking her scent.

Mmm, delicious.

"Have you seen today's schedule?" She shifted her glare from him to her own hand as her fingers snagged in a nest of tangled hair. "We—"

He batted her hands aside and combed her hair with his claws. "Allow me."

"We don't have time for whatever you're about to do," she snapped.

"I am Vri Cilvril. I have whatever time I require."

"Well, I'm not, and I'm missing my meeting with Jhoni, the first of *my* many meetings today," she groused, but despite her words and temper, she crossed her arms and remained still for his ministrations.

He sectioned three strands of hair at her right temple and began weaving. "You are not missing anything. Jhoni is waiting outside, being kept company by Avier, who is your true first meeting. Your elbow evaluation, remember?"

She groaned.

"You do realize that with Tironan exonerated, Jhoni is my top suspect."

"I'm aware." She met his gaze in the mirror. Had her eyes always been that deep and dark? "After today, I'll be able to officially confirm whether he's the guard I was working with."

"Good." Raveno refocused on his task before he lost himself and his purpose in those eyes. He grabbed an elastic from his stash, tied

176

off the weave just behind her ear, then turned her head to address the hair at her opposite temple.

"Another career option should your maniacal-overlord gig not pan out," she murmured.

"What is that?"

"Hair stylist."

He snorted. "This is personal hygiene, not a career option."

"On Earth it is. People style hair for big events like prom, weddings, award shows—"

"Award shows?"

"A public ceremony where people receive recognition for their accomplishments."

"Ah." Raveno nodded. "I am familiar with the concept. I have received many recognitions during such ceremonies."

"Of course you have."

"But I styled my own hair on those occasions."

She studied her tamed curls. "That's because you're good at it."

"After a lifetime of practice, how could I not be?" he asked, amused.

"Has Tironan not been styling his own hair for as long?"

"Tironan is not good at many things he has attempted to perfect with a lifetime of practice."

"Harsh."

"Accurate." He tied off her second braid and felt strangely proud of his own work, considering, as he'd just said, that he'd done the same to himself every first shift for a lifetime. "Now it *is* a great morning."

"Mmmm." She studied herself in the mirror, rotating her head side to side. "Debatable."

"People on your planet pay for this service!" He gestured to her hair in mock offense.

They locked eyes in the mirror, and she winked.

He grinned back, helpless not to.

He shouldn't allow her to tease him or insult his brother, no matter the good-natured humor behind it. He should take offense at her high-handed tone and appropriation of his calendar. And he most certainly shouldn't be amused by her laziness in oversleeping. But he wasn't insulted or offended, and he couldn't remember when his time had ever been better managed. Yes, the schedule she created was grueling, but it was efficient. There was nothing he liked better than efficiency. Plus, it wasn't just his schedule that she'd improved. Miraculously, he could find reports when he needed them now.

Organized and efficient and about to identify his traitor.

He would not tolerate oversleeping from his crew, but his crew was not as effective as Kinsley even when they were early, let alone on time.

Even without her inciting chaos.

Raveno placed his hands on both her shoulders. She stiffened, but he held firm and turned her to face him. "This arrangement may have been born from desperation—a snap decision to save your life on my part and a grudging acceptance of the lesser of two evils on yours —but I am both pleased by your organizational efforts and impressed by your training."

Her eyes widened. She opened her mouth as if to speak, but no words emerged.

"I am not generous in my praise, I know. But you have earned it, and I thank you."

She closed her mouth with a *clack* and nodded.

As Raveno exited the room, he caught her studying her reflection in earnest. She smoothed a fingertip delicately over the tight, precise braids of her woven hair.

His pride swelled, and Raveno quit the room before he did something regrettable. Even so, his gratification lingered all through first shift, even when Tironan failed to defend himself. Even when he realized that Kinsley had progressed more in ten lessons than Tironan had in a thousand. Even when he pitted Tironan against Svish and Bvet, his newest recruits, and watched his brother lose time and again. Thanks to Kinsley, he knew that Tironan wasn't his traitor, and that's what truly mattered. Soon, she would give his traitor a face and a name, and Raveno could arrive on Havar with a clear head, determined to finally set his plan to overthrow Josairo into motion without the gnawing worry of his plot being exposed before it had even begun.

Yes, indeed, it truly was a great morning.

AFTER SNEAK ATTACKING A DOZEN ALIENS, KINSLEY'S adrenaline didn't even spike this time. Kual had arrived for their scheduled meeting. She'd bullshitted her way through a brief interview under the guise of managing Raveno's files, and now, she just needed to wait until he turned around to exit the room before taking him out. Gaining the upper hand against someone was chillingly easy once you had their trust.

Or disregard.

Kual was her final meeting of the day. By the grace of some higher power, she'd managed to disable all twelve guards in the time allotted—a miracle, considering her late start. Everyone had arrived at Raveno's cabin as scheduled, and Kinsley had drugged each one, as planned. Minus her unexpected morning wake up, this first phase of her mission was falling smoothly into place. She should be thrilled.

Kual stood, clicked his heels, and turned around to exit the room.

Kinsley lunged forward and jabbed him in the neck with a dose of svirros.

Kual swung around, startled. He raised a hand, feeling for the syringe still protruding from his scales, but like the twelve guards before him, his eyes rolled, unconscious before his body hit the floor.

Kinsley winced as the entire room shook. Again.

She unlocked the passage to Raveno's secret office, hooked her elbows under Kual's arms, and heaved. His limp body was dead weight, but the leather-like material of his uniform slid smoothy across the hard chrome floor. With gritted teeth and possibly a developing hernia, Kinsley dragged Kual across the room and dropped his body beside the row of drugged aliens already hidden in Raveno's closet.

Kinsley straightened, dug her thumbs into her sore lower back, and groaned as her spine popped in a xylophone run of disk cracks from tailbone to neck. If only she'd had a dolly for today's mission! Or a partner. She took a moment to catch her breath and face the disturbing sight of a dozen limp bodies lining the dark hallway.

They were only unconscious, not dead, but the distinction didn't settle the unease curdling her gut because they weren't just bodies. They weren't even just aliens anymore. They were Kual and Svish and Bvet. They were Jhoni, who skipped his guard shift every day, worshipped the ground Raveno marched on, and couldn't meet her eyes without his ears blazing neon blue. They were Avier, who'd healed her multiple times now, against his better judgement. They were Raveno's brothers-in-arms: his to order, train, and punish.

His to protect.

They'd kidnapped me across the galaxy, Kinsley reminded herself. *Just last week, they tried to burn me alive!*

If Raveno saw them like this, he'd be devastated.

Kinsley massaged her eyes, trying—not for the first time—to squelch that nagging self-doubt.

It was the Dutch fishtail braids, she decided. They were sucking the joy from what should be the building momentum of her triumph. She could still feel the tickle of Raveno's claws that could so easily disembowel her, carefully parting her hair, gently tugging the braid tight, and deftly smoothing each strand into place. She could still see his expression in the mirror, the concentration and pride in his work, in her. And she could still taste the bitter pill in her mouth that she had yet to swallow: She *liked* working for Raveno.

I'm not getting paid, she reminded herself. She hadn't been given a choice when she was abducted, and she didn't have a choice now. Not really. Not when it wasn't just her own freedom at stake.

Besides, even if she wanted to—which she didn't!—she'd gone too far to lose her nerve now.

Kinsley stomped passed the dozen unconscious aliens, survived the dark passageway without hyperventilating, and entered Raveno's secret office. The dim glow of the security monitors offered a respite from the pitch-black darkness, and she focused on that meager light, forcing her heart to settle.

Riley raised an eyebrow in acknowledgment of her presence. "How many digital reports can one alien possibly need organized?"

"When you revamp his entire filing system? All of them." Kinsley met Riley's petulant expression with a grin. "But I'm not here to file."

"No?" He crossed his arms. "What task has he bestowed upon you today?"

"I'm not here for him. Today, I'm here for you."

Riley narrowed his eyes.

"Today's D-Day, my friend. Today, I bust you and everyone else out of jail."

"Don't joke." He swung his legs down from the chaise longue and sat up, his expression grim. "Not about this."

"I'm not." Kinsley's grin widened. "After one hundred and thirty-seven days, we are finally commandeering this ship."

Riley stared at her, frozen.

Not this again. Why was no one excited to escape? "I've already incapacitated twelve of Raveno's guards." Kinsley hitched a thumb back at the passageway. "They're unconscious, hidden inside the closet. When I unlock the cell doors from the control room, you need to leave, lock the closet door behind you with the new passcode I've programmed, and then climb into the incineration shaft until everyone in the brig completes their escape."

Riley broke his stillness only to shake his head, still silent.

Just as Kinsley was considering the merits of dragging one of the unconscious guards in to convince him of her sincerity, a smile split Riley's face—pure joy as bright and beautiful and vital as the sun. "You're serious."

"I wouldn't joke about us escaping."

He stood. "We're commandeering the ship today?"

"Today." She bobbed her eyebrows. "*Now!*"

"Yes!" Riley fist-pumped the air.

Finally, the correct reaction to this news! The giddy excitement she'd been expecting to feel all along rushed to the surface.

"You did it," he marveled, stepping up to the clear viewing pane. "This whole time you were filing and training and bowing like a little bitch, you were working to free us all along?"

The pull of her braids chafed. "Deserve an Academy Award, don't I?"

"You're amazing!" he said, laughing. "What's the plan?"

Pride swelled at his confidence, so she let the "bitch" comment slide. She jabbed a thumb at the security feeds. "Once the cell doors open, you'll see the cameras black out. Everyone will escape into the shafts, so when the guards rush into the brig, they'll find it empty."

"Let me guess. Once the guards rush inside, you'll lock the brig door behind them?"

"Bingo. And the remaining guards that Raveno thinks are on duty to help him will be here, unconscious."

"Nothing you haven't done a time or two."

Exactly, thank you very much! "And with a little added insurance." She pulled out her last two sedatives from her cleavage and wiggled them at him.

Riley nodded, still smiling, and Kinsley realized that she'd never seen him smile before. He had dimples when he smiled. Same as hers.

"Switch, I..." Riley cleared his throat. "I'm sorry I doubted you."

Kinsley waved away his apology. "I'm sorry I didn't know you were alive. That you were left in here alone for so long."

"Locked in with Leanne and Ben without you as a buffer, Martin has it worse."

Kinsley laughed. "True."

"After I lock the closet, how can I help?"

"I need you to hide in the incineration shaft and hold your position."

"Absolutely not." Riley pressed his palms against the clear viewing panel. "I want to fight by your side."

Kinsley shook her head. "These aliens are trained in combat. If the mission comes to blows we lose, so I need you to hold your position in the shafts and *avoid* any fighting."

Riley pounded the cell wall with the flat of both palms. "He burned me alive, Kinsley! I want him *dead*."

"We all want justice for what happened," Kinsley said carefully.

"I can't just hide and do nothing while everyone else rises up and fights."

"No one is fighting! Everyone else will be escaping through the incineration shafts and holding their position until the coast is clear, same as you," she reasoned. "While I'm in the control room, I *need* you here, locking the unconscious aliens in the closet. You're an integral part of my plan."

"What about Martin?"

"What about him?" she asked.

"Will he be hiding in the incineration shaft and holding his position?"

"Yes." Maybe the aliens had managed to mind meld after all, because without Riley having to say it, Kinsley knew exactly where this conversation was going. Unfortunately. "Martin will be holding his position."

The petulance returned to Riley's lips. He unfisted his left hand and held it steady in the air between them. "I'm like you, Switch. Nerves of steel."

Kinsley eyed that hand, annoyed. "I'm surprised you have any nerves left after being burned alive."

"I'm serious."

"That's the problem. This isn't the time, the place, or the circumstance, but somehow, as usual, you've managed to twist something that involves everyone into something just about you. *Everyone* is escaping today. *Everyone* has a role. And your role is crucial to the success of this mission. Can I trust you to lock the closet behind you and maintain your position in the incineration shaft or not?"

"Yes, but—"

Kinsley raised her eyebrows. "There's a *but* to trusting you?"

His jaw clenched.

She lifted her hand to his, the clear viewing panel of his cell between their matched palms. "This is bigger than hurt feelings and bruised pride. We're staking our freedom against our lives on this plan, and I need to know that you have my back."

His fingertips curled slightly, pressing hard against the glass. "I have your back."

Kinsley nodded. "Then stop concerning yourself with Martin and focus on your part of the mission. When the cell doors open, you escape, you lock the closet behind you, and you hold your position in the incineration shafts. Got it?"

Riley exhaled through his teeth. He was obviously still concerning himself with Martin, but he nodded back. "Give 'em hell, Switch."

The glowing pulse of her ankesh spiked.

Kinsley dropped her hand from the cell and fisted it at her side. "Always," she murmured, and left to do just that.

No matter how the braids made her scalp, and other inexcusable body parts, ache.

SEVENTEEN

RAVENO'S MORNING, ALONG WITH HIS OPTIMISM, WAS QUICKLY charring beyond recognition.

Training with Tironan had only been the first of several challenging sessions. Despite being healed and cleared for combat, Kual's hands somehow still pained him. He didn't complain—he'd die before admitting weakness—but he could barely grip his ezil. He dropped his pivz after every block and flinched with every strike. Kual's lingering injury was likely more psychological than physical, so when Avier didn't immediately answer Raveno's summons, Raveno cried mercy and sent Kual to Kinsley with orders to visit Avier afterward.

Dellao's injury, however, needed immediate medical attention.

Raveno wrapped the wound in a clean towel, calling for Avier and cursing himself. He hadn't even been distracted this time! Quite the opposite. He'd been focused and unwavering and finally sparring with a true opponent. Dellao's greatest asset, in addition to his stellar combat skills, was the wisdom he'd gained over a long, loyal career in Raveno's service. Emphasis on long, which Raveno should have noticed and made accommodations for *before* nearly severing his arm.

He'd managed to slow the momentum of his strike too little too late as the forearm was sliced to the bone, and the bone itself likely broken.

Second time within the same shift, however, Avier didn't answer his summons.

Raveno called for Kual—who, by will or wrath, should be visiting Avier by *now*—but Kual didn't respond either.

Raveno escorted Dellao to the infirmary himself and, finding it empty—*where the svik is everyone?*—sought a dose of svirros to ease Dellao's agony while they waited. He entered his access code into the dispensary and stared, stunned, at their supply.

The entire stock of svirros was depleted.

Their pharmaceuticals had been fully accounted for per Tironan's third-shift report. Raveno reentered the access code and blinked at the empty space before him, seething.

While he'd been reprimanding Tironan, despairing over Kual, and injuring Dellao, his traitor had had an entire shift to implement whatever plan required fourteen doses of sedatives.

Raveno's heart lurched. *Kinsley.*

She'd warned him. *"If he finds me now, I'm dead,"* she'd lamented, and now his traitor had enough sedative to kill her, his cabin was clear across the ship, and no one was answering their anku.

He abandoned Dellao to the empty infirmary with instructions to apply his own pressure and sprinted down the hall toward his cabin.

His mind filled with her face: her dimples, the wisps of those too-short hairs plaguing her eyes, the drugging bite of her scent nearly as sharp as her wit. Her nose wrinkles.

Avier was right, as he was in nearly all things—Raveno's admiration and lust for Kinsley was a risk to his mission, but suddenly, the consequences of not acting on his feelings seemed the greater risk. He'd already lost Tironan's trust and Cresha's love. How much more could he bear to lose in pursuit of this mission without losing himself?

If he found Kinsley in time, he would pursue more of her than those chaste memories.

When he found her in time.

A few minutes later—an eternity—Raveno reached his cabin, lunged inside, and scanned the room.

Empty.

No mess. No blood. No body.

No Kinsley.

Raveno checked his bathing room: nothing. He dropped to his knees and peered under the bed, knowing she wouldn't be there again and desperately hoping anyway: nothing. He tore the sheets from the bed, as if she were so small, he wouldn't be able to detect the lump of her body beneath them: of course, nothing.

He stood in the center of his cabin and studied the room in a slow pivot, his chest heaving. Thev sa shek, his ears were burning from tip to neck, and his vresls were quivering. He needed to breathe. He needed to calm.

He needed to think.

He was overreacting. Surely, she was simply busy. They'd had back-to-back meetings all shift, the both of them, so maybe...maybe she had identified his traitor and been silenced before she could relay her discovery.

Raveno swiped a hand down his face. No, the worst possible outcome was not reality. More likely was the possibility that she'd finished her meetings and was safely locked inside his private office, filing.

Raveno tore open the doors to his closet, nearly ripping them from their tracks, and halted midstep.

And there it went, the final morsel of his great morning burned to ash.

The passage to his private office was wide open. Jhoni, Kual, Svish, Bvet, all of them, even Avier, were lying on their backs, lined up in a neat row down the passageway, unmoving. Limp.

Dead?

Raveno knelt beside Avier, his heart throbbing. He slipped his first thumb between the limp folds of Avier's vresls, pinched the thin membrane, and closed his eyes.

He held his breath.

A beat, slow but strong, pulsed against his fingertips.

Raveno wiped his eyes, and checked each of his soldiers. They were all alive. All unconscious but alive and, judging by the delayed capillary fill on their vresls, drugged.

Raveno scanned their faces a second time, seething. Of the fourteen missing svirros syringes, twelve had obviously been used. With the exception of Dellao and Tironan, his entire crew was here!

And if Tironan wasn't his traitor...

No one knew about his private office except Avier and Kinsley.

And if Avier himself was drugged...

Raveno ran into the passage, ignoring the churning unease in his gut. Kinsley must have disclosed the location of his private office in duress. Yes, she could fight. She was quite good—lethal, even. But no matter her quick learning and natural skill, anyone could be overpowered if the right pressure was applied.

The door to his office slid open, and Raveno stepped inside.

No mess. No blood. No body.

Still no Kinsley.

The only person present was Riley, standing within his cell. His spine snapped straight at Raveno's entrance, and a sour burst of fear filled the room.

Raveno narrowed his eyes.

Riley was usually too consumed by anger to feel fear.

Raveno jabbed both thumbs over his shoulder. "What do you know about my unconscious guards?"

"Unconscious guards?" Riley crossed his arms, and with that movement managed to rein in his expression. He quirked an eyebrow. "They're falling asleep on duty again?"

"You know who's behind this," Raveno growled. "You can posture at me all you like, but I can smell the stink of your fear."

"You sure that's not your own stink you smell?" Riley asked, and contrary to his scent, he grinned. "You look rattled."

Raveno approached the clear viewing pane, determined to

remain rational. He was the killing hand to Vra Cilvril s'Hvri Josairo. He'd sacrificed his own leg to gain favor with a tyrant and had masqueraded as his loyal servant for years while plotting a revolution. Surely he could bend one stubborn human to his will without resorting to torture.

"Do you despise Kinsley so much that you would condemn her to death?" Raveno asked. "As if she had any other option but to align herself with me. As she said, she was only attempting to survive."

Riley opened his mouth, but no words emerged.

"You were friendly with her once," Raveno pressed, aching inside. "Such anger is born from deep feeling, and I can tell that you still feel for her. She's in danger, but I can't protect her if I don't know who I'm protecting her against. For her sake, help me. Please. Have you seen her? Do you know where she is?"

Riley uncrossed his arms and bobbed his shoulders.

That infuriating, unconcerned, human gesture!

"How can I know anything, locked in a cage inside a secret office within a hidden passage?" Riley asked. "I can't help you."

Raveno punched the viewing pane. "I will torture you for answers!" So much for remaining rational.

Riley raised his chin, and the stubbornness in that one-inch movement was miles wide. "You've already abducted me from my home, isolated me from my people, and stolen my freedom. I have nothing you can take from me besides my life, and you're not a murderer. Or so you claim."

"You will *wish* me a murderer by the time I finish extracting my answers from you!" Raveno pivoted on his heel and strode to the monitors. Despite his threats, they didn't have time for such nonsense, and he didn't require Riley's cooperation to locate Kinsley. With a few keystrokes, he accessed the ship's tracking program and waited for it to connect with her ankesh.

"You wouldn't *dare* torture me," Riley taunted. "Kinsley would disapprove, and from where I'm standing, she has you wrapped around her little finger."

"I assume by your tone that such an expression is an insult?" The tracking program connected with Kinsley's ankesh, and Raveno scowled at the screen. "What is Kinsley doing in the control room?"

A burst of fear soured the air. "Without your guards behind you, you're a coward! You wouldn't dare give me a weapon and face me on equal ground, man to man!"

Raveno turned to face Riley, incredulous. "Is that what you want? With my traitor striking and Kinsley in danger, proving your masculinity is most important?"

"She's only in danger because of you. *You* abducted her. *You* caged her. *You* forced her to minion for you, and you—"

"You truly believe anyone could *force* Kinsley to do something against her will?" Raveno laughed. "Kinsley is her own person with her own mind, a clever mind at that, and she knows precisely the advantages she gains by aligning with me. She—"

The locking mechanism on Riley's cell flashed from orange to blue, and the door slid open.

"She just unlocked your cell," Raveno whispered.

Riley grinned. "What were you saying about her aligning with you again?"

Raveno staggered back a step, stunned. "This was the truth diluting your anger. She feigned our alliance to gain my trust. She's still loyal to my traitor."

Riley bobbed his shoulders. "Kinsley's her own person with her own mind, a clever mind at that. Right?"

Svik, his chest ached! What would his traitor gain from freeing the humans? He couldn't possibly think to return them home. And to what end? Raveno choked as the final truth of this horror gripped him.

Kinsley had claimed that Tironan wasn't his traitor, but if she remained loyal to him...

Raveno turned around to stare at the pulsing dot that was Kinsley in the control room, devastated. "Tironan has betrayed me after all."

Riley didn't respond.

"You will get your wish. I will finally become everything I've fought to overthrow. To protect this ship and my people, I will become a murderer," Raveno hissed, low and rasping.

Silence.

"Nothing to say now?" Raveno bit out. "Have you finally, for once in your life, been rendered speechless?"

Raveno peeked over his shoulder, but Riley's cell wasn't just open. It was empty.

Raveno whipped around, tensed to sprint for the passageway.

Riley was at the office door. He'd never seen someone look more smug.

"I don't need to speak when I've already won the argument."

Raveno was across the room by the time Riley finished his sentence, but as fast as he was, he wasn't fast enough.

The door slid shut right in Raveno's face.

EIGHTEEN

Kinsley stared at the brig's floor plan on the monitor, transfixed by the blue bars outlining each cell. Their doors were unlocked. By now, Martin, Ben, Leanne, and everyone would be disabling their cameras. In another minute, they would be climbing into the incineration shafts and crawling to freedom. Kinsley imagined their faces as the doors slid open, the hope and fight returning to their eyes as they escaped, and felt an answering swell of hope burn her own eyes.

I did it. She covered her mouth. *We're free. And in another hundred and twenty-some days, we'll be home.*

Returning to Earth wasn't just a distant dream of a goal anymore; it was a real, viable possibility for the future. She'd breathe fresh air again. She'd have that round with Martin and soak in the sun's warmth at his barbecue. She'd drink that cold lager—oh, how she missed beer!—wear clothing that didn't double as armor, and feel vindicated once and for all watching Daenerys Targaryen and her fire-breathing babies win the game of thrones.

She'd have the opportunity to apologize to Reece.

The blue bars outlining each cell blurred.

Focus!

Kinsley swiped impatiently at her eyes and pushed aside her emotions. Tironan, Dellao, and Raveno were still unaccounted for. Three aliens and two remaining sedatives, damn it.

The cell doors wouldn't relock without the new access code she'd programmed—fingers crossed!—so she could leave the control room and wait at the brig for at least one guard to run inside. She'd trap him, sedate the other two, and *then* she could fantasize about watching TV and drinking beer and practice her "I'm sorry" speech to Reece.

The cockpit door slid open.

Kinsley whipped upright.

Tironan stood in the doorway.

No, no, no, no!

Her heart punched her esophagus with each beat of denial.

Kinsley forced her expression, if not her surging adrenaline, to remain calm even as Tironan's eyes flicked to the monitors. They widened, taking in all that blinking blue, then sliced back to her. His delicate, fine-boned features tightened.

He grasped the pommel of his pivz.

Fine, she'd sedate Tironan first, *then* run to the brig, trap Raveno, and sedate and/or trap Dellao before practicing her "I'm sorry" speech.

Resisting the impulse to unsheathe her own pivz, Kinsley clutched a hand to her heart in mock relief. "You've come just in the nick of time!"

Tironan's frill flapped out cautiously.

Kinsley gestured to the control panel, then lifted her hands in confusion. "I don't know what happened! But maybe you can help me?"

She fluttered her eyelashes, the picture of helpless innocence.

Tironan was Raveno's opposite in many ways—in size, bearing, confidence, and ruthlessness—but in that moment, as his wide eyes narrowed in suspicion, Kinsley could clearly see the resemblance.

He strode forward slowly, cautiously, to study the control panel. He released his pivz to type; a few swipes and a series of clicks, and Tironan had entered the old access code for the cell lock system.

The cells flashed red, then immediately returned to their blinking blue.

Kinsley grinned.

Tironan's head snapped up. "Svik!"

"Sorry about that," Kinsley murmured, delving into her cleavage for a sedative.

Tironan jabbed at the keys, frantic, as usual.

She uncapped the syringe, cocked back her arm, and aimed the needle between the scales at the base of his neck.

Tironan spun, blocked her strike, and locked her wrist in an iron grip. "No. I s-sorry."

Shit! Kinsley didn't know what stunned her more: his words or his strength. Tironan might be weaker compared to Raveno, but he was stronger than her.

She bit back her panic. "You speak English?"

"Just s-s-start learning. For y-you."

"How flattering." Kinsley stepped forward into him, locking her elbow and using her weight and momentum to break his hold. "Why?"

He squeezed her wrist harder and retained his grip.

Her hand spasmed. The syringe fell from her numb fingers, clattered to her feet, and shattered. *Shattered.* Sedative puddled on the smooth chrome floor, reflecting the blinking blue lights of the control panel.

Fine, *two* guards would need to be locked in the brig now. This was still fine.

"You c-c-close to Raveno. I learn English. I learn why." Tironan bared his fangs. They weren't nearly as long as Raveno's, but they were deadly all the same. "N-now, I know."

"You don't. Know. Anything," she gritted out, attempting to leverage his own weight against him.

Tironan, again, simply tightened his grip.

Kinsley stilled, gasping through the pain. He was going to break her wrist! "This is another test, and you're failing it! Again!"

"Lie!" He jerked her to him. She slipped on the broken glass and nearly speared herself on the lethal claw pointed at her chest. "N-n-not a test. Never a t-test."

Think. Think. Think. "Why did you save me?"

Tironan's lip peeled back on a sneer.

"You could've let me burn alive in the incin—er, heating duct. You probably should have, for your own sake, but you risked your life to save mine." Her pivz was more accessible than the second sedative, but would he notice her unsheathing it? "Why would you do that?"

His tongue flicked out to taste the air.

"I think you know that abducting me and all the other humans from Earth is wrong. I think you know that Raveno is wrong in everything he does, and you don't want any part of it. It's morally, fundamentally, terribly *wrong*."

Tironan's frill pressed flush against his chest, bristling.

"Do what's right," Kinsley breathed. "Let me go."

"W-w-what is right not m-matter. Raveno is brother, and I his h-hand," Tironan hissed. "You correct. I should have l-let you b-b-burn."

He released her arm, cleared his pivz from its sheath, and struck so fast that she felt more than saw his movement.

Kinsley gripped her own pivz, one in each hand, and caught his blade with both of hers inches from carving her face in half.

She fell back, absorbing the force of his blow into a side roll. She needed some distance to regroup, but he was on her just as she found her feet, nearly faster than she could dodge. Nearly harder than she could block. Nearly. She'd sparred with Raveno, after all. Thank God, because without that training, she'd have been dead on the second blow.

Strike after strike, their pivz clanged on contact, and block after block, Kinsley endured the impact of his rage. She wouldn't have the

195

stamina to match his intensity for long. She needed to make her own move before her arms tired. Before she slowed and missed a block. And one missed block was all he'd need.

Kinsley dodged another blow and jumped onto the pilot's chair, hoping to gain some advantage from the added height.

Where was his skill and speed coming from? She'd seen him spar. She'd witnessed ass kicking after ass kicking time and again and had felt a measure of pride at her progress compared to his skill, or lack thereof. The man fighting her now wasn't an inept little brother struggling to keep up. He was a warrior and willing to kill.

Apparently, Raveno wasn't the only alien on this ship with secrets.

Kinsley struck down, forcing Tironan to raise his arms to block. With his side exposed, she lunged from the chair and stabbed between his ribs.

Instead of blocking her, he rotated.

Damn it, her strike slid off the plate of his uniform.

He jabbed down at her neck.

Kinsley threw her hand up and caught his blade with hers just as its tip split her skin. It sliced across her collarbone instead of her carotid, but she couldn't stop her momentum.

She landed on her feet, and in a burst of agony, his pivz pierced her left shoulder.

She dropped her weapon.

Shit!

Kinsley lunged forward, the pivz still embedded hilt-deep, and tackled Tironan to the ground. He fell flat to the floor on his back with an *ooph*, but even with the breath knocked from his lungs, he managed to roll over her. She tried to wedge the blade still in her right hand between their bodies, to use his momentum against *him* this time.

He dropped his weapon, gripped her wrist, and squeezed.

Her hand spasmed—*no!*—and she dropped her second pivz.

Shit, shit, shit!

Tironan elbowed both their weapons across the floor and out of reach. She watched them disappear into a shadowed corner of the room as he restrained her right hand over her head to join her left. *This is it,* she thought as he pinned her body with his pelvis. *This is how I die.*

Old age had never been her preference, she reminded herself.

He gripped the handle of the pivz still embedded in her shoulder and yanked it free.

The pain, bone-deep, gushed. She screamed. Blood sprayed.

Three drops, like tears, landed on Tironan's prominent cheekbone, just under his right eye. Kinsley stared up at him, at her bright blood staining his grim expression, and stopped struggling.

Tironan flipped the pivz in his grip. He eyed her neck.

"Please." Kinsley panted. "Don't."

His gaze flicked up to meet hers. His jaw flexed.

He wasn't even out of breath.

"I didn't. Ask. To be here." She swallowed. "I'm just surviving."

He leaned down, and for one, crazy, hopeful heartbeat, she thought she saw sympathy light his eyes.

His lips peeled back from his fangs. "M-m-me too."

Tironan jabbed down, hard and fast and undoubtedly precise.

Something slammed into Tironan's temple, knocking him sideways.

Kinsley blinked.

Riley was standing over her, shaking the sting from his right hand.

Thank God he ignored my orders! "I take back what I said about fighting." Kinsley pointed. "Grab a weapon!"

Riley offered his hand to her instead. "I'm sorry. I heard you scream, and I couldn't just—"

Kinsley pointed. "Don't—"

Tironan swiped his leg, taking out Riley.

—turn your back. Damn it!

Riley fell in a hard double tap, slamming flat to his back then cracking the back of his head on the unforgiving chrome floor.

Kinsley scanned the room. Where was her pivz?

Like a snake, Tironan's arm shot out and wrapped around Riley's neck.

Small blessing, Tironan must have lost his second weapon, too, and with his hands busy strangling Riley, he couldn't wield the ezil still strapped to his back.

Riley gurgled, struggling.

Kinsley climbed to her feet and gripped the pilot's chair to keep from swaying. Four pivz were scattered around the floor somewhere. Surely, she could find just one!

Tironan stood to face her, holding Riley between them like a shield even as he continued choking him.

Kinsley squinted through the shadows, scanning the room, but even illuminated by the control panel, the room was too dark to find the lost pivz. She still needed a weapon, damn it! She needed more time. She needed...ugh, if only the cockpit had more than just monitors, a control panel and a rocket launcher! Was a light switch too much to ask for?

Kinsley stilled. The rocket launcher.

She spun to face the control panel, and there it was, her favorite orange button, pulsing at her. Calling her home.

The rocket would need something to hit.

Riley's body slumped, limp in Tironan's grip.

She flipped a silver switch, releasing a solo cruiser, then pressed all the blue buttons needed to throw the ship thrusters in reverse.

Tironan's head whipped up.

As the ship slowed, the solo cruiser came into view, floating in space before them.

Kinsley grinned and did the only thing she'd ever wanted: She pressed a button and watched the sparks fly.

The intercom whooped. Every button on the instrument panel flashed, and the monitor with its pulsing countdown sprang to life.

Tironan dropped Riley, gaping at her.

Kinsley stepped aside and gestured to all that beautiful chaos. "Happy disarming."

Tironan's frill sprang out from his chest. He knocked her aside on a shriek and dove for the control panel.

Riley was still on the floor. Still unmoving.

Kinsley dropped to her knees beside him. "Be alive. Be alive. Be alive."

She pressed two fingers to his neck. Caged together for how many months, and she'd only just discovered that he had dimples yesterday. How was that even possible?

"I will not grieve you a second time!"

"You grieved?" he rasped.

The air whooshed from her lungs so fast, she swayed on her knees. "Now's not the time for a nap." She patted his cheek. "Come on, look alive."

He made an indistinct garbling noise and flinched. "Throat's on fire."

"We both know that's a lie. You've experienced the real thing. A little strangulation is nothing in comparison, I'm sure." Kinsley leaned in close and whispered, "We need to *unray* to the *igbray*. Now."

Riley tried to speak, winced, then tried again. "What?"

"As much as I want to see this play out," she hitched a thumb at Tironan typing and squawking behind them. "We need to run." She stood and tugged Riley to his feet with her good arm. "Find a pivz."

"A what?"

"A weapon!"

"Fighting didn't pan out last time," he ground out.

"Nope." She leaned in and whispered the words directly into his ear. "We get to the brig, hide, and trap them as planned."

"Copy that." Riley glanced past her. "What about him?"

"Let him disarm the rocket." She scanned the floor, and— finally!—spotted the glint of a pivz in the hallway. She pointed at it.

"Hurry, while he's distracted. We've got three aliens and one sedative left."

Riley staggered into the hall to pick up the pivz. "Two."

"No, one of my sedatives broke while I was fighting Tironan."

"I meant we only have two aliens left. I took care of Raveno." He scooped up another weapon and passed it to her.

She holstered it, her heart thudding hard against her ribs. "You took care of him?"

Riley nodded, finding the fourth pivz between them.

"What exactly does that mean?" Her shoulder blazed with each breath, but the pain didn't prevent that pesky ache of obligation from constricting her chest.

"Raveno found the aliens hidden in his closet."

Kinsley choked back bile. "That was fast," she murmured.

"He barged into his office, searching for you, of all things," Riley laughed, shaking his head. "Worried that his traitor was striking again. Thinking you were in danger, he was frantic to save *you*. Isn't that rich?"

After everything she'd just endured, how was it that *now* she felt, inexplicably, on the verge of tears.

"But your timing was perfect. When the cell door opened, I slipped out while he was distracted and locked him inside his own office."

Raveno didn't deserve her loyalty. He didn't deserve anything but his own cage. Turnabout was fair play, Kinsley reminded herself, massaging her sternum.

"You ready? Which way do we go?"

"Go?"

"Your plan. The brig." His eyes dropped to her shoulder and hardened. "You've lost a lot of blood."

"My plan. Right." Kinsley blew out a breath and stepped into the hall.

Riley blocked her. "What's going on?"

"We're commandeering the ship." She gestured to the room around them. "Obviously."

He shook his head. "What's going on *with you?*"

Kinsley tried to shove passed him. "I'm fine."

"But you—"

The whooping alarms cut to silence.

Kinsley peeked back at the control panel and blinked at the sight before her, stunned.

Oh. Yes.

"—maybe we should—"

Kinsley grabbed Riley's chin and jerked his attention to the floor-to-ceiling view of space.

He shut up, silenced by the beauty before them.

The lir s'flis had launched.

Kind of.

One couldn't honestly describe the rocket's movement as having *launched.* It didn't blast off. There was no fire and most certainly no fanfare. It had more accurately *released* from its restraints and was propelling itself through space with three spitting thrusters. Kinsley stared, transfixed by its painfully slow progress as it distanced itself from the ship, then pivoted its nose down with tiny puffs of air.

The thrusters cut. The rocket continued rotating, moving by momentum alone until the pointed nose of the lir s'flis aligned with its target: the solo cruiser.

It froze.

A trickle of sweat beaded at Kinsley's hairline and rolled down the back of her neck.

The rocket disappeared, zipping across space nearly faster than her eyes could track.

Tironan shrieked.

Riley gripped her right shoulder.

Kinsley held her breath.

The rocket collided with the solo cruiser, and the black space in front of them exploded with light.

The flash of impact was blinding at first, but when her eyes adjusted, Kinsley watched as a double spray of shimmering starbursts fanned from what used to be a single occupant spaceship. Now the solo cruiser was nothing but floating ash. The detonation had the shape of a nuclear impact, but instead of clouds and flames, the mushroom was electrical, snapping with sparkling pops of blue and green and white light. Like fireworks.

In a lifetime of tripping switches, Kinsley had never witnessed anything so gorgeous.

Someone was shaking her, and Kinsley realized she was swaying, lightheaded. She inhaled—*must remember to breathe*—but she craved the explosion before her more than air. More than great hair, beer, and burgers. More than Earth.

More than life.

Every sparkling pop, every flash and snap of color, was everything right and beautiful and perfect, a language that only spoke to her. It buzzed through her veins and penetrated to the marrow of her bones, and suddenly, after so many hundreds of days in captivity, Kinsley felt something inside her click into alignment.

Air and food might keep a person alive. Hope and the promise of freedom might inspire the fight to stay alive. But this was something apart from survival.

This was the sun's warmth on her face after months of living in shadow.

Tears dripped down her cheeks.

The someone shaking her shoulder said something, but Kinsley straightened, a tingle of apprehension staining her bliss.

Instead of dying like an Earth firework after having burst into color, the explosion radius of the lir s'flis was expanding. The petals of scattered light burst again in a second blast of color and then again in a third, growing exponentially bigger and brighter and closer with each pop.

Too close.

Kinsley reached back, still unable to tear her gaze from the sight, and rapped on Riley's arm. "We need to go."

"That's what I've been saying!" The hand on her shoulder—Riley's hand—tightened, then tugged her back. "To the brig. *Now!*"

Tironan ignored them. His fingers jabbed at the control panel faster than the naked eye could follow, but Kinsley could see quite clearly that no matter what access code he managed to press, in the correct combination or otherwise, they needed to brace for impact.

Still, Kinsley hesitated. She reached for the last sedative, eyeing the back of Tironan's neck. He'd never be more distracted than he was at this moment.

Riley released her shoulder and grabbed her wrist. "Later. Someone needs to drive us away from that mess."

She didn't like it, but Riley was right. Kinsley turned her back on the deadly brilliance before them, gripped Riley's hand, and ran.

NINETEEN

ONE OF THE BRIG'S SECURITY CAMERAS WAS MALFUNCTIONING.

Raveno sneered at that blank screen with every fiber of his rage and frustration—and, if he was honest, his fear. The monitor should have splintered from the force of it. Just as the door should have splintered from the force of his fists, and his kicking feet and prying claws and straining back. But apparently, his ship had betrayed him too, because his exit code wasn't working. All he had to show for his escape efforts was two rows of raw knuckles and four broken talons. He'd commissioned the door himself and therefore knew it was impenetrable. He was an idiot for even trying to escape, but he couldn't just sit and do nothing!

Such was the depth of his distraction, he hadn't even noticed when the camera had first malfunctioned. Its connection to the server was strong, same as all the others, and according to his tech, the camera was still online and recording. He played back the footage to discover exactly when the malfunction had occurred and watched as one male human hoisted another onto his shoulders and smeared—Raveno leaned forward, frowning—*something* over the ceiling of their cell. Halfway into third shift, the moment after the cell doors unlocked and slid open, the human had covered the camera's lens as well.

And then, like bells tolling before a funeral, the alarm for a lir s'flis launch began its countdown.

Trapped in his office with that incessant alarm and without anything to do other than chew on his ugly thoughts, Raveno could feel that obscured camera spread hate like poison through his veins. Because it wasn't just any camera that was malfunctioning.

It was the camera in Kinsley's old cell. Whatever plan required fourteen doses of sedatives was Kinsley's plan. Or, at the very least, she was implementing it.

The countdown stopped. Finally.

Raveno pressed his fingers deep into his eyes, less careful of his own claws than was probably wise, but at this point, who cared?

The ship began to vibrate.

Raveno dropped his hand from his face, frowning. What now?

The ship jumped violently, knocking him from his chair. He sprawled on the floor and spat out a curse, and then he was flying through the air, smashing headfirst into the ceiling.

Thev sa shek!

He jabbed a claw into his anku. "To the control room! Gravity off! I repeat, gravity off and tactical maneuvers on!" Cry mercy, with his entire guard unconscious in his closet, Dellao likely bled out by now, and Tironan—Raveno shook his head, refusing to finish that thought. Who was he even commanding? "Is *anyone* receiving my signal?"

His wrist vibrated. "I—I—I receive, Vri C-C-C-Cilvril Hoviir!"

Before Raveno even had time to spit out another curse, he slammed back to the ground. And then, after his left elbow, knee, and chin had bashed into the unforgiving floor, his body was relieved of its weight.

"W-w-we have a situation."

Raveno rubbed his chin. "Oh, do we?"

"I—I—I—"

Raveno felt the slice of his claws, and forcibly removed his hand from his face.

"W-w-where are you?"

Raveno stilled. What was his brother playing at? "In my office."

"What are y-you—" A cough, and then, "W-we are under attack."

Was that not his plan? "I am aware."

"Th-th-then why—svik!" The ship shuddered. "W-what are your orders?"

"My orders." Raveno shook his head, biting off the urge to laugh. Perhaps Kinsley was fighting back after all. "Even if you released me from my office and begged my forgiveness, do you think we could come back from this? Do you think *Father*," he gagged out, "will allow such incompetence to go unpunished?"

"I—I—I—" Tironan's stutters ended on a high shriek, and the ship jolted.

Raveno rolled his eyes. Only Tironan would blunder his own uprising.

Then again, Raveno was the one caged inside his own office.

"Give me a m-m-moment."

"Sure. Take your time." As if the ship wasn't doomed, with tactical maneuvers in Tironan's hands.

Raveno closed his eyes, shutting out the sight of that black camera, but it still soured his thoughts. Unbidden, his mother's final wishes flashed before him: *You're the spark that gave my life meaning, Raveno. Sight beyond the present to a better future. Be the spark for them all.*

He'd taken her letter to heart, but he should have seen her words for what they were: love and farewell. But not truth.

Raveno dropped from his three-inch float back to the floor with a grunt, the weight of his own body nearly crushing.

A minute later, his anku glowed. "I've n-navigated us out of r-r-range of the explosion and s-s-stabilized the ship."

Miracles do exist.

"I—I—I'm in your o-office, Vri C-C-Cilvril, but I don't s-see you."

"You're here?" Raveno sat up. "To *release* me?"

"Here w-where? Your c-c-cabin is empty!"

Raveno opened his mouth and froze, hesitant to trust the uncertain hope seeping into his heart.

"Was she s-s-speaking the truth, then?" Tironan asked, his voice suddenly flat. "Was this a t-t-test?"

Raveno found his footing and stood. "Open my closet. Push aside my clothes, and at the far back, to the right, there's a panel." He took a steadying breath and gave Tironan the access code.

"Your c-c-code isn't working," Tironan informed him.

Of course it wasn't. "Return to the control room and reboot the access code system."

"R-r-r-r—"

"You heard me, Tironan," Raveno growled.

"But all access-code operated s-s-systems will disengage. We'll need to r-r-reprogram them all by hand. We—"

"What systems are you really worried about keeping locked at the moment?" Raveno snapped.

"Y-y-your will by my h-hands," Tironan muttered.

Raveno waited a long moment in silence.

"Tironan? Did the system reboot?" Raveno attempted to activate the door, but the lock refused to disengage. "Do you receive?"

Another minute passed. The lock flashed blue—finally!—and the door slid open.

Raveno ran from the office and through the passage, but he stopped short at his closet exit.

Tironan had returned from the control room and was kneeling before Avier, looking stricken by the sight of their crew. His braids were completely undone. His circlet was askew. His weapons were missing.

Raveno had never seen a more welcome sight, even as his heart threatened to vomit from his throat.

Tironan looked up. "The entire c-c-crew. Are they..."

"They're drugged, but they're fine." *Hopefully.*

Tironan stood, blocking the doorway. "This entire t-time, it was her, wasn't it? Kinsley," Tironan hissed her name like a curse. "The svirros shortages. The c-c-constant chaos and m-mistakes."

"It's more complicated than that. She's working for me, helping me to identify—"

"Kual l-l-lost three fingers!"

"A well-deserved punishment," Raveno countered. "Focus, Tironan! I can't regain control of this ship from my office."

"From your c-c-closet, you mean," Tironan grumbled.

Of all times, *now* Tironan found his nerve?

"She was r-right," Tironan said, his voice quaking. "This m-m-m-mission. Trafficking shols against their w-will. I don't care what J-J-Josairo's orders are. It's wrong."

"*I know.*"

"You do?"

Without his ship and crew, without even one ally at his side, what remained to salvage this catastrophe but the truth? "That's why I'm planning to overthrow Josairo and take command of Havar."

Tironan stared at him for a hard moment. "Exp-p-plain," he hissed.

"For some time now, I...I..." Svik, now *he* was afflicted. "I've used Josairo's missions to conduct my own covert meetings with our off-world allies."

Tironan didn't react. He didn't speak or even blink, and his vresls remained firmly flush against his chest.

"That's why Bazail, Iroan, and Fray sent willing warriors to compete in the Intergalactic Frisaes. They weren't competitors so much as spies, confirming my reports to their respective leaders. When they realized I spoke true, that other planets' civilians are being trafficked against their will to compete, Bazail, Iroan, and Fray swore to support my efforts to overthrow Josairo and remain our allies should Haven attempt to retake Havar during our revolution. I wanted Lorien's support as well, but..." Raveno released a disappointed huff. "Well, you saw how that turned out."

"Yes, I d-did." Tironan crossed his arms. "They s-s-sold us the humans, as promised. Y-y-you betrayed *them*."

"I thought they wanted to meet under the *pretense* of selling us humans. I'd hoped to finally meet their Lore'Lorien in person while maintaining my cover as Josairo's loyal Vri Cilvril. If all had gone according to plan, everyone would think *she'd* reneged on our deal by *not* selling us the humans. We'd have fired at one another and missed, and I'd have returned to Havar seemingly empty-handed, but having solidified another ally." Raveno released a low hiss. "But I was wrong about the Lorien, and now, instead of another ally, we have a ship full of enslaved people."

"If y-y-y... If this has been your plan since our m-m-mission to Bazail..." Tironan's eyes swept over him, taken aback. "Cry m-m-mercy! It's been over seven thesh!"

"Ten, actually."

"Why d-d-didn't you t-tell me?" Tironan stepped forward. "All t-this time! I could have h-helped you!"

"Helped me overthrow Josairo? Helped me commit treason?" Raveno's hand swept through the air. "Helped me murder our father?"

Tironan didn't even flinch. "Y-y-yes, please!"

Raveno laughed. He wasn't sure if he was more shocked or amused by Tironan's enthusiasm. "If I'm unsuccessful—if I fail to kill Josairo—he'll execute me and everyone caught as my allies."

"F-f-from what I'm seeing, you're not on the path t-t-toward success." Tironan leaned closer. "Y-y-you *need* my help."

"I won't have you executed beside me."

"We won't be if we're s-successful."

A creeping blush burned Raveno's ears. "I promised our mother that I'd protect you from Josairo," he admitted. "Embroiling you in a plot to assassinate him isn't protecting you. I couldn't protect her, but for you—"

Tironan pointed a claw at Raveno's chest. "Y-y-you are not to blame for M-M-Mother's death."

"I should have been there."

"I w-w-*was* there," Tironan said flatly. "I should have p-p-p—"

"Stop. Please." Raveno pressed his fingers into his eyes, physically damming the tears within their sockets. "I didn't expect you to protect her. I—"

"You *should have* expected it!" Tironan shouted, his words, for once, as clear as his anguish.

"She followed her heart," Raveno forced out. "She did what she thought was right."

"And I—I—I should have h-helped her."

"We both should have."

"S-s-so now that you're picking up where she left off, let me do what I should h-h-have done all along. Let me help you. Your will by m-m-my hands."

Oh, Tironan.

"F-F-Father doesn't need to know about t-this—" Tironan gestured to their unconscious crew. "M-mishap."

Raveno snorted. "Sure. We'll just excise this entire shaoz from the ship's log, security cameras, and the crew's memory, assuming they even remember any of this after waking up."

"No one would d-dare refuse an order of silence from y-y-you."

"Because they fear me." He shook his head. "They fear Josairo more."

"They hate J-Josairo more."

"I'm his killing hand. They hate me too."

"Y-y-you may be his hand, but he's the one g-g-giving the orders, and they know from experience the c-c-consequences of disobeying orders. They hate Josairo m-much more." Tironan smirked. "Or m-maybe Kinsley had the right idea. Maybe this was another t-t-test."

"You spoke to Kinsley?" Raveno felt his vresls lift slightly. "She speaks Haveo?"

Tironan rolled his eyes. "I s-s-speak English."

"Since when?" Raveno scoffed.

"S-since you brought her into your confidence over m-m-me."

Raveno's ears blazed a second time.

"So. W-w-we restore order on the ship, and when the c-crew wake, we t-t-tell them they've failed another test."

"Why am I testing them so much?" Raveno asked the ceiling.

"B-b-because you're a thev sa shek, and you do as you p-please."

Raveno barked out a laugh. "All right, then."

"W-w-what of your plan to unseat Josairo?"

"What of it?" Raveno asked, sobering.

"Even w-w-with the support of off-world allies, it's not as if y-y-you can simply stride up to Josairo and r-run him through with your ezil." Tironan's upper lip peeled back to expose both his top fangs. "No m-m-matter the immediate, personal satisfaction that might b-b-bring."

Raveno stared at his brother, stunned by the reality before him: Tironan at his side and guarding his back instead of plotting to stab it, their wills and minds aligned. He reminded himself of his promise—he should be choking on guilt—but the strength of his love for, pride in, and loyalty to Tironan didn't leave room for feeling anything but awe.

Tironan's eyes slid sideways then returned. "W-what?"

"We will discuss my plan to unseat Josairo and everything it still lacks after we regain control of this ship." He grunted with a sudden burst of derisive humor and shook his head. "I can't maintain control of my own vessel. How can I possibly assume to maintain order on Havar?"

"Y-y-you can't."

Raveno met the fierce determination in Tironan's gaze.

"N-not alone." Tironan swept aside his hair and tipped his head, exposing the vulnerable scales at his throat.

Raveno tried to swallow and nearly choked.

"We're in this t-together."

Raveno shook his head, stunned.

"Y-y-yes."

This was real. His brother was before him, knowing the truth, and still pledging his loyalty.

This was everything.

Raveno closed the distance between them, bowed, and brushed the curve of his front incisor carefully across his brother's exposed neck. He straightened, tipped his head aside, and his brother returned the gesture.

"T-t-together?"

Raveno straightened. "Together."

Tironan grinned.

Raveno met Tironan's dark eyes, so similar to Kinsley's. Identical to their mother's.

"What else did Kinsley say?" Raveno asked ruefully. "That was her lir s'flis launch, wasn't it?"

Tironan stiffened. "Y-y-yes, it was."

"Who is she working with?"

Tironan winced and rubbed the back of his neck. "It sounds c-c-crazy, but she's partnered with the human you executed. He's alive and helping h-her."

"She's working *with* Riley?" Raveno asked, taken aback. "You're sure?"

"P-p-positive."

"Who else?

Tironan cocked his head.

"Jhoni, perhaps? I originally suspected that he—"

"Jhoni isn't h-h-helping her. He's right here," Tironan pointed at his unconscious body, "d-d-drugged in your closet along with everyone else."

"But considering his missing brig shifts—"

"H-h-he skips his brig shifts because he can't abide what we're d-doing. Caging p-p-p-people and trafficking them across the universe —it's s-sick."

"But he—"

Tironan knifed his hand between them. "No. He confided his cconcerns to me, and I was the one who s-s-s-suggested he swap shifts when possible."

"He didn't swap shifts. He skipped them."

Tironan blew out a breath. "He's young. I'll talk to h-him."

"Then who's helping her?"

"W-w-who remains?"

Raveno gritted his teeth. Perhaps Dellao hadn't bled out after all.

TWENTY

RUNNING THROUGH THE SHIP'S HALLWAYS WITH RILEY SHOULD have been cake in comparison to Kinsley's usual method of crawling through the incineration shafts solo: no stinging metal, no dripping sweat, no risk of burning alive, no panic attacks. Cake! Instead, Kinsley was sprawled on the floor, having just dropped from the ceiling—thank you, gravity—and fighting a losing battle to keep the contents of her last meal within her stomach. At least with the gravity back on, if she vomited, it wouldn't float midair.

She tried to brace against the wall to stand and fell sideways with a gasp. How could her arm simultaneously be numb and in excruciating pain?

"You okay?"

Kinsley peeked up. Riley was swaying unsteadily but had managed to remain on his feet. He extended a hand.

Kinsley gripped his wrist and clung on tight as he helped her stand. "Is it just me or is the ship still spinning?"

"It's not just you, but I don't think it's the ship either." Riley covered his mouth and shuddered. "How far do we have left to go?"

"The brig is just around that corner." Her stomach heaved. "I think."

Riley scowled. "You think?"

She grimaced as bile burned its way up her throat. "I've only ever entered the brig from the incineration shafts. Never from the hallway."

"Well, there's only one way to find out." Riley eyed the hallway the way one might the prospect of a colonoscopy.

"We'll be fine. We've only got Dellao and Tironan left, and at the moment, we know Tironan's occupied." Kinsley released Riley in favor of her pivz and shuffled forward. "Cover my six."

"*Only* Dellao and Tironan," Riley muttered, but he turned to cover her back, as requested. He followed her down that last hallway and around the corner, so close that when she halted, he rammed into her, nearly knocking her flat.

But nothing could flatten her more completely than the unfathomable sight in front of them.

The brig door was unlocked and open, as it should be. All ten cell doors, five on each side of a long hallway, were wide open too, as planned. The hallway itself was empty. No guards in sight. Nothing prevented Kinsley from squinting through the darkness into the brig, into each cell, which should also be empty by now, with everyone having escaped through the incineration shafts.

But by the glow of the hallway baseboard lighting, she could see that three dozen people were still sitting in their cells. Reclining on their couches. Lying in their beds.

Everyone.

"Christ, people, move your asses!" Kinsley sheathed her pivz and sprinted into the brig, shouting into each cell as she passed. "Get up! Let's go!"

Several people startled upright.

"What are you waiting for, an embossed, hand-delivered invitation? Climb into the heating ducts!"

Why were they staring as if *she* was crazy? *They* were the ones still tucked inside their unlocked prison cells.

"*Escape*, damn it!"

Kinsley skidded to a halt in front of her old cell. Benjamin and Leanne were spooning on the chaise longue. Spooning! They should be running for their lives! At least Martin was standing, but even he was standing *inside* their cell.

Inside their *open cell*.

She should have known better than to think the sheep would move without being herded.

Why hadn't Martin done any herding?

Benjamin, Leanne, and Martin stared at Kinsley with varying degrees of regret, puzzlement, and resentment shaping their expressions, and Kinsley realized she'd spoken that last thought out loud.

Martin raised his hands, as if the sight of his palms could placate her! "I went cell to cell, just like you asked. I told everyone about today's escape plan."

Kinsley eyed "everyone." The few people who weren't fawning over Riley had poked their heads into the hallway, listening to her conversation with Martin. But no one had escaped. "Clearly."

Martin's jaw tightened. "They didn't believe me."

"Didn't believe you?" Kinsley swept her arm out, then winced as her shoulder blazed in protest. "When the doors unlocked and slid open, what was there not to believe?"

His eyes dropped to her shoulder. "You should sit."

"*You* shouldn't even be here."

"They weren't convinced that escaping through the incineration shafts was their best option." He bridged the distance between them and pointed at her shoulder. "May I?"

"Sure, why not?" Kinsley laughed. "It's not like we're sitting on a ticking time bomb here!"

Martin peered at her wound. "They didn't have the benefit of you rallying their spirits with the hope of escape all this time."

"Fuck the *hope* of escape! I'm giving them the real thing!" Kinsley burst out hoarsely, ignoring his probing fingers.

"They watched Riley burn alive," Martin reminded her oh so reasonably. "No one wants to die like that."

"If they escape, they won't die here at all."

With a frustrated grunt, Martin gave up on whatever amateur medical exam he thought he was performing. "We don't have anything clean to wrap this in."

"My shoulder is hardly our biggest concern at the moment," Kinsley muttered.

Martin opened his mouth, undoubtedly about to argue that point, but his gaze slid sideways. "Welcome back to the land of the living."

Kinsley peered over her shoulder. Riley had finally caught up, having extracted himself from the outpouring of congratulatory hugs and handshakes at his resurrection.

"More like the land of the lounging." Riley looked around at them, baffled. "Why is everyone still here?"

Leanne's head snapped up. "Riley?"

Benjamin's face split into a wide grin. "You're alive!"

Kinsley rubbed her forehead. Her entire plan was falling apart.

Leanne bolted to her feet—for *Riley*, she bolted to her feet, but not for an open door?—and lunged into Riley's arms.

Riley staggered back, but he managed to catch her and keep his footing. "It's good to see you too, Leanne."

Benjamin was suddenly at his side, clapping Riley on the shoulder. "It's a miracle."

"Yes, it's wonderful," Kinsley conceded. "Now, let's get everyone into the incineration shaft and—"

"The plan isn't working," Leanne interjected, and she had the absolute nerve to appear completely calm about that statement. Where was her urgency?

"The only reason it's not working is because no one is escaping. You—" *Idiot!* Kinsley closed her eyes for a second to rein in her panic. *Make it work. Just make it work.* She turned to project her voice

217

down the brig to the dozens of terrified faces watching them. "Riley and I took out thirteen of the aliens, so there's only two left. When they come for us, I'll lock them inside the brig. Then we can *return home to Earth*. But to trap them in the brig without us inside, we need to climb into the incineration shaft."

Riley glanced doubtfully around at the full cells.

"This plan will work," Kinsley insisted. "We're running out of time, but if we leave now, *right now*, I'll make it work."

"You say there's only two remaining as if taking on even one of those monsters is conceivably possible," a man spoke up from his cell. "I'm a black belt in Taekwondo, and even I can admit that I wouldn't stand a chance against them."

Kinsley scanned the doorways and found him. A tall, fit man, maybe in his early fifties, had poked his head from his cell to speak up. Kinsley met his eyes. "I'm not asking you to fight the aliens. I'm asking you to escape them."

"How will we survive?" a woman shouted back. "We don't know the first thing about traveling through space."

Kinsley found the woman, a girl, really, clutching the frame of her cell as if she might tumble out if she didn't hold on tight enough. "I can navigate us back home."

"Are you an astronaut?" the girl asked, sounding nearly as hopeful as she was terrified.

"I'm a Special Forces operative. An explosive ordinance disposal specialist. I—"

Someone snorted. "And I'm a rocket scientist!"

People laughed.

Kinsley clenched her teeth. "After weeks of training, I assure you, I can fly this ship."

The man ducked his head back into his cell. "She thinks she can fly an alien spaceship," he scoffed, jabbing his thumb at Kinsley.

"Maybe she can," the girl argued.

"Maybe she's delusional."

"She opened the doors, didn't she?"

They didn't have time to debate this! Words were just words after all. Kinsley faced Martin. "If we get this party started, maybe they'll follow suit." She ran into the cell and wove her fingers together to provide a leg up into the fire vent. "Who's first? Riley? Benjamin?"

Martin approached her slowly, shaking his head. "That arguing out there? They've been going back and forth like that all day. Instead of covering their cameras."

Kinsley met Martin's calm, resigned eyes and straightened. She could still make this work. *She could!* "Fine. We cover their cameras ourselves, and *then* we escape."

Martin lifted his hand and cupped her right shoulder. "Will you personally lift each person into the incineration shaft too? You said so yourself, we're running out of time."

Something inside Kinsley shattered. "Then we leave the idiots behind and escape ourselves! Just the five of us!"

"There's a problem with that too." Martin shifted his eyes to Leanne, still cozy in Riley's embrace.

"Leanne is one of the idiots refusing to escape?"

"We've talked about name-calling," Benjamin chided.

"I still prefer option two," Leanne said, still so damn calm even against Kinsley's animosity. "Keeping a low profile and waiting on your alien to return us to Earth is the better bet. If you shut the doors now, they'll never know we tried to escape."

Kinsley blinked at her. "It's too late for option two now."

"No, it's not. All this could be another ship malfunction, like you've done for other missions," Leanne suggested.

"That's not a terrible idea," Martin said.

"It's a shit idea!" *Breathe.* Kinsley straightened away from Martin and put every morsel of her energy into speaking without screaming. "I can't twist this as another ship malfunction because Tironan saw me in the cockpit. He knows it was me this time."

Martin made a rough noise in the back of his throat. "They caught you?"

"Again?" Benjamin plopped onto the chaise, exasperated.

"As if I wanted to get caught," Kinsley snapped.

Leanne sat on the chaise and curled into Benjamin's side. "You shouldn't have let them see you."

"*Let* them?" Kinsley couldn't stop blinking. "Even if I'd managed to pull off my end of our plan without revealing myself, Raveno isn't stupid. He knows how much I've fantasized about launching that rocket. I'm the only one who would dare blow up that solo cruiser, and only a human would disable the cell locks. Who do you think is the only human with the knowledge and opportunity to accomplish all that? Sherlock isn't the only one who could make that deduction!"

"No one asked you to do this," Leanne said, shaking her head. "I didn't want this."

"You didn't want to be free?" Kinsley asked, incredulous.

"We're fine as we are: alive."

"You prefer being caged like an animal?"

"That's my preference to death, yes!"

Kinsley rubbed her pounding forehead. "All you had to do was crawl through that vent and save yourself."

"To be fair," Riley chimed in. "It's a vent that spits fire."

Kinsley thought of the pile of unconscious aliens she'd left in Raveno's closet and shuddered. "I know you're scared. I'm scared too." Kinsley knelt in front of Leanne and took hold of her hand. "But don't think about what we're risking by escaping. Think about what we might gain: beer and bacon onion barbecue cheeseburgers. Mani-pedis. The ending to *Game of Thrones*. That spa appointment is still in your future if you just reach out and take it!"

Leanne sandwiched Kinsley's hand in hers, and just as Kinsley's hope hitched, Leanne flipped her wrist and pointed at her ankesh. "They turned you into one of them."

"W-what?"

"You're wearing their uniform, you're braiding your hair in their style, you've got their glowing blue dot, whatever that is."

Kinsley snatched her hand from Leanne's grip. "It's an ankesh. It—"

220

"There's no point, Kinsley," Martin said grimly.

"No point?" Kinsley stood and whipped around to face him. "If we don't leave, not only will we not be free, we'll be dead." She held up one finger. "We launched a rocket." Two fingers. "We blew up one of their solo cruisers." Three, four, five fingers. "We're escaping, commandeering their ship, and returning to Earth." Kinsley waved her hand at him, a bit hysterical now that she was listing all her offenses. "If Raveno finds us before we trap him, we're dead."

"We didn't do any of those things," Leanne said. "*You* did."

Kinsley flinched, taken aback. "What did you just say?"

"They saw *you* in the control room. They saw *you* blow up a solo whatever. They'll kill *you*." Her lips trembled. "And I'm sorry about that, I *am*, but I didn't ask for this. When they come for you, I'll be here, exactly where I should be. Caged and miserable, but alive," Leanne said. "Until we get off this ship, *that's* our best option."

"We're never getting off this ship unless we fight for it." *Why did that even need verbalizing?*

Leanne looked away.

"Like I said," Martin said, glumly. "There's no point."

Kinsley covered her mouth, and for the first time, maybe ever, she couldn't see a way forward. "You're on board with this? With staying here and letting me take the fall for this mission? With letting them kill me?"

The anguish in his dark eyes was piercing. "One life versus thirty-five." His jaw flexed. "Do I have a choice?"

"Thirty-four." Riley nudged her good shoulder. "Let's go, Switch. Leave the idiots behind, like you said."

Kinsley didn't know when she'd started shaking her head, but she couldn't seem to stop even as she fell back a step. "You gave me your word."

Martin covered his face with his hands.

She whirled on Leanne. "When I visited yesterday, I asked if we were on for today's mission, and you nodded. You might not have wanted this escape plan, but you *did* agree to it."

Leanne snorted. "Bullied into it, you mean."

Kinsley locked eyes with Benjamin. "And do you remember what you said?"

Benjamin looked away.

"'It's a risky plan, but it's better than no plan at all.' We were in this together!"

Riley tugged on Kinsley's elbow. "Come on. We need to move."

How the tables had turned: someone telling *her* to move!

Kinsley tore her arm from Riley and strode into the hall. It didn't matter what she said, how loud she screamed, how solid her plan, what she risked for them, if the guards were returning or not. They hadn't reached Havar, they didn't even have an ankesh with his ouk, but Raveno owned them all the same.

They were strangers. She'd felt a kinship with them, a responsibility toward them, because they were human. But they were strangers.

She should have just saved herself.

"Fucking sheep," she whispered, but it wasn't enough. It wasn't nearly enough. Kinsley spun in a circle, seething. "You motherfucking *sheep!*"

"Looks to me like you are the one being left for slaughter."

She froze at the sound of that deep, hissing voice behind her.

Raveno.

All the heads poking out from their doorways and gaping at her disappeared back into their cells, like bugs scattering from the light.

Kinsley nearly laughed. Nearly.

She closed her eyes. She took a deep breath, attempting to suck in all the courage and fortitude she could muster, and while her back was still to him, she slipped her last syringe from the wedge of her cleavage and palmed it.

She opened her eyes and faced him.

Tironan was standing just inside the brig's doorway, which was a bit of a surprise, but it probably shouldn't have been. All his panic had been replaced with cold intent.

Next to him stood Raveno. Half a head taller and nearly twice as wide as Tironan, he blocked the entire exit. Despite his murderous tone, his expression mirrored hers: rage, resignation, disgust, and, strangely enough, fear.

What could Raveno Hoviir, the killing hand of his king, possibly have to fear in this moment? She was the one who'd been kidnapped. She was the one who'd been betrayed by her own people. She was the one facing the man who would sentence her to a brutal, fiery death.

Raveno pressed his hand to the door's locking panel.

All the cell doors slid shut with a whoosh, trapping the sheep in their cells as the door closed behind Tironan and Raveno.

Trapping them all together in the brig.

TWENTY-ONE

RAVENO DIDN'T LIKE LOOSE ENDS. QUESTIONS THAT REMAINED unanswered were usually the ones that caused the most grief, so he'd ordered Zethus to update their translators. According to his intelligence, an IED was an abbreviation for an Improvised Explosive Device, a homemade weapon consisting of five components: an initiator, a container, a charge, a power source, and lo and behold, a *switch* that activated the device.

The Kinsley before him now was more than just a switch, however. Exploding with rage and fear and—he inhaled, and without conscious thought, his vresls rattled—passion, she *was* the device, even as the force of her resolve activated something within him. The fire in her eyes quickened his heart. The determination in her stance blazed through the tips of his ears like twin torches. The husk of urgency in her voice threatened to splinter his resolve. From the warrior's braids he'd added to her hair, to her posture, poised to run, dodge, attack—whatever necessary—she was riveting.

Raveno sealed shut his nostrils against all of it and stalked forward.

Kinsley edged back. Riley matched her step for step, staying behind her, his eyes locked on Raveno. Her gaze took flight around him, darting from the heating ducts to the doorway to Tironan—Was that a flash of apprehension in her expression? Aimed at *Tironan?*—and back to the heating ducts. Eventually, she focused on him, resigned but not beaten, even seeing there was no escape.

"I am impressed," Raveno murmured.

"My purpose in life," she quipped. "To impress you."

"If not for Tironan's loyalty, I would still be caged in my own office." He swept a hand at the cells around them. "Then again, had your plan succeeded, you might have caged me inside my own brig."

Her eyes flitted sideways to glance at her people. Her face flushed a bright red.

All her humans were at their viewing panes, lined up shoulder to shoulder on either side of the hallway. Although they were the ones caged, strangely, Raveno suddenly felt on display.

He refocused on Kinsley. Her right hand was resting on the pivz sheathed at her hip. Her left arm was cradled against her stomach, immobilized by a punctured shoulder. The blood he'd tracked through the hall from the control room to the brig had probably dripped from that injury, but the wound had already clotted. It probably wouldn't even need rapid repairing to heal.

Despite such logic, Raveno resisted the urge to help her. To apply pressure and call Avier to ensure she wouldn't suffer lingering muscle or nerve damage.

Avier couldn't help anyone at the moment, least of all her.

Because of her.

"You did well by him," Raveno said, forcing a note of indifference into his voice. "Even as you served your own purposes."

"Him?"

"Do not play coy," he chided. "Did Dellao know about your plan to fire the lir s'flis?"

Her eyebrows jumped into her hairline.

"Ah, the explosion was not part of the plan, then? Just you improvising. As usual." He forced a chuckle. "Dellao must have loved that."

Kinsley bit her lip, and thev sa shek, he could practically see the cogs grinding and repositioning themselves in her mind as she, even now, attempted to maneuver the situation to her advantage.

A spike of panic spiced her scent. No advantage to be found, he supposed.

Raveno resealed his nostrils. "I understand why you did it. Why you chose Dellao."

Her eyes narrowed.

"You had a lot of choices to make. Whether to betray Dellao by switching loyalties to me. Whether to betray me by remaining loyal to him. Whether to betray your people to save yourself."

Riley's back hit the end of the hall. He cursed, and Kinsley stopped her retreat.

Her hand curled into a white-knuckled fist around the hilt of her pivz.

Raveno leaned down so his face was inches from hers. "I understand that in the end, you had options, but no choice."

"You don't know anything about my choices."

"I know you chose wrong. These people, *your* people, obviously don't care about you half as much as you care about them."

"They're too terrified to care," she said, but her voice, like the rest of her body, trembled.

"Are *you* not terrified?" He reached up and very slowly—very carefully, considering her trembles and the close proximity of his claws to her face—wiped a tear from her cheek and displayed it for her on his finger. "Yet you still find the courage to care. To the detriment of all you attempt to accomplish, you care very much."

Her eyes, those dark, impossibly familiar eyes, locked on his and blazed. "They didn't kidnap me. They didn't brand me. *They're* not my enemy."

"They did not, as you say, have your back."

A muscle in her jaw ticked. "What do you want from me, Raveno?"

"I want to hear it from your own lips. I want the truth," he said, and was shocked by the yearning ache constricting his chest. He didn't want the truth, not at all, but he couldn't have what he really wanted.

His vresls quivered.

Tironan cleared his throat. "R-R-Raveno—"

"You want the truth?" She shook her head and snorted. "That's rich. You've never wanted to hear the truth before. Why start now?"

Riley reached out and squeezed her uninjured shoulder. "Switch—"

She wrenched away from his hold. "My very first words to you were the truth, but you refused to listen. But you're right about one thing. For me, there was no choice."

Kinsley dropped to one knee, her weapon still sheathed.

Raveno frowned, as confused by her actions as he was by her words. What truth was she referring to?

Tironan knocked Raveno back with an elbow to the gut and lunged forward, a pivz in each hand.

Tironan barely had the nerve to sneeze without asking permission. What was he—

Raveno caught sight of the syringe in Kinsley's cupped palm and choked on his order to stand down. He watched, stunned, as his brother—his meek, uncertain, untrainable, too smart, too trusting, unkempt little brother—took the hit meant for him.

Kinsley stabbed the syringe between the scales of his upper thigh.

"Switch!" Riley lurched forward. "Watch it!"

Tironan jabbed at Kinsley with his pivz. She sprang to her feet and drew her own weapon, too little too late. The pivz punctured her left biceps.

"Shit," Riley hissed.

She gripped the wound, gasping. "I'm fine."

Tironan fell to his knees.

Kinsley could have struck while he was down, but she too just watched as Tironan collapsed between them, unconscious. His pivz lay within the loose grip of his dead hands, stained with her blood.

"He's only knocked out, not dead," she rasped. "Like the rest of your crew."

Raveno didn't remember unsheathing his pivz, but its handle was suddenly in hand. He tensed to strike.

Kinsley dropped to one knee again, but she wasn't holding another syringe.

The tip of her pivz was poised over Tironan's neck.

Raveno froze, seething.

"Let me leave the brig, and I'll let him live." Her voice cracked. Her breath hitched. Her injured left arm shook violently.

But her right hand gripping the blade poised over Tironan's neck didn't waver.

"Fight me." Svik, *his* voice cracked.

"It's so nice to finally see brothers getting along after all this time."

"Fight *me!*"

"I can't," she said, raggedly. "No choice, remember? I wouldn't win a fight against you."

"Is that the only reason?" he purred.

Her lips sealed against the truth of that answer. Her cheeks reddened, and her eyes darted sideways for a moment.

A moment was all he needed.

Raveno lunged, tackling her back and to the floor. He clamped onto her wrist, applied pressure, and the pivz slipped from her hand.

A wrenching, broken sound clawed from her throat.

Raveno leaned back slightly, his heart leaping. Had he squeezed too tightly?

Something moved in his peripheral vision.

Raveno blocked the strike with the side of his arm—not the best shield—but effectively protecting his neck as the point of a pivz pierced bone-deep.

Raveno stared at the hand still holding the pivz's hilt and followed the arm to Riley's wide, shocked eyes.

Before Riley could react, Raveno squeezed Riley's wrist.

"Ah!" Riley's hand spasmed, releasing the pivz. "Fuck."

"Run!" Kinsley gasped hoarsely.

"I'm not leaving without you." Riley drew a second weapon with his nondominant hand.

"Do you want to burn again?" Kinsley choked out. "Go!"

Raveno gripped the hilt of the pivz imbedded in his arm, gritted his teeth against the pain, and ripped the blade free.

Their human audience pounded their fists on the viewing panels in warning.

Riley's frantic eyes flitted between Kinsley and the heating duct. "But I can't fly the ship! There's no more sedatives! I—"

Raveno threw the pivz hilt over blade.

Riley tried to dodge it, but there wasn't much room to maneuver. The blade sank into Riley's upper thigh.

The humans were screaming now, or seemed to be. Whatever warnings or encouragements were probably issuing from their open mouths couldn't breach their cell walls.

Riley dropped to the floor, clutching his leg.

"Get up!" Kinsley screamed. "Run!"

Raveno swung his arm in a backhanded punch just as Riley was attempting to regain his footing. Riley's head whipped back from the blow. He was unconscious before he even hit the ground, and Raveno worried for a moment that perhaps he'd struck him too hard.

But no. If he strained, Raveno could still hear his heart beating.

"No," Kinsley sobbed.

Their audience dropped their hands to their sides, silent.

"He's only knocked out, not dead," Raveno growled.

Kinsley closed her eyes on a groan.

"The truth between us, Kinsley! Is that really so difficult to face?" Raveno's chest was heaving. He wasn't sure when he'd lost his breath. His control. "What was Dellao's purpose in all this? Yours, clearly, was to escape, but what did *he* stand to gain from a deep-space uprising?"

Kinsley shook her head, refusing to open her eyes.

Blood had smeared from her punctured biceps, across her collarbone, and up her neck. Raveno unclenched his fist—bah, his hand was trembling at the sight—and very carefully, he stroked the underside of her jaw with his knuckles. "Or was the uprising your own agenda?" Raveno asked. "What do you have to lose by telling me now?"

Her lips disappeared into a wrinkled line, and then a burst of air exploded from her mouth on a loud, "Pah!"

Raveno's vresls sprang out around his head.

Her shoulders were quaking. Her face flushed in red patches. Her lips parted a second time and released a lurch of hysterical laughter.

Laughing. She was *laughing?*

"You're right," she wheezed between gasps. "I have nothing left to lose. I could take the truth to the grave when you burn me."

Burn her? Something dark and bitter chilled his veins. She still thought him capable of murder.

"I could leave you haunted by everything you still don't know: Why did Dellao betray you? What did he have to gain? How did he accomplish such a feat? When did he approach me?"

Raveno endured the stab of each question with unflinching stoicism.

"Because no matter who you burn, no matter how long and diligently you dedicate yourself to the endeavor, you'll never find the answers to those questions. *Never!*"

Raveno frowned. "I can be quite persuasive."

"Of that I have no doubt. But you're asking all the wrong questions." Her lips stretched apart, more sneer than smile. "You can't discover why or how or when Dellao betrayed you. *Because he didn't.*"

Raveno reared back, unsure what she was implying. "But then who—"

"No one!" She barked out another laugh. "The day we met, when you caught me in the control room, you asked me my purpose in escaping through the incineration shafts. Do you remember? I told you the truth from the start! And what did you do?"

"I don't—"

"You ripped my shoulder from its socket. Ha!"

Not on purpose, he thought, annoyed, but otherwise, she was right. He *had* questioned the purpose of her insane crawl through the heating ducts, and her response had been ludicrous. Something about commandeering the ship and returning home to Earth.

Which she'd nearly just successfully done. "You were working *alone* this entire time?"

She nodded.

"There is not a traitor on my ship?"

"Not that I know of," she said, calming her laughter with a few deep gasps. "Oh, my stomach."

"Why lie about that? Why—"

"Why pretend to know that a member of your crew was betraying you, thereby preventing you from pulling my other arm out of its socket? Why convince you that I was a useful asset, thereby gaining your trust and securing a means to commandeer the ship and return home? Yeah, why *by will or wrath*, would I ever do that?" She snorted. "Everything I did, I did for me. Well, for us." Her eyes flitted aside to the humans still watching shoulder to shoulder from the safety of their cages.

Her laugher hitched on a sob and died.

Raveno stared at her in awe. "What am I supposed to do with this information, Kinsley?"

"You wanted the truth." Her dark eyes, which had been wild with laughter just a moment before, dulled with resignation. "You do whatever the hell you want with it, Raveno."

The nerve it must have taken to traverse the heating ducts, knowing they could incinerate her, was one thing—her bravery bordered on insanity—but the cunning to hatch such a plan, the patience to implement it, the fortitude the stay the course... Had she not been betrayed, she would have succeeded.

She would have commandeered his ship.

Was it only one shift ago that he'd sworn to pursue less-than-chaste memories of her if he found her in time? Well, here she was before him, spitting the truth in his face and revealing the yawning depths of her deceit, her will fierce even in defeat.

He'd found her in time.

And he knew exactly what he wanted.

Raveno dropped his head, buried his nostrils in the soft valley of Kinsley's chest, closed his eyes, and inhaled.

Sweet musk. Smooth smoke. A bite of spice.

Instantly, his head swam. His heart slowed, then bolted to match hers. His groin throbbed in rhythm, yearning so deeply, it ached. His vresls rattled, although he wasn't certain when they'd lifted, and his entire face, not just his ears, burned for her. Even the hair follicles beneath the tight rows of his braids seemed to throb.

Her breath caught.

Raveno pulled back and opened his eyes, but the floor and ceiling and cells and everything around them was nothing but a fuzzy kaleidoscope of color and flame. He blinked several times, fighting to bring her into focus.

Kinsley stared back at him, tense. Uncertain. Waiting.

She didn't understand. How could she? He needed to demonstrate his feelings in actions familiar to her.

He placed a gentle hand on her cheek, leaned down, and as was *her* people's custom, pressed his mouth to hers.

TWENTY-TWO

HE WAS KISSING HER.

Despite the obvious—him pressing his lips to hers—Kinsley hadn't been exactly sure what was happening at first. She'd been expecting him to throw her back into one of the cells, at best. At worst, she'd been braced for the immediate blow of a pivz through her heart, or possibly a public burning. He'd incinerated Riley for requesting extra rations, for heaven's sake. What was the consequence for leading a failed uprising?

A public snogging, apparently, because Raveno Hoviir, the captain of this human-trafficking operation and the killing hand to his planet's tyrannical overlord, was unequivocally, impossibly, definitely making out with her. On the brig's hallway floor. With Riley and Tironan splayed unconscious next to them. For the avid entertainment of the entire cellblock, Martin undoubtedly included—someone was pounding on the viewing panels again.

She should play along—kissing was preferable to dying, after all—but that would require a level of deception beyond her at the moment. Perhaps she'd sustained a concussion during all that hand-to-hand combat, because to her severe annoyance, she didn't need to pretend.

He was as talented a kisser as he was a fighter.

The protrusion of his fangs behind those deceptive, soft lips should have been alarming, but her body apparently cared more about soft lips than the deadly fangs behind them. The gentle caress of that second thumb echoing the first—one along her cheek and the other across her jaw—should have made her cringe. His touch was strange, but both thumbs were gentle and careful and touching her as if she were precious. The vibration of his frill rattling against her chest should have cooled any heat his lips might have sparked, but her nipples weren't protesting the position of that vibration. On the contrary, tightened to taut, aching peaks, they'd never protested less.

Yep, she was unquestionably concussed.

Oh, this was not...

His lips shifted to a better, deeper angle.

This was not...

He found a rhythm. His lips were more than just pressing against hers, they were stroking, and his fervor, as unfamiliar as it was unexpected, was genuine and drugging.

This was happening.

If she wasn't concussed, her judgment was obviously being impaired by adrenaline or terror turned relief or the lingering hysteria of dropping truth bombs everywhere, exploding her cover and her mission and all hope of survival, let alone escape. Because she wasn't just not alarmed, not cringing, not protesting his touch. She was *enjoying* it.

And then she was closing her eyes and actively participating in it.

She bit his lip, and his frill vibrated faster. He cupped her cheek with his other hand, framing her face, and she licked the seam between his lips, urging them apart. He licked her back with his long, flexible, bifurcated tongue. Instead of snapping back into the reality of what should have been a nightmare, her brain took a hard left, parting with reality completely and thinking, *That tongue is going to be heaven elsewhere.*

Her body throbbed.

She thought of him finding his unconscious crew and how his first instinct had been to search for her, worried that *she* was in danger. The familiar ache that she could no longer pretend was the weight of obligation filled her chest.

She wanted this.

Her body wanted him. *Him.*

She moved her lips urgently against his, taking where he'd been giving. How the scales on his lips could be so soft when the scales everywhere else on his body were so impenetrable was a mystery. Just one of a thousand concerning Raveno, but one she could actually explore. She tried to lift her hand to touch his body, to test the feel of his scales elsewhere, everywhere, and cried out.

Fuck, how had she forgotten about her injured arm?

Because, as usual in Raveno's presence, she'd lost her fucking mind.

Raveno leaned back slightly—*he* was the one who broke the kiss, *my God*—and frowned down at her, concerned.

"What—" she breathed, because she refused to admit she was panting. "Was that?"

He cocked his head. "You don't know? It's true, I haven't seen you engage in one, but... I'm told it's called a kiss. It's to express affection and give pleasure and—"

"I know what it is," she snapped.

"You just asked—"

"It's proper for a man to take a woman out to dinner first before sticking his tongue down her throat."

"We have shared a dinner previous to this." His inner eyelid swiped across his eyes. "What does eating have to do with expressing affection?"

Expressing affection? "Never mind dinner. That's the least of my grievances. What I meant was *why* were you kissing me?"

"To express—"

"Affection. Yeah, I heard you the first two times. But *why?* I just tried to overthrow you as captain of this ship. I just admitted that I've been lying to you. That I deliberately encouraged you to distrust your crew, knowing there was no one to distrust. I could think of a lot of emotions you might express, and affection isn't one of them."

"You told me to do whatever I wanted. So I did." Raveno caressed her cheek again, just two inches of both his scaly thumbs stroking her skin, and her body lit. "But I want something more, if you are willing to listen."

Kinsley raised her eyebrows at that. *More. He wants more.*

"I want you to have my back in truth," he murmured. "As I will have yours."

Not quite the more she'd braced for, and damn her confused body for deflating. "Come again?"

"What if I confided in you? What if I disclosed the full truth of my mission, and what if that truth, and my goals, aligned with yours?"

Without the distraction of his kisses, her wounds were becoming insistent. She tried to wedge some distance between them and flinched. "What goals might those be?"

"Our mutual goal to return you home to Earth and ensure that no one is trafficked across the galaxy by havari ever again."

Perhaps the pain was affecting her hearing—her judgment, more likely—but no, he was in earnest. "Knowing that I just betrayed you, you want to bring me further into your confidence?"

"You betrayed me because I didn't listen to your truth." His frill flexed. "Are you willing to listen to mine?"

Kinsley narrowed her eyes. "Just to be clear—you're not planning to burn me alive?"

His frill clamped flush again his neck. "No."

"Promise?"

"I give you my word."

"Well, then. Confide away. What choice do I have, and as usual— ha!—what do I have to lose?"

Raveno narrowed his eyes on her speculatively. "Your life, which you very much value."

He stood. The absence of his heat and weight should have been a relief, but nothing was as it should be.

"As do I." He held out a hand to help her to her feet.

Kinsley ignored his hand and attempted to stand on her own, but the ship swayed.

"Kinsley?"

Someone cut the gravity again, and her head floated off into the air even as her body somehow remained on the ground, the ship somersaulting in dizzying loop-de-loops around her.

"Thev sa shek!"

Two strong arms with biceps of steel gripped her, one under her knees and the other around her back. A boulder was cradling her head against another even larger boulder at her ear, and then her body was floating too, her feet swaying midair as the ceiling rushed by. As far as boulders went, they were quite warm, and the one beneath her ear had a drum inside it, beating in steady acceleration.

"Stay awake, Kinsley!" A rush of spitting hisses in another language. "We are nearly at the healing bay. Kin—"

HER BODY WAS ON FIRE.

Kinsley opened her eyes—when had she closed them?—and just that simple act of moving her eyelids was nearly impossible as her skin melted. Her throat was raw. Someone was screaming. She tried to move, but the most she could manage was a finger twitch, and even that small victory was hampered by a restraint. Something hard. Something surrounding her.

She wrenched her eyes open. Had they closed *again*? Raveno was standing over her, but his face was distorted. Elongated. Blurry.

Someone was crying.

She forced her arm up through the flames, but her knuckles clunked against the restraints and fell limply to her side.

"Just another few minutes!" Raveno looked like he was shouting, but she could barely hear him. His frill was stretched out and quivering around his head, appearing even longer by the strange distortion of the curved glass around her.

Ah, she was in a translucent tube. And why not? They had incineration shafts on their spaceships. Was it so farfetched that they'd have incineration tubes too?

"I know it hurts!" he yelled at her. "Stay strong!"

Both his palms pressed flat against the glass.

Huh. He had scales even on his palms. Tiny little scales the size of ladybugs.

"Just another minute!"

Did his planet have ladybugs?

"Kinsley!"

KINSLEY OPENED HER EYES, AND IT WASN'T A STRUGGLE THIS time. She wasn't on fire, she wasn't in an incineration tube, and she wasn't alive. She couldn't be, because Tironan had impaled her shoulder and punctured her bicep, and Raveno had burned her alive after giving her his word that he wouldn't after...after kissing her. She should still be in agony, but her body's most pressing discomfort was the crusties scraping the corners of her eyes.

She was lying in bed, a warm and cushy bed with blankets over her body and a pillow under her head. The room was small and spartan. And familiar. An instrument panel, monitor, and ergonomic swivel chair were on her right. No doubt a floor-to-ceiling window showcasing the awesome magnitude of the universe would be on her left.

She was back in her cabin—well, *Raveno's* cabin—in his bed and still aboard his spaceship.

So. Not dead after all.

Or still in a coma. Or still enduring her penance in hell.

But either way, nothing had changed.

Someone gently squeezed her hand.

Kinsley turned her head.

Well, perhaps one thing had changed.

Instead of showcasing his muscles on bulging display beneath his strappy leather uniform, Raveno wore a lightweight green robe. The material was shiny and slick, like silk but thicker. Intimate. It crossed in front and was held in place with a wide band, kimono style. He seemed different, younger—naked, somehow—without his usual trappings. How a man could look naked when he was wearing *more* clothing was a puzzle, but when had anything between them ever been normal?

He wasn't wearing his headband.

She'd never seen him without it. *His forehead's exposed,* she thought and then nearly laughed at herself. An exposed forehead! The scandal! Yet she found herself unaccountably staring at that smooth, broad expanse of opal scales.

He hadn't braided his hair either. Combed straight back from his forehead, his thick platinum locks hung damply over one shoulder, puddling on his kimono.

He'd just showered.

Now that she thought of it, she must have showered too. Her hair was damp, soaking the pillow under her ear. She was naked under the blanket, *again,* and when she tucked her nose down slightly to sniff a waft of herself from under the sheet, she smelled pleasantly delicious from his scented shower gel.

"We have to stop meeting like this," she croaked. Jesus, her throat was sore!

He sandwiched her hand in both of his.

Her left hand, which was attached to her healthy, unburned, uncut, pain-free left arm.

"How are you feeling?" Although his expression was as taciturn as ever, his blood-orange eyes pinched at their corners.

"Obviously suffering from the effects of rapid healing syndrome."

"Impossible." Raveno sniffed with bruised dignity. "Avier assured me that he could not have healed you better himself."

"Too late to say otherwise. What—" She swallowed. Even saliva burned her throat! "Why does my throat hurt so much?"

"You injured your throat in the chamber because *someone* wasted our entire stock of svirros. You endured the healing process... cold chicken. Is that correct? Without the aid of pain-relief medication."

"Cold turkey." She waved a hand. "Close enough."

"Why are so many of your idioms associated with birds?"

"They're not *my* idioms. I didn't invent them." She winced through another swallow. "What does that have to do with my throat?"

"You were screaming." His lips flattened. "A lot."

"Ah." Her face flamed, as if a little screaming was the most embarrassing aspect of this situation. "Listen, Raveno, we need to talk. You..." *Would have kissed my socks off, had I been wearing socks.* "Er, I..." *Should have hated every moment of it.*

How were his eyes so damned orange? Practically glowing neon in the dim room. She covered her eyes, trying to find the appropriate words, since she obviously couldn't voice the truth, not even to herself.

"Allow me." He passed her a cup of water from the bedside table.

Her arm shook, but with his help, she took a sip, shamelessly stalling.

"You may ask me anything you wish," he said, taking back the cup. "But it might be easier if you allow me to speak first."

Was this the same man who'd ripped her arm out of its socket during interrogation? Who had burned Riley alive to reinforce his reputation as an evil son of a bitch? Who was trafficking people across the galaxy in a spaceship prison?

Kinsley waved her hand between. "Yes, by all means, speak." *So I don't have to.*

His rattling frill pressed nearly concave against his chest. "I must apologize."

"You? The next great killing hand of Havar, *you* must apologize?"

"I took without asking." He cringed. "In regard to the kiss, I mean. I was so relieved to have found you alive that I failed to account for your feelings in the spell of the moment. I failed to discern the magnitude of your injuries. Such puncture wounds would not have weakened an havari to the extent that—" He clacked his mouth shut. "I will not make excuses. I realize now that the last thing you would have wanted was a demonstration of my affection."

The last thing she'd wanted was to *want* a demonstration of his affection.

"I apologize and promise that such a failure will not happen again."

Kinsley stared at the straining cords of muscle beneath his opal scales.

She forced her gaze away. "Apology accepted."

He inclined his head on a heavy sigh. "Secondly, I finally told Tironan the truth about my plan to overthrow Josairo, and he did not betray me, as I feared. We..." His lips twitched into a grin. "We are allies, true brothers, once more."

Kinsley raised her eyebrows. "I noticed."

"Thanks to your use of svirros, most of my crew does not remember who attacked them, although many are speculating correctly. Per Tironan's suggestion, I told them they failed another test, which most accepted without question, speculations aside, except for Dellao. I brought him into my confidence along with Tironan and Avier. And, I hope, after this conversation, you." Raveno smoothed a hand down the wrinkle-free perfection of his kimono. "Additionally, I wiped the security footage, so all the evidence that remains are the witnesses themselves. With their rooms muted, they could only see us, and since none of your humans speak Haveo and none of my general crew speak English nor have access to translators, I think we are, as you say, in the clear, yes?"

"Sure. But that has always bothered me."

"What has you bothered?"

"That you're fluent in English," Kinsley said. "I understand why Tironan learned, but I still don't understand how you and Avier were fluent from the start." She held up a hand. "And don't give me that crap about it being common for modern civilizations to know off-world languages. No one but you and Avier knows English."

"Many havarian diplomats are conversational in multiple languages to communicate with off-world planets, but you are correct. I know more than most. Earth, ridiculously, has roughly six thousand five hundred spoken languages, which would be impossible to learn, even for me. When I thought humans might be potential allies in my mission to overthrow Josairo, I focused on the top three most commonly spoken languages on your planet: English, Mandarin, and Spanish."

"You speak Spanish and Mandarin too?"

"Si. Es mi favorito de los tres. Me gusta rodar mis Rs."

Her jaw dropped.

"But once I realized you and your people spoke English, I had Zethus, my scout stationed on Earth, focus on English for his translator updates."

"You have a scout on Earth? Right now?"

"Of course."

He'd left behind an alien spy on Earth. Of course. Jesus. "Doing what?"

"Observing behavior, social interactions, habits, diet, updating our translators. You know: scouting. Although I could not return you to Earth until I took command of Havar, I needed to ensure that I could properly care for you and your people in the interim."

"Right." She bit back giggle of hysteria. Aliens were on Earth.

"Understanding and communicating with potential allies was critical to my mission. One does not effectively appeal to other planets for aid without learning to speak their language and respect their customs. At one point, I nearly approached Earth as one of those allies, but after careful consideration, I decided to move on to more promising prospects."

"More promising prospects?"

"Your countries are constantly waging ethical wars similar to Havar's. I needed allies who had already won those wars and had the means and willingness to help me win mine." He shrugged, his vresls lifting along with his shoulders. "Plus, you still do not have the technology capable of intergalactic travel."

Kinsley couldn't hold back her laugh at that. "Plus, I'm not sure that helping you wage an ethical war on Havar would be our main priority after discovering the existence of aliens."

"Would they be discovering me if I approached *them*?"

"They would think so."

He snorted.

"So..." Kinsley struggled to sit up. "You—"

Raveno took hold of her shoulders to lift and prop her upright.

"I can do it," she grumbled, but she couldn't, so Kinsley let him help her even as she protested, snatching the sheet to her chest. "Thanks," she muttered, settling back against the pillows he'd just fluffed.

"You are welcome."

"So, everything you told me before, about you waging a revolution against your tyrannical overlord and your intensions to return me to Earth. All that's true?"

Raveno nodded. "And I want you to have my back in this mission."

"Me."

"If your near commandeering of this ship is any indication, you will be a great ally." The very tips of his ears tinged a bright blue. "And the one scrap of good to emerge from this mess."

"How can I possibly help you? And why would I want to?" Kinsley shook her head. "You expect me to believe that *you're* the good guy in this story? That the monster who kidnapped me and burned Riley alive is the hero plotting to free his entire planet from a corrupt king?"

"I am *not* a hero. But I *am* plotting to kill Josairo and return you to Earth." Raveno scrubbed a hand wearily over his face. "The persona I developed in my pursuit to unseat Josairo is not the person I truly am, but I could not find allies and gain their support without becoming Vri Cilvril, our king's killing hand. And then I could not continue as his killing hand without doing his killing to maintain appearances." He leaned forward, his eyes fevered. "I never wanted to take you from your home, but returning you and your thirty-five humans to Earth would have exposed my plot early, preventing me from preventing *him* from trafficking more people in the future."

"The needs of the many outweigh the needs of the few?" she asked warily.

He nodded. "But my trip to meet the lorienok was not a complete waste." His blood-orange irises pinned on her meaningfully. "Assuming I do gain one ally."

Kinsley laughed. "Yeah, I'm a great replacement for an entire planet as backup."

"Not in terms of numbers or weapons, perhaps, but consider what you nearly accomplished here on *Sa Vivsheth*. With allies who have your back, imagine what you will accomplish on Havar. What *we* will accomplish."

Kinsley shook her head, baffled. "What do you expect from me?"

"You will continue to spy for me, but you will do so in truth this time. No more hidden agendas. No more attempts to overthrow my ship. And once we reach Havar, no attempts to overthrow me. You will report to me and me alone. You will be loyal to me and me alone, and together, along with my remaining allies, we will overthrow Josairo and gain everyone's freedom, including yours."

Kinsley licked her lips. "What can I expect when we reach Havar? What does Josairo want with us?"

Raveno leaned back, his fervor leaking out on an exhausted sigh. "Do you know what a frisaes is?"

Kinsley lifted a single eyebrow.

"A frisaes is a one-on-one public combat to the death. Winning such a frisaes is how havari progress through our military and political ranks, either by challenging a superior for their position or by competing for a recent vacancy. Many thesh ago, before I was born, our warriors were renowned for their combat skills, so much so that we began hosting the Intergalactic Frisaes, an event to which our allies sent their greatest warriors for the privilege of fighting *our* greatest warriors." Raveno winced and rubbed his jaw. "Eventually, the Intergalactic Frisaes lost popularity among our allies—their greatest warriors rarely won—but it did not lose popularity among our people. About ten thesh ago, Josairo modified our fleet of luxury destination ships, such as *Sa Vivsheth*, into prison transport vessels and sent us on covert missions to purchase people from other planets and bring them to Havar to compete in the Intergalactic Frisaes."

"But *you* didn't," Kinsley clarified. "You said that you approached your allies instead and brought spies, posing as competitors, with you to Havar."

"Correct."

Kinsley narrowed her eyes. "But you've been training me to compete in this Intergalactic Frizzies. That's why you've been improving my combat skills, isn't it?"

"Frisaes," he corrected. "I've been training you because I claimed you as my Vri Sa Shols. I needed to put on a show of sparring with you, as I would if you were truly mine to fight."

Kinsley crossed her arms. "What does being your Vri Sa Shols really mean in the context of this combat competition? I'm not just your unpaid personal assistant, am I?"

"Um. No." Raveno clasped his hands into a tight knot. "When we land on Havar with our shols—the competitors in the Intergalactic Frisaes; in this case, you and your humans—there are several ceremonies. The Welcome Ceremony in which Josairo and our people welcome us home. The Selection Ceremony in which the havari who intend to compete in the frisaes bid on their own Vri Sa Shols, whom they will battle against. The Sparring Ceremony in which the havari spar publicly with their Vri Sa Shols, so spectators can prepare their bids. The Remembrance Ceremony, to honor those who lost previous frisaes. And then, finally, the Intergalactic Frisaes itself, in which the havari and Vri Sa Shols fight, and our people bid on the outcome."

"So..." *Breathe. Must remember to breathe. Breathing is important.* "No one is planning to eat us, then?"

Raveno scrunched his nose at *her*. "The Intergalactic Frisaes was a prestigious event for havari and shols alike for many thesh when both parties came willingly for the honor of testing their skill in such a battle. But now that the shols are shipped in against their will..." Raveno stared at the ceiling and shook his head. "It's a monstrosity, and more often than not, a slaughter."

"And you want me to fight in this combat to the death?" Kinsley squeaked. "Against *you?*"

"Svik, no!" Raveno reached forward and squeezed her hand. "I only claimed you as my Vri Sa Shols to save your life after Tironan found you in the heating ducts. I only train you to improve your skills and continue the ruse. We will need to continue the ruse on Havar, but it will not progress so far that we will fight in a frisaes against one another."

Kinsley chewed on that a moment. "What happens if I refuse your offer?"

Raveno leaned forward and brushed her bangs from her eyes. He studied the waves of her hair as they slipped through his fingers as if her frizz was the most fascinating thing he'd ever seen. "If you refuse my offer, we will continue as we are. You will remain here in my chambers, and when we reach Havar, you will be my Vri Sa Shols. I have already set that in motion. But you will have no obligation to spy for me or help me in any way. Once I succeed in overthrowing Josairo, you will return to Earth."

"*If* you succeed in overthrowing him," she muttered.

The blue at the tips of his ears spread to stain the lobes as well. "I stand a better chance of success with you at my back."

Kinsley couldn't argue that point. "But how do I trust you, Raveno? After everything you've done, how do I know that what you're saying now is true? That your motivations are true? That your intent to keep your end of our bargain is true?" Kinsley shook her head. "We have a saying on Earth: actions speak louder than words. Your actions don't speak, Raveno. They scream."

"I have saved your life on several occasions."

"That doesn't count when you're the one endangering it."

"I have taught you to navigate this ship and improved your hand-to-hand combat skills."

"With the intention of battling me in a fight to the death!"

He leaned back, looking as pained as he did thoughtful. Kinsley shifted, uncomfortable under such scrutiny—he was the one on trial, here!—but then he broke their gaze. He lifted his left leg over his right knee. Grasping his calf in both hands, he squeezed three fingers into his calf muscle and three into his shin. Something clicked, and he twisted his leg—*his leg!*—like the lid of a pickle jar. His thigh, knee, and upper calf remained in place, but his lower calf and foot rotated ninety degrees until his toes pointed inward at his body.

Kinsley gaped, stunned.

He separated his lower calf and foot from the rest of his leg and held his leg aloft in his right hand.

Raveno had a prosthetic leg.

The prosthesis was nothing like she'd ever seen before. The leg seemed to function exactly like a natural leg—it had scales and toes that moved independently, and those toes even had claws—but it didn't have a socket. Instead, it locked into a component permanently affixed at the base of his residual limb. Was it—

Raveno cleared his throat.

Kinsley jerked back, realizing she'd been caught staring.

"I sacrificed my soul for this mission," he gritted out, low and deep. "I sacrificed my future with a lovely, kind, beautiful woman who eventually couldn't stand the sight of the man I'd become. I nearly sacrificed my own brother, trying and failing to protect him. But in the very beginning, when I first realized that I'd need to ingratiate myself with Josairo in order to overthrow him, I sacrificed my leg."

TWENTY-THREE

Raveno reattached his prosthetic leg, feeling suddenly, strangely, nervous under Kinsley's rapt attention. He wasn't sure if this would convince her of his sincerity, but at least she wasn't shouting accusations anymore. She was quiet and waiting and finally willing to listen, just as he'd hoped. But now that he had the opportunity, he was struggling to find the words.

He'd never had to explain it before. Ever. All of Havar knew how he'd lost his leg. Svik, the story had become glorified nearly beyond recognition, so anyone who hadn't witnessed the spectacle had had it shoved down their throats at birth as propaganda: the highest standard of loyalty and dedication to Havar.

Only Avier and Zethus knew the truth about *why* he'd lost his leg.

Now, so would Kinsley, and if his heart beat any harder, it might very well explode from his chest.

"I was born with a rare leg deformity called *hevrch sha*. I should have asked Zethus for the translation, but I did not anticipate... I do not speak of this often."

Kinsley nodded, patient and encouraging.

249

Raveno flexed his vresls, attempting to maintain a semblance of control. "Children born with this condition often suffer from one or more of their extremities being, shall we say, *twisted* in the wrong direction. My left foot was curved in on itself, so the side of my ankle touched the ground instead of the flat of my foot."

She took that in stride without even a blink.

He leaned forward slightly. "You are familiar with this condition?"

"From what you describe, I think some human children are born with it too. Or something similar."

He nodded, and for a moment, silence throbbed between them, with their heads bobbing together in unison.

"My condition could not be rapidly repaired. There was nothing, technically, to heal. The limb was healthy. With supportive assistive devices, I could walk and run and use my leg like anyone else, but Josairo was not pleased, to say the least." Raveno swallowed. "He saw my foot as a personal affront."

"Why would Josairo concern himself with your foot, let alone be offended by it?" Kinsley asked, baffled. "As if you could help being born with a congenital deformity. Surely, as king of *an entire planet*, he has bigger concerns than one citizen's medical condition."

"I am not just any citizen," Raveno murmured. "I am his son."

Kinsley froze. "His son?"

"Yes, Vra Cilvril s'Hvri Josairo is, regrettably, my father."

"Uh, what are you saying? That you're a...a—" Her mouth shaped a few words in silence until she found the ones she wanted. "You're a *prince*?"

Raveno waved a dismissive hand. "On Havar, title and position do not automatically pass down a blood lineage by the fortune of birth. One must earn his place in society."

"You're the son of the king of your planet," she said, deadpan, and then eyed his bare forehead in sudden realization. "It's not a headband. It's a crown."

"It is an ornamental circlet, and Josairo is less a king and more an overlord, as you've said on occasion. All of which is less important than the fact that I am his killing hand."

Suddenly, she gaped. "Tironan's a prince too."

Raveno snorted. "Tironan is a fyvrili. *My* helping hand, remember? Forget Josairo as our king. He *rose* to political power. He was not born to it."

"He's more like a president?"

Raveno scrubbed his face. "Our people do not vote for political leaders anymore."

"Then how did he 'rise to power'?"

"He challenged the previous Vra Cilvril s'Hvri in an official frisaes and killed him."

"Even if you weren't overthrowing Josairo, *someone* would need to fight and kill your father in order to change leadership?"

He nodded. "Several have tried. All have failed, and at the moment, I fear I would fail as well. Even if by will or wrath I did win, I probably do not have enough off-world allies to prevent another war with Haven. Our sister planet has wanted to regain power of Havar since they lost it. Recruiting Lorien would have helped tremendously." He covered his eyes on a groan. "Not to mention that without adequate on-world allies, many warriors would demand their own frisaes. I would best some of them, but eventually..." He sighed. "The frisaes frenzy that could potentially spur from the power void of Josairo's death might be unavoidable, but if I manage to gain power of Havar, I would prefer to reduce the number of people I am required to murder to maintain it."

Her small, warm hand slipped over his shaking fist and squeezed.

Raveno stilled. He dropped the hand from his face and considered their entwined fingers, straining to contain his emotions.

"What happened to your leg?" she whispered.

Her eyes were so dark.

Raveno cleared his throat, but the words were still rough when he finally spoke. "I passed the requirements to enter our military academy, and I rose through the ranks. Despite my condition, I was more skilled, and because of it, I was more ruthless, determined to prove myself. Determined to win Josairo's admiration."

Raveno closed his eyes, his vresls throbbing.

Her grip on his hand tightened.

Thev sa shek, his eyes were burning.

"At the time, my mother was Josairo's killing hand. While I was seeking his approval, she was establishing off-world alliances and building on-world allies."

"Sounds familiar," Kinsley murmured.

"Apparently, she'd tried reasoning with him to soften his grip on power and sway his decisions, but when all her efforts were exhausted..." Raveno felt the burning drip from his eyes and turned away. "She challenged him to a frisaes."

Kinsley smoothed her small thumb over the ridges of his knuckles.

"She lost."

"I'm so sorry, Raveno."

"I missed the battle, off conducting some inane mission or another. But Tironan was there. He watched Josairo impale our mother with his ezil. He said that she managed to throw both her pivz even *after* having been mortally wounded. Both hit slightly off target. She'd been dying, after all."

Kinsley blew out a hard breath.

"I—" His voice broke. He coughed to cover it and tried again. "I should have been there for her."

Something ripped, and Raveno realized that the claws of his free hand had sliced into the mattress.

"Had I known of her plans, we could have stood against Josairo as a united force and bested him together. Instead, I was off carrying out Josairo's will when she needed me most."

She tightened her grip on his hand. "I didn't know her, obviously, but I doubt she would have placed you in harm's way against your own father."

Raveno shook his head. "We are all in harm's way under Josairo's

252

rule. She knew I had the skill. She knew I had the strength. Unlike Josairo, she believed in me. What she didn't believe was that I believed in her." No matter how many times he cleared his throat now, his voice still shook, but he cleared it anyway. "She saw my determination and unrelenting efforts to impress Josairo and thought that I supported him. I didn't. I hated him even then, but I didn't think another way of life was possible. He was Vra Cilvril s'Hvri. Changing that and the world he'd built was as impossible as...as changing the color of the sky or the...the flow of lava beneath the land. Not just impossible. Inconceivable. But she attempted it. Alone."

Kinsley grazed her thumb across his knuckles. Raveno focused on the unfamiliar, not-unwanted warmth that constricted his chest, and he forced out the rest.

"In her letter of passing—her will, I believe you call it—she asked me to protect Tironan and begged me to open my eyes. To succeed where she failed. My every effort since then has been to satisfy her dying requests. I fought for my place as Josairo's killing hand to retake the reins of my mother's mission, but even after having earned my place, I was denied the position. Josairo forced challenger after challenger upon me. I won against them all." His voice cracked. "I killed them all."

"Oh, Raveno..."

"He knew I would tire and eventually die, and *someone* would be his killing hand. Just not me, not with my twisted foot." He impatiently wiped at his eyes. "So I cut it off."

Her thumb stilled over his middle knuckle. "You what?"

"In the center of the arena, between challengers, I called him out. 'I earned my place at your side, Vra Cilvril s'Hvri,' I said. 'I know it is not me you reject, but my deformity. Your will by my hands.' And I used my own ezil to slice my foot off."

Kinsley covered her mouth. She might have swallowed.

"It worked. Josairo finally acknowledged my claim to the position of Vri Cilvril. After the wound healed, and I was fitted for a prosthesis, I began cultivating my reputation as an infallible weapon, Josairo's best and truest killing hand. And Josairo! Ha!" Svik, how long had his vresls been bristling? He forced them down, but they still chafed. "He exploited my actions like the zealot he is: commercials, posters, children's dolls, even. One cannot exist without seeing my face at least five times a shaoz in various mediums and media, all with the same message: to sacrifice is to serve. I became his recruitment slogan."

He was laughing, and he wasn't sure when he'd started that either. He wiped his eyes again and forced himself to continue.

"But eventually, all this sacrifice *will* serve. I will run *him* through with my ezil, and Havar will be liberated from his rule. I will stare into his eyes and whisper the sealing vows, 'My will in Havar's hands,' and he will finally know the truth, that my will is my mother's and has never been his."

Kinsley's head and her thumb had ceased their slow back-and-forth, and in her still silence, he couldn't interpret her expression.

"You will need to speak for me to know your thoughts," he whispered, and even that scant murmur of sound was nothing but ground gravel.

She removed her hand from his.

Raveno closed his eyes. Something other than his heart throbbed within his chest.

She wrapped her arms around his waist, rested her head under his chin, and she squeezed, just like she'd squeezed his hand, but this time, she squeezed his entire self.

Raveno shuddered, collapsing into her embrace.

Kinsley was holding him. Hugging him. That was what that bloom of throbbing warmth had been all along: She was comforting him.

That something lodged deep within Raveno's chest heaved.

"I'll need a translator," she whispered.

Kinsley leaned back, and Raveno had to physically restrain himself from caging her in his arms. "What?"

"To be an effective spy, I need to know not just what your people are doing, but what they're saying. And I'll need to learn to read and write in Havar."

Raveno didn't grin. His vresls didn't flare, and his ears didn't color, but that throbbing thing within his chest skipped a beat and then burst through his body like thunder. "Haveo," he corrected roughly. "Havar is our planet. Haveo is our language. And I will teach you myself."

"If he agrees, I want Riley given the same choice. The same combat and language training and anything else we need."

Raveno's inner eyelid swiped sideways. "*Riley?*"

She nodded.

"I don't trust Riley."

"But you trust me, and I trust Riley. He had my back when I needed it most. He deserves the same choice." She stared him down. "If you want me, you get him too. Everything I get, he gets."

Raveno envisioned her beneath him on the brig floor and the intoxicating musk of her scent. *He might not want everything you get.*

She must have simultaneously thought something similar, because her face flamed.

"Fine." Raveno hissed through his teeth. "Agreed."

"And you and me..." She jabbed her pointer finger between them. "We're equals in this mission. I might be *pretending* to be your unpaid personal assistant and sparring partner, but in truth, while we plan and execute this mission, I'm your equal. Not your helping hand or killing hand or any hand. Equals."

"Yes, we are," he murmured.

"Okay, then." She held out her palm. "Allies?"

He eyed her hand uncertainly. "This is what you call a handshake, yes?"

Kinsley nodded. "On Earth, when people come to terms, they clasp hands and shake on it, binding their deal."

"On Havar, we have a similar gesture." He lifted his gaze and studied her face. "No more plotting against me? No more crawling through heating ducts without my knowledge? No more secret missions?"

"That's what *allies* means."

"I want nothing but truth between us."

Kinsley rolled her eyes, but she nodded. "Agreed, agreed, and agreed."

"No more playing with the artificial gravity."

"I wasn't *playing*, and that last time was Tironan, not me."

"No more stealing other people's access codes."

She opened her mouth.

He held up a finger. "You will receive your own. No more explosions. No more—"

Her eyes widened, nearly panicked. "No more explosions?"

"Unless it serves our mission," he added.

She huffed. "Fine."

Cry mercy, were they truly coming to terms? "Then you, Kinsley 'Switch' Morales, agree to spy for me and, together with my other allies, help me overthrow Cilvril s'Hvri Josairo Hoviir?"

"I do. As long as you, Raveno Hoviir, agree to immediately return me and my fellow humans to Earth after Josairo is overthrown."

"I do."

Kinsley grinned. She wiggled her fingers.

Raveno extended his hand to clasp hers. He wrapped both his thumbs and all four fingers around her delicate palm, very careful of the placement of his claws so close to that vulnerable wrist and all those unguarded veins.

Her grip tightened. She pumped their clasped hands.

When she released him, he slid his hand across her palm to her wrist and pulled her closer. "We are bound by human ritual: a handshake. Now, we must honor havarian custom with a lasvik. No sudden movements."

Raveno bent his head down over her smooth neck, swept aside her dark hair, opened his mouth, and brushed the curve of his front incisor across the delicate skin over her throbbing pulse.

She didn't make any sudden movements, as requested, but she didn't remain completely still either. Her skin immediately puckered in response. The fine hairs across the back of her neck stiffened, her muscles tensed, and her scent, all pepper and musk this time, engulfed him. He lifted a hand to steady himself on her shoulder and mistakenly grazed her collarbone. Her breath caught. He dragged his incisor across her neck in the opposite direction. Her pulse leapt. The bumps that had pebbled the back of her neck swept down her chest to disappear beneath the sheet.

He shuddered under the spike in her scent for a lingering moment, longing for more.

She didn't pull away.

He closed his mouth and forced himself back.

"Your turn," he whispered hoarsely. He bent his neck to her.

Kinsley leaned in and mimicked his movements exactly. Her tiny, dull incisor grazed the side of his throat, just over his own throbbing pulse. She wouldn't be able to feel its jump or acceleration beneath the thick, protective layers of his scales. Her insensitive human nose wouldn't detect the added pheromones in his scent, and she was too close to see the telltale burning at the tips of his ears.

Her fingers grazed across his collar, an exact mirror of his touch from moments before. He tried to keep his reaction in check, but her warm breath tingled across his neck and shot down his spine. His vresls stiffened of their own accord and quivered, desperate and embarrassingly eager. She swiped her incisor across his pulse point a second time, completing the gesture and sealing their arrangement— along with his doom, he was certain.

Her incisors weren't lethal, but she slayed him just the same.

She eased back, both her eyebrows arched. Without needing to scent the air, he could easily interpret the challenge in that stare.

He forced his vresls to settle—an award-winning feat—and nodded.

"Allies."

TWENTY-FOUR

Two hundred and thirty-one shaoz later.

Kinsley absorbed her first view of Havar from the vantage of *Sa Vivsheth*'s level-five disembarking ramp. Or tried to. The sun couldn't penetrate the ash blanketing Havar's atmosphere, leaving the planet in perpetual shadow, so initially, Kinsley could only discern her immediate surroundings. *Sa Vivsheth* was docked alongside a dozen rows of other prison transport vessels: their fleet of kidnapping ships. Before investing in intergalactic human trafficking, havari must have loved going on vacation.

Now they loved ruining people's lives.

As her eyes adjusted, Kinsley could finally see beyond those rows of docked spaceships to study the surrounding landscape.

She sort of wished she couldn't.

It took every ounce of her self-preservation not to let her mouth drop in breathless, heart-rending shock. Her breath did catch. Her heart did lurch. But her expression held: calm, strong, and, most importantly, unsurprised. To everyone else, she was Vri Cilvril Raveno Hoviir's Vri Sa Shols, and surely his shols in truth would have been prepared for such a sight. Although Raveno had

258

mentioned that Havar's surface climate was hot, that "her lands had separated and turned molten," he'd never warned Kinsley that Havar was a volcano.

It didn't *have* a volcano. It wasn't a paradise like Hawaii that had been made *by* a volcano.

It *was* a volcano. Or, at least, it was what Kinsley imagined the insides of a gigantic, planet-sized volcano would look like.

Deep, jagged chasms separated Havar's land masses as far as the eye could see, which wasn't particularly far, considering the haze of ash blocking the sun and obscuring her vision. The land was singed, desolate, and black, blending into the black sky at the horizon, so one couldn't truly discern where land ended and sky began. And far below, at the bottom of those wide, snaking fissures, was the flow, pop, and ebb of scalding lava.

Every pore on her body instantly began sweating.

Surely the entire planet wasn't this unbearably hot and bleak and molten?

Kinsley glared dubiously at the sky and then glared at the scorched earth. Not much could grow in such conditions. The havari had obviously come to that same conclusion and given up on Havar's surface. They'd drilled what looked like ant hills into the petrified rock. Many of the guards had already disembarked, disappearing through those ant hills into the underground city beneath, and too soon, Kinsley would follow, leaving behind *Sa Vivsheth* and the familiarity of her and Raveno's shared cabin for a new cage. Between language lessons and combat training, Raveno had attempted to help her overcome her claustrophobia in preparation for living in a subterranean city fashioned from her worst nightmare, but as proficient an instructor as Raveno was, nothing could truly prepare her for this moment.

Riley stood at her right and Raveno at her left, surveying the procession below.

Raveno's eyes notched sideways, watching her. "Welcome to Havar," he whispered.

Kinsley glowered at those dreaded anthills. Some welcome. She didn't return Raveno's look, and she didn't dare glance down, either, because following the march of guards from the brig below was a line of humans.

They seemed just as hale and hearty as she'd last seen them. Their hair was washed and brushed. Their skin was clean, if a bit lackluster from so many months without the benefit of sunlight. Some had obviously taken advantage of the personal gym in their cell. Others, perhaps not so much.

But they were shackled.

Everyone wore thin silver bracelets, one on each wrist. Delicate and unobtrusive, they didn't hamper their stride or constrict the swing of their arms as they walked. One by one, each human exited *Sa Vivsheth*, and one by one, they stopped dead in their tracks, gaping at the abyss of lava and ash. Truly, Havar was spawned from a Tim Burton fantasy. When the people walking in front of them reached a certain distance, the people who had stopped to gape were yanked forward by some unseen tether jerking their wrists. Kinsley supposed if they worked together—ha!—and all ran as one group, an escape could have been possible.

Had there been anywhere to run.

Most of the humans were too overcome by their surroundings to notice anything else, but a few spotted her and gaped as they passed, their surprise and resentment as stark as the silky white kimonos covering their bodies.

Kinsley was all too aware of her own appearance: her hair, the longest it had ever been, was swept back from her face in five Dutch fishtail braids, two at each temple and one in the center—her own addition to Raveno's style—that met at the crown of her head and merged into one braid that hung over her left shoulder. She still wore the uniform Raveno had altered for her, her warrior corset, as Riley was so fond of calling it, as if he looked so much less absurd in his gladiator skirt. Three pivz were strapped to each thigh, and all she needed was an ezil strapped to her back to pass as Raveno's female mini-me.

They'd betrayed *her*, she reminded herself, watching the humans pass. If they'd had her back, they'd be crash-landing on Earth instead of marching onto Havar. She didn't deserve their censure. They weren't the only ones who were shackled.

Her ankesh glowed in steady pulses at her wrist.

No matter her righteous anger, her breath still caught when she spied *them* in the procession.

Leanne's glare was hot and accusing. Benjamin's eyes widened, flicking between her and Riley, looking confused and a little hurt. Kinsley clenched her teeth against their rancor, but her heart leapt to clog her throat when Martin lifted his head and met her gaze.

She couldn't wink. She couldn't grin. She couldn't do anything other than play her part at Raveno's side, but remembering Martin's last words to her as he'd solidified his betrayal helped firm her resolve: *One life in exchange for thirty-five: Do I have a choice?* They'd both had to make impossible choices. He'd made his. And so had she.

Something lit in Martin's face, something warm and...proud? He nodded, subtly but unmistakably, before his wrists jerked up and yanked him forward to keep pace behind Leanne. He turned away, and Kinsley watched his back as he followed the line of humans off the docking platform.

Apparently, she didn't need to explain herself. Even after all this time, they still shared a brain.

Kinsley dragged in a lungful of ashy air, trying not to cough.

She could do this. Not that she had much of a choice, but still, despite the lack of options—the lack of light and air and reprieve from this suffocating heat—she could do this.

Raveno's attention snapped straight. His vresls quivered silently before he could suppress their movement, and he strode forward.

Keeping pace beside him, Kinsley disembarked *Sa Vivsheth* and took her first step onto the hot, barren hell that Raveno called home.

PART 2

Havar (noun): an Earth-like planet with a nitrogen-oxygen atmosphere, three moons, and one sun, inhabited exclusively by nocturnal creatures and carnivorous plants. (noun): hardened lava. (verb): to burn with no flame; to smolder.

TWENTY-FIVE

Before his own face frowned back at him from billboards and broadcast recruiting propaganda, before dozens of his biggest fans began camping outside his home and chanting his name, and long before he'd ever stepped foot in a frisaes arena, let alone competed in one, Raveno Hoviir played goal guard for the capitol's youth *sheshzi* team with Avier and Tironan. More crystalline in his memory than the games were their antics. Celebrating wins with sickening mounds of losths. Daring Avier to play an entire game one-handed. Collecting bets from Tironan when Sheso refused to pass. Ever. In all fairness, Tironan was hardly ever open. Not for lack of trying.

Raveno took in the frisaes arena surrounding him now, similar in form and purpose if in no other way to his childhood sheshzi arena, and ached for that simpler time. A time when he hadn't wanted anything more substantial than to share desserts, pull pranks, and win bets. A time when Josairo's eyes rolled in despair rather than fixing too knowingly and too proudly upon him. Back when Avier and Tironan had smiled as equals beside him instead of dourly supporting him. Raveno should count his blessings that they were still alive and still supporting him after all they'd learned and endured, but it was difficult to focus on anything against the deafening roar of the crowd.

RA! VE! NO!

RA! VE! NO!

RA! VE! NO!

All 200,674 arena tickets had sold for the Welcome Ceremony, as usual, so the stadium's fifteen levels were packed shoulder to shoulder with spectators. The cacophony of their chanting echoed around him, nearly physical in its volume and energy. Some people clapped in rhythm with the syllables of his name. Others waved shred banners or cranked hand sirens. The crowd undulated in organized chaos, thousands seemingly transformed into a single organism.

Josairo's Vri Shavrili were staged on the jutting second-tier dais. All four were outfitted, armed, and poised in tense readiness: Jzoeshi, Rez, Veilon, and—was that Sheso on stage? When had he won a promotion? Raveno shook his head.

Cresha was seated among the general population, only a few seats from the dais, and easy to spot, as always. He'd asked her once, after that first Welcome Ceremony following their separation, why she still wore her ornamental circlet. Maybe if he hadn't been half out of his mind with *phosh* at the time, she'd have answered.

The arena seating was too high above the stage for Raveno to distinguish anyone else in the crowd. He knew the view was similar for the spectators. Anyone above the third tier would strain to see his face if not for the live display projectors. Anyone above the fourth tier, well, he often wondered why anyone would pay to attend an in-person event when their view wasn't any better than it would have been from home. Then again, he wasn't the sole entertainment during this ceremony, just the excuse.

Citizens who hadn't nabbed a coveted ticket to the live event could watch from the comfort of their homes. According to Jzoeshi's analytics, home viewership had risen to an all-time high of 96.7

percent during the previous Intergalactic Frisaes. As if people had anything else to watch.

As if there wouldn't be consequences if they skipped it.

"Home sweet home," Kinsley muttered.

Raveno peered down at her and nearly cursed. He wasn't the only one struggling to maintain his composure. Kinsley was flushed and tense as she took in the crowd with wide, darting eyes.

Breathe, he thought at her, because he could tell by the strain in her corded neck that she wasn't. With the live display projectors capturing every nuance of his expression, he couldn't say the words. No matter how he felt for her, he couldn't take her hand. To the 200,674 people surrounding him, the two billion people watching from home, and, most importantly, the one person about to make his grand entrance, he wasn't Raveno Hoviir, no matter how loud they chanted. He was Vri Cilvril, and as such, his heart could beat only for Havar.

Raveno widened his stance so the heel of his boot kissed the toe of hers.

Kinsley released a shaky breath.

The glowing rails bracketing each tier dimmed, and the roaring crowd quieted. The silence was jarring, but not nearly as unsettling as being reunited with his father. The projectors swirled, Raveno braced himself, and in the next moment, five giant projections of Josairo's face appeared at various levels above them as a six-tier-tall, full-body live projection of him materialized on the dais.

The crowd burst into screaming, waving, cranking applause.

Josairo's vanity knows no bounds.

Reading of Josairo's projections in Jzoeshi's reports and witnessing their reality in person were two very different things. Raveno feared he couldn't keep the disgust from his expression, but luckily, no one was watching him anymore.

Josairo smiled magnanimously, striding past his Vri Shavrili to the center arena, where he raised his hands to settle their cheers. The arena fell silent. He took a moment to circle the platform, meeting their anticipatory stares with an intensity that the projectors captured and reproduced perfectly. *Even with eyes shaped by prisms, I see you,* they said.

Finally, he opened his mouth—could he possibly drag this charade out any longer?—and his voice echoed from every speaker, from all sides.

"Two thesh and sixty-one shaoz ago, Raveno Hoviir, my son and killing hand, embarked on a mission to greet and transport the competitors of our fifty-fourth Intergalactic Frisaes." Josairo paused a beat, letting his echoing words—"FRISAES-AES-AES"—fade from the arena. His eyes—enlarged on the projector screen to the size of an entire person—locked on to his audience. "Two thesh and sixty-one shaoz, we waited for his safe return." He waited once again, longer this time, for his echoes to settle, and the ensuing silence buzzed through the crowd like a shot of phosh. "Now. Our patience has been rewarded. Now. Vri Cilvril Raveno Hoviir and the crew of *Sa Vivsheth* have returned, their mission complete!"

Josairo, beaming with joy and pride, chopped his miles-long arm down at Raveno.

The crowd burst into shouting applause.

Raveno braced against their exuberance as he would an ezil aimed between his scales.

Josairo held up his hands for silence.

Instantly, 200,674 people complied.

"Welcome home, my killing hand. My son. And I welcome the most anticipated of all, the skilled and courageous competitors of our fifty-fourth Intergalactic Frisaes!" The audio popped, and for a moment, Josairo's words came from his mouth a second after his lips appeared to form them. "Humans of Earth, we salute you!"

Josairo clicked his heels together, and as one, 200,674 people mimicked him. The reverberation of their synchronized heel clacks shook the stadium like thunder.

On that exciting display of power, the projectors cut from Raveno and his crew to a pre-scripted sponsorship plug.

While his face was his own for the moment, Raveno glanced aside to see how Kinsley was coping.

She was gaping at Josairo's frozen projection on the dais.

He leaned down. "What is wrong?"

Her head and body remained still as if carved from stone, but her eyes snapped to his. "We can talk?" she asked, and he marveled at her ability to form words without even moving her lips.

He nodded. "It is what you call a commercial break. No one is looking or listening."

"What happened?" she asked.

"How much of his speech did you not grasp?" Raveno shook his head. "No matter. It was all nonsense anyway."

She leaned in. "I understood what he said, but why is he a hologram?"

Raveno snorted. "Because there is little Josairo likes more than his own image everywhere."

Kinsley raised both her eyebrows.

"According to the Vri Shavrili and their streams of drivel, ratings skyrocketed during our previous Intergalactic Frisaes, the first time he projected himself. Viewership improved, even in the outlying districts watching the ceremonies from home. Something about theatrical manipulation. People find it more entertaining. Bigger is supposedly better." He rolled his eyes. "Having finally witnessed the spectacle for myself, *I'm* not impressed, but profits don't lie, so Josairo is hosting the ceremonies as a projection again."

"We're being filmed and broadcast to home viewers?" Her eyes darted around. "Is that what the swarm of drones are for?"

"Drones?"

"The flying video cameras?"

"Ah. They are projectors, not video cameras."

"They're," she reminded him, but with considerably less relish than she normally showed when encouraging his use of contractions.

"They-r," he tried, but as usual, his tongue slipped out on a hard trill. He waited on her chastisement, but Kinsley ignored him in favor of staring at Josairo's paused projection.

"The projections *aren't* recording us?"

"No, *they-r* projecting us from real life into 3D reproductions—"

"Holograms," she murmured.

"Then that reproduction is enlarged and projected to our audience here and broadcast to homes for the benefit of people who couldn't attend in person." He cocked his head, considering. "I suppose the projectors do have what you would consider video-like capabilities."

"But they don't keep a record of what they broadcast? For people to watch later?"

"The central processing unit that stitches the image together has a record of the entire broadcast, but each individual projector only captures parts of a person. One is dedicated to the back right leg, one to the front right leg, one to the torso, and so on. I heard once that nine are dedicated to the face alone."

Instead of clarifying her confusion, the wrinkle between her brows only deepened.

"What is't?" he asked.

She blinked at him uncomprehendingly.

He sighed. "I was attempting a contraction."

"A contraction of what?"

"*Is it.*"

"There's no contraction for that."

"Ther-s no contraction for *is it* but ther-s one for 'it is'?"

Kinsley waved away his question. "Forget contractions. Why—"

"Forget this entire conversation," Avier hissed in Haveo. "Maybe no one up there can hear you, but they have eyes, and the crew down here has ears."

Raveno and Kinsley peeked over their shoulders.

Avier's expression was the epitome of calm dignity. Only the autonomic, near microscopic throb of his vresls indicated he felt otherwise.

"Something to say?" Raveno asked, just as calm, still in English, back at Avier.

"No, and that's the point," Avier gritted out, still in Haveo.

"The p-p-projectors will activate any m-moment," Tironan added.

Raveno focused on Tironan, but his brother could finally meet his eyes now without impersonating a shetn.

"D-d-did you want the projectors to activate and c-capture y-y—"

"You flirting with a shols?" Avier finished for him.

"My Vri Sa Shols," Raveno corrected him, but still, his ears blazed. "I wasn't—"

Kinsley inhaled sharply. "We weren't—"

"Oh, no?" Avier asked. His voice leapt into falsetto. "There's no contraction for that."

Kinsley coughed. "Since when is correcting someone's grammar flirting?"

"Since you started correcting his grammar," Avier said smoothly.

"Listen, you—" Kinsley began, slipping into Haveo.

"English only," Raveno ordered.

Her eyes darted around. "You said no one was listening."

"This conversation is over," Raveno bit out, ears blazing.

Avier gave him a brisk nod, a more gracious ally than Kinsley for resisting an "I told you so."

As if on cue, the projectors activated, and Josairo's projection reanimated. He pontificated a while longer, regaling everyone with the history of the frisaes, the great honor of competition, all his "service is sacrifice" rhetoric, the same droning speech thesh after thesh, until finally, he began to wind up to his grand finale.

"Now, on the eve of our fifty-fourth Intergalactic Frisaes Selection Ceremony. Let. Us. Begin!"

Josairo lifted his arms overhead, and, showcased between the V of his holographic arms, a firework exploded.

The crowd went wild. The firework was followed by several more

—fifty-four, to be exact—and Raveno bore each explosion with the gnawing resolve of a man receiving a life sentence.

Fifty-four, Raveno thought. And of those, seven injustices. Seven planets robbed of loved ones. Seven horrendous debts their people would never be able to repay. His vresls bristled. Yes, this was their fifty-fourth Intergalactic Frisaes Selection Ceremony, but by will or wrath, it would be their last.

TWENTY-SIX

KINSLEY HAD THE DISTINCT AND DISTURBING IMPRESSION THAT, despite their lack of eyes, the plants decorating the stadium's perimeter were watching them. She'd normally have attributed such paranoia to oxygen deprivation, but no, lightheaded as she was, she was not mistaken. The stage beneath her feet had begun to rise mid-firework display—by hidden levers, hydraulics, drones, magical levitation?—and the higher it rose to meet the platform where Josairo's hologram was standing, the higher the plants lifted their buds. When their buds (heads?) couldn't lift any higher, the plants bloomed, their blossoms separating into two pedals (jaws?) revealing four neat rows of clear, needle-thin, serrated teeth.

Yep, jaws. On plant heads. Watching them with no eyes.

As much as Raveno had hyped Josairo as their primary target, Kinsley's most pressing concern at the moment was staying conscious and not, say, passing out, tumbling off the platform, and falling into one of those gaping, hungry flower mouths in front of an audience of millions.

Raveno hadn't been lying when he'd warned her that "All eyes will be upon me," but she hadn't fully comprehended what he was

273

trying to convey. Who could until one experienced it in person? The crowd. The chanting. The blown kisses and screaming faints. The swarm of flying cameras—the drones were fucking filming, regardless of how Raveno attempted to twist reality with technicalities—zooming in for high-definition, 3D detail of every scale and scar on his face.

It was bananas. Full on, Gwen Stefani-level B-A-N-A-N-A-S.

The word he'd been searching for in English was *celebrity*.

Raveno was a celebrity.

As overwhelming as the event was, however, the attention hadn't been her trigger. She'd already been hovering on the razor's edge of near panic for hours, long before enduring this sham of a welcome home party.

The walls only *felt* like they were closing in. Her lungs weren't *actually* being crushed, not yet, anyway, but she couldn't quite convince herself that she wasn't trapped this time.

The havari had created an illusion of the outdoors. The stadium was "normal" if one overlooked the mob of millions, the floating 3D animated hologram heads, a dozen-plus stories of stadium seating carved from volcanic rock, and the carnivorous plants waiting for someone to wander too close. A smattering of stars lit the evening sky along with three moons, and wisps of clouds floated by on a fresh breeze. Unseen above their heads, however, between them and the real ash-filled sky, were miles-thick layers of hardened volcanic rock under a miles-deep ocean of bubbling molten lava.

The lovely *Tron*-like glow of their midnight, carnivorous Fern-Gully was nothing but a pretty illusion. They weren't really outside. They were deep underground, Kinsley's worst nightmare made reality.

A sophisticated, pressure-support system that was "beyond her comprehension," kept the lava dammed and prevented a cave-in. Raveno wasn't an engineer, but if he'd managed to explain the mechanics behind such a system rather than spout a gruff, "Havar hasn't collapsed in centuries. It certainly won't collapse in the short time you're here," maybe she'd have been able to breathe without gasping. But he hadn't, so she couldn't, and here she was, going on three, maybe four hours—*an eternity!*—without being able to inhale enough oxygen to keep from feeling on the verge of passing out.

As the rising stage drew even with the jutting platform, the final, fifty-fourth rocket launched into the air and exploded overhead. Unlike fireworks on Earth, fireworks on Havar exploded in a cascade, similar to the rocket launcher on Raveno's ship. Each explosion doubled and tripled and quadrupled with each subsequent burst, forming moving images in the sky. Kinsley stared, transfixed. She'd always felt a soul-deep kinship with bombs, but this was something more than heat and power. This was art.

Even so, she hadn't realized the show's significance until the end, when she began to recognize the images. They were more than just random pictures, beauty for beauty's sake. The images told a story, and not just any story, it seemed, but a retelling of recent history. She saw now what everyone else had been watching all along: Raveno slicing off his foot, Raveno kissing Josairo's neck, Raveno at the helm of a ship. And everyone's cheering adoration exploded on.

Kinsley studied Raveno. His frill was still, relaxed, even, but its tips, just that last inch of bone that resembled a talon necklace, stuck stiff and straight out from his scales.

Now was obviously not the best time to ask him about the mechanics of Havari fireworks or their cost. But damn, this entire event was the Superbowl on crack: the spectators and cheering, the cameras, the special effects, the entertainment. If the Welcome Ceremony was this widely attended, how popular was the main event? Kinsley couldn't even imagine the millions all this raked in. Someone was rolling in it.

Kinsley straightened, startled by her own thought. Someone, or several someones—she scanned everyone standing up on the dais—were benefiting financially from this spectacle. From intergalactic human trafficking.

Was Raveno approaching his revolution from the wrong angle? Maybe all this insanity wasn't just about politics and power.

Raveno must have felt her startle, because he peered sideways at her.

Kinsley met his eyes, and her heart lurched.

With more effort than she cared to admit, she refocused on the dais. She'd managed to leash her increasingly conflicted feelings for two hundred and thirty-one shaoz, however long that equated to on Earth time. Forever. She could keep those feelings, and herself, in check a few shaoz longer to concentrate on what really mattered: the mission, liberating his people and returning home. Nothing was more pressing than that. Nothing.

Not even the leashed longing in his eyes.

He'd kept his promise not to kiss her again. For the remainder of their journey, he'd been the perfect gentleman while preparing her for life on Havar, but part of her, a larger part than she intended to acknowledge, wished he wasn't quite so honor bound.

His nostrils flared, then sealed shut.

Focus on the mission, Raveno, she willed.

He faced Josairo and marched forward.

Kinsley blew out a relieved (disappointed?) breath, stepped forward, and the parade behind her followed him onto the platform toward Josairo's hologram.

As much as Raveno despised his father, he spoke of Josairo the way one might a god: all-knowing, all-seeing, unbeatable in battle. Invincible. Tironan and Avier supported Raveno's assessment of Josairo's character, but after so much preparation and training, Kinsley had anticipated finally meeting the man and judging him for herself. Meeting a hologram of him wasn't at all what she'd expected, but perhaps that was a sort of verdict in and of itself.

After all, one can't assassinate someone who isn't physically present.

Tironan and Raveno were nearly polar opposites in every conceivable way, yet both of them resembled Josairo. Even from the pixilated holographic display, Kinsley could see where Raveno had inherited his brooding intensity and Tironan his delicate features. Josairo was a magnetic combination of beauty and strength. His big, lavender eyes beamed with focused, convincing, determination. His long, fine-boned hands gestured with purpose and resolve. His lean stature filled his strappy uniform in all the right places, and although his strength was less overt than was common for havari, the bone-studded headdress braided into his waist-length, golden hair put even Raveno's Conan crown to shame.

Josairo was well preserved for his age. Granted, Kinsley had never seen an older havari to compare. Did their scales wrinkle or hair thin? If their bodies did show physical evidence of aging, then Josairo truly was a god among his people. Judging solely by the holographic version of Josairo, Kinsley would have never guessed that he was a father with adult sons. He appeared equal in age to Tironan.

Perhaps Josairo took advantage of more than just size when projecting his image.

Raveno halted in front of the holographic wall that was Josairo's person-sized boot and clicked his heels together in salute. His crew followed suit. The clack of their respect echoed in the void of silence following the final blast of fireworks.

Josairo's projection faced Raveno. The edges of his projected body suddenly swirled around him in a misty cyclone. His projection began to shrink. The crowd oohed and ahhed as if his adjustment to a life-size person was the result of fairy-godmother magic and not just a programmed light display.

Once he was life size, the swirling mist absorbed back into his body, and Josairo's image spread its arms wide in welcome, a god willingly diminished for the benefit of his son.

Kinsley narrowed her eyes skeptically. Raveno stood head and shoulders above most of his crew. Only Dellao rivaled his height, and even then, only nearly. Josairo's projection stood taller than Raveno's impressive eight feet, but with his lean stature, he was a bit too evocative of Slender Man: His arms and legs were gangly in proportion to his too-short torso, as if the person programing the projectors had incorrectly adjusted his aspect ratio.

Raveno hesitated and then leaned forward, fangs bared to perform a hollow mockery of a lasvik, their lethal handshake, brushing the tip of his incisor over Josairo's neck. Kinsley choked back a grunt. The entire transaction, which was intended as a display of mutual vulnerability and trust, was ludicrous with a hologram.

Josairo returned the gesture, but where Raveno had been as mindful of his fangs in proximity to Josairo's hologram neck as he would real flesh and blood—well, scales and blood—Josairo wasn't mindful in the least. Had his fangs been corporeal, they would have pierced Raveno's scales and severed his carotid, violating the very trust their gesture was designed to demonstrate.

Maybe she was reading too much into it. A hologram didn't have depth perception, after all, and it wasn't as if Raveno could feel pain from a holographic fang. Perhaps he didn't even know what Josairo had done. No harm, no foul.

Kinsley bit her lip.

Josairo straightened, grinning indulgently. So proud. So genuine.

One of the drones shorted, and for a moment, so quickly one might have sneezed and missed it, his left eye flickered to a hollow socket.

Josairo surveyed the crowd, and the arena erupted with insane applause. On that cue, the mist returned, and Josairo swirled into a crazy growth spurt, catapulting up one story, then two, then five, then passing the highest row of seating into their fake sky. His feet rocketed up from the platform, springing back up to his head like a snapped rubber band. On impact with his head, they exploded into a dazzling blast of strobing light. His image lit the sky, then burst again and again and again until the entire illusion of sky sparkled with the remnants of fake fireworks from the projection of Josairo's hologram body.

The crowd went wild over Josairo's grandiose light show, then began cheering at the field below the stage. Kinsley followed the direction of their eyes and jolted.

Jesus! The gaping, toothy-mouthed plants had slithered from the field's perimeter to fill the entire field. The way their long stems were wiggling and gyrating in rhythm, all of them were... They were... Kinsley sighed. Hell, they were dancing.

Raveno elbowed her side.

Something was more important than dancing Venus flytraps?

Kinsley tore her eyes from those grooving plants. Two women were approaching, one of Josairo's advisors and a civilian.

Kinsley knew they were women because they were just as Raveno had described. Unlike superficial human indicators of gender —hair, physique, facial features—havari woman could be identified by their lack of a specific organ: that bony, rattling frill called a vresls.

Otherwise, female havari presented much like the males, and they styled themselves similarly. The two women approaching them had long, straight hair braided back at their temples. Their bodies were lean and muscular, and their uniforms had strips buckled across their flat chests. No postpartum style corsets for these ladies. They didn't have babies to nurse.

Besides those few gender generalities, the two women couldn't have been more dissimilar. One was Kinsley's height. Her strawberry-blonde hair was darker than Tironan's, but her crown was identical, just a thin, corded band. Her lips, even compressed in a frown to rival Raveno's temper, were generous. Her nose was wide, but fit the proportions of her mouth, unlike her eyes, which were beady. But what they lacked in size, they made up for with striking lime-green irises.

The other woman was tall—shockingly, taller even than Raveno—with delicate features, a button nose, and deep-set purple eyes turned up at their outside corners. A thick, raised scar sliced diagonally across her left temple. Several scales around her left eye were missing, revealing the dark, vulnerable, navy-blue skin beneath. Her top lip was bee stung, slightly larger than her bottom lip even when she was smiling, which she was—unlike her companion—ear to ear. Her black hair was glossy and gorgeous and braided into a fancy bone-studded headband.

Kinsley stared at that headband a moment, then studied Raveno's matching crown.

Something cold and brittle and unacceptable curdled and sank to the pit of her stomach.

In synchronized, military precision, both women halted before Raveno, clicked their heels together, and belted out: "Vri Cilvril!"

The scowling redhead tipped her face down. Her thin lips smirked. Her eyes gleamed. And Raveno, the honored son and killing hand to the king of this planet, rolled his eyes on a long-suffering snort. He opened his arms and wriggled both hands in a reluctant come-hither wave.

Kinsley watched, agog, as the woman's expression cracked into a beaming smile. She threw her head back, laughing, and launched herself into Raveno's arms.

And Raveno caught her. He shook his head, his scowl deepening, but he didn't set her aside. He wrapped his arms around her, dipped his head, and brushed a fang across her neck.

The woman returned the gesture. "I missed you!"

His scowl eased somewhat. "Yes, it's been too long, but even for you, *little sister*, I should probably maintain a semblance of dignity."

Ah, so this was Raveno's sister, one of four advisors—they looked more like bodyguards—to the king, their father. Kinsley struggled to remember her name: Veela, Veena, Veega?

His sister waved a hand. "The projectors are off."

Tironan stepped forward, his arms outstretched. "You kn-kn-know as well as I do that the projectors are never t-truly off, Veilon."

Ah, that's it! Veilon.

She leaned in to accept his hug, but just as Tironan wrapped his arms around her, she chopped him in the bony chest flap.

Tironan staggered aside with a yelp.

Veilon giggled. "Gets easier every time."

Tironan's ears glowed a bright blue.

Avier's frill bristled before he remembered himself.

"By will or wrath, some dignity! Both of you!" Raveno's eyes were blazing, but Kinsley had seen true rage on his face. This wasn't it. The vein in his temple wasn't throbbing.

Veilon nodded deeply. "You're absolutely correct, brother," she said, contrite, and opened her arms a second time to embrace Tironan.

Tironan eyed her suspiciously, still rubbing his neck.

She smacked his shoulder at his hesitation. "I wouldn't sting you again—not so soon, anyway." She grinned. "It's no fun if you're expecting it."

They exchanged fangs, and afterward, she squeezed him in a third hug for good measure. "I've missed you too."

While everyone else was warily riveted by the siblings' royal rivalry, Kinsley's attention was pulled off stage. The spectators had become active participants in the ceremony and were tossing sparkly somethings at the toothy plants. Instead of dancing, the plants were chomping and battling over whatever was being thrown at them. The floating 3D jumbotron showed some sort of scoring system. Half the crowd was cheering with insane exuberance while the other half was screaming with equally insane rage.

A typical sporting event, then.

The woman wearing a twin replica of Raveno's Conan headband stepped forward. "Tironan. I hope you're doing well. Veilon's welcome notwithstanding."

Tironan's pained expression eased. "You look well."

"I am. Thank you. Welcome home." She turned, and those bee-stung lips pinched as she met Raveno's eyes. "Raveno."

"Cresha," he said, equally stiff.

Apparently, that was that, and Raveno marched onward, passing Cresha and striding across the platform toward the stadium's interior. As he neared, the three advisors clicked their heels together in quick succession, then pivoted in the opposite direction, toward Kinsley and the line of humans behind her.

Kinsley sidestepped them to follow in Raveno's wake. The Venus flytraps were growing, and she did *not* want to stick around to see them draw even with the raised stage.

Another guard blocked Kinsley's way.

She tried to sidestep around this one as well, but he was expecting it this time and sidestepped right along with her, halting her progress.

Raveno rounded the corner and disappeared into the bowels of the stadium.

Great.

The guard pointed behind her, and when Kinsley followed his finger, she realized that all the other humans were being herded to a different exit, as Raveno had predicted.

Here we go, Kinsley thought, bracing herself. She pointed at the exit where Raveno had disappeared. "I'm with him, asshole," she said sweetly in English, knowing full well the guard wouldn't understand her.

The guard shook his head and, calm as could be, shooed her to join the line of humans.

"Nope." Kinsley lifted her arm, wrist out, and flashed her ankesh, just as Raveno had instructed.

The guard jerked back, his vresls flapping out in surprise.

Kinsley suppressed a grin along with the perverse part of her that took some twisty satisfaction from his reaction. She was branded, but damn if that brand didn't give her security clearance.

"That's right. I don't listen to anyone but the big guy." Kinsley sidestepped the guard a third time. "So if you'll just excuse me, I'll be—"

"What, by will or wrath, is going on?" Cresha demanded. "Is that shols already selected?"

Veilon whipped around. "Surely you're mistaken."

Kinsley walked faster.

"Vri Shavril Jzoeshi Lo! Detain that shols!" Cresha ordered.

Someone grabbed her wrist—Jzoeshi Lo, assumedly—and yanked her back.

Kinsley glanced at the exit where Raveno had disappeared, then back at Avier. *This is not going as planned.*

Avier was still glaring at Raveno's timely exit as well before meeting her eyes.

She raised her eyebrows. *Time to improvise?*

Avier shot her a quelling glare, then confronted Jzoeshi. "Vri Shavril Jzoeshi Lo. Is there a problem?" he asked, as if he hadn't just heard Cresha shout at the top of her lungs to detain her.

Jzoeshi's eyes shifted from Avier to Kinsley, and then, slowly, they slid sideways to Cresha.

"There most certainly is a problem." Cresha leapt into the silence. She swatted Jzoeshi's hand aside, took up Kinsley's wrist, and aimed the glowing ankesh at Veilon. "Surely I'm *not* mistaken."

"Well." Veilon blinked. "That's unexpected."

Avier activated his anku and muttered something under his breath.

"Yes. Do call him back." Cresha's sharp purple cat eyes sliced sideways to meet Kinsley's gaze. "This we must discuss."

Her outraged expression didn't change, not one searing inch of it, but her grip on Kinsley's wrist turned clammy.

Did scales sweat?

The pounding of Raveno's boots preceded him, and then he was striding around the corner, haughty annoyance shadowing every line of his scowl.

"Vri Shavril Jzoeshi Lo," he growled.

Jzoeshi's stiffened. "Vri Cilvril Rav—"

"What is the meaning of this?" Raveno barked. "You've detained my Vri Sa Shols?"

"I, erm—" Jzoeshi studied his hands, as if checking that both were free and not detaining anyone, then lifted them uncertainly. "Vri Cilvril Cresha ordered me to—"

Raveno leaned in so close, they nearly touched eyeballs. "Who did what, now?"

The other two advisors, who'd maintained their impassivity up until that point, froze where they stood. Their eyes locked in shared chagrin.

"Vri Cilvril Cresha Zami," Jzoeshi said. "She ordered me to detain this shols."

Raveno jabbed a claw at Cresha, his vresls bristling. "Cresha Zami is not Vri Cilvril."

The naked skin around Cresha's scarred eye crinkled.

"Yes, but— Well, erm—" Jzoeshi's eyes darted to the veritable crown adorning her dark head. "Are you sure?"

Avier coughed, but his shoulders shook.

"Am I sure?" Raveno asked, low and rattling. "Am *I* sure?"

Jzoeshi didn't seem sure about anything, but considering Cresha's crown, Kinsley did think it a valid question.

"Cresha Zami can't give orders, not to you and certainly not to me, and if she did *ask* something of you, you are not required to fulfill that request." His eyes sliced to Cresha. "Not anymore."

Whether or not scales had sweat glands, Cresha's palm was definitely damp and had developed a slight tremor.

Raveno homed back in on poor Jzoeshi. "I *am* Vri Cilvril, and every order I give, whether it sounds like a request or a demand, should be followed immediately and precisely." He tilted his head. "Yes?"

Jzoeshi stiffened. "Yes, Vri Cilvril. Your will by my hands."

Kinsley fought against a grin. There was nothing like a proper dressing down.

"Release my Vri Sa Shols," Raveno hissed. "Immediately."

Jzoeshi lifted his empty hands. "But I'm not—"

Cresha released Kinsley and clasped her trembling hands behind her back.

"And step aside. I haven't been home in over two thesh. At this rate, it'll be three."

Jzoeshi and the other two advisors leapt back, parting like the Red Sea to create an unobstructed path to the exit.

Raveno stepped forward.

Veilon slid smoothly into the newly cleared path to the exit and held up both hands to stall him. The pulse of an intricate ankesh glowed from her right wrist.

Kinsley frowned. Shouldn't she bear the dot of an anku, like Raveno and the rest of his crew?

Veilon pouted. "You can't think to return immediately to your rooms."

"You presume to tell me what I can or can't think?"

"As you just said, it's been over two thesh. Let's share a phosh and catch up. You've been stuck on *Sa Vivsheth* with Tironan for too long if you're returning home before third shift after your Welcome Ceremony."

Tironan scowled.

"I have over two thesh worth of gossip to catch you up on," she tempted coyly.

Raveno chopped the flat of his hand at her. "And I'll enjoy hearing everything you have to discuss. Tomorrow, at Selections."

"I rather think we should meet *before* Selections," she insisted.

"I rather think not."

She narrowed her already narrow eyes. "I know what you're doing."

Kinsley's heart skipped a beat.

"Oh?" Raveno crossed his arms, seemingly unconcerned, but the vein at his temple was throbbing now.

Veilon's eyes gleamed. "I want in."

All three of her fellow advisors looked like they might have swallowed their tongues.

Cresha's eyes darted around the stadium. "We're still on stage," she warned, but no one was watching them. The entire stadium was engrossed in whatever sideways basketball game they were playing with the Venus flytraps, which were now alarmingly tall, as if they hadn't been alarming to begin with. The toothy plants had reached at least fifteen feet in height and were still growing, their heads nearly even with the stage.

Raveno leaned into Veilon, his arms still crossed, his expression still impassive, his temple still throbbing. "Bid on your own shols. This one is mine."

"I can't bid on something already bought," Veilon countered.

"I returned home with thirty-six shols for you to—"

"One hundred and sixty fewer shols than expected."

Raveno's frill rattled.

"There's obviously something special about this one. Perhaps something you think will save you from Josairo's wrath?" Veilon leaned in. "Or have you forgotten how he punishes those who disobey his will?"

"The only thing forgotten is procedure," Cresha interrupted smoothly. "You can't bid on a shols until Selections. Everyone in attendance tonight has the right to bid."

Raveno homed in on Cresha, meeting her eyes directly this time. "Does anyone have more *avish* than me?"

"No, but—"

"No matter how long or well anyone plays tonight, could they ever earn more *vit* than me?"

He gestured to the stadium, and Kinsley followed the wave of his hand. Christ! The plants had grown even with the stage. As if it could sense Kinsley's attention, one rotated its bud/head in her direction.

"That's not the point," Cresha argued. "You can't just—"

"I can, and that's exactly the point. My bid stands." Raveno grabbed Kinsley's wrist and held the ankesh before them like a shield. "She's mine."

The seam between the plant's petal lips curved up at the corners, then split to expose its spiny sharp teeth. Smiling.

Veilon's grin widened, but her jaw was clearly clenched. "She?"

"Even you are not above the law," Cresha hissed.

"Correct, because I *am* the law." Raveno leaned in so close, his next words made the wisps of Cresha's long black hair flutter. "My will by your hands, remember?"

"How could I ever forget?" she murmured. "You've been away too long, I think."

"That we can agree on."

The plant opened its mouth into a wide, toothy gape, begging for a sparkly treat or preparing to swallow someone whole—who was to say? From this angle, Kinsley had an unhindered view straight down its gullet, and from its proximity, she could see that her wild musings were accurate.

The plant had swallowed at least one someone whole already.

The person inside the plant didn't look well, but neither did he look dead. And he was undoubtedly a he, biologically, because he had a chest flap, just like Raveno's albeit tattered and limp. His opal scales were peeling, many of them having flaked off to reveal what should have been navy-blue skin beneath. His skin was milky, as were his eyes, which had a sort of film clouding them. They were open and staring, but they weren't glazed in death. They didn't move and they didn't blink, but Kinsley swore they were seeing. His head lolled along with the plant's movements. His jaw fell open. His teeth had rotted, so all that remained were pitted gums. A high whine emitted from his mouth.

It wasn't a Venus *fly*trap. It was a Venus *person*trap.

Kinsley released a hysterical laugh-scream and stumbled back at the same moment that Raveno must have won his argument with Cresha. Or, at the very least, he'd given up on it. He plowed forward between Cresha and Veilon and past all the rest, keeping hold of Kinsley's wrist this time as he strode off stage and into the stadium. His expression was cold and sneering, his bearing haughty, and his tone unwavering. But his palms were just as clammy as Cresha's had been, even if they didn't tremble.

TWENTY-SEVEN

THE ARENA'S RESIDENTIAL LIVING WING WAS THE CLOSEST thing Raveno could claim as home on Havar. He preferred *Sa Vivsheth*, which could fly him as far from Josairo as possible—no distance was far enough—but his suite within the arena was a close second. It certainly had more amenities and comforts than *Sa Vivsheth*: his sleeping room had a larger bed and was separate from his office, as if he was ever technically off duty. He had four guest sleeping rooms and three bathing suites instead of one, each with proper plumbing and heated intimacy loungers. Not that he entertained often. Ever. And he had individual rooms for relaxation, dining, and cooking, if he ever had the time or inclination for such pursuits.

Mostly, however, he appreciated the fact that neither Josairo nor Cresha had ever set foot in his suite since the wing's construction. Raveno's space within these walls and the memories he made here were his alone and the one place, if only for a shift or two, where he didn't need to give orders or maintain appearances. A respite from expectations. The relief of solitude. He'd never appreciated the silence that came with anonymity until he'd lost it, but here and only here, it remained.

Raveno unlocked his suite, and the door slid open. Ah: peace, serenity, the stillness of complete seclusion.

Riley's head popped up from behind the couch. "Hey, partners! Nice of you to finally join the party."

Raveno groaned.

Riley's near-perfect Haveo managed to grate on Raveno's last nerve; a character flaw within himself, no doubt, and not one he intended to work on.

Tironan strode past Raveno into the room. "T-t-technically, *you're* the one who missed the party. Not that y-y-you missed much."

"Agree to disagree," Kinsley purred in English.

Raveno turned to her. She'd stopped beside him, crossed her arms, and was eyeing him pointedly, as if waiting on an answer. But she hadn't asked a question.

"Problem?" he asked calmly, reverting to Haveo just for the pleasure of being contrary.

"What was that freak show back there?" she hissed back in English.

Avier slipped behind Raveno into the room, clapping him on the shoulder as he passed. "Good luck with that."

Raveno's anku vibrated. "Fyvril Zethus Rysheer to Vri Cilvril Raveno Hoviir. Do you receive?"

"Signal received," Raveno said on a sigh. "Stand by."

Dellao appeared from the back office, marched to Raveno, and clicked his heels. "Vri Cilvril. Zethus has signaled?"

"Yes."

"I'll connect him to the room's projection system."

Raveno nodded, then opened his mouth to encourage Kinsley to enter his suite so they could argue in the privacy of his home. As if there was any privacy to be had at the moment.

"Additionally," Dellao continued, and Raveno closed his mouth, "Riley is smuggled in from *Sa Vivsheth* and secure in your lodgings."

Riley waved, smugly watching the proceedings from his perch on the couch.

So I can see. "Well done, Dellao," Raveno said instead. "Thank you."

"You know what *wasn't* well done?" Kinsley interjected. "Preparing me for that circus back there."

Riley's grin widened.

Raveno didn't curse, not in word or gesture. He didn't sigh a second time. He didn't about-face and leave all these people and their demands behind, no matter how he longed for unattainable seclusion. Despite the knot gathering over his left eye, Raveno ushered Kinsley into his home, slid the door shut behind them, and locked himself inside with all these people and their never-ending tsunami of needs. His loyal, trusted people.

Distrusting everyone had been so much easier.

He faced Kinsley and her raised eyebrow. "We reviewed the ceremonies in detail during phase three of our curriculum," he reminded her calmly. Rationally.

"You know, I admit I'm not the best student, but even I would remember if you'd informed me that dancing Venus persontraps would attend the Welcome Ceremony and that they stored half-dead bodies inside their stems."

"I did mention it once, but you claimed to not want the details."

"Half-dead bodies?" Riley sounded more intrigued than horrified.

"Venus *p-persontraps?*" Tironan asked, genuinely confused.

Kinsley crossed her arms. Her left foot began tapping impatiently on his floor, and Raveno wondered at her ability to tap in rhythm with the stabbing pulse at his temple.

"The plants you speak of are called *ushelz*," he explained.

"Ah." Tironan nodded.

"They consume people. *Dead* people," he hastened to add. "The ushelz cannot survive past maturity without a host. They are..." Raveno circled his hand in the air, thinking until the word struck

290

him. "Parasites. They gain nutrition from the body they consume, and only by preserving that body within their own do they thrive."

"Parasites preserving and feeding from dead bodies." Kinsley shuddered. "Your planet's the setting for a horror movie!"

"It *was* a movie," Riley interjected. "You never saw *Little Shop of Horrors*?"

"At least Twoey was potted!" Kinsley laughed, sounding a little hysterical. "Until the end."

Dellao leaned into Tironan. "What is *too wee*?"

Tironan shook his head, looking as baffled as Raveno felt.

"It's the nickname for a person-eating plant from another planet," Riley said, clearly enjoying himself. "He's a mean green mother from outer space."

Kinsley threw her hands in the air. "The Twoeys here are plants too! They have roots, don't they? How do they move like they're not...not..."

"R-r-rooted?" Tironan finished for her.

"Exactly!"

Raveno rubbed his eyes. "The ushelz have roots, but they don't use them the way Earth plants do. Our soil doesn't have nutrients to help them thrive. Without a source of sunlight either, young ushelz use surface roots to move above ground and scavenge for their food."

"People," Kinsley spat, clearly disgusted.

"*Dead* people," Zethus clarified. "To be precise."

"N-n-not helping," Tironan muttered.

Riley's grin widened. "Where exactly do these dancing Twoeys scavenge for dead people to host?"

"In addition to their surface roots," Raveno interjected before Zethus could clarify anything else, but Kinsley was already shaking her head, "the ushelz use heart roots—which are much longer and can slither underground—to both anchor themselves and travel to places as part of a larger, moveable, mycelial network. They—"

"You said that no one would eat me!" Kinsley shouted. "That, and I quote, 'Despite the tangled mess I have made of my life, that is the one thing I can absolutely guarantee,'" she mocked in haughty English.

"One, I do not sound like that," Raveno said. "Two, I maintain that assessment. A ushelz might consume your *dead* body if you lost a frisaes. Which you won't, because you're not competing in a frisaes. Therefore, no one will eat you."

Avier covered his face, so it wasn't clear whether he was sighing or laughing.

"The plants consume the losers of a frisaes?" Kinsley asked.

Thev sa shek. "Not all the plants," Raveno qualified, as if that would ease the blow. "Just their young who don't already have a host."

"*Why?*"

"Would you rather they consume living bodies?"

"People you know and love have lost frisaes. Your friends, your—" She swallowed.

Raveno grimaced. "Our bodies don't burn. Our soil requires significant effort and resources to excavate. With depleted resources for the disposal of our departed, the ushelz became a convenient solution to a growing problem for both our species' survival."

Kinsley's face softened on a sigh. "You should have warned me."

"I did," Raveno said, proudly maintaining a levelheaded tone— not without effort. "I told you the plants on Havar are carnivorous. That they eat people."

"Plants that eat people are one thing. Real life Twoeys incubating an army of zombies is something entirely different."

"It's not as if you don't have parasites on earth," Raveno snapped.

"We don't!" Kinsley snapped back. "Not like that!"

Raveno's anku buzzed, and suddenly, Zethus's voice echoed through the room in sync with the words broadcast within Raveno's ear. "Actually, you do," he said in perfect English.

Was he developing a Southern accent?

Raveno shook off that ridiculous notion. "Not now, Zethus." At this point, perhaps he should simply apologize and move on.

"What did he say?" Dellao asked.

"He's claiming we have plants that make zombies on Earth," Riley said, clearly delighted. "This I must hear."

"They're called *Cymothoa exigua*, commonly known as the tongue-eating louse," Zethus said, oh so helpfully. "It eats a fish's tongue and then affixes itself in the tongue's place."

"Ha!" Kinsley burst. "You made that up."

"I found it in your worldwide digital database. Am I connected to the room's projection system?" Zethus asked, switching to Haveo.

"Yes," Dellao said.

"Transmitting a photo to you now."

Raveno rubbed his forehead. "That's not necessary."

"He has internet?" Kinsley asked, surprised.

Riley leaned forward, intrigued. "I always imagined him skulking and spying on people in the woods like a creeper. Not stealing Wi-Fi from Starbucks."

"It is not internet the way you know it."

A photo uploaded to the screen. A fish was gaping into the camera, and inside its mouth, instead of a tongue, was another creature, its beady little eyes gleaming.

Kinsley gasped. "What the hell is that?"

"If you're seeing the photo I just transmitted, that's an unfortunate fish harboring a tongue-eating louse."

"On Earth."

"Yes."

"I can't. I just can't." Kinsley about-faced and plopped herself on the couch between Riley and Tironan. "Next time, we'll swap places, Riley. I'll nap in luxury while you play undercover human with the zombie plant army."

"Thank you, Zethus," Raveno said flatly. "Dellao, would you please?"

Dellao deleted the photo from the screen.

"You're most welcome, Vri Cilvril," Zethus said, either oblivious or impervious to everyone's mood.

Kinsley turned to Tironan. "How feels your neck?" she attempted to say in Haveo, knowing Tironan was more comfortable speaking his native language.

She never gave Raveno the same consideration.

Tironan sighed. "It's f-f-fine."

"It's bruised, is what it is," Avier grumbled. "But Veilon's right about one thing. You do make it easy for her."

"Excuse m-me?"

"Have you frozen vegetables on this planet?" Kinsley asked, prodding at Tironan's neck.

He winced. "I'm n-n-not hungry."

"That brings me to another question—" Kinsley said, pivoting to interrogate Raveno in English.

"Shocking," Raveno muttered.

"Had you better prepared me for today, I wouldn't have so many," she countered. "Why does Veilon have an ankesh instead of an anku?"

"She has neither," Avier said, returning from the kitchen with an ice pack. "Well, I suppose that, technically, she has a modified anku, but she calls it an ankis."

"Ankis, ankesh, anku," Kinsley whined. "And you wonder why my Haveo sucks."

"I wonder no such thing," Raveno groused. "I know exactly why your Haveo sucks."

"It's an impossible language! Everything sounds the same!"

"Oh, like English is so different," Avier said, switching to English. "*There*, a distant location. *Their*, a possessive person. *They're*, a contraction."

"Yes, but—"

"*Witch*, a sorceress. *Which*, a choice. *Wich*, something you combine with sand to make a meal," Dellao added.

"You don't—" Kinsley shook her head. "I get your point. *But*—"

"H-*here*, a close location. *Hear*, to l-listen."

Kinsley raised a hand as if to chop Tironan's neck, and Tironan feigned a flinch.

Dellao laughed.

Avier plopped the ice on Tironan's neck, making him flinch in earnest.

"At least English doesn't have all that impossible tongue hissing."

Raveno pointed an accusing finger at Kinsley. "Hard trills aside, you can't speak Haveo because you refuse to immerse yourself in the language. Even now, you respond to our Haveo in English."

"Fine, fine." Kinsley switched to Haveo. "What is ankis?"

"Veilon modified her anku after Josairo, well..." Avier peeked at Raveno. "Suffice it to say that Raveno isn't the only one of Josairo's children to suffer a permanent injury during a frisaes."

Tironan leaned in and whispered, "P-p-pivz to the eardrums. B-both ears."

Kinsley winced. "During frisaes?"

"Afterward," Raveno said. "Josairo inflicted the injury on her himself after she'd won the battle. He'd claimed her cries during the frisaes had pierced his ears. So he pierced hers."

Kinsley inhaled through her teeth. "I sorry."

Raveno nodded. "The damage to her hearing was permanent even after the eardrums were physically healed, so she invested in several engineering companies that manufacture anku and produced a device of her own invention. Where the ankesh transmits two-way communication regardless of distance, her ankis transmits one way at only close distance. Now she can hear via electronic pulses to her brain."

"She invented a kaklee ur implant," Kinsley murmured in English.

"A what?" Raveno frowned. "In Haveo," he added.

Kinsley rolled her eyes. "We having similar technology on earth, without a glowing wrist."

"H-h-her company, Cershys, has proved quite l-lucrative," Tironan chimed in, sounding proud of his big sister in spite of the ice pack pressed to his neck. "Sh-sh-she even managed to combine translation t-technology in her most recent upgrade."

"Cershys? What does that mean?"

"In English? I d-don't know." Tironan tugged at a lock of hair, tilting his circlet further askew. "It's a w-way to see by hearing. By the echo of s-sound."

"Echolocation?"

Tironan scrunched his nose. "Underw-water."

Ah! "Sonar."

"Veilon isn't our greatest concern at the moment, but she did voice my greatest concern," Avier interjected. "Has Josairo commanded an audience with you yet to discuss the fact that we returned to Havar with thirty-six and not two hundred shols?"

Raveno blew out a hard breath. "Miraculously, no."

"Good." Avier leaned against the couch back, crossing his arms. "We need to avoid that confrontation for as long as possible—"

"My thoughts precisely," Raveno agreed.

"Because thanks to Cresha's little outburst, we didn't slip Kinsley in without protest. All eyes are upon you now, not just his," Avier finished.

Raveno snorted. "All eyes are always upon me."

"Speaking of avoiding conversations," Kinsley began, sliding back into English, as usual. "Who's Craysa?"

Must they pry open that wound now *of all times?* "Cresha," he said, correcting her pronunciation.

"Just Cresha? No hand to speak of?" Kinsley narrowed her eyes, and Raveno fought to maintain his impassivity under the heat of her scrutiny. "Because if I'm not mistaken, someone back there addressed her as Vri Cilvril, and she's wearing a pretty impressive crown." Kinsley reached up and flicked one of Raveno's braids. "It matches yours."

Svik Cresha, and svik her inability to move on. He had! "Yes, it does."

"But I thought your crown indicated your lofty status as Vri Cilvril."

Raveno clamped his teeth together. "Yes, it does, but it's not a crown. It's an ornamental circlet."

"See? This is you"—she poked a finger into Raveno's chest—"avoiding a conversation. Also known as a lie of omission, and if you recall, we promised one another only truth going forward. No more lies."

"I didn't divulge the details of my extra bowel movement last shift," Raveno said, glaring at her jabbing finger. "Should I have informed you of that as well?"

"Yes, from now on, that might be best." Kinsley crossed her arms, staring him down.

Raveno crossed his arms, refusing to relent.

"How do they do that?" Dellao murmured, sounding awed.

"W-w-what?"

"He's speaking Haveo, but she's arguing back in English."

"It's their usual form of communication," Avier said.

Dellao was still shaking his head. "It's fascinating."

"It's something," Riley muttered.

"It's a s-s-sstrange relationship," Tironan interjected, nodding.

Kinsley's eyes whipped to Tironan. "We're not in a relationship."

"We're not arguing," Raveno snapped simultaneously.

Silence.

Kinsley refocused on Raveno. "Why was Cresha wearing a matching circlet if she's *not* Vri Cilvril?"

"After six thesh, who knows why she still wears it?" he growled.

"I could hazard a few guesses," Avier muttered.

"Raveno," she said carefully. Deliberately. "Who is Cresha?"

"Her ornamental circlet doesn't have any true meaning anymore, and I don't know—"

Kinsley reached out and clasped Raveno's shoulder.

Raveno swallowed, but he couldn't seem to dislodge the knot in his throat.

"Who is Cresha to *you?*" Kinsley whispered.

"She is, *was*, within me. We..." Thev sa shek, he couldn't hold her gaze. "We made promises to be one person, so when I became Vri Cilvril, so too did she. But once we were broken into two people again, she lost that privilege."

Kinsley blinked hard. "Cresha is your ex-wife?"

"Not quite."

"Yes," Avier said flatly. "She is."

Raveno shot another hot glare in his direction. "In human marriage as well as in divorce, its bond, or its breaking, is sealed with signed legal documentation. On Havar, such ceremonies are more complicated. We—"

"N-n-not *that* much more c-complicated," Tironan muttered.

"Like you would know!"

Kinsley released his shoulder, cupped his cheek in her hand, and forced his attention on her. "You and Cresha were in a romantic relationship. You made vows to stay together. And then you broke up. Yes?"

Raveno felt his vresls bristle. "Yes."

"Who broke it off?"

Gah, he'd rather someone impale him with an ezil than have this conversation! "Cresha. She never wanted the notoriety. She wasn't political. She despised Josairo as much as I did, but when faced with the ramifications of my decision to overthrow him..." Raveno shook his head, and the sigh that escaped him was acidic. "She couldn't cope with the man I'd become."

Kinsley raised her eyebrows. "But she knew the truth about your mission?"

"Like most civilians, she doesn't know how corrupt the Intergalactic Frisaes has become, that the shols are unwilling captives and not willing competitors. But she knows that I became Josairo's killing hand to overthrow him."

Kinsley stared at him like she'd never seen him before. "She knows you're undercover."

"Why do you look so surprised? We were one person at the time."

"You didn't even tell Tironan for how long? Ten thesh?"

Tironan straightened. "I never thought of it that w-way."

Raveno glowered at her, his jaw now ticking in rhythm with his throbbing forehead.

Kinsley winced. "Sorry."

Avier shook his head at the ceiling.

"So Cresha knows the truth," Kinsley pressed. "She resented the man you became and broke it off... But she's still wearing a crown to match yours."

"Ornamental circlet."

"Maybe she wants you back."

Raveno laughed. "She's just keeping up appearances."

"She's taking advantage of the freedoms and power her position at your side provides," Avier interjected.

"Cresha wouldn't—"

"You saw how she ordered Vri Shavril Jzoeshi Lo, and how he immediately jumped to do her bidding."

Raveno grunted.

"But if she did—want you back, I mean—would you have her?" Kinsley asked, and the moment she spoke the words, her expression puckered, as if something had soured in her mouth.

No one in the room even breathed.

Tironan bit his lip.

Riley's smarmy grin froze.

"No," Raveno said.

Kinsley raised an eyebrow. Just the one.

"What are you trying to say with that expression?"

"This," She circled her face with a finger, "is my face not believing you. I think you *would* take her back."

"No, I wouldn't," Raveno repeated more firmly. "She abandoned me when I needed her most. I don't blame her, but neither do I trust her." Raveno locked eyes with Kinsley. "I could only be one with someone I trust." *I trust you.*

She held his gaze for a scorching moment.

Never had he been more aware of having an audience.

"We need to plan for tomorrow's Selection Ceremony," Avier interjected. "And decide which unallied planet to approach next."

Kinsley turned to Avier at that. "I've said it before, but I'll say it again—"

"Of course you will," Avier muttered.

"Gathering more off-planet allies is a waste of time."

Would the throbbing in Raveno's temple never ease? "Avier is concerned, *with reason*, that without Lorien, we lose the advantage of numbers. We can't win a battle against Josairo only to lose a subsequent war with Haven should they attempt to take advantage of a transition in power. Bazail, Iroan, and Fray will support me, but that's still only three against Josairo's five remaining contracted allies: Lorien, Marzes, Ioali, Ku, and—"

"It took you two years to complete this latest mission," Kinsley reminded him.

"Only to return empty-handed," Avier reminded her right back.

"I wouldn't consider myself completely empty-handed," Raveno murmured in English, glancing at Kinsley.

Avier rolled his eyes.

Riley huffed.

Dellao leaned in to Tironan. "What did he say?"

Tironan shushed him.

Kinsley forged ahead with her argument despite the raging blush blotching her cheeks. "My point is, I'm not waiting another two years for you to *maybe* gain another ally. Your rebellion is happening in the next few days, *before* everyone competes in an Intergalactic death dual."

"We need off-world allies to secure the reign of our next Vra Cilvril s'Hvri," Avier insisted. "Without legitimate political off-world allies, Haven may see a coup as the weakness it is and attempt to regain control of Havar."

"Haven *may* attack, which also means they may not. We can face that problem if and when the time comes," Kinsley said. "But Josairo's reign ends now. Not two years from now. Not another three allies from now. *Now.*"

Kinsley and Avier stared at one another, then, as if choreographed, everyone in the room, including the two of them, faced Raveno.

Svik, his brain might just explode through his left temple.

"W-w-without legitimate *on-world* allies, the p-power void will only spur a frisaes frenzy," Tironan chimed in.

Raveno closed his eyes. *Really? Tironan is bringing this up now?*

"The people in the room are l-l-loyal to you. That's it. That m-m-makes only six allies."

"Seven," Zethus added.

"You're o-off-world," Tironan reminded him. "J-Josairo has nearly *all* the on-world political support. Officially, anyway. Unofficially, he has n-n-no one."

Raveno narrowed his eyes. "I'm not sure I like where this conversation is going."

Avier rubbed his frown. "I know I don't."

Dellao flicked his eyes back and forth, obviously not sure where the conversation was going and whether he liked it or not.

"Dellao and I are not the o-only people who would b-be swayed to your side after knowing the t-t-truth," Tironan said. "W-we must gain more havari allies."

Kinsley pointed at Tironan. "This plan I like more."

"Tironan's right," Dellao agreed. "People look up to you, Vri Cilvril. If more people knew the truth, they would choose you over Josairo."

"Would they, though?" Riley asked. "When they find out that their leaders have been buying and enslaving people to use in their Intergalactic Hunger Games, will they really trust the poster child for the current world order to bring about change and justice?"

"Who is h-hungry?"

Raveno crossed his arms. "My people will follow me when they witness me slay Josairo."

Avier shook his head. "Our people will follow you, as we all have, after they know the truth."

"And how is killing Josairo a *new* world order and not just more of the same?" Riley asked pointedly. "If you're the one who kills Josairo—"

"I will be," Raveno hissed.

"Then you can't be the new leader of your planet. Not if you truly want change."

"Who would be Vra Cilvril s'Hvri if not Raveno?" Dellao asked.

"With that logic in mind, it couldn't be anyone with military or political affiliation," Avier added.

Raveno scrubbed his face. "But it must be someone our allies know and trust, with my support."

"That's a narrow m-margin."

Avier snorted. "Nonexistent."

Kinsley laughed. "From what I just witnessed, your people don't want a new world order."

Raveno reared back. "Of course they do! Josairo's a tyrant. He's evil, manipulative, controlling, and people on- and off-world are suffering for it."

"No one was concerned about our arrival: the evidence of intergalactic human trafficking. In fact, they were cheering! And I'm sure they'll be just as excited to bid on us tomorrow during Selections."

Thev sa shek, he was exhausted. Raveno eyed the empty cushion on the couch longingly, but it was next to Riley. "They don't know you're here against your will."

"They have eyes. They can see a line of shackled, scared people, not warriors."

"They can't see the shackles. The humans are too far away and not featured in the projections."

Kinsley scowled. "You're telling me that not one civilian on this entire planet knows that shols are here against their will?"

Raveno opened his mouth.

"People talk!" Kinsley continued. "You think your crew doesn't— don't shake your head at me."

"My crew wouldn't dare talk."

"Take Jhoni, for example. You truly think that he didn't tell his girlfriend or mother or best friend, *someone*, about his experience serving under the great and powerful Vri Cilvril Raveno Hoviir?"

Raveno frowned.

"And you don't think that after hearing all the shit that went down on board—us working together to test the crew, guards being dosed with sedatives, what seemed like a failed prison escape that, funnily enough, was just another test—that someone less starstruck by you won't see through the bullshit and tell someone else who then tells someone else that you keep shols in cages?"

"Less s-s-starstruck?" Tironan laughed. "You saw the a-arena, yes?"

"Despite Raveno's wild popularity, some people talk," Avier said. "Ten thesh ago, ninety-eight percent of the population believed that Josairo had their best interests at heart. The following thesh, his popularity returned to one hundred percent, even in the few outlier districts further from the capitol. Also, according to more recent polls, one hundred percent of the population feel safe thanks to our government's efforts. And one hundred percent would lay down their life for him. They have remained at one hundred percent ever since."

"That's ridiculous," Kinsley laughed. "No one has that kind of unanimous popularity. And doesn't that disprove your point?"

"These polls tell a different truth."

"And what truth is that?"

"One hundred percent of the population is terrified," Avier said. "They're telling us what they think we want to hear to avoid being that two percent who disappeared."

Kinsley rubbed her temple.

Raveno knew the feeling.

"But we digress." Avier chopped a hand at Raveno. "We need to ensure the new Vra Cilvril s'Hvri has enough off-world support to prevent a second war with Haven."

"There w-won't be a new Vra Cilvril s'Hvri w-w-without enough on-world allies."

Dellao nodded. "People will follow where you lead, Vri Cilvril. Your will in our hands."

Riley grunted. "Will you keep the same slogans or create fresh ones for your new world order?"

Raveno's anku vibrated. "I propose Earth be reconsidered as a potential ally."

"Cry mercy!" Raveno shouted to the ceiling.

Everyone succumbed to silence.

Raveno locked eyes with Avier. "Research our next three best candidates for off-world allies and develop a plan to—"

Kinsley stiffened. "I'm not waiting—"

"—*and develop a plan* to approach them that will take less than a thesh. We have the time it takes for Haven to reach Havar to convince them that we're better allies than Josairo." He glanced at Kinsley. "After we overthrow Josairo in the next few shaoz."

Kinsley settled back, appeased. For now.

Avier clicked his heels. "Consider it done."

Raveno turned to Tironan. "Get closer to Veilon and the rest of the Vri Shavril."

"B-b-b-but—"

"And determine who, if any of them, we can trust enough to sway to our side."

"I—I—I—"

"You will confide in more people?" Avier asked, shocked.

"For several thesh, you begged me to confide in Tironan. I refused, and it nearly cost both our lives. Now, not only do we have Tironan, we have Kinsley and Dellao at our side. We've never been stronger than we are now since I've learned to trust."

"And me," Riley interjected. "You have me too, oh killing hand."

Raveno ignored him. "If Tironan can convince me of their loyalty, we should expand our on-planet allies. Especially if you determine that we can't expand our off-planet allies."

"I will not determine that," Avier said flatly.

Tironan sighed, giving up on whatever reservations he'd been attempting to communicate. "Your will by m-my hands."

Raveno turned to Dellao. "Find me potential candidates who we can consider as prospects for Vra Cilvril s'Hvri. Someone besides the people in this room. A civilian with military ties who we can trust."

"He could pluck a person from thin air more easily," Avier muttered.

Dellao stood and clicked his heels. "Your will by my hands."

"Fyvril Zethus Rysheer?" Raveno asked.

"My connection is still live," Zethus chimed in

"Earth will not be up for reconsideration. Prepare to return home to Havar."

Silence.

Kinsley raised her eyebrows.

"Fyvril Zethus Rysheer," Raveno tried again. "Do you receive?"

"Signal received. However, I would prefer to remain on Earth."

Raveno sighed. Of course he would. Who in their right mind would *want* to return to Havar? "Noted. However, I need as many allies as possible. On Havar."

"You may need further intelligence when we return the displaced humans to Earth."

"We have actual humans who can provide such intelligence."

"You may need someone on site. A few Lorien aboard the carrier vessel we destroyed managed to survive." A pause and then, "It's possible they crash-landed on Earth."

Raveno froze. "How possible?"

"Ninety percent. I found several downed emergency pods, but I haven't found any survivors."

"Yet," Raveno corrected him. "You haven't found them yet."

"Yes, Vri Cilvril." Zethus cleared his throat.

Raveno didn't want to ask, he truly didn't, but— "Is there more?"

"I am not the only person to discover the emergency pods."

Raveno closed his eyes. *Don't say it. Don't say it. Don't—*

"The humans have found the pods as well."

Raveno hung his head. *Svik!*

"And Reece Morales is among the team investigating the scene."

Kinsley straightened. "Did he just say Reece Morales? *My Reece?*" Kinsley paused, and when Zethus didn't immediately respond, she confronted Raveno, as if he was on Earth and had answers. "*My sister knows about aliens?*"

"Not yet," Zethus finally said. "It's her...I believe the correct term is *canine unit* that is searching."

"Reece has a canine unit?"

"She began investigating your disappearance when it became clear that Earth's law enforcement had more new cases with better leads to prioritize. She's identified nearly all the missing humans we have on Havar, and suspects 'foul play,'" Zethus said, sounding impressed. "She's the one who found the Lorien escape pods."

"How is she doing all this *and* completing her residency?" Kinsley breathed, shaking her head.

"What residency?"

Kinsley's mouth remained open for a moment, but no words emerged.

"Do you receive?" Zethus asked.

"She doesn't work at the hospital anymore?" Kinsley asked.

"No. Unlike Earth law enforcement, she has dedicated all her time and energy to this one task. She is incredibly focused and persistent."

"How is she earning money? Paying for her rent? Her—" And then a strange look overtook Kinsley's expression. "Why do you know so much about my sister?"

"I made it my business to know. Per my orders to—"

"Thank you, Zethus," Raveno cut in hastily. "You may remain on Earth for now. Keep me informed of the situation."

"And protect my sister," Kinsley added. "If dangerous Lorien are running around Earth, I don't want this investigation putting Reece in harm's way."

"Your will by my hands," Zethus said and cut the transmission, not making it precisely clear whose will he was handling.

Raveno faced Kinsley. "And you and I will—"

"How about we discuss you ordering Zethus to spy on my sister without telling me?"

Cry mercy, he'd need to amputate his head from his body to find relief from the stabbing pulse in his skull. "Everyone dismissed."

Avier, Tironan, and Dellao click their heels, belted out a clipped "Vri Cilvril," and marched out.

"Just when the argument was finally getting somewhere good," Riley muttered.

Raveno turned to glare at Riley, but he'd already disappeared into one of the four guest sleeping rooms.

The suite door slid closed behind Dellao, the sleeping room door slid shut behind Riley, and suddenly, wonderfully, terrifyingly, they were alone. His vresls quivered, just slightly and just for a moment. He forced them flat.

Raveno faced Kinsley.

She raised her eyebrows, waiting.

"I didn't order Zethus to spy on your sister," Raveno said carefully. "I ordered him to gather as much intelligence as possible about humans in general—diet, language, non-verbal communication—as well as specific information about the humans who were abducted. Which included you, and consequently, your sister. I needed to know what your Earth law enforcement knew and keep abreast of their investigation in case they discovered the abduction and launched a rescue mission."

Kinsley's expression flattened. "Earth doesn't have the technology to launch an intergalactic hot pursuit in space."

"I know that *now*, thanks to Zethus's intelligence." Raveno reached out to touch Kinsley's shoulder, then hesitated. "Kinsley—"

She glanced at his suspended hand.

He let his arm drop to his side. "This is the first I'm hearing about your sister's involvement in such an investigation. I'm sorry my mission has affected her life as well."

She bit the inside of her cheek, then nodded reluctantly.

Raveno edged closer to her, wanting to broach another subject, one that had been gnawing at him for some time. With this new revelation from Zethus, it seemed inappropriate for him to change the subject, but if he didn't speak now, they might not have time later. And he didn't want—

"Oh my God, Raveno, what is it?" Kinsley snapped.

Raveno startled. "Pardon?"

"You have something to say. Just say it before you dig a hole to your brain with all that forehead rubbing."

He dropped his hand to his side, but now that he had her attention and permission, he couldn't find the words.

"What do you want, Raveno?" she asked, her tone suddenly wary.

Nothing I can have, Raveno thought. He inhaled, searching for patience and steadfast resolve, and instead caught the scent of her own longing.

Nothing I deserve, he amended, and sat on the cushion next to her.

TWENTY-EIGHT

How could a room with fewer people feel more crowded? Raveno was to blame, always Raveno: his proximity, his riveted attention, his drive, and if Kinsley was being honest with herself, his inaction. And not just in regards to overthrowing Josairo.

The revelation that Reece had cared enough about Kinsley's disappearance to not just grieve but put her career—the most important facet of Reece's life, second only to breathing—on hold should have been stunning. And it was, but who could focus on something light years away with the swell of Raveno's biceps less than an inch from her face? She could feel the heat of him without even touching.

Raveno was only sitting on the couch cushion next to her. A simple action. Innocent, even. And her heart leapt. His weight dipped into the cushion, tipping her minutely toward him, and her breath hitched. She leaned away in an attempt to inconspicuously keep her distance, and that tingling awareness she'd been ignoring for countless weeks crept across the back of her neck.

Raveno's chest flap quivered. The movement was barely visible and practically inaudible, but unmistakable.

Kinsley scanned the room, attempting to focus on something safe while she got a grip on her circulatory system, but the view of his apartment wasn't much better for her sanity. The room was too normal, with its dining room table and living room couch and kitchen stovetop. Kinsley squinted: was that metal box on the kitchen counter, with its hinged door and curved handle, a microwave?

No. And even if it was, she'd pretend it wasn't, because after traveling across the galaxy to a subterranean culture with human-sized carnivorous plants, discovering that Raveno warmed his evening shenesls in a microwave same as she did her leftover spaghetti was just too much.

They were very different people from different planets of different species with different cultures and traditions but—she glared sideways at the microwave, because that was undeniably what it was, damn it—with the same appliances in their kitchen.

Not everything was exactly the same. She focused on those discrepancies to keep her grounded, but really, such fixed concentration only highlighted how few there were: the soft glow of illuminated floor panels instead of light fixtures, the living room furniture surrounding a metallic ball instead of a television, the walls carved from volcanic rock rather than being constructed from drywall. That was about it.

A bachelor pad on Havar was apparently still a bachelor pad, no matter the species.

It made her wonder how many other people were out there on various planets, happily ignorant of her as she was of them, thinking themselves special and their problems so uniquely insurmountable as they unknowingly, simultaneously, reheated their dinners? How many others were, at this moment, being kidnapped in their own corners of the galaxy? How many were plotting assassinations and thinking themselves the heroine of their own story? That their story was the be-all and end-all of all stories?

Raveno raised his hand and paused with it midair between them.

Kinsley stiffened, her heart pounding.

He has claws, for Christ's sake, she thought, staring at that hand.

And retractable fangs and scales and a bifurcated tongue, and a spy on Earth keeping tabs on her sister. But her heart just kept on pounding.

Raveno abandoned whatever he'd intended to do and dropped his hand on a sigh. "Your training has progressed well," he said in English.

"Thank you," Kinsley replied to the microwave, and because his attention was scalding even when she wasn't looking at him, she added, "I had a great teacher."

"My tutelage has been clear and thorough."

Kinsley managed not to snort. *By will alone*, as he'd say.

"But even with clear and thorough tutelage, my crew often does not—does-nt—progress as well or as quickly as you. So I can-nt take all the credit."

"How magnanimous of you."

"That said, I feel I have been remiss in other aspects of our bargain." He shook his head, frowning. "Arrangement?"

Kinsley stared hard at that metallic ball that wasn't a television.

"Relationship."

"Deal." Her gaze snapped to his. "What we have is a deal."

The vein in his temple throbbed. "I have focused primarily on your training, per our *deal*, as I sensed you wanted."

"As always, your senses are stellar."

"And despite my personal feelings, our mission does take priority. But—"

"No *but*. I completely agree with your priorities."

Raveno swiped sideways with his inner eyelid. Suddenly, the tables were turned, and he was the one speaking to the microwave. "There-sss another lie of omission between us that I must confess if you require complete truth between us," he murmured. "In my single-minded focus to train you, I have avoided a truth regarding my personal feelings about you."

"I've," she corrected. Jesus, could a beating heart physically bruise the inside of a person's chest?

"What?"

"The contraction. 'I have' becomes 'I've.'"

He refocused on her and cocked his head, a bird studying its prey. "You claim to want truth between us, then distract me with technicalities."

"Lies of omission only apply to the mission. Whatever you're not telling me about your feelings is fine. Just keep it to yourself."

"My feelings have to do with us, and we have everything to do with the mission," Raveno said in the same grave tone he might use in a confessional. "I have promised you only truths, and I will honor that promise."

Kinsley shook her head at the ceiling. "I was wrong to demand you tell me everything. Some things are personal, and I don't—"

"I trust you as an ally, and I respect you as an equal." He swallowed. "And I care for you deeply."

Kinsley shifted her eyes to the microwave that couldn't be a microwave and shook her head.

"Deeper than friends. Deeper than allies. Deeper than—"

"I get the point."

"I promised not to kiss you again, and I intend to continue honoring that promise, as well," he forged ahead. "But I want to make it clear that should you reciprocate the depth of my feelings, you may kiss me."

"Why are you saying this now?"

"The next few days will be dangerous. We may not survive my attempt to overthrow Josairo. While I still had the opportunity, I wanted you to know the truth of my feelings and give you permission should you want to pursue them."

Kinsley stared at him, at a loss. She couldn't seem to stop shaking her head.

"Is that no, you don't believe me, or no, you don't want to kiss me?"

"I...I..."

"In your presence, activities that should be labor are fresh and exciting."

Oh Lord.

"Combat lessons are more invigorating. History lessons more interesting. Language lessons..." His lips twitched. "More entertaining."

Kinsley rolled her eyes. "At my expense."

"Nevertheless, what I am trying to say is—"

"Christ, I know what you're trying to say."

"—I want you to want to kiss me."

She snorted. "Yeah, okay."

He hesitated. "Your words agree, but your expression—"

"It's called sarcasm." She crossed her arms. If her hands were tucked around her own body, they weren't touching his. "You don't actually want to kiss me."

"I do-nt?"

"No. And stop separating the contraction like that. It's one word: don't. Not 'do ont.'"

"Stop trying to derail the conversation," he hissed back, flipping to Haveo. "Why don't I want to kiss you?"

Kinsley chopped a hand between them. "You don't have kissing in your culture."

"A pity."

"I'm serious."

"So am I. Having tried kissing once, I feel it imperative that I try it again before passing judgment."

The only thing Kinsley knew with unerring certainty was that she wanted off this godforsaken planet. Everything else that she felt in his presence—heart-racing, skin-prickling, hair-raising, suffocating heat—was uncertainty personified.

His nostril slits flared.

Kinsley narrowed her eyes. "Tell me you didn't just sniff me?"

The tips of his ears began to glow. "Your longing is, what is the word in English? Consuming? Delicious?" He frowned. "Distracting into poor judgments."

Kinsley closed her eyes. Desire—was that what this was? Because it felt... "Raveno—"

"Intoxicating."

She choked. "Is this sort of direct approach common for all havarian men or just you?"

Raveno clasped his hands together in his lap. "Such expression is usually not needed. We can smell—"

"Yes, you just mentioned everything you can smell. So convenient." *So mortifying.*

"But you can't."

"I don't need to smell you to know what you want."

Raveno straightened. "Then why haven't you said or done anything about it?"

"Because it doesn't matter what I smell like. I don't know what I want!"

He nodded. How was it possible that even his flexing neck muscles were toned? "We are trusted allies, and that alone is more than I deserve."

Kinsley huffed. "What I want doesn't matter anyway."

Raveno reared back. "What you want is the only thing that matters."

"I want to go home."

His ears began to glow a bright blue. "I know."

"So let's focus on making that happen, shall we?" Not the most graceful subject change, but tact—along with controlling her scent, apparently—was beyond her at the moment. "Tomorrow is the Selection Ceremony."

Raveno slumped and scrubbed his eyes with both hands. "Must you remind me?"

"Someone must," Kinsley muttered.

"I managed to avoid Selections for the last several ceremonies. This will, as you say, suck."

"Hence why you need reminding, or you'll continue procrastinating."

Raveno dropped his hands with a scowl. "Procrastinating?"

"You've only gained three off-world allies in how many years? Without me, Avier would still be your only on-world ally. And now, when we should be planning my counter mission for Selections, you want to talk about your *feelings*. You—"

"You think developing and maintaining alliances with multiple planets galaxies away without breaking my cover is easy? Or quick?" He scoffed. "Iroan has loyally supported Josairo throughout his entire reign, but they are also staunch supporters of the Intergalactic Equal Rights Coalition. To gain their alliance, I needed to obtain evidence of Josairo's crimes against the coalition and then manufacture a mission that sent me to Iroan to present that evidence. Fray, on the other hand, is less likely to involve themselves in foreign politics unless it impacts their own planet. To gain their alliance, I—"

"Okay! I get it!" Kinsley raised a staying hand. "I take it back."

"*To gain their alliance*, I needed to obtain evidence that Josairo's crimes also impacted the Frayans, and then manufacture a mission that sent me there. And Bazail—by will or wrath—Bazail has a space compressor!" Raveno said in the same tone a less ambitious man might say *And Brad has a Maserati!*

"I'm sorry I belittled your efforts. You—"

"It may have taken me two thesh just to travel to Bazail, but that time was well sacrificed. With the space compressor, the return journey took only ten shaoz. They are as close as on-world allies. Or enemies." His eyes blazed. "But thanks to me, they are allies."

"You haven't been procrastinating," she acquiesced.

The crease of his frown deepened. "I admit, I wish we were closer to a frisaes than we are."

"Maybe I can help speed the process?" Kinsley leaned forward, resting her elbows on her knees. "I want to meet Josairo in person."

Raveno's vresls flared out wide, then snapped flat against his collar. "Ideally, the next time I face Josairo will be our frisaes."

"I know it's your life's ambition to avenge your mother, right your father's wrongs, and save your people from his rule, but Riley did have a good point. You can't start your own reign by following the rules of your father's reign. Don't shake your chest flap at me, I'm serious. You—"

"I don't need to rule. I just don't want Josairo to rule."

Kinsley stared. "You would give up the future of Havar?"

"To secure its future, I would do anything."

"Fine. Whatever. But when do *I* meet Josairo in person?"

Raveno heaved a sigh. He was certainly staying well oxygenated throughout this conversation. "Never."

"What I want is the only thing that matters, right?" Kinsley asked pointedly. "I want to meet him."

"No, you don't," Raveno grumbled in Haveo.

"I think I know better than you what I want and don't want."

Raveno flared his nostrils in a sniff.

"In regard to the mission," she specified.

Raveno tented his hands over his mouth, his blood-orange eyes burning. "Unless he summons me directly, no one from my crew— not you, not me, not Tironan, not Avier, not *anyone*—is meeting with Josairo in person. He executes people on a whim. For breathing at him the wrong way. And you do have a habit of breathing loudly."

Kinsley huffed at that, and then laughed ruefully.

"By bringing home thirty-six instead of two hundred shols, I've directly disobeyed his orders. He's executed entire crews for less grievous offenses." The pain in Raveno's eyes sliced bone-deep. "We must play this carefully and strategically."

"I understand. I *do*," she added at his withering glare. "But I made a living from blowing things up, remember? Sometimes, blowing *people* up." Damn it, her voice shook. She swallowed, but the quiver remained. "I convinced myself that because they were evil people, the world was a safer place without them. Maybe that's true, and maybe that's not, I don't know, but I *do* know that blindly following orders killed my partner and broke my sister's heart."

"Your Sergeant Colt Brandon."

She touched Raveno's knee and squeezed. "Never again."

He exhaled, and his vresls rubbed together like sandpaper. "I will think on it."

Kinsley frowned. "Well, while you're thinking, I'd like to actually do *something*."

The left corner of Raveno's lips pulled up into a wicked smirk. "You think I gave orders to Avier, Tironan, Dellao, and Zethus, but I didn't have a mission in mind for you?"

"You didn't have a mission for Riley," she quipped.

"You want me to give your mission to him?" he threatened, but the right corner of his plump lips stretched up to match the curve of the left.

Kinsley deliberately shrugged, knowing how much the gesture annoyed him. "Depends on the mission."

"You and I are going to study the financial records for the Intergalactic Frisaes."

Kinsley gripped his knee with both hands, all pretense of indifference forgotten. "It's like you read my mind! With all those in-person spectators and an entire planet of viewers tuning in from home, the Intergalactic Frisaes is probably worth millions of whatever your currency is."

Raveno's frill flared out and rattled. "Yes, but attendance, either in-person or at home via live broadcast projection, has always been required. Increasing profits through viewership, as Jzoeshi's reports claim, doesn't make sense. Profits don't lie, but people do."

"You think others, besides Josairo, are benefiting financially from the Intergalactic Frisaes?"

"That's what I'd like for us to discover. After Selections, shols meet with their selectors. Instead of the usual greeting and sparring, we'll review the financial records."

Kinsley nodded. "Great. What's the plan?"

"I just stated the plan."

"For stealing the financial records, I mean."

He just continued staring.

"Are they digital or hard copy? Is this a hacker mission or a physical heist? I can mix up a localized e-bomb, perfect for disabling electrical locking mechanisms, but we have—"

"Ah..." Raveno patted her hands, which she suddenly realized were still gripping his knee. "Although your knowledge of explosives is admired and appreciated, this mission does not require your expertise. I am the great Vri Cilvril, remember? I have clearance to access financial records."

"Oh." Kinsley slipped her hands from his and leaned back, deflated.

His twitching lips stretched into another wide smirk. "If I did-nt know you better, I would say you-er disappointed."

"The mission will eventually require me to blow *something* up."

"I am certain it will." His expression was the definition of sincerity.

Kinsley narrowed her eyes.

His grin stretched into a smile wide enough for the tips of both his fangs to peek out from behind his upper lip. "Is there anything else you wish to plan tonight? Any other grievances you must bring to light?" He leaned forward slightly. "Any truths *you* wish to confess?"

Kinsley crossed her arms. "No."

He met her gaze with those strange, beautiful, reptilian eyes with their elliptical pupils. The inferno Raveno could spark with a single look was just as dangerous as the mission itself.

Kinsley clung to her decision as one might the edge of a cliff.

"All right." He expelled a heavy breath and stood. "Then I wish you a restful sleep. We have only half a shift before we must wake for Selections."

Kinsley waved a hand. "Good night."

Raveno shook his head. "On Havar, it is *rest well*."

"Rest well, then." She snatched a blanket from where it was artfully draped over the back of the couch.

Raveno hesitated. "What are you doing?"

She glanced over her shoulder. "Preparing to rest."

"We have a separate room for that." His eyes narrowed. "As you do on Earth, yes?"

"Yes, but..." *We can't share a bed.* Kinsley clamped her lips against the words. Did she really have so little self-control that she couldn't lie beside him and *literally* sleep? She stood and swept her arm out. "Fine. Lead the way to your bedroom."

He blinked. "*My* sleeping room."

"Yes, that's what I meant. Your *sleeping* room."

He continued blinking.

"Is there a problem?"

"No," he said gruffly. "No problem."

Raveno about-faced, and Kinsley followed him as he marched across the living room and into his as if he were walking the green mile.

TWENTY-NINE

IS THERE A PROBLEM?

Kinsley's words echoed in Raveno's mind as his bedroom door slid shut behind her. Was being alone with her a problem? Was sharing a bed with her a problem? Was the possibility of becoming intimate with her a problem? Because he knew for a fact that humans often slept together in the same bed while intimate, a custom his species didn't share, but Kinsley had just claimed to not know her feelings.

Yet here she was, in his sleeping room, fluffing and positioning one of his pillows as he removed his boots, turning down the covers as he unstrapped his uniform and untied his ornamental circlet, and —cry mercy, there she goes—slipping into his bed as if she belonged.

His mind, as unhinged now as his hopeful body, imagined the parts of him that could slip into her as if he belonged.

Raveno clamped his vresls tight to his chest before they rattled.

Although Kinsley had slept in his bed aboard *Sa Vivsheth*, he'd deliberately separated their shifts, so they'd never slept together. He thought she'd appreciated that privacy. He certainly had—although, he suspected, for very different reasons. Now, he didn't know what to suspect.

Her scent told him yes.

Her words told him she didn't know.

Her actions...

The backs of his eyelids didn't have the answers. Nor did the ceiling nor the closed door when he studied the surrounding room for inspiration. Even more baffling, she was still fully dressed, uniform and all. He donned a robe, knowing full well the fabric would only twist around and strangle his torso in bed, but he couldn't rest naked with her fully clothed beside him and still remain true to his word that she controlled the pace of their deal.

Raveno rubbed the frown between his brows, fearing his forehead was becoming permanently creased in her presence.

Your will by my hands, he thought and turned down the covers on his side of the bed, resigned.

She stiffened. "Wait."

Raveno froze, the covers pinched between his claws.

"Maybe we should, I don't know, sleep head to feet," she suggested.

"Head to feet?"

"To keep it from getting weird." She snatched his pillow from the head of the bed and tossed it to the other end, beside her feet.

He dropped the covers and stared at his newly positioned pillow, unsure what was happening or how resting with his head beside her feet would *prevent* anything from getting weird.

Kinsley tucked herself under the covers, giving him her back.

Unless Zethus's research was incorrect—doubtful, but possible—this was not the beginning of an ill-advised intimate encounter.

He didn't know what it was the beginning of, but he suspected it wasn't the beginning of sleep either—which, if intimacy was beyond the sight of possibility, he most definitely wanted to achieve.

He held his breath, lifted the covers at the foot of the bed, and stiffened his vrels against her scent. Feeling the full weight of the "weird" she'd been hoping to avoid, Raveno sat, removed his prosthetic leg—gah, why were his ears burning?—and tucked himself into bed with both of Kinsley's feet inches from his chin.

And suddenly, he was holding his breath for an entirely different reason.

Not that his unwashed foot wasn't ripe—it probably was—but this hadn't been *his* idea.

He scowled at her feet and then leaned in. Were those scales on her heels?

He rolled his eyes at his own ridiculous curiosity. He was not doing this. The only thing he was doing, his most important mission at this very moment, was pursuing sleep. Not answers. He knew very well from experience that pursuing answers about Kinsley led inevitably to more questions.

He rolled away from her, and his robe instantly hitched up to strangle his torso. As he'd known it would.

"What"—Kinsley pounded both fists into the covers—"are you doing?"

"This is insufferable," Raveno muttered, tugging but failing to free himself from the grip of his twisted robe.

Kinsley peered over her shoulder and rolled her eyes. "Just close your eyes and relax," she said, but as she curled onto her side, her scaley heel struck out and kicked the back of his head.

"Oussss," he hissed, rubbing his bruised skull. "If I fail to fall asleep, you intend to knock me unconscious?"

"Sorry," she claimed, but the hiccup in her voice sounded suspiciously amused. "That was an accident."

"Only truth between us," he growled. "That hurt!"

"You know, the last time you *accidentally* hurt me, you dislocated my shoulder."

Some sins, it seemed, would never be forgiven. "That *was* an accident."

"So was mine."

"You said it with sarcasm!"

"Oh, *now* you have the ability to detect sarcasm?" She waved a dismissive hand. "My kick barely knocked your crown askew. Deal with it."

"Ornamental circlet," he gritted out. She knew this. "And why would I wear it to bed?"

She bobbed an unconcerned shoulder. "You wore a robe to bed."

"What would be more 'weird,' sleeping head-to-head or sleeping naked while you remain clothed?"

Her heel connected with the back of his head again.

"Kinsley..."

She flipped over to face him. "That *was* an accident. I swear."

Raveno narrowed his eyes. "You did not swear the first time."

Kinsley's eyes slid sideways.

He inhaled, ignored the insanity of his still-quivering vresls, and gave his robe a mighty tug. It gave with a sudden rip, and his fist jerked sideways into Kinsley's calf.

"Ow! *That* hurt!"

His turn to lift a shoulder in unconcern. Ha! "We are even, then."

"Not nearly! I'll definitely have a bruise!"

"And I won't?"

She rubbed the sting from her leg. "I think you underestimate the hardness of your scaly knuckles."

"As you underestimate the hardness of the scaly heels on your stinky feet," he muttered in Haveo.

She made a choked noise in the back of her throat. "I may have trouble speaking and writing in your language, but I understand it just fine!"

Raveno released an exhausted groan and flopped onto his back. Her feet were so close, he could feel the heat of them against his shoulder through the robe. "Humans truly sleep under such ridiculous circumstances?" He lifted his head and pinned her with a glare. "I will check with Zethus."

She snorted. "Zethus doesn't know everything. It's me you should rely on for Earth intelligence."

"He knows most everything."

Kinsley crossed her arms. "He didn't know that human women develop breasts during puberty, not pregnancy."

"Well, no, but—"

"And he was convinced that corn had the ability to hear."

"That intelligence had some merit."

Kinsley raised a skeptical brow. Just the one.

"They call them *ears* of corn, do they not?"

"Plants can't hear!"

"Plants on Havar do."

"He's not on Havar, now, is he?"

Raveno dug his palms into his eyes. "I need sleep."

"I wasn't the one disturbing the peace with my robe yanking."

He let his hands fall to his sides, defeated. "If we are not going to share the bed properly, then why are we sharing it at all?"

"You didn't want me on the couch."

"You could have used the guest sleeping room."

Silence. When she spoke, her voice was strangely monotone, every word distinct. "You. Have. A. Guest. Sleeping. Room?"

"No."

Kinsley sat up slightly and narrowed her eyes at him.

"I have *four* guest sleeping rooms, counting the one Riley is occupying."

Kinsley flopped back and slapped her hands over her face. "*Why didn't you say so?*"

"You told me to lead you to my sleeping room. I even repeated your words to confirm they weren't a figment of my hopeful imaginings. I asked, 'My sleeping room?' and you said, 'Is there a problem?'"

"I know what I said. But I thought you were correcting—"

"*I* did not have a problem sharing my bed. I was delighted, in a nervous sort of confused way, considering all your, as you say, mixed signals, but now that I know sharing my bed requires feet-to-head injuries, I am less inclined to share."

She'd sat upright sometime in the middle of all that, but now she just stared, breathing at him.

"What?" he snapped.

"You..." She shook her head.

"I what?"

"Gah! Just go to sleep!" She flopped back, rolled away from him again, and with the movement, swiped the covers from his body in one swift yank.

Raveno stared at the wall, debating the merits of simply giving up his room and using one of the guest rooms himself.

A minute passed. He was still staring, still debating. Still coverless.

"Raveno?"

He sighed. "What?"

"How do your fireworks create moving images in the sky?"

Raveno rolled onto his back. "What?"

"On Earth, fireworks move, but just from the fall of gravity. They don't move like they're animated."

"Lots of things on Havar are different than they are on Earth," he said vaguely.

"Well, on Earth, once the fuse is lit, it sets off a charge that ignites the gunpowder. This propels the firework into the sky. Once the firework is in the sky, more gunpowder within the firework ignites and bursts the stars across the sky."

Silence filled the room as Raveno processed that. "Okay."

She poked his foot. "Well?"

"Well, what?"

"This is the part when you share how fireworks work on Havar."

Raveno closed his eyes. "I thought you wanted to sleep."

"There could be multiple timed charges within each firework," she speculated.

"There could be," he said, hoping that would be the end of it.

"But even then, are they computerized in some way to counteract gravity? Maybe programmed to—"

"Kinsley..." Raveno sighed. "I don't know how they work."

"They must be computerized."

"Just don't think about it."

"I'll be able to stop thinking about it once I know how they work."

"We can examine explosive weaponry later. How about, for now, we just *try* to fall asleep?"

She muttered something under her breath, but at least her complaints no longer required a response.

A minute passed before he realized he was still staring at the wall. He forced his eyes closed.

"Raveno?"

"I thought we were sleeping," he muttered.

"What's the metal box on your kitchen counter?"

"The one next to the stovetop?"

A pause. "Yes."

He peeked over his shoulder at her, but she still had her back to him. "Are you hungry?"

"No. It's just another something that's bothering me."

Everything bothered her. "It is a cooking appliance. It utilizes a type of low radiation to vibrate, ah—what is the word for the smallest pieces of something's structure?"

"Molecules," she whispered.

"Yes. The radiation vibrates molecules to heat food quickly."

She laughed into her pillow, but the tail end of the laugh morphed into a high groan. "That's what I was afraid of."

He scowled at the back of her head. "You? Afraid of a kitchen appliance?"

"Forget it," she murmured, squirming deeper under the covers.

He grunted and settled back into his pillow, ignoring her feet, which were now shoved under his side, and the fact that he was still lying splayed out in the open without any covers. It was her first night on an unfamiliar planet, a planet she hadn't wanted to visit, an entire thesh of intergalactic travel from her home. He wasn't happy here either, and this *was* his home.

So. Raveno closed his eyes and tried his very best to at least pretend to sleep. Maybe one of them could find some rest.

"RAVENO."

No, not yet. Raveno rolled away from the voice.

Someone grabbed his shoulder and rolled him back. "Your tablet's been chirping for an hour."

"What is a tablet?" he grumbled, knowing exactly what she was referring to—he could hear it—but by will or wrath, he'd just closed his eyes.

"Your yensha. Come on! We need to mission prep."

Kinsley. He considered opening his eyes, if only to see her newly woken beside him, but the next thing he knew, someone was shaking his shoulder again.

"Raveno!"

He rolled away from the voice and found the sheet. *Ah, yes.*

"No, no, no."

The sheet was nearly ripped from his grasp, but he held on tight and forced it over his head. Who would dare fight *him*?

"Today is Selections. We need to review our plan."

Ah, that's right. Kinsley. "You're already selected," he muttered. "Nothing to review."

"That's what you said about the Welcome Ceremony, and then Josairo was a projection instead of a person, and there were millions of spectators and flying cameras and dancing humanoid plants with dead bodies inside them. We need to prep."

"On Havar"—he yawned—"would they not be considered havarianoid?"

Silence. And then a chill backdraft doused his body as the sheet was ripped away entirely.

He groaned, covering his face with a hand. Why were the illuminators on full blast? They were scalding his retinas even with his eyes closed.

"You cannot possibly tolerate this intensity of blinding light," he growled.

"This is how I *prefer* it." She wrapped her arms around him.

He opened his eyes. Suddenly, he wasn't nearly so exhausted. His vresls quivered.

She slapped his shoulder. "Don't get all excited."

"You're touching me."

"I'm waking you."

"You are."

She released him and sat on the edge of the bed beside him. "I'm nervous."

Raveno forced his vresls down and sat up. And promptly toppled over without the wall to lean against. Svik, that's right: he was at the foot of the bed. Ridiculous.

Kinsley scowled sideways at him, clearly unimpressed.

Deep breaths. He sat up of his own volition and met her eyes. "Do not be nervous."

"Oh, wow. Just like that"—she snapped her fingers—"I'm not nervous anymore. You're a miracle worker."

"Good."

"*Sarcasm*, Raveno."

"Yes. Me too."

She opened her mouth, hesitated, then released her own sigh.

"Listen. Everything is the same as yesterday, so you can expect no surprises. The only difference is I will stand on the second-tier dais beside Josairo—or rather, his projection—and you will be center stage with your fellow humans."

"Joy."

"When your bid begins, I-ll officially select you. A formality as you are already mine," he said, pointing to her glowing wrist. "After all the humans are selected, you-ll be led to a private room. I-ll join you the following shift, but instead of sparring as the other humans undoubtedly will be with their partners, we-ll review the financial records."

She nodded, but her teeth gnawed on her bottom lip.

"Is your concern beyond the Selection Ceremony?"

She shook her head, still gnawing.

"Because even if it comes to a frisaes, which it will not, you will face me in the arena, and we will fake our fight." He paused a moment, then clarified: "I will not kill you."

She rolled her eyes. "It's not that."

"Then what is wrong?"

"I hate that I'm not *doing* anything. I just"—she waved both her hands in the air, indicating everything and nothing—"stand there for sale. With Martin." Her lips pinched. "And Benjamin and Leanne and the rest of them," she added quickly.

Too quickly.

"That *is* you doing something," Raveno reasoned. He could do nothing to smooth her reunion with her former cellmates, but he could give her clarity of purpose if that's what she needed. "While all the other humans gave up on their freedom, you are still fighting for it. What did you call it? Taking cover?"

"*Under*cover. I know," she said, but she didn't look like she knew.

"I do-nt *want* to select you," he continued. "I do-nt *want* to have anything to do with this corrupt event, but here I am, having trafficked you across the galaxy to convince them of my loyalty while I too remain undercover. This is not an easy job. But we can do it." He grunted. "We have done worse."

"*I know.*"

Maybe he should try a different tack. "Not every mission is flash and danger. Not every mission requires something to explode. In fact, the mission is often better if *nothing* explodes."

At that, she finally grinned. "That's up for debate."

Something cleaved Raveno's chest. Not at the sight of her, which was admittedly dubious. She'd slept in her uniform, which had creased her skin. The lines of her braids were straighter, the braids themselves *more* even than when she'd first begun weaving her own hair—a steady improvement—but by no means were they straight nor even. And while her energy told one story, the dark shadows under her eyes told a different tale.

His chest hadn't been cleaved by the smell of her either, because after a night of their unwashed bodies sharing a bed, if not a sheet, her feet were no longer the only part of her that was ripe.

He couldn't quite pinpoint what about her had cleaved his heart, but he suspected it had something to do with that grin. With her dip into sarcasm even when she was nervous. With the fact that anything pertaining to explosives was only slightly self-deprecating because given the opportunity, she'd light it up. Whatever *it* was nearly didn't matter.

Little did she know that more often than not lately, *it* was every part of him, body and soul.

But this moment wasn't about him.

Raveno faced her directly and gripped her shoulders. "I know you are more comfortable with action rather than inaction. So am I. Although I cannot say that I understand your love of fire and explosions, I understand they are your strengths. And I too prefer missions that play to my strengths."

Kinsley didn't pull away or argue, so he pressed on.

"I understand your need to feel in control. Nearly everything about the present mission is out of your control, and I am sorry for that." He stroked his thumbs across her collarbone and didn't breathe. He didn't dare. "Tell me what you need. Tell me what I can do to make this a little better for you."

"There's nothing you can do," she whispered. "There's nothing anyone can do."

Raveno tightened his hold. "Our efforts today are the final few steps toward stopping Josairo. Take courage and comfort from the fact that, thanks to you and the risks you take, you and your humans will be the last species brought to Havar for his entertainment."

She tilted her head. "What are you saying?"

"You are not fighting for just your freedom. You are protecting all the people who would suffer in future Intergalactic Frisaes should we fail."

Kinsley's mouth went slack. Her dark eyes were suddenly huge, and Raveno realized that maybe such weighty responsibility wasn't as motivational as it was crushing.

"But we will not. Fail, I mean," he said quickly. Too quickly.

She huffed, and her breath trembled.

Svik! "That is to say, today is just a small step toward that overall goal. A tiny step. Baby step, as you say. You just stand there, and I select you. Anyone could do today's mission, really." Cry mercy, his ramblings were as helpful as a strip of bandage against a severed artery.

She met his gaze, and yes, tears were in her eyes. *Thev sa shek!*

She threw her head back, laughing.

Raveno released her shoulders and scrubbed his face. Why did he bother trying when he obviously knew nothing of her mind?

"Are we safeguarding the entire galaxy?" she asked, clutching her stomach. "Or could just anyone complete today's baby step mission? Which is it, Raveno?"

He glared at her through the bars of his claws.

"Oh, the panic on your face! Ha!"

"You said you were nervous. I was just trying to..." He glanced away, shaking his head.

"You were trying to help." She touched his arm, and Raveno froze. "You were trying to screw my head on straight by putting the mission into perspective." She sighed out the remainder of her amusement. "And it worked. Thank you."

"I was trying to comfort you." He laughed ruefully. "I should know better. I am the *reason* you need comforting. Not the source of it."

"That's not true," she said, and then looked startled by her own words. She was staring at her hand on his biceps and said again, as if in revelation. "That's not true."

Something in her expression shifted. Before he could pinpoint exactly what was different, her eyes darted down to his lips. She swayed into him slightly—whether deliberately or unconsciously, he wasn't sure—and bridged the distance between them.

She won't, she can't, she doesn't want to, she—

She leaned away and bit her lip.

Raveno tried not to feel disappointed. At her essence, she smelled as she always did: sweet musk, smooth smoke, and that bite of spice that made his vresls rattle even against his will. But more than that—more illogical, more incredible, and more imminent—he could smell that her needs matched his own.

No matter what she claimed not to know about her own feelings, she ached for him.

His vresls quivered.

Her eyes dropped and watched their movement. "I'm insane," she muttered. "We're not even the same species."

"Then I have caught the same affliction." He shook her lightly. "Look at me, Kinsley."

She sighed, then peeked up through her lashes at him.

"Are the differences between our species really any stranger than, say, Cresha, having black hair instead of blonde? Or wide eyes instead of narrow?"

She coughed. "Glad you're thinking about your ex-wife while you're in bed with me."

His hands tightened. "The differences between us only matter in so far as they make you, you. And me, me." He leaned in. "And I want *you*."

"Raven—"

"Kins—"

His sleeping room door slid open. "Rise and shine!"

Kinsley lunged away from him and nearly fell off the bed.

Riley leaned against the doorjamb, grinning. "Sorry to interrupt."

Raveno pointed a claw at him and glared. "Sarcasm."

"Can't get anything past you, Slick."

Kinsley strode from the room, knocking into Riley's shoulder as she passed. "We were just finishing mission prep."

"Just in time, then. Your escort's here." The heat in Riley's eyes as he followed Kinsley from the room was discomfortingly familiar. Raveno couldn't tell if Riley was more frustrated, annoyed, or in love. A confusion that Raveno was intimately familiar with.

"You r-r-ready?" Tironan stood in the relaxation room, looking barely ready himself.

"No," Kinsley muttered in Haveo. "Let us face shit."

Tironan smiled. "Your g-grammar still leaves something to be desired, but y-y-your meaning is p-precisely accurate." He slid the door open and waved his hand for Kinsley to precede him into the hall.

Raveno cinched the belt tight around his torn robe, reattached his leg, and stepped from his sleeping room. Three people in his suite, and he was still wearing the same robe he'd slept in. His hair was a disgrace, even compared to Tironan's, and by will or wrath, if he were to crawl into bed at this moment, he'd fall asleep before his head even fully settled into the pillow.

What was becoming of him?

"You must guide her step where the illuminators are dim," Raveno reminded him.

Tironan clicked his heels. "I w-will."

"Especially in the corners where the younger ushelz have grown. They need a host, so they'll be motivated to stretch beyond their usual reach."

"I—I—I know."

"And when you get to the arena, don't—"

"What happened to not being nervous?" Kinsley's head reappeared in the doorway, sideways. "What happened to not needing to prep?"

"I thought you *were* mission prepping when I walked in," Riley cut in.

Kinsley blushed.

"You are prepared," Raveno said, ignoring Riley. "For Tironan, I prefer to prep."

"Y-your confidence in me is s-stunning."

Raveno jabbed a claw at him. "When you arrive at the arena, don't let Cresha or Veilon distract you. Get Kinsley to the stage with the other shols without delay, and get yourself to the dais. I want you at my side during Selections."

"Of c-c-course." Tironan's eyes widened. "You think Veilon or Cresha would p-p-p—" He swallowed. "Stop me?"

"I think Veilon wants what she can't have, and Cresha—"

"Cresha w-w-wants what she can't have also."

"Cresha is not happy with me."

"Was she ever h-happy with you?"

"She—"

"I'll meet you there," Kinsley snapped. Her head disappeared from the doorway, and instantly, something banged into the wall. She grunted out a curse.

"Cresha delayed us yesterday," Raveno interjected before anyone could interrupt. "Don't let it happen again."

Tironan blew out a swift breath and nodded.

Raveno waved a hand in dismissal. "Hurry, before she loses an arm or worse."

Tironan clicked his heels and jogged from the room.

"Nice of you to join me," Kinsley said from the hall.

Sarcasm, Raveno thought, grinning as the door slid shut.

"It's never gonna happen. You know that, right, Romeo?"

Raveno faced Riley.

Riley was leaning his hip against the couch, arms crossed. His upper lip was curled back—the same hate-filled sneer, even after all this time—as he took in Raveno, head to foot.

"All those long looks and sweet words. It's all a lie," Riley murmured. "She's undercover, remember?"

Raveno didn't laugh—sweet words from Kinsley, ha!—only

nodded. "If that is truth, then what ally are you to her, breaking her cover?"

Riley's jaw clenched.

The door behind Raveno slid open.

Riley's eyes widened.

Raveno braced for whatever crisis he needed to solve next, but as he turned, something stung his neck.

"Oh, shit." Riley lunged back into the guest bedroom.

Raveno slapped his hand over the injury, but whatever had struck was gone.

"What..." He began, but suddenly, he didn't have a tongue to speak. He reached for his pivz, but had no hands with which to grasp them. Not that he was even wearing a pivz—or any weapon, for that matter. The room tilted sideways. The illuminators dimmed. He blinked, and a pair of stylish boots were inches from his face.

And then he was nothing at all.

THIRTY

Raveno wasn't on the dais.

Millions of spectators were once again in attendance, their roar just as deafening as yesterday. The camera drones were flying, the *humanoid* body-snatching plants were grooving, and a nervous Tironan had claimed his place on the dais between Avier and Veilon. But Raveno—literally the only person she needed in attendance— wasn't here.

Josairo wasn't on the dais either, however, so maybe the two of them would make a grand entrance together: king and his killing hand. Father and son. A united front for all the world to celebrate.

Kinsley snorted. Raveno would love that.

"You look great."

Kinsley hated that her heart squeezed and jumped in response to that low voice, but she had to acknowledge him eventually.

Eventually was apparently now.

Martin.

Kinsley tried not to see that he looked great too. She refused to notice the toned evidence of regular exercise, the tight outline of his black boxer briefs, the clipped thickness of his trimmed beard. The hesitant hope in his dark eyes. Instead, she focused on the pair of silver cuffs locked around his wrists. As he edged closer to her, the woman behind him was tugged closer to him by the invisible sensor tethering the cuffs on her wrists to his.

He chose those chains when he betrayed me, she reminded herself as she met his eyes.

He flinched slightly, as if holding her gaze hurt.

Good. Meeting her gaze *should* slice him up inside.

It certainly felt like she was bleeding.

"I like the braids. You've earned them." He raised his hand as if to touch one, then froze and let his arm drop. "Like Khaleesi," he clarified, as if she wouldn't understand the *Games of Thrones* reference.

"I thought my braids meant I had, how did you put it?" She tapped her lip, then held a finger aloft in recollection. "Ah! That I had 'turned into one of them.'"

"It was more the uniform," Leanne piped up from behind her. "And the glowing blue dot in your wrist."

"You promised to play nice," Benjamin whispered, then raised his voice and added, "Although the braids didn't help."

Benjamin had sidled up to her left, and behind him stood a strangely optimistic-looking Leanne. And because Leanne was tethered to the man beside her and that man to the woman behind him, everyone had shuffled in.

Christ, she was surrounded.

"Listen, Switch, I'm sorry." Martin placed a hand on her shoulder. "I—"

Kinsley shrugged off his touch. "You're sorry? Oh, let me guess: Now that we're here on Havar instead of back on Earth, you realize you were wrong? You should have followed my lead and escaped while you had the chance? You'd take it all back if you could?"

"No. I made a choice, and I stand by it," Martin said. His tone was firm, calm, and certain, but his expression was unbelievably sad. Grieving. "But I'm still sorry."

"I made a choice that I stand behind too," Kinsley said. She opened her mouth to say more, then turned her back on the three of them and focused on the dais before she choked on all the regret clogging her throat. Why did she suddenly feel like she should be apologizing too?

After a moment of pointed staring, Kinsley finally snagged Tironan's attention. She glared at Raveno's empty spot meaningfully and raised her eyebrows. *Well?*

Tironan spread out his hands.

Ha! Surprise of the year: Tironan didn't know what was going on.

She stared at Avier next. It took a little longer, but eventually, he noticed. He followed the movement of her eyes to Raveno's empty place, then patted the air with his hand.

Easy for him to pump the breaks on panicking. He wasn't the one up for Selection.

He tapped the inside of his wrist.

Yeah, yeah, yeah. She was already branded as Raveno's Vri Sa Shols. But if his claim was so official, why was she up for Selection?

"So..." Benjamin cleared his throat. "Those plants are crazy, huh?"

You have no idea, Kinsley thought.

"Forget the vegetation," Leanne groaned.

"The plants are the present danger, I think." Benjamin's finger shook as he nudged his glasses higher up the bridge of his nose. "If I'm not mistaken, they have teeth."

"Who cares? After how many years behind bars, the only thing that matters today is if our plan is still in place." Leanne sidestepped in front of Kinsley, and everyone tethered behind her jerked forward. "Will he keep his promise?"

"Who?" Kinsley blinked. "What promise?"

"Your alien boyfriend. Option two," Leanne said, and for the first time in all the months that Kinsley had known her, Leanne's face didn't pinch like she was sucking on a lemon. "How long before he completes his mission so we can go home?"

So much for Raveno's mission being *covert*. Kinsley skimmed the arena, but no one seemed capable of overhearing their conversation in the chaos of the teeming crowd.

"It hasn't been years," Benjamin corrected Leanne, consulting his watch. "We were abducted three hundred and sixty-three days ago."

Kinsley sucked in a sharp breath at that. "It's been one year since our abduction?"

"Almost." Benjamin peered over the rim of his frames to meet her eyes. "It's been approximately eight months since we saw you." He glanced aside at Leanne and added, "Not enough months to count as years."

"It feels like decades," Leanne lamented.

"Ignore them," Martin said, his face grim. "What's happening today, Switch? What is all this?"

Kinsley studied the three of them—Martin, Benjamin, and Leanne—and refused to feel. She'd considered them friends. She'd risked her life for them. She hadn't particularly *liked* all of them but she'd... She shook her head. After *eight months* with only the aliens who'd abducted them for company, not one of her former cellmates, not even Martin, had asked how she was coping.

After enduring their betrayal, how stupid would she have to be to feel disappointed?

Kinsley swallowed her hurt, locked eyes with Leanne, and answered the only relevant question pending. "I don't have an alien boyfriend, but if I did, his promises wouldn't pertain to you."

A swarm of drones converged over the dais, and Kinsley ignored Leanne and her incensed gasp in favor of today's true danger: the Selection Ceremony. The glowing rails bracketing the stadium levels dimmed, and on that signal, the crowd quieted. The projectors swirled as one unit, and in the next moment, five giant holograms of Josairo's face burst into the air above them. A thirty-foot-tall, full-body projection of him materialized on the dais.

Josairo was here as a live projection. Again.

Everything will be the same as yesterday, Raveno had assured her. *Expect no surprises.*

The crowd erupted in crazy, screaming applause.

Josairo smiled magnanimously, striding past Veilon, Tironan, Avier, and his other minions to the center of the arena. When he raised his hands, the stadium fell silent, and he took a moment to circle the platform, soaking in the attention and power.

"Two thesh and sixty-one shaoz ago, Raveno Hoviir—my son, my killing hand—embarked on a mission to greet and transport the competitors of our fifty-fourth Intergalactic Frisaes." Josairo paused a beat, letting his words echo. "Two thesh and sixty-one shaoz, we waited for his safe return." He paused again, waiting longer this time, and the silence following those echoes buzzed with energy and anticipation. "Now. Our patience has been rewarded. Now. We begin our fifty-fourth Intergalactic Frisaes Selection Ceremony!"

Josairo clicked his heels together, and as one, everyone in the stadium did the same.

Kinsley stared, stunned. Yes, everything was the same, but should everything be *exactly* the same. Nearly word for word?

Martin leaned in. "What's he saying?"

Kinsley waved him back. "It's just ceremony fluff at the moment."

"It can't all be fluff," Leanne argued. "What are they planning? Why are we here?"

Kinsley raised an eyebrow. "We wouldn't be here had we managed to commandeer the spaceship."

"You're right. We'd be dead."

Benjamin jabbed an elbow into Leanne's ribs. "You promised!"

Kinsley shushed them. "I can't hear with everyone nattering at me."

Josairo droned on for a bit, giving the same TED Talk as yesterday. He let the last words of his speech echo into a dramatic pause. And then: "Now, on the eve of our fifty-fourth Intergalactic Sparring Ceremony. Let. Us. Begin!"

Josairo lifted his arms overhead, and the crowd went wild.

One of the drones shorted, and for a moment, so fast one might have sneezed and missed it, Josairo's left eye flickered to a hollow socket.

Just like yesterday.

This wasn't a live feed. This was a recording. And practically the same recording as yesterday, with only a few details edited to pass as a Selection Ceremony speech instead of a Welcome Ceremony speech.

Kinsley scowled at the empty spot where Raveno should be. Was this what he'd really meant? That Josairo's speech would *literally* be the same? But Raveno—Mr. I'm Not Nervous, Mr. We Don't Need To Mission Prep—was still Mr. No-Show.

Raveno should have been here by now.

Cold, sickening dread curdled in Kinsley's stomach.

Raveno had her back. She'd stake her life on it. She *was* staking her life on it. Which meant that something had happened to prevent him from attending today's ceremony.

Or someone.

Avier must have come to the same conclusion, because after activating his anku and engaging in a heated whisper fight with Tironan, Avier's vresls flattened. His mouth pinched, and his eyes slammed down to meet hers.

Kinsley brushed a shooing hand at him. *Go. Find him.*

Avier shook his head.

Kinsley tapped the inside of her wrist, reminding *him* this time. She was already selected. All this was just a formality.

Avier froze for a moment—thinking, considering, panicking?—then, without further hesitation, he muttered a final order to Tironan, pivoted on his heel, and left the dais.

Tironan looked about ready to vomit.

Josairo's projection swirled into a crazy growth spurt. His feet rocketed up from the platform, springing back up to his head as if his body was a snapped rubber band, and on impact, exploded into a dazzling blast of strobing light.

Again.

One of the guards stepped forward: Jhoni. Long time, no see. He eyed Kinsley nervously as he passed, entered a combination into Martin's cuff, then gestured for him to move away from the group.

"Kinsley?" Martin's voice quavered. "What's happening?"

But Kinsley didn't have words of comfort, not for him. Not for any of them.

Not even for herself.

"There's a plan, right?" Benjamin asked. "You always have a plan."

Kinsley shook her head. "The plan is fucked."

Leanne's face crumpled. "Again?"

"Behold, our first shols!" announced one of Josairo's advisors. "Legendary for his skills with the *logar*, he is undefeated in his class."

Martin shuffled forward, oblivious to the beautiful lies being spun regarding his skills and accomplishments. Not only was he apparently legendary and undefeated, his speed and stamina were unparalleled. He held records in both sprinting and long-distance running events, and he was a notorious...breeder?

Kinsley chewed on her translation. Ah. Lady's man.

"Behold! Finech the Ferocious!"

The crowd went wild.

The Vri Shavril allowed a moment of celebration. When the crowd's enthusiasm diminished from ear-piercing to merely deafening, he shouted, "Selections begin!"

Several dozen people began hurling sparkly balls at the dancing Twoeys, same as yesterday—again—except only spectators from the third level participated this time. A dozen names with correlating numbers flashed on the scoreboard, ranked from highest to lowest. The Twoeys caught the balls in their jaws, excitedly at first, still grooving, and as the number of balls being thrown increased, so did the numbers on the scoreboard. The names swapped, keeping the person with the most thrown balls (bids?) at the top of the chart. As the scores increased, some of the participants dropped out, and as the quantity of balls decreased, the plants became more aggressive, snapping at each other as well as the balls.

Eventually, the bidding war whittled down to two people. They tossed sparkly ball after ball as the plants pitched themselves into a vicious, hissing frenzy. The two top names on the scoreboard chased one another, swapping positions with every throw.

Until one of the competitors stopped throwing.

She had a ball in hand. She tossed it up and caught it several times, like a pitcher, considering her next throw. The plants watched that ball—even without eyes, they watched—their heads bobbing up and down in sync with each toss. Waiting. Anticipating.

The stadium fell into a hush, millions of people holding their collective breath.

She dropped her hand and stepped back from the rail.

The top score on the board remained in first.

"Selas Nayess has won this Selection! By will or wrath, congratulations!"

The winner—Selas, presumably—lifted both her hands overhead, her expression rapturous.

Marathon runners had crossed the finish line for gold at the Olympics with less joy.

The crowd went berserk, screaming and clapping and whistling.

The plants slumped.

Jhoni escorted Martin "the Ferocious" across the stage, around the corner, and out of sight.

The entire Selection process had taken maybe twenty minutes. Kinsley eyed the three dozen humans beside her. This was going to be a long day.

Shaoz, she corrected herself since Raveno wasn't there to remind her: without a rising or setting sun, days and nights didn't exist on Havar. Only shifts and shaoz.

Kinsley bit her lip. *Where are you, Raveno?*

Jhoni approached, just as wary as before, but once again, he bypassed her to escort the petite woman beside Leanne to center stage.

"Our second shols..."

As the hosting Vri Shavril droned out another stat sheet of false accomplishments and credentials, Kinsley considered the stadium, the millions of people watching both here and at home, and their willingness to believe these proceedings were real. Their willingness to actively participate.

Their willingness to see only lies.

"Skull Crusher Keeras!"

The crowd erupted.

Kinsley did a double take. The woman up for Selection was five-two, maybe one hundred and five pounds, and pushing seventy. She didn't seem capable of crushing a grape, let alone a skull. Granted, appearances were deceiving. But really? Skull Crusher? If they were going to fabricate warrior backstories for everyone, shouldn't they stay somewhat within the realm of plausibility?

The bidding frenzy began.

Just like the Welcome Ceremony, Selections ran flawlessly without Josairo's help. Was that truly indicative of his reach and how greatly his people feared him? Or did it indicate how deeply his rule had influenced his people? Because no one looked particularly afraid.

Even if Raveno successfully gained enough on- and off-world political support to assassinate Josairo and replaced him as their leader, would the havari people accept Raveno and his rule if that meant a different way of life?

"Our third shols..."

Raveno claimed his people couldn't see the chains, but did they just not *want* to see them? Because of fear? Because of convenience?

Because of indifference?

"Our fourth shols..."

Kinsley surveyed the fire-code nightmare that was the frisaes arena and its sardine-stuffed spectators and dreamed a different dream. A familiar dream. The havari were fire-resistant, but was their stadium?

When burning the world to the ground and starting fresh was her best solution, had they already lost?

Did it matter if that was her ticket back to Earth?

"Our fifth shols..."

Jhoni stood in front of Kinsley and ushered her center stage.

The stadium fell silent.

Raveno was still absent.

"An expert weapons specialist with a concentration in pyrotechnics, aviation, and engines, she can build and disarm bombs—"

What now? Kinsley met Tironan's eyes, but he seemed just as shocked.

"—fly human-made as well as havari-made air and spacecrafts—

No. No, no, no—

"—and speaks fluent Haveo."

Kinsley closed her mouth. Gaping didn't look good on anyone.

"Behold, Kinsley 'Switch' Morales!"

So much for being undercover.

"This sh-sh-shols is already s-s-selected!" Tironan belted out, but without a microphone, Kinsley could barely hear him.

"*Before* Selections?" Veilon asked, her voice loud and clear through the stadium speakers. Perhaps only Vri Shavril received microphones? "That's impossible."

"Her ankesh shows otherwise." Tironan gestured to Kinsley.

If Kinsley thought she'd been the center of attention before, she was mistaken. Every eye in the stadium and every flying camera drone fixed on her in simultaneous, question-soaked attention.

Kinsley lifted her arm above her head and flashed her ankesh.

"As you c-c-can see, she is already s-selected by Vri Cilvril Raveno Hoviir."

Veilon cocked her head speculatively. "When was the last time an ankesh had a person's name on it?"

The crowd murmured uncomfortably. A few chuckled.

Tironan frowned. "I—I—I—"

"I see an ouk, the symbol of the Hoviir family," Veilon said. Her voice sounded genuine enough, but people eating their favorite flavor of ice cream licked their lips less. "My symbol."

"And m-m-mine."

"As our dear brother mentioned, no matter how long or well anyone bets, they can't earn more vit than him. And only Raveno earns more vit than me." She glanced left, then right, then spread her arms wide as she returned her attention back to Tironan. "Since he's not here, feel free to waste all your vit if you want. But I've already won."

Silence. Even the Twoeys had stopped moving.

"Y-y-y-y—"

Veilon waited, serene as he stuttered—so calm, so patient—knowing he wouldn't get the words out.

Come on, Tironan, Kinsley thought, biting her lip. *Be the warrior I know you are.*

Tironan took a moment, and incrementally, the rage in his face subsided. "You can't intend t-t-to spend all your vit today."

"No, not all of it. Just enough to outbid you." She cocked back her arm.

One of the Twoeys opened its mouth. Just the one. She tossed a sparkly ball at the waiting plant. It caught the ball in its massive jaws, and the scoreboard flashed Veilon's name with a number next to it. Kinsley couldn't read the symbol, but apparently, everyone else could.

No one else bothered to bid.

Toss your bid. Toss your bid. Toss your bid, Kinsley thought at Tironan, but he just glared at the scoreboard along with everyone else.

"Vri Shavril Veilon Hoviir has won this Selection!" the announcer gushed. "By will or wrath, congratulations!"

No.

Veilon beamed and dipped into a deep bow at the stadium's roaring applause.

Tironan looked about ready to vomit. Again.

Jhoni gripped Kinsley's upper arm and escorted her to the other side of the stage to stand beside the other selected humans.

No, no, no, no.

Martin leaned in. "Why do you look like you just choked down a bite of ostrich wing?"

Kinsley shook her head, less in answer to Martin than a physical manifestation of the only word her brain could focus on: No!

Veilon, Raveno's little sister, had selected her. For a frisaes. For a fight to the death.

Tironan locked eyes with Kinsley. A dozen drones were projecting his face in massively enlarged 3D detail for all the world to see. He couldn't say anything. He couldn't so much as twitch without everyone and their grandmother noticing. But Kinsley knew that dead-eyed non-expression all too well. It was the same look he'd worn right before punching her to save face in front of the crew after saving her from the incineration shaft.

He was sorry. Very sorry.

Because they were both very screwed.

THIRTY-ONE

EVERY TIME KINSLEY THOUGHT CAPTIVITY COULDN'T POSSIBLY become more luxurious, the havari proved her wrong. She had an entire one-bedroom, bathroom, workout suite to herself this time, with actual walls instead of a viewing pane—although, any increased sense of privacy was probably an illusion, same as in the brig on *Sa Vivsheth*. Just because she couldn't find a security camera didn't mean they weren't watching, so Kinsley minded her expression while exploring the apartment, even as the knot in the pit of her stomach grew spikes and anchored.

Unlike on *Sa Vivsheth*, the furnishings were earthy (havary?) instead of chrome and utilitarian. The bed in her new cage was larger and softer. It had that pleasant freshness of newly laundered sheets, over a dozen throw pillows, three body pillows, and warming/cooling controls. Its headboard and footboard, the surrounding tables, and the coffee table in the center of the room all resembled custom furniture hand-carved from reclaimed wood, with unique grains, curved lines, and misshapen artistry. Havar's surface was a craggy, lava-wrinkled wasteland, not a tree in sight, so the furniture were antiques, perhaps? Imported from another planet? Or maybe they had subterranean orchards, same as they had subterranean stadiums.

The connecting bathroom didn't disappoint either. The havari once again provided a paradise of scented soaps and lotions and sprays. The tile was immaculate. The mirrors spotless. But more impressive than the five-star housekeeping service were the bathing accommodations. The shower wasn't just a stall. It was an entire room unto itself, complete with waterfall and body shower heads, a separate, handheld shower massager, and three curved in-water pool loungers. All three had strategically placed pulsing water jets.

The inclusion of *three* pool loungers in a private room gave her pause.

Same as in Raveno's suite, her living area had a silver ball in lieu of a TV and a kitchen with a stovetop and a chrome metal box that couldn't possibly be (but was) a microwave. Despite those three pool loungers, she didn't have any guest bedrooms, but in addition to the adjoining personal gym, she did have another space the size of a room. If the hooks, bars, and hangers were any indication, the room was a walk-in closet.

Kinsley stepped into the closet and, after a brief moment debating the insanity of her sudden suspicion, she gave in to paranoia and slid her fingers along the closet's inner edges and corners. She leaned her ear in close and knocked on the walls, pressed firmly on imperfections in the wood-like molding, and knelt to examine the baseboard lighting. If someone was spying on her, they were probably reevaluating her mental state—hell, she knew what she was doing and *still* felt crazy—but a part of her couldn't help but hope that perhaps Raveno had missed Selections on purpose. Maybe he'd intended for his sister to select her. Maybe he'd been instrumental in assigning her to this room. Maybe he was behind this wall at this very moment, about to emerge from another secret closet office, and explain, oh so reasonably, why he'd kept her out of the loop on this latest mission, despite their promises.

And no matter how much she'd resent him for betraying her trust, that was the preferable outcome to the one she suspected.

Nothing short of death would come between Raveno and his mission, and the next step of that mission had been to attend Selections.

Kinsley gave up pressing on the seam where the baseboard met the back wall and covered her mouth.

She thought of Raveno as he'd been this morning—exhausted, gentle, concerned, as futilely careful with his words as he was with his fangs—and that spiked knot anchored in her stomach began to churn, shredding her insides.

She shouldn't have pulled away.

What if she never got the choice to lean in or pull away ever again?

Nothing short of death.

Something outside the closet whirred and beeped.

Her suite door had just unlocked.

Had Raveno been conjured by will alone? Kinsley whipped up, lunged into the main room, and inhaled so hard, she nearly choked on her own tongue.

Cresha.

The knot dropped from Kinsley's throat and sank back into her stomach.

Cresha stepped inside, and the door slid shut behind her—whir, beep, red light—entombing them together in screaming silence.

She wasn't wearing her wedding headband. The thick, raised scar across her left temple was more prominent without it, and her long black hair hung nearly to her waist without the benefit of braids. She was still dressed in gladiator gear and armed with several pivz strapped to both her left and right thighs. Her ezil was fancier than Raveno's. More intricate swirls and symbols were etched into its sheath. Kinsley pondered a moment the status perks of being Raveno's wife—the fancy crown, the obedience of his crew, the respect of Josairo's advisors—all without having to win a frisaes. She'd only had to win Raveno, because on Havar, being married meant being one person.

Ex-wife, Kinsley reminded herself. They *had been* one person. Past tense.

And Kinsley refused to analyze why that distinction filled her with strength.

"Is it true?" Cresha whispered in Haveo.

Kinsley tore her eyes from Cresha's ezil and looked up, and up—shit, she was tall—and met her deep-set, gorgeous purple eyes.

"Tell me it isn't true." Cresha's voice shook.

All the world, literally, believed she was an explosives expert who spoke fluent Haveo. Which technically wasn't true. She barely spoke *passable* Haveo. Still, any hope of keeping her strengths undercover were completely blown after today's disaster of a Selection Ceremony. So.

Kinsley replied in Haveo. "Who are you?"

"I, ah, sorry." She clicked her heels together. "My name is Cresha Zami. I'm a *bresha* for a company called Only Will."

"A...bresha?"

"It's a paid occupation. I ensure that people obtain the help and resources they need to improve their life."

Huh. An alien social worker. Didn't see that one coming.

"We have a saying on Havar: by will or wrath."

Kinsley nodded. "This I have heard."

"I believe that by will alone, people can improve their life. Wrath is not needed." Cresha wrung her hands, then forced them to her sides. "I've dedicated my life to helping people thrive in difficult circumstances. And it's come to my attention that perhaps you are in a difficult circumstance?"

Kinsley considered her words carefully. "How did this attention come to you?"

"The how doesn't matter," Cresha said, taking as much care in finding her words as she did maintaining her expression. "What matters is if it's true."

"If what is true?" Kinsley hedged.

Cresha fisted her hands at her sides. "Were you taken from your home planet and forced to come here against your will?"

Maybe some people *were* willing to see the chains. Yet...Kinsley eyed Cresha's claws in such close proximity to the pommels of her pivz.

"Tell me that Raveno didn't, that he didn't..." Cresha cleared her throat. "Tell me the truth of how you came here."

Was there harm in confirming the truth of her abduction? The real secret was that Raveno was a double agent, which Cresha supposedly already knew.

If I was pissed at my ex-husband for committing treason, would I join forces with his father against him?

Kinsley studied Cresha's face—her downturned lips and pinched brows and pained eyes—and didn't know what to think. Even if Cresha was in league with Josairo, even if the shock and disgust in her expression was an act, the truth of Kinsley's abduction didn't blow Raveno's cover. If anything, it solidified it.

And on the heels of that thought came another to poison her resolve: *As Raveno's ex-wife potentially in league with Josairo against him, does she know why Raveno missed Selections?*

"Humans have chains." Kinsley circled one wrist with her other hand and mimed being pulled along by the makeshift cuff. "What do *you* think?"

"They're leads for your protection. You can't see well in the dark, and on an unfamiliar planet with the young ushelz starving and the crowds..." Cresha blinked several times. "It would be careless to let you to walk blind among such dangers without the benefit of..." Her voice broke. "They're shackles, aren't they?"

Kinsley nodded.

"Cry mercy," Cresha whispered. She wiped a heavy hand down her face. "And all that was said, that you can fly havari-made air and spaceships as well as human-made? Was all that even true?"

"Yes, true about me. Not true about the other humans."

Cresha inhaled, and the effort seemed to cost her. "I can smuggle you home."

"You can..." Kinsley coughed. "What?"

"If you know how to fly, I'll give you my cruiser." Before Kinsley could fully process what she was saying, Cresha began pacing the small confines of the room. "It'll be a long journey. At least one thesh. And dangerous without a crew, but between the two of us, we could—"

Kinsley staggered back. "Two of us?"

"Yes, my cruiser only holds two passengers, and we don't have a crew, not one I can trust, anyway. Svik, not after all this." She waffled her hand at Kinsley.

"That is not my meaning. I—"

"Without the crew on board, we could probably squeeze in an additional passenger." She floundered a moment, likely at the prospect of traveling an entire year across the galaxy with only two aliens for company. She pivoted when she reached the wall and strode across the room a second time.

"You and I fly to Earth? Together?" Kinsley asked. This couldn't be happening.

Cresha's face fell. "I can't. I don't know how to fly, but if you can, my cruiser is yours."

"You *give* me spaceship to fly home," Kinsley clarified. She had to be translating this incorrectly.

"Yes. I'll come with you to ensure that you reach your destination."

"But how you return home if you not fly?"

Cresha waved that question away as one might a gnat. "I'll figure something out."

"No."

Cresha stopped pacing. "What do you mean, 'no'?"

Kinsley raised an eyebrow. "Not yes."

"If you can't fly, I'll find a pilot. I'll buy their loyalty. I—"

"No."

"I'm not sure you're understanding me. I—"

"I understanding you. *You* not understanding *me*. I—" Kinsley clamped her mouth shut against the words. If this was an elaborate ploy by Josairo to trick Kinsley into outing Raveno, it was fucking brilliant. "I not leave."

"Yes, you can. I have a ship. You can fly it. Or someone will, and we—"

"I *can* leave, yes. But I not to leave. Not without my people." *Not without taking down Josairo.*

"Do you understand what's happening? Why you're here?" Cresha gestured at the room around them. "You were selected for a frisaes. A fight in which you must—"

"A fight to the death." Kinsley nodded. "I understanding."

"You're not supposed to be here against your will," Cresha snapped. "You're supposed to *want* to be here."

"Who *want* to fight to the death?" Kinsley snapped right back. "How no one know the truth?"

"It's an honor to travel here for the Intergalactic Frisaes," Cresha said, indignant. "People from all across the universe train a lifetime in the hope of battling our greatest warriors and returning home victorious. They..." She hesitated, deflated. "They used to, anyway."

Did they, though?

Cresha lifted her hands, pleading. "We must get you home. And tell your planet—Earth, is it?—what's happened. They can come in force to rescue the others. They—"

"Earth has no spaceships. If we go, all humans die in frisaes."

Cresha shook her head. "Some will live."

"They fight to death."

"But some will live," she insisted. "And—"

"No. All will die," Kinsley said grimly. "No one train. Not for lifetime. Not ever."

"Okay. So. I'll..." Cresha blinked several times, then seemed to steel her spine and settle into whatever she'd decided. "I'll appropriate a carrier vessel."

Oh, sweet Jesus.

"It'll take longer. I'll need a full crew to maintain it. And weapons. They'll pursue us. Svik, Raveno might..." Cresha closed her eyes, anguished, but after a long sigh, she opened them, her expression cold. Resolved. "I'll try. I...*we'll* get everyone home."

Damn it, Kinsley did not want to like this woman! "I not leave."

"I said I'd take everyone home. Everyone!" Cresha waved her hands in the air as if the everyone she referred to was in the room. "I'll take all the humans, you and all your people, home. Back to Earth."

"No," Kinsley whispered. Christ, how she wanted to say yes!

Cresha shook her head. "Is there something else you're not telling me? Is there something else you're afraid of? Let me help you."

Kinsley nodded and pressed one hand to her chest. "I not first person taken." She waited for a sign Cresha understood her, then, keeping one hand pressed firmly to her chest, she added, "But I last person taken."

Cresha nodded. "Like I said, let me help."

Kinsley met Cresha's gorgeous, anguish-filled eyes and considered the possibility that she was genuinely offering her aid.

"Please. Kinsley, is it?"

She nodded. "Friends call me Switch."

Cresha lifted her arms out, pleading. "Please, Switch. What do you need?"

"I need..." *Raveno,* she thought, or at the very least, some C-4 and a cell phone so she could bust this joint and find him herself.

Nothing short of death.

Kinsley shook her head before panic could sink its claws in her mind as well as her heart. She needed to think logically and survive. She wouldn't be any good to Raveno dead, and until she created an opportunity to find him without blowing both their covers, she should continue the mission as planned.

"I need the Intergalactic Frisaes money books," Kinsley said.

Cresha frowned, uncomprehending.

"The books. Of money," Kinsley tried again, changing her inflection, but she was butchering the pronunciation beyond recognition, assuming she'd found the right words to begin with.

"The books of money..." Cresha murmured slowly, phonetically, until her accent kicked in, and she said it correctly. Her purple eyes widened. "The financial records?"

Kinsley nodded.

"I may know someone with access to that information."

Yes, you certainly do. Kinsley grinned darkly. *And despite the divorce, you're still posing as one person with him.* "Lucky me."

THIRTY-TWO

"T-T-TAKE HIS SHOULDERS. I-I-I'VE GOT HIS LEGS. READY?"

"No. I'll treat him here."

"We should g-get him to medical."

"His vitals are stable, and we've already secured the room."

"I'm his brother, and I s-s-say we leave for medical."

"I'm his doctor, and I say we stay here."

A pause and then. "D-D-Dellao? What do you s-say?"

"I'm just his soldier," Dellao said without hesitation. "I don't have a say."

"This is a new world order, remember? For Josairo, you don't have a say, but for Raveno, we're equally screwed if we get caught committing treason. So speak up."

"I don't think—"

"You've f-f-faithfully served Raveno his entire c-career. You know h-h-him. Advocate for him!"

A sigh. "He wouldn't want us stirring up a media circus, no matter his injuries. This is a medical issue, so I say we follow Avier's lead."

"S-s-svik."

357

Raveno felt his legs drop to the floor.

What was he doing on the floor?

Raveno tried to move. He tried to speak, open his eyes, wiggle his fingers, something—anything!—but all he achieved from his efforts was frustrating, inconceivable nothing.

"So we bring m-m-medical to him."

"Are you seriously suggesting that we, what, carry an entire RRC here, into his suite? Because *that* would be less conspicuous than carrying his unconscious body."

"Are you s-s-seriously suggesting we d-do nothing?"

Another stretch of silence. "Waiting is often the most difficult mission of all."

Someone squeezed Raveno's hand.

From their voices, Raveno recognized Avier, Tironan, and Dellao, but for the life of him, he didn't know who else was in the room, holding his hand. Not Kinsley, of that he *was* certain.

"C-c-can't you just give him a-a-a shot of adrenaline or something?"

"Not without knowing how much sedative he was given. And even then, considering metabolism and timing, it would be an approximation. Better to just wait it out."

"W-w-we don't have the time to w-wait."

"We have time."

"Tell that t-to Switch."

Switch? Raveno's heart stuttered on a surge of fear. What had happened to Kinsley? He struggled to sit up a second time. There! He'd managed to lift a claw. Hadn't he?

"Kinsley's the least of my concerns at the moment," Avier muttered. "She can hold her own."

"She c-c-can't."

"She kicks your ass in training," Dellao said.

Tironan muttered something that sounded suspiciously like: "I let her."

"What's that?"

"N-n-never mind."

Now, Raveno had moved for sure. He heard his claw clack against the floor this time.

"Did you see that?"

"What?"

"I think he's waking up."

"R-R-Raveno? Can you hear m-me?"

"Try slapping him," Riley suggested. He'd recognize the grate of *that* voice anywhere. "Might help speed the process."

Raveno strained to open his eyes. He managed a squint and groaned. Svik, how had his life come to this? He was indeed lying on his relaxation room floor. Tironan and Avier were kneeling on either side of him, staring at him with an intensity that was alarming, even to him.

By will or wrath, Tironan was the one holding his hand.

Dellao was standing behind Avier and Tironan, arms crossed, and Riley was lounging on the couch, enjoying the drama.

Raveno sat up. The room tilted on its axis, and his stomach immediately revolted.

"Whoa!" Avier caught him and eased him gently back to the floor. "Take it easy, Raveno. Slow and easy."

Raveno closed his eyes. Of his own volition. He *chose* to close his eyes—to block out the room's sick spinning. "What is wrong with me?"

"We w-w-were hoping you c-could answer that question."

"You were obviously drugged. Blood tests will confirm my suspicions."

Cry mercy, what were they rambling on about? "And what are your suspicions?"

Someone snorted. "It's not like we haven't experienced these symptoms before," Dellao grumbled.

Raveno sighed. "Are you saying that Kinsley drugged me?"

"I'm saying that *someone* drugged you."

"It w-w-wasn't Kinsley. I was with her the whole t-t-time."

"When were you with her? You were supposed to be compiling a list of potential on-world allies." Raveno squinted an eye open just in time to witness Avier and Tironan lock eyes. "What happened? What did I miss?"

"Y-y-you. Well, I—I—I—"

"Perhaps we should focus on your own incident."

"Kinsley was involved in an incident?" Raveno struggled upright. "What sort of incident?"

"Calm down," Avier gasped out, half supporting Raveno's weight and half forcing him back to the floor. "You were attacked. We must deal with that first."

Raveno scanned the room. "Where is she?"

Everyone, even Riley, looked at each other, but remained silent.

"I order you to—"

"She's safe," Avier insisted. "I need you to focus. What's the last thing you remember?"

Raveno could have pushed Avier and his concerns aside in favor of finding Kinsley himself if the floor would only cease rocking! "I'm not sure. I was in my sleeping room with Kinsley. We'd just woken up. We were..." Memory lit his mind like an approaching dawn, and suddenly, the pounding in his head wasn't quite so painful.

Kinsley had nearly kissed him.

Raveno cleared his throat. "We were 'mission prepping' as she says."

"D-do you remember what h-happened next?" Tironan asked.

Raveno nodded. "Riley interrupted our discussion—"

Riley raised his eyebrows. "That's what they call it these days."

"And she left with you...for..." Raveno's mind blanked for a split second even as his stomach heaved. He sprang upright, and will alone kept him standing. "*Selections!*"

"Stop." Avier wrapped an arm around Raveno's shoulders, more in restraint than support. "Breathe deep and calm."

"I must get to Selections!"

"You c-can't."

"Why aren't you there now?" Raveno asked.

Tironan peeked at Avier.

"And you," Raveno said, rounding on Avier. "You should be there too. And you..." Raveno shook his head at Dellao. "Guarding my unconscious body required all three of you?"

Dellao's lips compressed into a thin line. His vresls bristled.

"We must leave now. Before—"

"It's t-t-too late," Tironan said grimly.

"What's too late?"

"You m-missed it."

Raveno froze. "Tell me precisely what I missed."

Tironan glanced at Avier.

Avier sighed. "The Selection Ceremony ended four shifts ago."

"*I was unconscious for an entire shaoz?*"

Dellao huffed. "I was unconscious for six shifts after she dosed me."

Tironan scowled. "Kinsley didn't d-dose him."

"Thev sa shek!" Raveno gripped Avier's shoulder and attempted to use him as a crutch to reach his sleeping room. "Help me to her. She'll think I skipped, that I am 'procrastinating,' as she says. I must explain and apologize and—why is no one helping me!"

Silence.

Tironan glanced *again* at Avier.

Dellao stared at the ceiling.

Avier met Raveno's eyes—finally!—but his expression was stoic. Raveno knew that look: a soldier who had nothing but bad news to report.

"Sit." Avier's voice was gentle, belying the steel in his grip as he forced Raveno toward the couch. "And I will tell you."

Riley patted the cushion beside him.

"Fine." Raveno sat. "Now, report."

"Kinsley is not here."

Raveno massaged his eyes. "I know she must be furious, and I

361

also know how formidable she can be when provoked, but you can't just let her wander the hallways. The ushelz—"

"'Let' her." Riley snorted. "As if anyone *lets* Switch do anything."

"We're in a precarious enough situation without taking unnecessary risks." Why did this even need saying?

Avier covered his eyes.

"What?" Raveno snapped.

Tironan nudged Avier. "Just s-say it."

"If it's so easy to say," Avier muttered from behind his hand, "then *you* say it."

"I order someone to say it!"

"She's not your shols," Riley said, clearly feasting on everyone's anguish.

Raveno slouched into the couch. "I'm out for a few shifts and you develop a sense of humor. Wonderful." If they were joking, the situation must not be as dire as their expressions had led him to believe.

"Since you w-w-weren't there," Tironan said, his voice haunted. "Veilon insisted that the Hoviir ouk didn't claim Kinsley as s-s-strictly yours. I—I—I tried to select her on your behalf, b-b-but—"

Raveno sat up. "Veilon did what?

Tironan winced. "I c-couldn't outbid her."

Raveno turned to Avier.

"In your absence, Veilon selected Kinsley," Avier said, but as slow, clear, and distinct as his voice was, Raveno couldn't comprehend what he was saying.

Raveno turned to Dellao.

He nodded. "Kinsley is now Veilon's Vri Sa Shols."

Raveno scrutinized their reactions, and one by one, Avier, Tironan, and Dellao all met his gaze, equally grim.

Riley discovered a sudden fascination with the underside of his blunt claws.

"Where is she?" Raveno growled.

Tironan blew out a hard breath. "Who knows with V-V-Veilon? You know how she gets w-w-when—"

"*Kinsley!*" Raveno roared. "Where is Kinsley!"

Avier gripped his shoulder. "She's locked in the shols's residential living wing."

Raveno tensed to stand, but he was too weak to fight Avier's hold. Even so, Dellao moved to block the door, and Tironan stepped directly in front of him.

"Release me," Raveno hissed.

Avier's grip didn't waver.

Tironan wrung his hands. "You can't go to h-her. Not yet."

"I order you to—"

"Broadcast System on," Avier commanded. "Security Channel two. Room six."

The Broadcast System flashed, projecting an image of room six, per Avier's command. Kinsley's room, apparently, because there she sat on her bed, her legs crossed in front of her, head bent over a yensha. He narrowed his eyes on the docking station where his own yensha was still charging, and frowned. How had she—

Cresha crossed the room and sat next to Kinsley. She joined Kinsley in studying whatever was displayed on the yensha, their mouths moving.

Kinsley and Cresha. In the same room. Together. Talking.

Raveno collapsed back into the couch and rubbed his eyes. He'd never been more exhausted in his life.

Finally, Avier released him.

Raveno flung an arm at the screen, keeping the other over his eyes. "What is Cresha doing in there?"

"They're talking."

"That I can see! She didn't even loop the feed!"

"Sh-sh-she probably doesn't know the r-room is bugged."

Raveno glowered at the projection through the bars of his claws. "What could they possibly be talking about?"

"Similar to his f-f-frugalness while modifying *Sa Vivsheth,* J-J-Josairo didn't invest in audio m-m-monitoring systems when he converted the arena's guest accommodations into holding cells."

Tironan flicked his eyes sideways at Raveno. "So we d-d-don't know what they're s-saying."

Raveno glared at Tironan. "Tell me something I don't know."

"The only thing they have in common to talk about is you," Riley offered.

Raveno groaned. That, he also knew.

"Although Kinsley might not be located where you want her, she's alive and well. You, however, I discovered unconscious on your living suite floor." Avier ordered the projection off and sat on the couch beside Raveno. "What do you remember after Tironan escorted Kinsley to the arena?"

Raveno shook his head, still staring at the air where Kinsley had been projected a moment before. "Riley and I spoke a few words, I can't even recall the topic, and then I woke up on the floor, surrounded by you and this mess."

Avier straightened. "You spoke a few words to Riley?"

"Yes."

"Y-y-you spoke to him here in this r-r-relaxation room?"

"Yes." Raveno frowned in thought. "Kinsley left with Tironan, and then I spoke to Riley. He was leaning against the couch, charming as always. I must have been attacked from behind."

"You're certain?" Avier leaned in. "Because you just said you couldn't recall your conversation."

"I can't recall our exact words, but he was here. Annoying me with his complaints."

Tironan and Dellao peered up at Avier, but Avier was glaring at Riley.

"What am I missing?" Raveno asked, annoyed that he even had to ask.

"If you were attacked from behind while you were talking to Riley, then Riley should have seen your attacker," Avier said flatly. "But according to Riley, he was in the sleeping room during your attack."

Raveno turned slowly.

Riley was slumped against the couch, arms crossed. He met Raveno's eyes. "You're mistaken. I was in my room."

If Raveno could, he would raise an eyebrow. Just the one. "You were here in the relaxation room. Standing right there." Raveno pointed a claw at the other side of the couch.

Riley shook his head. "I heard a thud from my room, and when I came out to investigate, you were already unconscious on the floor, the room empty."

"You were facing the door as we spoke." Raveno said, realizing the truth even as Riley lied straight to his face. "You saw who came in."

"You were drugged. You can't trust your memories."

"No matter Kinsley's assurances, I obviously can't trust *you*."

Riley bobbed his shoulders. "The feeling's mutual."

"I've trained you to fight. I've taught you Haveo," Raveno growled. "Despite my better judgment, I've included you in this mission. And this is how you repay my trust?"

"I couldn't give a shit-soaked svik about you or your mission," Riley said with a smile. His expression was nearly as grating as his perfect Haveo. "Kinsley may have let herself forget that you're the enemy, but I never will."

Avier sighed wearily.

Tironan stiffened.

Dellao kept one eye on Raveno, the other on Riley, and his hand on his pivz.

Raveno laughed. The sound hurt his throat. "The purpose of the mission you care so little about is to gain your freedom and return you to Earth."

Riley snorted. "The purpose of your mission is to kill your father. Our freedom is just a happy byproduct."

"That's not true."

"If you truly cared about Kinsley, you would let her go and finish your mission solo." He jabbed a finger at Raveno. "But you want her for yourself more than you want her freedom."

"I gave her the choice, and she chose to help with this mission."

Riley cocked his head. "One of her choices was to return to Earth?"

"I plan to. After—"

"*Before* getting your revenge?"

Raveno gritted his teeth. "Who attacked me?"

Riley looked him square in the eyes, grinned that annoying grin, and bobbed his shoulders.

Raveno rubbed his eyes and regretted—not for the first time or, he was sure, the last—that he'd only *faked* Riley's death.

Dellao shifted his weight.

"Something to say, Dellao?" Raveno asked.

"If Riley saw your attacker, then your attacker likely saw him," Dellao said. When everyone only stared blankly at Dellao, he added. "And they left Riley here. Alive. Even after Riley saw their face."

Raveno felt his ears burn down to his cheeks. He faced Riley. "Who are you working for?"

Avier slapped his face. "Not this again."

"G-g-good job," Tironan hissed at Dellao.

"It's possible!"

"I was in the bedroom," Riley stubbornly insisted, but his grin died. "I didn't see who attacked you, and whoever attacked you didn't see me. If you don't believe me, burn me. Again. That's sure to get you on Switch's good side." And with that, he rose from the couch and padded to his room.

Dellao lunged forward in pursuit, but Raveno lifted a stalling hand. "Don't."

"He's lying."

"I know."

"He saw who attacked you, and—"

"And short of torturing the information from him, we've exhausted our efforts on Riley." Raveno sighed.

"But—"

"You want to burn him alive this time?" Raveno snapped.

Dellao closed his mouth with a *clack*.

"Once we have Kinsley back, we'll continue this investigation. Until then, we need to focus on her."

Tironan's eyes darted to Avier, and Avier sighed at the ceiling.

Dellao nodded. "Your will by my hands," he said, but he was the only one.

THIRTY-THREE

Kinsley lay back flat on the couch and scrubbed her face, trying to work up a good rage at her latest predicament—kidnapped on a strange planet, her mission unraveling, and caged in nearly the same circumstances as she'd begun those twelve long months ago, having been *abducted by aliens*—because rage was infinitely more palatable than the emotion she was currently feeling. But the rage wouldn't come, not as sick and fierce and immediate as it used to. Not when her heart was already sick for an entirely different reason.

The door's lock was unbreakable and unpickable. She'd tried both with the limited supplies at her disposal and failed. The incineration shaft over her bed had a bolted cover blocking the vent, and those bolts weren't just screwed on tight; they'd been soldered permanently in place. She didn't have a weapon or the means to create one. She couldn't communicate with her havari allies, Riley, or her fellow humans—not that they'd be much help, but it would have been *something* to work with.

Something would have been better than nothing.

Kinsley glared at the ceiling, at those soldered bolts anchoring the incineration shaft's vent cover firmly in place, and steadfastly ignored the tears slipping down her temples.

The closet was just a closet.

Raveno hadn't intended to miss Selections.

If he'd been attacked, even if she wasn't too late, she didn't have the means to find and save him.

She groaned and scrubbed her face harder. She should be more concerned about saving herself! About the fact that had she accepted Cresha's offer, she might be rocketing back to Earth at this very moment. Toward beer and fresh air and bright skies and freedom. Toward Reece and that overdue apology. Sunshine. T-shirts and sweatpants. Chili cheese fries!

And away from Raveno.

Assuming she hadn't already lost him.

Kinsley covered her mouth, as if she could physically push the panic back down her throat. She needed to calm down and reexamine her options, damn it. She needed—

The latch whirred and beeped. The door slid open with a swish.

"Forget a thing?" Kinsley muttered in Haveo from behind her hands. She'd worked up a great wallow and didn't particularly want to see Cresha's perfect hair and gorgeous eyes again.

A pair of muscular arms wrapped around her shoulders, bringing the bright scent of eucalyptus and oranges.

Kinsley startled upright. "Raveno?"

His breath was ragged against her ear. "Kinsley."

"Raveno!" She struggled to see his face, but he'd buried it in her neck. "Are you okay? What happened?"

He inhaled deeply, lingering a moment.

She gripped his forearms, the only part of him she could reach, and squeezed. He was trembling. "Raveno?"

He stood, walked around the couch, and sat on the cushion beside her. His eyes darted down her body. "You're unharmed?"

"I'm fine. But you—"

"What's this?" He swiped his thumbs across her cheek and exam-

369

ined the slick of her tears. She'd have interpreted the twitch of his lips as amusement if only his eyes weren't bright and welling too. "I worried for you as well."

Kinsley swatted at his finger, and that lip twitch tipped to amusement, thank God. "What happened? Did something detain you?"

"Not something. Someone." Raveno caught her hand and held it, his fingers still wet, but warm and capable and *here*. "After everyone left my suite, I was attacked from behind, Kinsley-style."

"Meaning what?"

"Avier hasn't finished processing my blood sample, but he's confident that I was drugged."

"Drugged." Kinsley leaned forward. "With svirros?"

"So it would seem."

She scanned his body, forcing her eyes over his flexing neck and shapely chest and bulging biceps without lingering overlong on any one linger-worthy feature. "But you're okay?"

"I'm fine."

She raised her eyebrows.

He smirked, decidedly amused this time. "My version of fine, not yours."

She caressed the textured ridge of his palm and savored the hard flex of his jaw as his teeth clenched at her touch. Yes, had she accepted Cresha's offer, she might be rocketing back to Earth at this very moment.

Thank God I didn't accept.

"What did your attacker take?" Kinsley asked.

Raveno tipped his head. "Take?"

"From your apartment. While you were unconscious."

"Ah. Nothing." The vein at his temple ticked. "I believe their intent was for me to miss Selections."

She frowned. "Why?"

"It's not as if my desire for you as my Vri Sa Shols was a secret. Someone knew the perfect way to wedge between my scales, desired to do so, and succeeded."

Kinsley shook her head. "More than that, someone knows how I attacked your crew on *Sa Vivsheth*."

"I considered that, but we scrubbed the brig's security footage, and the crew was unconscious from svirros," he reasoned. "How would anyone know? Unless..." His expression blanked. "I refuse to consider the possibility that Avier, Tironan, or Dellao are traitors."

"Agreed. But maybe someone else on your crew remembers more from that day than they let on. People talk."

The tips of his ears began to glow in earnest. "What did you and Cresha talk about while I was unconscious?"

"How do you... I knew it!" Kinsley glared around the room. "Where is it?"

"Where is what?"

"The security camera."

"Where else?" Raveno pointed a claw at the incineration shaft.

Kinsley flipped off whoever was watching.

"Tironan is looping the feed at the moment," he said, amused.

"I don't care. It makes me feel better." Kinsley dropped her hand on a sigh and flicked one of his warrior braids. "Better brace yourself. My conversation with Cresha was a whopper."

"I am unfamiliar with this 'whopper,' but there is little you could say that I have not already imagined." He cringed. "Just confess."

"Cresha offered to smuggle me off Havar and return me to Earth."

Raveno blinked with both his inner and outer eyelids and continued staring. Guess he hadn't imagined that.

"When I refused," Kinsley continued, "she assumed I couldn't bear to leave my people behind, so she offered to steal a carrier vessel to return *all* the humans to Earth."

Raveno flopped back on the couch, slapping both hands over his face. "Arrrggggh!"

"I told you to brace yourself."

"She knows I'd be forced to pursue her!"

"Yep, she said as much," Kinsley said, still reluctantly impressed by Cresha's grit. "But she was willing to risk it anyway."

"That's not a risk. That's a suicide mission!"

"I know." Kinsley crossed her arms. "Because you'd be the one killing us."

"You'd be forcing my hand! Making me choose between maintaining my cover to overthrow Josairo or—"

"Or overthrowing him without the on- and off-world allies that you need. *I know.*"

Raveno stared at her from between his claws, his ears blue, his vresls throbbing, the vein across his temple pulsing. "Why didn't you accept her offer? It's everything you've ever wanted. At this very moment, you could have been boarding a vessel bound for Earth, saving your ungrateful humans, and escaping this wretched planet and me."

"You think I didn't consider it?" Kinsley leaned over him. "You think that every word out of her mouth wasn't everything I wanted to hear? That it wasn't everything I've been dreaming of hearing *you* offer me?"

Raveno's vresls rubbed together like sandpaper.

"I gave you my word. I promised, no more plotting against you and no more secret missions. We're a team, you and I," she said, poking his chest. "We have a mission, and I intend to see it through. And I—" Kinsley snapped her mouth shut, her heart throbbing in her throat.

Raveno's vresls perked. "And you?"

"And that's all I have to say about it. Besides," she forged ahead, forcing out a snorting laugh. "My luck, Cresha's a double agent for Josairo just trying to get me to admit we're planning his assassination."

Raveno shook his head. "Cresha's not a double agent. She'd never serve Josairo, not in any capacity."

Kinsley shrugged. "Did you think she'd offer me a suicide escape mission?"

Raveno's vein continued throbbing.

"Maybe you don't know Cresha as well as you think."

"I know her to her core."

"You *knew* her. And then you broke her heart, right?"

Raveno grimaced, nodding.

"That changes a person."

"Maybe." He dropped his hands from his face and relaxed back to muse at the ceiling. "But if what you just said is true, that she offered to help you and all the humans escape despite devastating odds against her, then perhaps she hasn't changed much at all."

Kinsley pursed her lips, wondering why the hell the admiration in his voice made her want to vomit.

"What did you tell her?" he asked.

"About what?"

"Your excuse for refusing her offer?"

"I told her the truth."

Raveno sat up and met her eyes. "The truth?"

Kinsley nodded. "I told her that I wasn't the first person abducted for havari entertainment, but I intended to be the last. To prove her sincerity, she helped me search through the IF financials. Which *you* were supposed to do. But you were busy, you know"—Kinsley wrinkled her nose—"getting drugged unconscious."

He hesitated at that. "The IF?"

"'Intergalactic Frisaes' is a bit of a mouthful, don't you think?"

"You think everything in Havao a mouthful." Raveno rubbed his forehead, and his laugh sounded just as painful as hers had been. "Svik!"

"We don't have to abbreviate its name if you feel *that* strongly about it."

Raveno waved his hand dismissively. "Cresha thinks that you're planning *my* assassination, and she's just"—his arm whipped out, gesturing to everything and nothing—"she's just going to let it happen. Worse, she's aiding and abetting you!"

373

"Better than aiding and abetting me off Havar and back to Earth!"

"Cry mercy," Raveno begged the ceiling.

"Ask me the best part."

"None of this is for the best," he grumbled.

"I determined who's benefiting financially from the IF's corruption." Honesty made her add, "Kind of."

"Explain this 'kind of'?" Raveno crossed his arms, the closest he'd ever come to petulance.

Kinsley steadfastly did not notice the strain of his muscles against his strappy gladiator gear. "Examining the IF's event-over-event profits from the events that were legitimate to present, the profits have remained roughly the same, but for the last two thesh, the investment of those profits has changed. Instead of reinvesting in the next IF, all the profits from the previous event were invested in something called a... vreeshelly?"

"Vriusheli," Raveno said, correcting her pronunciation. "They're a botanical organization dedicated to the research of ushelz. It's a play on words, literally translating to 'a hand of ushelz.'"

"They research the Twoeys?"

"The ushelz. Yes."

"Why would money from the IF be legitimately invested in such a company?"

Raveno shrugged. "The ushelz are an integral part of the ceremonies. Investing in their upkeep is not such a stretch. What concerns me is that the Intergalactic Frisaes's profits haven't increased. You're certain of this? Not even since Josairo began projecting himself?"

"I'm positive, *and* supposedly Josairo hasn't noticed *with his all-seeing eye* that his Vri Shavril are lying to him about those nonexistent profits?" Kinsley tsked her forefinger. "Why would Josairo, the mastermind behind the IF's illegitimacy, *not* be intimately familiar with its financials?"

"Unless Josairo and the Vri Shavrili are both benefiting financially from the Intergalactic Frisaes." Raveno shook his head. "But that is inconceivable."

"Why? That seems plenty conceivable to me."

"In that scenario, whatever con they're running, they're in on it together. Veilon would have told me."

"Maybe she's not in on it," Kinsley offered. "There's four of them, after all."

"I can't imagine Jzoeshi, Rez, or Sheso conspiring with Josairo behind Veilon's back. She has Josairo's complete confidence."

Kinsley bit her lip. "Then maybe she *is* in on it."

"I will not suspect another sibling of treachery without evidence to support such an accusation," Raveno said hoarsely. "All of this is just speculation."

"And I have more speculation to consider."

Kinsley didn't know which gesture oozed more exasperation: Raveno's rolling eyes or his waffling hand.

"Maybe someone is cleaning the money," she suggested.

"Cleaning...as in washing?"

"Cleaning as in laundering. Money laundering."

"I am unfamiliar with that phrase."

"On Earth, when people sell something illegal, like drugs, they use a legitimate-looking business as a front to avoid the notice of the feds." At Raveno's blank stare, she added, "Our all-seeing eye."

"You think that somewhere on Havar, there's a business that's hiding the Intergalactic Frisaes's corrupt profits as their own legitimate earnings?"

"Yes." Kinsley frowned. "Although why someone would claim there's a profit and then go through the effort of cleaning it doesn't really make sense."

"Whatever their motivations, their efforts have worked for seven thesh."

Kinsley blew her bangs out of her eyes. "We're missing something."

"So we find this cleaning business and interrogate whoever is profiting to discover the full truth."

"Considering the entire purpose of this business is to *hide* the money, I'm not sure how we'd find it."

Raveno dropped his head into his palms. "I do." His vresls bristled, and when he spoke, his voice was more a garbled growl than actual words. "I need to speak to Josairo myself. In person."

Kinsley stilled. "I thought you were worried about his wrath. That he might execute the entire crew for arriving with hundreds fewer shols than ordered."

"I am and he might." Raveno slumped so far down into the cushion that he was nearly lying down. "But now I'm wondering why he hasn't done *anything*. He hasn't welcomed me in person, not to bait my wrath nor to take pleasure in outright punishment. I must tread cautiously, but I can't continue avoiding this confrontation." He rubbed his eyes. "Perhaps I can use the financials as leverage to protect the crew."

Who will protect you? Kinsley took Raveno's hands and pulled them from his face before he cut himself on his own claws. "Maybe we should focus on the man *behind* the curtain instead of the projection in front of it."

Raveno held on tight. "What curtain?"

Kinsley leaned back with him, so they were shoulder to shoulder. "It's from a movie. A city is ruled by an all-powerful, terrifying wizard, but in the end, the wizard was just an illusion, a projection, controlled by an ordinary man hidden behind a curtain."

"A curtain is a piece of hanging fabric, yes?" Raveno asked, baffled. "Could the city's citizens not simply pull the fabric back to break the illusion?"

"They were too scared to question what had always been."

"Josairo hasn't always been a projection."

"Only someone with fresh eyes could see that something was wrong."

"We have no curtains. How does this pertain to us and our mission?"

Kinsley sighed. His stubbornness knew no bounds! "Stop being so literal. Who controls the projections?"

"The projectionist. He sets up the live projection, so that—"

"But Josairo's projection isn't live."

Raveno startled. "What do you mean it's not live?"

"At Selections, it was pretty clear that the projection was prerecorded. Josairo's speech and movements and mannerisms were all the same as the Welcome Ceremony. *Exactly* the same." She leaned forward. "Identical. No one could manage that precision of sameness."

Raveno stared at her—stunned? seething?—but she wasn't certain how to read the intensity in his expression.

Kinsley swallowed. "So...does Josairo give the projectionist the prerecorded message himself?"

"I—" Raveno's gaze drifted to study the wall. "I don't know."

Kinsley firmed her grip on his hands. "This is what I'm thinking. If talking about the financials becomes too dicey during your meeting with Josairo, ask him which of his Vri Shavrili advised him to continue using projections at public events. Tell him you want their help to further improve viewership and ratings and you need them to... I don't know, to pull an analytics report for you. Something that reveals who's giving the false reports without incriminating them in case they're just a pawn. And without incriminating yourself."

Raveno smoothed his thumbs across her knuckles. "That might work," he murmured. He turned his head, and suddenly, their foreheads were inches apart. "You're such a pivz."

Kinsley blinked. "Excuse me?"

"Practical. Unassuming." He smirked. "Capable of wedging right between the scales."

"Good thing I'm on your side, then, huh?"

"I may not be the aim of your strike, but I am still slain," Raveno murmured, slipping into English.

Oh, but his irises were like liquid fire. Both their color and their heat, which scalded through her veins at his attention. Kinsley licked her lips, suddenly, unaccountably self-conscious.

Raveno's eyes dropped to her mouth. All four of his thumbs rubbed across her knuckles, and the shiver that jolted through her body was electric. Four thumbs. Christ, she should be freaking out. Four thumbs, claws, scales, a forked tongue and snake eyes and flapping chest frill and...

He was Raveno.

And he was alive.

She might or might not have survived this mission without him, but for the first time, she knew without a shadow of doubt that she wouldn't want to.

For eight months he'd kept his word, training her in hand-to-hand combat, teaching her Haveo, and acting on her advice. For eight months, Kinsley had bided her time, waiting for his actions to live up to his words. Waiting for all his plans—*their* plans, now—to result in her freedom.

I may not be the aim of your strike, but I am still slain.

What if his attacker had dosed him with the intention to kill? What was the point of waiting on freedom if it meant stopping herself from living?

Who was keeping her caged now?

You must be the one to kiss me, she recalled him saying.

Heaven help her. Kinsley bridged the distance between them and pressed her mouth to his.

Raveno's entire body stiffened. His thumbs froze, ceasing their hypnotic touch, and for a crazy moment, Kinsley thought he might pull away.

He did. He released her hands.

Her heart throbbed.

He cupped her jaw in both palms, returning her kiss, and Kinsley moaned against the twin bars of his hard fangs behind his soft lips.

How was it possible to feel so much frustration and still so much desire simultaneously? For one person? Everything about Raveno was maddening. Skin covered in scales shouldn't be this smooth. Someone consumed by so much bitterness shouldn't taste so sweet. A mouth filled with such lethal fangs shouldn't respond with such sensitive care. The friction of his dualities had always rubbed Kinsley raw, but if she was honest with herself, and him, that rawness felt just right.

Kinsley slanted her mouth, deepening the kiss.

He mimicked her movements—the caress of her tentative touch, the lingering press of her parted lips, that slow swipe of her tongue, teasing, encouraging, savoring—and her breath hitched.

Oh, that tongue!

She attempted to unbuckle one of his chest straps, but he cupped the back of her head and tilted her face to nuzzle her neck. His tongue lashed out and danced across her collarbone.

Incredible, how skin could simultaneously burn and shiver. Could scales?

She skimmed her nails down the tendon of his neck, taking an unhealthy amount of pleasure in his immediate, visceral response: the clench of his teeth, the surrender of his groan, the flex of his grasping hands.

His chest frill flared out and quivered.

Yes!

She tried unbuckling his chest straps again, but her fingers were trembling, distracted by his caresses—around her ears, down her neck, across her chest—but when he reached her breasts, he hesitated.

She opened her eyes and met his gaze.

His nostrils flared, obviously hoping. Hovering. But waiting.

She smiled and nodded.

He cupped her breast, or rather, the molded leather cup of her uniform. She nearly laughed—as if she'd feel anything through the padded cups!—and then he used just the perfect amount of pressure to clamp her nipple between his knuckles even with her uniform between them. Oh! Lightning zipped from her breasts through her body, pulsing in her pelvis, lighting her skin, burning her toes. Her head lolled back on a moan of seismic proportions.

She was loud, embarrassingly loud, except for the fact that his neck was still rattling like a maraca on crack. Apparently, they were both beyond shame, beyond thought, beyond excuses and boundaries and—

Oh, just screw his damn buckles! Kinsley reached under his gladiator skirt, pushed aside his leathery shorts and wrapped her hand around...

"Thev sa shek!"

Kinsley was definitely holding a penis in her hand. Its shape was familiar, if jarringly large, and positioned between his legs, as anticipated, but she wasn't certain of the jutting appendage *above* his penis. By feel alone, she couldn't quite understand what was touching the back of her hand. Similar to the penis *in* her hand, the appendage was slick scales wrapping steel. It was the same cylindrical shape, the same generous size, the same...

Did Raveno have two...

Raveno jerked back, removing himself from her curious grip. He wedged a hand between them and blurted in Haveo, "Stop! Please, stop."

Kinsley couldn't quite comprehend his words, let alone the meaning behind them. She was riveted by the sight of his hand on her chest, holding her at bay, and the sudden realization that perhaps his thumbs weren't the only twin appendages on his body.

THIRTY-FOUR

SWEET MUSK. SMOOTH SMOKE. A BITE OF SPICE.

The scent had exploded from her and surrounded him, first in the air, then on him, and finally *in* him before he'd even realized that he'd inhaled. He'd cleared his nose twice now and sealed his nostrils, but cry mercy, his head was still swimming. His heart was still beating in sync with hers, his groin throbbing in hopeful anticipation. Her hands were at her sides—he could see them with his own eyes, her fingers lightly curled in her lap—yet her grip was still upon him. He chuckled humorlessly: a phantom grip.

Svik, he craved her more than he craved air.

Kinsley seemed strangely consumed by the sight of his hand holding her at bay. Considering the liberties that hand had just taken, he couldn't imagine why she was so riveted by its current position on her stomach.

Maybe she was just as lust high? As far as he knew, humans didn't crave scent as intensely as havari, but maybe something else about him had her drugged into distraction.

His vresls rattled, unaccountably pleased by the notion.

Her hair certainly looked how he felt: ragged, yanked lopsided, and disheveled. He'd mussed her tidy braids. He was the cause of her tousled confusion. For the first time in his entire life, he observed complete disarray and felt a swell of pride.

If only he could finish what she'd started.

His heart throbbed along with his body, but he ignored both, waiting for her senses and sense to return.

Eventually, longer than he'd expected—a second source of pride —Kinsley returned to herself. She leaned back, seeming to shake free of whatever mental grip his hand had held, and refocused on him. "Why are we stopping?"

Svik, for the life of him, he couldn't hold her gaze. As it was, even with his eyes riveted to the wall beside her head, he could still feel the tips of his ears blaze on either side of his head.

The skin between her brows wrinkled. "Is something wrong?"

As she appeared unlikely to re-embrace his person, Raveno dropped his hand from her stomach. "I haven't been intimate with anyone since Cresha."

"But you and Cresha broke up, like, years ago."

"Seven thesh ago to be exact."

"You haven't had, er, *been intimate with* anyone in seven thesh?"

Could his ears possibly blush any hotter and not boil his brain? "Correct, and until your hand was upon me, I didn't realize that I... that I hadn't...that I'm not quite ready."

Kinsley peered down at his hand still cupping his groin. "You felt plenty ready to me."

"Ha! In that way, I've been ready long before now, but you don't know certain differences about me, my body, and our customs. I've had the benefit of Zethus and his research to understand you, and I didn't realize until you took me in hand that you didn't understand—" He chortled. "How could you..."

Kinsley slapped her hands over her mouth. "I didn't obtain your consent," she whispered.

"What?"

"You obtained my consent to touch my breast, but I just grabbed your penis. I didn't ask—"

"It's not that." *If only it was that.* "When we are intimate, you may grab my penis without asking first. In fact, I encourage it."

Kinsley's lip twitched. *"When* we're intimate?"

"Yes, when. I just need time. I must educate you on a few havari customs, but at the moment..." He pressed the heel of his palm into his groin and winced. "I am not ready."

Her eyes flicked down to his hand. "It has something to do with me grabbing you."

"Yes," he admitted. "But not anything to do with obtaining my consent. You already have it."

Kinsley frowned. "Raveno..."

Perhaps he shouldn't have said anything. Perhaps he should have let her live in ignorance and simply endured her touch rather than risk losing it entirely.

"When you didn't show up for Selections, I was terrified."

"I'm sorry," Raveno groaned. "I should have been there for you. I—"

"I was terrified that something had happened to *you.*"

His vresls perked. He hadn't expected this turn of conversation.

"Nothing short of death would keep you from our mission, and attending the Selection Ceremony was the mission. I thought—" Her voice hitched.

Raveno leaned forward. "You thought I might be dead?"

"It was a thought." Kinsley laughed up at the ceiling. "There was a time when I'd not only wanted you dead, I'd dreamed of being the person to trip the switch!"

Of course, Kinsley's revenge fantasy was to blow him up. "But now?"

"Losing you felt like a physical wound." Her eyes darted to his prosthetic leg. "Like losing a piece of myself. And not because of how devastating losing you would be to the mission and my hope of returning home. Losing you would be devastating of its own accord.

To me." Kinsley reached out—slowly this time, as if waiting on his permission—and squeezed his hand. "However long it takes until you're ready to share your Havari customs with me is nothing compared to the eternity I endured thinking you might be dead. I'm happy to wait. To..." She blushed. "Anticipate."

Kinsley's dark eyes seemed to see through his scales, through his skull and brain to his very core. Never had someone expressed such feelings for him and their feelings so mirror his own.

"So." Kinsley cleared her throat. "We do have a pressing problem, a *mission* problem, we have yet to address."

Raveno spread his arms wide. "I have many ears."

"The phrase is *I'm all ears.*"

"At least I-m *trying* to speak your language," he said sweetly.

She scrunched her nose. "You may not have heard, but without you in attendance, Veilon selected me. I'm your sister's Vri Sa Shols."

Raveno released a hard breath. "I heard."

"If we don't overthrow your father in three days—shaoz—and put a stop to the IF, I'll be facing your sister in a public fight *to the death.*"

He scowled at her, feeling the heat of rage war in equal measure with fear beneath his scales. "I will not let that happen."

"Unless we trust her enough to tell her the truth about your mission and convince her to throw the fight, I'm dead."

"Not necessarily. Next shift, when you spar with Veilon in preparation for the public Sparring Ceremony, get a feel for her technique. Her strengths and weaknesses. I've trained both of you, and I assure you, she's not as good as me."

"But better than me, I'm sure," Kinsley laughed darkly. "She's won frisaes before to earn her place as Vri Shavril. She's *killed* before, Raveno."

His ears blazed. "Yes. We all have."

"And she's planning to kill again: me."

"Not during a sparring session, she won't. And after your sparring session, we still have the Sparring Ceremony and the Remembrance Ceremony before the actual frisaes."

Kinsley scrubbed her face. "Jesus, all your fucking ceremonies."

"Yes, praise your deliverer from sins, because such ceremonies give us precious time. While you occupy Veilon, I'll meet with Josairo about his projections. I'll determine which Vri Shavril is cleaning the financials and root out who is benefiting from the IF." Raveno tipped her chin up with a coaxing finger and smoothed several of her untamable locks of hair back into their braids. "We will figure this out *before* your frisaes with Veilon. I promise."

Kinsley closed her mouth, dropped her hands, and nodded, but her lips compressed as if she'd accidentally swallowed a vespers whole.

Not the reaction he'd been attempting to inspire. "Speak the words before you choke on them."

Kinsley's face twisted uncomfortably. "What if Veilon is the Vri Shavril cleaning the financials?"

Raveno shook his head. "She doesn't know the Intergalactic Frisaes is corrupt."

"You claim havari citizens aren't close enough to see our chains. But she is. She's not a helpless citizen at the mercy of her government. She *is* the government."

"Josairo maimed Veilon's eardrums because she didn't win a frisaes in a manner acceptable to his standards," Raveno growled. "Helpless citizen or not, we are *all* at his mercy."

"Raveno—"

"If she knows about the IF's corruption—*if*—then she's just like anyone else who may suspect that terrible truth—too terrified to do anything about it."

"That's possible," Kinsley conceded, but when she sandwiched his hands in hers, he could tell the concession was words without feeling. "It's also possible that she likes her comfortable life and has decided to look the other way."

"No." Raveno slipped from grip and crossed his arms. "That's not possible."

"You sound very certain."

"I'd bet my life on it."

"Then why not tell her the truth?"

Because I wouldn't bet your life on it, Raveno thought and scowled. "The same reason I never told Tironan: to protect her. I don't want her dragged down with me should I fail."

"Have you regretted telling Tironan?"

He compressed his lips, refusing to acquiesce.

She lifted her eyebrows. "Maybe it's time to trust your sister as much as you do your brother."

"Maybe," Raveno said, but his vresls bristled.

"That's a no." Kinsley rolled her eyes. "What if I tell her—"

His chest flap snapped out so fast it ached.

"—that I've been abducted against my will, just to see how she reacts. Then we'll know whether she already knows and how she feels about it."

Raveno's throbbing temple intensified to stabbing. "What if she guesses the truth of my plot to kill our father?"

"That would be quite a leap of logic," Kinsley argued. "Cresha didn't guess the truth. She knows about your undercover mission, and she *still* thinks you abducted me against my will."

"I did."

"*My point is,* that if your ex-wife, who knows your true motives regarding Josairo, still believes you're capable of being an evil, kidnapping bastard, then so will your sister!"

Raveno slid his hand to cover his eyes and laughed. "How far I've fallen that this is what we're hoping for!"

"You've played your part well."

Raveno groaned.

"If I reveal myself as the sad, stolen person that I am, Veilon should have a similar reaction to the news as Cresha. Right?"

Raveno grunted noncommittally from behind his hand.

"And then, having confirmed that both Cresha and Veilon have hearts of gold, you can tell them the full truth about your mission and gain two powerful on-world allies, killing two birds with one stone."

Raveno dropped his hand and met her eyes. "What are we doing to birds with stones?"

"Er, it's just another bird idiom. It means you'll only have to confess the one time to two people. Easy peasy."

Despite her nonsensical rhyme at the end, her plan was logical, as her plans usually were, but Raveno couldn't stop shaking his head.

"You need allies." She placed her small hand on his leg, and although it was his knee that she squeezed, his heart felt her touch. "If you can't even tell your ex-wife, who already knows the truth, and your sister, who else are you going to trust?"

Gah! More logic! "Yes! Fine! You're correct!"

"I know."

"Reveal to Veilon that you're not a willing competitor in the IF, but that's it." Raveno pointed a claw at her. "Do not reveal the truth of our relationship nor our mission. Just observe and report her reaction to me after your sparring session."

Kinsley raised her fingertips to her forehead. "Sir, yes, sir."

Raveno frowned, but before he could reply, his anku vibrated. "Avier to Raveno. Do you receive?"

"Signal received," he said, still glaring at Kinsley. "Proceed."

"Josairo has assigned guards to patrol the residential hallways during first shift."

Raveno startled upright. "*Now* is first shift."

"Affirmative."

"He's never assigned guards to this quadrant of the arena before. How would the shols even escape? Why would—"

"Would we have thought an escape possible on *Sa Vivsheth*?"

Raveno ground his teeth. "No, but it's as if someone knows they tried."

"We can debate that *after* you're out of her room."

Avier cut the signal, and Raveno turned to her. "I need to—"

She stood and shoved him toward the door. "Yeah, I got the gist. Go before your guards find you fraternizing with your sister's Vri Sa Shols."

387

Raveno dug in his heels. "Are you ready to spar with Veilon?"

"Are you ready to confront your father?"

"Fair enough." Raveno shooed away her pushy hands. "Remember your training, and you'll be fine. Rely on your instincts rather than your eyes. You've got great instincts. Do not strike her. Strike *through* her."

"I know."

"Anticipate her movements, and if you can, improvise around them. And—"

"If you weren't able to teach me the basics in eight months, what makes you think a one-minute reminder will make any difference?"

Raveno hissed. "Her preference is the five-blade, even though she fights better with the ten, and she knows it, some nonsense about tradition, but don't let her sway you. Stick with the three. Even though she'll beat you in reach, it fits better in your hand."

"Raveno—"

"But if she's come to her senses in the last two thesh and picks up a ten, you pick up a ten too." He puffed out a breath. "You strike first and fast, and you end the fight as quickly as possible. You're strong, but the stamina required to sustain a long fight with the ten is beyond you."

Kinsley punched her fists onto her hips. "You do realize that you're giving me advice on how to kill your sister?"

Raveno shook his head. "I'm giving you advice on how to survive sparring with her."

THIRTY-FIVE

TRAINING ROOMS ON HAVAR WERE AT LEAST DOUBLE THE SIZE of the one Kinsley was accustomed to on *Sa Vivsheth*, but the room's layout was nearly identical. A fully stocked weapons rack lined the far wall. The floor was covered—one hesitated to say *cushioned*—by mats that supposedly eased the impact of being slammed to the ground. Fresh towels were folded and stacked next to a sink beside the weapons rack, and a vacuum bin for used towels was built into the wall above the sink.

Granted, it wasn't the same room, but memories of those training sessions with Raveno came flooding back. They'd sparred on *that* center mat when she'd slipped a strike past his unbreachable defenses and managed, for the first and only time, to pierce his scales. They'd stood next to *that* sink when he'd poked and prodded her injured elbow in his best imitation of a medical exam. They might have kissed for the first time, right *there* instead of in the brig, had Avier not interrupted.

Oh, the good ol' days when she was merely trying to commandeer an alien spaceship instead of an entire planet! She'd thought herself so clever, planning to turn all of Raveno's teachings against him, and look at her now, nearly right back where she'd begun, on a sparring mat with an alien who might or might not care if she'd been kidnapped.

If she hadn't been cuffed, she would have felt right at home.

The training room was nearly pitch-black. Someone had graciously activated the illuminators lining the floorboards. The room wasn't as bright as she'd prefer, but neither was it as dark as she was accustomed to.

As I'm accustomed to. Kinsley shook her head. *When did that happen?*

She supposed she could thank Raveno for all the many beatings—one hesitated to call them *sparrings*—he'd forced her to endure nearly blind.

Jhoni stood sentinel beside her, having escorted her through the labyrinth of inner arena hallways to the training room where Veilon had just racked her pivz.

Kinsley squinted, but she couldn't tell which size Veilon had been warming up with.

Jhoni clicked his heels in salute. "Vri Shavril Veilon Hoviir!" he belted out.

Veilon nodded at Jhoni, but as she approached, she addressed Kinsley. "Although Havar has offered an entire ceremony to welcome you, I'd like to extend you my personal welcome. It's an absolute pleasure to meet you and an honor to have you as my Vri Sa Shols, Kinsley Morales."

Kinsley raised an eyebrow. "The pleasure not mine."

Jhoni stiffened.

Veilon's smile faltered slightly. She gestured to the cuff. "Kinsley isn't in the hall anymore. What are you protecting her from in here? Me?"

"I. Ah. Your will by my hands." Jhoni released the laser connection between her cuffed wrists so she could move her arms freely.

"My apologies," Veilon murmured.

Kinsley tipped her head. "Why apologies?"

"For the necessity of using leads to guide you safely through the arena. Our vegetation becomes quite ravenous during our ceremonies."

Kinsley opened her mouth to ask if that accounted for why her room was locked—to keep the plants out?—but Veilon focused on Jhoni. "And how are you?"

Jhoni straightened. "Very well, Vri Shavril. Thank you."

Veilon's gaze flattened. "Please, as I've told you many times, call me Veilon. In weapons training, I remember you calling me much worse."

The corners of Jhoni's lips hitched even as his ears blazed. "You didn't have a title back then."

"But I'm the same person now as I was then," she countered.

Jhoni puffed out his cheeks. "Very well."

She tilted her head, waiting.

"Veilon."

She grinned indulgently. "And Fis? She must be thrilled to have you home after such a long mission."

Jhoni nodded deeply. "Especially now that she—" Jhoni bit his lip.

Veilon leaned forward. "Out with it. She what?"

"It's still early. I wasn't supposed to say anything."

"Yet you already have."

Jhoni bit his lip. "She's expecting."

Veilon clasped her hands together under her chin. "She's pregnant?"

Jhoni's watchful expression split into a wide smile. "Yes. Our first."

"Oh! Congratulations!" Veilon closed the remaining distance between them, which admittedly wasn't much, and wrapped her arms around Jhoni with the same leaping joy she'd thrown at Raveno and Tironan upon their return.

Jhoni returned her hug, and despite the formality of his address a moment ago, the movement was natural. Familiar. Friendly. They'd hugged before. "Thank you."

"Give Fis my best." She pulled back and squeezed his shoulders. "We should plan a celebratory dinner. My treat."

"Fis would love that. *After* she tells you herself. I didn't breathe a word of it."

"Breathe a word of what?" Veilon winked.

Winked!

Kinsley stared at them, dumbfounded by Veilon's charm and Jhoni's oozing respect and warmth. Jhoni had been nothing but nerves, ineptitude, and dour duty on *Sa Vivsheth*. Two hundred and thirty-one shaoz of training side by side with him, and she hadn't even known he'd had a partner waiting for him at home, let alone that they were trying for a child. Did Raveno?

Veilon inclined her head. "Thank you, Jhoni. You're dismissed."

Jhoni clicked his heels and left the training room.

"Now," Veilon clapped her hands. "Time for some fun."

Kinsley raised her eyebrows. *Fun?*

Veilon strode to the weapons rack, practically skipping. "Select the pivz of your choice. Personally, I've always been partial to the traditional five-blade."

As expected. Well, no time like the present. "You know I the only human having pivz preference, yes?" she asked in Haveo.

Veilon picked up two five-blades and hefted them, testing their balance, one in each palm. "Everyone has a preference."

"I the only *human* with preference."

"And why is that?" Veilon flipped both pivz in the air. The blades rotated midair before both hilts fell flawlessly back into her palms.

"I the only human who train to fight. My people taken from home. Abducted," Kinsley waited a moment to let that sink in. "We not want to be here."

Veilon's vivid lime-green eyes remained riveted on the blades. In shock? In stunned horror?

"We want to fly home," Kinsley clarified, on the chance that her terrible Haveo was preventing Veilon from understanding.

"You mistake my meaning." Veilon turned, her weapons in hand. "Of the ship full of humans my brother kidnapped, why did he train only you?"

Kinsley swallowed. "You know we kidnapped?"

"As if you're the first. We've had seven welcome ceremonies in which Raveno or another of Josairo's hands has 'escorted' the contestants to our planet." Veilon tilted her head. "Why do you think that is?"

Kinsley blinked.

Veilon waved her pivz on a long-suffering sigh. "Don't get me wrong. I love my brothers dearly, but having them home is like being given saltwater when you're dying of thirst. The very thing you need to survive is finally within your grasp, yet tainted."

"I not understand your meaning." Kinsley hesitated on her next move, not even sure if she was translating Veilon's words let alone her metaphor correctly. "You not like that Raveno kidnap us?"

"I *not like* a lot of things, but at the moment, I have the opportunity to change one thing I *not like*." Veilon approached the mat, no longer skipping. "Select a pivz."

Kinsley approached the weapons rack warily and selected two three-blades, as Raveno had advised. "You know the truth?" She faced Veilon. "And you do nothing?"

Veilon gestured with her pivz, and Kinsley approached the mat in front of her.

"I certainly am doing something." Veilon lifted her arms, one straight out, the other bent at the elbow, prepared to strike. "I'm ensuring that you don't kill my brother."

Kinsley reared back at that. "I not kill your brother."

"Lift your weapons. Bend your knees. Very good."

As soon as Kinsley assumed the ready position, Veilon sprang forward in attack.

Kinsley blocked her first strike, absorbed the impact into a roll just as Raveno had taught her, and pivoted to the side.

Damn, this conversation isn't going well. Kinsley lifted her pivz just in time to block Veilon's second strike.

"I learned from a young age that happiness isn't something you can find," Veilon said, so casual in her tone that she could have been strolling through a meadow instead of trying to spear Kinsley's kidney. "Happiness is a choice."

Kinsley blocked a third strike, her arms already heavy. Had Tironan been going easy on her? Had Raveno?

"And one must protect that which makes them happiest." Veilon pivoted into a drop roll without needing to block. Kinsley anticipated her movement a second too late, and Veilon's pivz pricked Kinsley between the straps of her corset.

Shit!

Veilon jabbed with her pivz in a second, identical strike.

Anticipate her movements, and if you can, improvise around them.

Kinsley ducked and rotated, so the blow glanced off her shoulder strap. It would leave a nasty bruise, and the move didn't allow for a counterattack, but at least she hadn't been stabbed a second time.

Veilon laughed, but the sound was harsh and disbelieving. "He trained you. He really trained you." Veilon advanced on her. "Of all the idiotic—"

Jab to the sternum. Kinsley hopped back but managed to keep her feet.

"—selfish—"

Slice to the carotid. Kinsley threw herself back, Matrix style, and the blade missed her nose by inches. The unforgiving mat slammed the wind from her lungs.

"—short-sighted—"

Pivz to the face. Kinsley tried to roll, but Veilon sat on her, pinning her hips in place.

Oh, the pain in her ribs was exquisite.

Kinsley managed to jerk an inch to the left, and the pivz aimed at her face sliced through a lock of hair and sank into the mat next to her head.

Do not strike her. Strike through her.

Kinsley feigned a stab at Veilon's chest with her right pivz, and as Veilon blocked that strike, Kinsley pounded her other pivz into her back, careful to find the seam and puncture through scales to flesh, but only flesh, not organ.

Veilon stiffened with a screech.

Kinsley rolled over onto Veilon so she was on top. "What if Raveno train me?" Kinsley asked between pants. "Jealous?"

"You don't understand," Veilon said, striking out in defense, but from her prone position, she wasn't as quick. A snake's strike instead of lightning.

"Correct. I not understand. Just speak truth."

"You're too wrapped in your own problems to understand. Or you would have seen the truth for yourself."

"Help me see."

Veilon pounded both pivz in a double strike at Kinsley's chest.

Kinsley blocked the hit with her blades, but Veilon used her momentum to thrust Kinsley off her.

"We all survive in different ways," Veilon said, assuming the ready position.

Kinsley did the same, except where Veilon stood calm and steady, Kinsley barely kept her feet.

"I exercised my brain as hard as my muscles to climb beyond Josairo's reach. He couldn't kill the mind behind his greatest technological advances in intergalactic communication."

Kinsley dodged a jab instead of blocking it, missing an opportunity to strike. Raveno would be screaming at her to anticipate *and* improvise, but just breathing was agony now.

"Tironan exercised his ineptitude to sink below Josairo's notice, and consequently, his judgment. A huge risk, but when Raveno is your brother and protector, effective."

Kinsley managed to squeeze in one strike between dodges, punching *through* just as she was taught, but Veilon anticipated her movement, pivoted, and used Kinsley's missed momentum against her.

She fell into Veilon's blade.

Kinsley peeked down. The pivz was buried up to its hilt in her gut. Yet not bleeding.

Funny, how deep wounds could make you feel like your bones were on fire. Even without any bones in her belly.

Veilon tore the blade from Kinsley stomach.

Ah, now the blood gushed.

Kinsley collapsed. She didn't feel her face hit the mat, although it did—she watched it happen with her own eyes—and it must have hurt. Her teeth rattled. She might have bitten her tongue.

Veilon rolled her to her back and pinned her a second time. "Raveno escaped Josairo's wrath by becoming his greatest weapon. But knowing Raveno, I imagine he's sick of the role he crafted for himself, isn't he? Yes, he's risking that survival. And for what? For you? For love? For a dream future he thinks to make a reality? Ha!"

Shit, Veilon was jumping to conclusions. Maybe not the conclusions Raveno had feared, but conclusions all the same. Kinsley tried to stab Veilon while she was monologuing, but only managed to punch her with a fist and scrape her own knuckles against Veilon's hard scales. Where were her pivz?

"I'll tell you the reality I see," Veilon hissed. "Raveno trained you to fight in anticipation of selecting you as his shols so that you could put on a good show...but survive the frisaes. You both win on a draw. You both survive, and you both enjoy a long, happy future together. So sweet."

Veilon stabbed the pivz through Kinsley's left shoulder, pinning her arm to the mat.

Kinsley screamed.

"So delusional. Raveno hasn't been home in two thesh, so he doesn't know that Josairo doesn't allow draws anymore."

Veilon stabbed her second pivz through Kinsley's right shoulder.

Kinsley tried to breathe.

"Last thesh, there was a draw for the position of fourth Vri Shavril. An uneven advisor count is unacceptable. We might vote with a majority on matters. Could you imagine?" Veilon's laugh was haunted. "So the draw was considered a *losing* tie, both competitors were consumed, and the position was filled by a person of Josairo's choosing."

Kinsley tried to speak, but she couldn't quite get her voice and tongue into alignment.

"Had I not intervened, Raveno would have selected you. He would have tied with you during his frisaes, thinking to save you. And then you both would be dead."

"Why not tell him?" Kinsley finally managed. "Why do this? Why select me and fight me and—"

"I see how he looks at you." Veilon grinned, but her eyes were devastated. "How he touches you when he thinks no one can see. He'd kill for you, would he? Yes, even himself, but I won't let that happen. He'll never forgive me for winning a frisaes against you, but he'll be alive to hate me for a lifetime. I can choose to be happy with that ending."

"You do anything for family," Kinsley whispered.

"I'd do anything for my brothers," Veilon corrected.

"And your father? What you do for him?"

"I'm his advisor, so I advise. Just as Raveno is his killing hand, so he kills. We do what we must to survive."

"But you wrong. Raveno not love me. He—" Kinsley bit her lip. This hadn't been the plan, but Veilon was killing her. All Veilon wanted was to protect her brother and survive her father. Her motivations were sound and justified.

Rely on your instincts. You have great instincts.

"Is this room recording?" Kinsley asked.

Veilon cocked her head. "No."

"You correct. Raveno train me, but not for love. He train me for survival. He sick of his killing hand, so I help him."

"You help *him*?"

Why was it so hard to breathe? Like trying to inhale through water. "I help him kill Josairo."

Veilon stared at her a long moment.

Kinsley stared back, mostly just trying to stay conscious.

Veilon threw her head back and laughed.

Kinsley licked her lips and tried again. Maybe her pronunciation was off and skewing the meaning of her words. "We plan to kill him."

Veilon clutched her stomach and moaned, laughing even harder. "Oh, stop. Please. I heard you the first time." She covered her mouth, still laughing, and Kinsley went back to just attempting not to pass out.

"You can't kill him," Veilon said, her uproar dwindling to chuckles.

"We can. We have plan and support. We—"

"You think Josairo is the only threat to this planet?"

"We know he not and find who help him."

"Oh? And how exactly will you do that?"

Kinsley wrenched her eyes open, not sure exactly when she'd closed them. "I read...Intergalactic Frisaes money books. I find... where he hides money."

"Such ambition," Veilon said consideringly. "But I suppose you're highly motivated. Freeing our planet from Josairo would free you and your people as well." Veilon rested her hand on the pivz imbedded in Kinsley's right arm and leaned in close. "Let me confirm my understanding. Raveno and you have gathered allies in preparation to assassinate Josairo and usurp his rule?"

"Yes."

Veilon snorted. "He's two thesh too late for such heroics."

"Never too late to do right."

"On this we must agree to disagree." Veilon wedged her claw into her anku. "Veilon to Avier. Do you receive?" She paused a moment. Then, "Your services are needed in sparring room two. Thank you."

Veilon stood, gazing down at Kinsley almost sadly. "To survive our father's reign, I became his brain, Raveno became his weapon, and Tironan became invisible. I wonder. What will you become?"

"You think we not win," Kinsley murmured.

"I think I've seen it all before and been disappointed by the results." And with that, Veilon quit the room, leaving Kinsley pinned to the floor like a butterfly on display.

THIRTY-SIX

RAVENO MARCHED THROUGH THE HALLWAY TO THE INFIRMARY. He didn't run. He didn't hiss. He calmly nodded to people as they saluted him in passing. His expression was impassive—haughty, even —because Kinsley wasn't his Vri Sa Shols, and besides the bitterness of Veilon having claimed what he'd clearly wanted, why should he care who might or might not have needed medical attention after their sparring match? Raveno had always taken public opinion in stride, mostly because, as evidenced by their chanting and swooning and manic cheers, public opinion was favorable, but all he could feel toward them now was a searing resentment.

Avier had promised that Kinsley was fine. That in and of itself was worrisome, hearing Kinsley's word—*fine*—issuing from Avier's mouth, but he'd promised that her injuries were nothing he couldn't heal.

He'd also refused to catalogue those injuries.

Raveno marched faster.

The ushelz rotated their heads as Raveno passed, following his progress down the hallway as they'd done his entire life, but their attention chafed now. Logically, he'd always known that the preserved bodies of fallen competitors resided within their bloated stems. He'd attended countless frisaes, both regular and intergalactic, and had witnessed their young consume countless people, but for the first time in nearly twelve thesh, he suddenly couldn't pass the ushelz and not wonder which one had consumed his mother.

Why had he never wondered it before? He'd just accepted that she'd been consumed, that her preserved body was somewhere within these halls, feeding one of the ushelz. He didn't truly think she was a zombie, I mean *really*, but if the process by which the ushelz attained their nutrients preserved cells—even brain cells?—could the people inside them be healed enough to think and feel while trapped inside the ushelz? His mother included?

Only someone with fresh eyes could see that something was wrong.

Raveno turned the last corner toward the infirmary. The hallway was empty, so he sprinted the final stretch and rushed inside, his heart bursting.

Avier had his arm around Kinsley's bare waist and was helping her from the RRC. She looked wrecked. Granted, he'd seen her in worse shape. At least she was conscious and hadn't been—nope, she *had* been sick. And if her green pallor was any indication, she was about to be sick again. Imminently.

"Bucket," she gagged.

"No point now," Avier grumbled, but he produced a bucket from somewhere and held back her hair with his free hand.

Raveno winced, ready to rush forward.

"Better now than later when Raveno arrives," Avier added.

"He's coming?" Kinsley cursed between heaves. "I told you not to tell him yet!"

Raveno froze midstride, scowling.

Avier grunted. "And what would happen to me, do you supposed, should you die without Raveno even having been informed of your injury?"

So much for Kinsley being "just fine" if she'd been at risk of death. Avier's definition of the word was becoming as loose as Kinsley's!

"So much for patient-doctor confidentiality," she grumbled.

"What's that?"

"Exactly." She heaved, but nothing emerged.

Avier set the bucket aside and handed her a damp towel. "Cry mercy! He was bound to find out eventually."

"Sure. *Eventually.*" She wrapped the towel around her chest and wiped her mouth with the back of her hand. "Not in the next few minutes. Not *again.*"

Raveno ignored the sting from his fisted claws.

Avier pointed at the towel. "That was for..." He shook his head. "Let's just get you sorted before he arrives, and—" Avier glanced up, caught sight of Raveno in the room, and flinched.

Raveno held up a staying hand and backed into a shadowed corner of the room.

"—and you'll be good as new," Avier finished smoothly. He helped her from the chamber and steadied her against him as her knees tried to buckle.

"You can bring people back from the dead, but you can't manage it without making them puke up their guts?"

"I can, just not you. Not yet," Avier said, sounding suddenly indignant. "The RRC was developed to heal havari. Luckily, I was able to modify the technology for humans. For *you.*" He sighed. "I still have a few kinks to work out."

"Technically, you modified it for Riley first."

"Don't remind me."

Kinsley laughed, but she leaned heavily against Avier as he led her to the bathing room.

Raveno waited until her exhausted chuckles disappeared behind the shut door, then slid the infirmary door shut behind him. "Avier? Kinsley?" he bellowed.

A pause, then: "In the bathroom!" Kinsley shouted. "Give me a minute!"

Raveno closed his eyes and tried to rub the ache from his skull. Something in the room was beeping. The noise was stabbing his temple, as if his temple needed help throbbing. "Are you all right? I heard that sparring with Veilon didn't go well."

"I'm fine!"

Right.

What was that beeping? Raveno whirled around on a snarl. The RRC monitor was flashing. Raveno approached the machine, intending to silence it, and glimpsed Kinsley's health summary.

He considered the closed bathing room door, lowered his vresls, ground his teeth, then gave in to temptation.

- Puncture wounds: Skin pierced at both the left and right shoulders, muscles torn, blood lost. Repaired.
- Concussion: Hairline skull fracture to the right temporal lobe. Repaired.
- Internal musculature and organ failure—

Raveno closed his eyes.

Breathe. She's her definition of fine, which means alive.

You saw her walking and talking and complaining with your own eyes.

Breathe.

Raveno opened his eyes and forced himself to read.

- Internal musculature and organ failure: Punctured abdomen. Pierced long intestine and digestive organ two. Blood loss. Repaired.

Raveno inhaled, blew out his breath and inhaled again, repeatedly, until his heart stopped aching.

A quarter shift later, Kinsley emerged from the bathing room. "What's with your siblings trying to beat me to death?"

Kinsley was clean, her hair dried and braided, and she was

dressed in a fresh uniform. She looked sharp, strong, and confident as she walked toward him, steady on her feet. Her skin was pale, but no longer green.

Had he truly arrived when he'd pretended to, he never would have known of her grave condition.

She sighed dramatically. "If I didn't know better, I'd think they didn't like me."

How many times had she pretended to be fine in her life?

How many times had she pretended to be fine *with him*?

A cold knot twisted his gut. He met her halfway across the room, fell to his knees, and enveloped her in his embrace.

"Oof," she wheezed.

Raveno loosened his grip, but only slightly.

"I told you! I'm fine. See?" She attempted to lean back, her arms spread wide to showcase her condition, but Raveno shook his head and buried his face in the curve of her stomach.

"I saw..." He cleared his throat. "I saw the RRC's repair report and feared the worst."

"Well, your fears were unfounded."

"She is healed," Avier concurred, padding up softly behind her.

"Avier, will you give us a moment?"

"That's not—"

"Of course, Vri Cilvril." Avier clicked his heels and quit the room.

"Oh, now you're suddenly his Vri Cilvril," Kinsley grumbled. "Convenient of him to acknowledge your title *now* of all times."

"Yes. Very convenient." Raveno savored the relief of having her healthy in his arms with one last squeeze, then loosened his hold enough that he could lean back and see her face. "What—"

"How was your second shift?"

Raveno sputtered. "*My* second shift?"

"If you read my repair report, then you know exactly how my second shift was. So. How was yours?"

Raveno let her distract him. "Unproductive, but I hesitate to complain, knowing the shift you just experienced."

"Please, complain. I encourage it." Kinsley wriggled from his hold, walked to one of the chairs beside the RRC and sat. She met his eyes, smiled—genuinely, if wanly—and patted the chair beside hers.

Her right hand, resting on the chair arm, was trembling.

She'd needed an excuse to sit.

Raveno stood, strode to the chair and sat beside her. "I attempted to meet with Josairo."

"Ah." Kinsley winced. "How did that go?"

"Not well." Raveno admitted. "I was unable to obtain an audience."

"At all?" Kinsley raised her eyebrows. "Even for a scheduled appointment, like, in the future?"

"Correct. His schedule is completely full."

"Even for his son."

Raveno met her gaze. "Even for his Vri Cilvril."

"That's interesting," Kinsley said carefully. "What if you just barged into his office unannounced and forced a meeting?"

"I attempted that. He wasn't there." Raveno rubbed a hand down his face and groaned into his hands. "Tironan even hacked into this schedule. I followed it, meeting to meeting. Each one was via anku."

"When was the last time *anyone* had an in-person meeting with Josairo?"

Raveno bobbed his shoulders, his head still cradled in his palms. "When I interrogated his vrili, they all said the same thing. It's faster and more efficient to communicate via anku. Why would they meet in person now that we have the technology to meet within our own minds?"

"And no one questioned how strange or out of character it is for Josairo to stop in-person meetings?" Kinsley asked, incredulous.

"They know better than to question Josairo's orders. He once executed an entire crew because one Fyvril disobeyed him. Vesso, *Sa Riluuz's* captain, had been devastated and, in his grief and rage, challenged Josairo to a frisaes." Raveno stiffened against the echoing stab of those memories. "I'd never much liked Vesso before that incident."

Silence stretched between them.

"It's why I was so hesitant to confront Josairo regarding our shols shortage. Nothing good ever results from an in-person meeting with him."

Kinsley stroked a soft finger along his inner wrist.

"So no, I wouldn't expect anyone to question his orders, even ones that don't make sense. I suspect that, like me, they don't *want* to see him. They're so grateful to dodge a confrontation that they haven't questioned *why* they haven't met in person." He hissed. "Now that it's the one question I can't answer, it's all I can think about!"

"Have you interrogated his Vri Shavrili?"

"Not yet. Before I could plan my approach, I received word of your injuries." Raveno tugged lightly on one of her undulating locks of hair that refused to remain braided. "Tell me what happened during your sparring session with Veilon."

Kinsley, who always had something to say even when he didn't want to hear it, turned her head to stare at the far wall in silence.

"Did you reveal that you're here against your will?"

"Yep."

"And? How did she react?"

Kinsley leveled him with a look. "If you read my repair report, then you know exactly how she reacted."

Raveno scowled. "She discovered you're a victim of, as you say, human intergalactic trafficking, and decided to kill you for it?"

"She..." Kinsley bit her lip. "She didn't discover anything. She already knew."

Raveno's heart jumped up his throat.

"She doesn't believe anything can be done about it, so instead she's taking control of the one problem in her life that she can get rid of: me." Kinsley rubbed the rib that Veilon had cracked and laughed bitterly. "If Reece is half as fierce in her search for me as Veilon is in protecting you, Reece may find me here on Havar before I ever make it home."

"What are you implying?"

"Veilon deliberately selected me as her Vri Sa Shols to protect you from me. She knows that you wouldn't kill me in the arena, so really, I suppose she's protecting you from yourself."

"You don't know—"

"She told me so!" Kinsley burst. "She's probably the one who drugged you. Planned it from the beginning. And when Veilon fights me for real—"

"She won't."

"—she'll kill me. Without a doubt. I'm no match for her. She *will* win, and I *will* die."

Raveno weaved his fingers through Kinsley's, raised their joined palms, and kissed the back of her hand. But she wasn't trembling anymore. His fierce Kinsley. "I admit, it's an uneven match, but even so, you are skilled—"

"She's *more* skilled."

"With the element of surprise, you might—"

"I'm telling you, I can't win. Not against her."

Raveno bit off his first response to that defeatist attitude and took a moment to caress his thumbs over the ridges of her smooth knuckles as he composed his thoughts. "Did you watch and anticipate her movements?"

"I tried, but she was improvising too."

"Well, yes. I taught her to fight."

"And you did a damn good job."

"I did just as well by you."

Kinsley shook her head.

"She chose the five-blade?"

"Yes, and I picked up the three, just like you suggested. But I could have been wielding a toothpick for all the good it did me." Kinsley rubbed her left eye, but he knew from experience that such efforts wouldn't quell the coming headache. "We need a plan, and we're running out of time. We only have two days before I'm plant food!"

"Two *shaoz*. Don't worry about the frisaes. I'll talk Veilon into a draw."

Kinsley laughed, but it was her brittle, I-want-to-blow-you-up laugh, not her genuine one. "According to Veilon, draws are considered a tie for a *loss*. We'll *both* be plant food."

Raveno straightened. "What? Since when?" he shouted. Then, hearing the echoes of his own bellow, he tried again. "Sorry. Start from the beginning. What did she say?"

"Last year—*thesh*—there was a draw for Vri Shavril, but Josairo wouldn't let it stand. Something about having an uneven number of advisors."

"Who was the challenger?" Raveno asked.

Kinsley bobbed her shoulders with unconcern. Gah!

"The challenged must have been Yariz, since he's no longer Vri Shavril...but Josairo had them *both* consumed?"

She nodded. "That's what Veilon said."

"Who did Sheso fight to earn his position?"

"Who?"

Patience, Raveno reminded himself. She'd been badly wounded. She'd had a concussion. She was less fine than she ever let on. "The new Vri Shavril."

"He didn't fight anyone. Josairo appointment him."

"That's impossible," he scoffed.

Another shoulder bob. "I'm only relaying what Veilon said."

"You had a concussion. You're mistaken about what she said."

Kinsley narrowed her eyes, unimpressed. "Look it up. You have a record of such things—of promotions or successions or whatever—don't you?"

"Yes, but it doesn't make sense. Draws have always meant two winners. No matter the position."

"What it means is that we need a new plan." Kinsley looked like she might vomit again. "One that I may have already set into motion."

"What did you do?" he asked carefully.

"Veilon will be a great ally."

"I told you I'd consider it."

"She hates Josairo. She already knows that the IF is corrupt. And I think you're right. She's terrified to do anything about it. But she's willing to do anything to protect you. She loves you."

Raveno snorted. "Her love and fierce loyalty to me were never in question." And then it dawned on Raveno what she'd said, that she'd *already* set a plan in motion. "You—" Raveno began, but the words were so unthinkable, he couldn't say them. "What did you tell her?"

"I believe that everything she told me was the truth." Kinsley's dark eyes met his. "With my life on the line, I told the truth too."

"What did you do, Kinsley?"

"I did what I had to do."

"What did you do?"

"She was turning me into a human shish kabob, Raveno!" She flinched. "You're crushing my hand."

"Say it." He released her hand and took hold of her shoulders. "Offer me the same consideration: the truth."

"I told her that I'm helping you save Havar. That we're going to kill Josairo."

Raveno couldn't speak for a moment. He couldn't even breathe.

"We need her on our side," Kinsley reasoned, reaching up to cup his cheek.

Raveno dropped her shoulders and dodged her touch. "You blew my cover?"

"I had to tell her something, and in the moment, I couldn't risk anything less than the full truth."

"We discussed this in advance of your sparring," he snarled. "You specifically agreed not to tell her!"

"My days blindly obeying orders are over!"

"I wasn't ordering you! We agreed on a plan. A plan which specifically involved *not* implicating my sister in treason against our father!"

"I was in the field, and I made a judgment call. Sometimes plans change."

"Sometimes do promises change too?" Raveno swallowed so he could communicate without growling, but when he spoke again, his voice was still all gravel. "Because you promised nothing but truth between us."

"Why do you think I'm telling you all this?"

"No playing with the artificial gravity. No stealing other people's access codes. No unplanned explosions."

Kinsley blinked. "I didn't—"

"No side missions! No sabotage!"

"You told me to follow my instincts, that I have great instincts!"

"You do! And you told me to suspect Veilon of colluding with Josairo and/or his other Vri Shavrili!"

"And you said that was inconceivable!"

"It *is* inconceivable! Everything about this mission is inconceivable! Josairo missing, the Vri Shavrili lying, the possibility of my own sister..." Raveno gritted his teeth and shook his head. "Your pride is going to get us all killed."

"My *pride*? I'm not—"

"Your overconfidence. Your unwavering belief that you are correct no matter if you have evidence to support your claims or only speculation." Raveno pointed a claw at her chest. "You better hope you're right about Veilon, because if you're not, you've blown more than just my cover. You've blown our entire mission and risked my life, yours, the lives of my people, your people, and the lives of all the future people Josairo—or whoever the svik is 'behind the curtain' issuing orders these days—decides to abduct."

Kinsley's expression cracked. She reached out. "Raveno..."

Raveno jerked back and stood. He couldn't bear her touch at the moment. Her smooth fingertips, her scent, her fathomless eyes—svik, everything!—drew him in even against his will. So. By wrath alone he would resist.

She dropped her hand to her lap and leaned back in the chair, but somehow, in the absence of her touch, *he* was the one who felt crushed.

"I will order Jhoni to escort you back to your room," he said flatly.

"Back to my cell, you mean," Kinsley murmured, but her voice hitched. "I think I can manage."

"I know you can. That is my concern. How well you manage."

She crossed her arms and held his gaze. Not stopping him. Not begging him. Not that he wanted her to.

Cry mercy. Raveno quit the room. The door slid shut between them, and he strode down the hall, seething. At himself. At her. At everything between them that made her actions and words so searing.

The halls had never felt so suffocating. The ushelz watching him had never felt so invasive. Knowing now that perhaps there were two pairs of eyes seeing him when their jaws gaped, Raveno couldn't look back.

Back to her cell, indeed.

The entirety of Havar was a cell.

THIRTY-SEVEN

Was it possible to become accustomed to the *Tron*-like glow of a carnivorous, zombie-making FernGully in only three days? Well, three-ish shaoz. Nine shifts. The arena was jam-packed, as usual, with thousands upon thousands (millions?) of spectators stretching as far as the eye could see. Which, admittedly, wasn't very far with her eyes, considering the lighting, or lack thereof, but Kinsley could tell the crowd numbered in the thousands, if not millions, by the volume of their fanatical screaming. Their chanting physically vibrated through her chest.

RA! VE! NO!

RA! VE! NO!

RA! VE! NO!

Could soundwaves physically trip a person's heartbeat? Kinsley struggled to breathe past that unnerving sensation, but if she was being honest with herself, it wasn't just the screaming fans or the lurking Twoeys or the constraint of shackles affecting her heart.

Kinsley stared up at Raveno—his bone-studded crown held firmly in place by the precise plaits of his warrior braids—standing resolutely on the dais among his many hands and adoring fans, knowing he stood alone. Well, except for Tironan, who was little more than a yes-man, and Avier, who'd been applying adhesive bandages to severed arteries for years. They might have his back, but she was the only one who challenged him, who demanded he be better, who wasn't afraid to defy him. Raveno needed her.

Or so she was trying to convince herself in the wake of their fallout.

"What's happening?"

Kinsley groaned at the sound of Martin's deep voice behind her

"Does it matter?" And there was Leanne. "Whatever plan she had is fucked, remember?"

"I'd still like to know and brace myself for what's coming." Benjamin sidled beside them in a close third, as usual.

Kinsley braced to face the three of them—her albatross triplets—and startled. Her old cellmates weren't the only shols—er, humans—in attendance. She'd been so wrapped in her own misery, she'd failed to notice the three dozen human gladiators cuffed behind her. She'd known that her corseted uniform was Havar's standard battle garb, but somehow she hadn't made the leap to anticipate that everyone would be wearing it today.

Kinsley scanned the motley crew they presented and swallowed a burst of laughter. Everyone looked ridiculously uncomfortable, tugging at straps and complaining over corsets. One person had undone his buckles and was letting the uniform hang loosely from around his neck. Another kept wedging her fingers under the seam where the edge of her bustier was digging into her underarm. A particularly nervous gentleman had sweated through his uniform, staining the neck and pits in dark moons.

Unlike the masses, Martin wore his uniform well. His muscles had always been impressive, but framed by all that not-leather, they somehow appeared even bigger. The bulge of his pectorals strained his chest strap. As he lifted his hand in greeting, his biceps flexed against his bracer. His washboard stomach disappeared behind his gladiator skirt, but the skirt was short enough to showcase the thick cut of his upper thighs.

No matter his muscles, he was no Raveno.

For the first time, Kinsley could own the truth of her feelings and not cringe, and what had she done with all that personal growth? She'd managed to ruin everything before it had even blossomed.

Steadfastly ignoring the pang in her chest, Kinsley glanced aside at Benjamin, who looked, well, like Benjamin, but dressed like a nerdy gladiator for Halloween—without having sprung the extra cash for contact lenses.

Leanne also looked prepped to attend a costume party, but with her long limbs and subtle curves, at least she pulled it off. She didn't look like a warrior by any means, but she looked good.

Kinsley eyed each of them with a feigned gasp of horror. "You're wearing their uniform!" She pointed accusingly at their wrists. "You've got their blinking blue dot!" She slapped her cheeks "They've turned you into one of them!"

Martin's lips quirked.

Benjamin blushed.

Leanne tossed the highlighted tips of her dark hair over her shoulder. "I've been naked forever. I'll live with being a hypocrite if it means finally wearing clothes."

"Technically, you weren't naked," Benjamin reminded her.

"You wear a sheer teddy and tell me whether or not you feel naked."

Benjamin blinked at her from behind his black frames. "I was *actually* naked."

"Switch." Martin shook his head. "Kinsley. Please. Why are we dressed like this? What are these glowing symbols in our wrists? Why did we receive a karate lesson yesterday?"

"You received a karate lesson?" Benjamin squeaked.

Leanne frowned. "Mine was more like kickboxing."

Benjamin's eyes darted between them, concerned. "Why didn't I get a lesson?"

Kinsley sighed. Had she ever felt more exhausted in her life? "Believe me, you don't want to know. Not about the Intergalactic Frisaes or your ankesh or any of it."

Martin drilled her with a knowing look. "If you could turn back time, would you prevent yourself from knowing?"

Her eyes were suddenly, unacceptably scalding. If she could turn back time, she would do a lot of things differently.

Martin startled. "Is it really that bad?"

"You're about to participate in a public sparring match with an alien warrior." Kinsley wiped her eyes. "Hope you learned something from your karate and kickboxing lessons. You're gonna need it."

"I sucked at kickboxing!"

"I didn't get a lesson!"

"Why a sparring match?" Martin asked calmly.

"In preparation for the main attraction," Kinsley blurted, the words vomiting from her mouth nearly faster than the tears pouring down her cheeks now. "Tomorrow will be a Remembrance Ceremony to commemorate everyone the aliens have murdered for their entertainment. And the day after that, we battle them in one-on-one fights to the death."

Leanne covered her mouth.

Benjamin groaned.

Martin pursed his lips, grim.

"Those carnivorous parasite plants"—Kinsley jabbed a thumb at the nearest Twoey—"will eat whoever loses each battle, and their body will remain whole and preserved as the plant feeds from their organs for decades."

Benjamin blinked at her from behind his black glasses.

Leanne gaped at the plants, horrified.

"I thought as much," Martin said flatly.

Kinsley hiccupped into a surprised laugh. "You did not."

"I did."

"You did *not* think the plants were going to eat you and siphon nutrients from your dead, preserved body."

Martin chortled. "No. But I figured we were about the go out gladiator-style."

"Yes, well, the uniform doesn't leave much to the imagination, does it?" Kinsley turned to Leanne and, for her own sadistic personal pleasure, added, "You should know, your outfit is a postpartum uniform."

Leanne's head whipped up to Kinsley. "*Excuse me?*"

A swarm of drones converged over the dais. The glowing rails bracketing the stadium levels dimmed. The roaring crowd quieted. The drones swirled as one unit, and in the next moment, five giant projections of Josairo's face burst into the air above them. A thirty-foot-tall, full-body projection of him appeared on the dais.

Here we go again.

The crowd erupted in crazy, screaming applause.

Kinsley sighed, too annoyed to be angry anymore.

Josairo smiled magnanimously, striding past Raveno and all his minions to the center of the arena. "Two thesh and sixty-one shaoz ago, Raveno Hoviir—my son, my killing hand—embarked on a mission to greet and transport the competitors of our fifty-fourth Intergalactic Frisaes." Josairo paused a beat, his words echoing in the still silence. "Two thesh and sixty-one shaoz, we waited for his safe return. Now. Our patience has been rewarded. Now. We begin our fifty-fourth Intergalactic Frisaes Sparring Ceremony!"

Josairo clicked his heels together, and as one, the million people in the stadium did the same.

Blah blah blah. Same droning speech as yesterday and the day before that, and surely the years before that.

Kinsley hesitated mid-eyeroll. A word was changed here and there to maintain the illusion, but it *was* the same prerecorded speech. The same hand movements. The same for years.

Like those Whitney Houston and Michael Jackson hologram performances in Vegas.

What if one of Josairo's speeches had been recorded years ago and was being dubbed and replayed for these current events?

Like Whitney Houston and Michael Jackson...

What if Josairo wasn't just missing? What if he was dead?

Kinsley scanned the hands standing guard on the dais. If Josairo was dead, who would have access to his recordings? Besides Raveno, Josairo's advisors were second in command in Havar's government hierarchy. Veilon wasn't on the dais, but the other three were. Two she didn't know by name, and Josairo's newest advisor—Shezi or Sheso or Shensu, *something*—was the only one who hadn't earned his position. It had very conveniently been granted to him by Josairo.

Who might or might not have been alive to so very magnanimously break with tradition to offer him such an honor.

Kinsley refocused on Raveno.

Raveno, who had been staring at her, flinched and quickly looked away.

Were they in middle school? Kinsley waved her arms like an aircraft marshal.

By the sheer effort he put into *not* making eye contact, he'd obviously regressed to high school, at the least.

Kinsley wedged her fingers at the corners of her mouth and let loose a high whistle.

Raveno's vresls twitched, but if anything, he stared even harder at the empty air.

For the love of—

Kinsley considered her options, and after careful deliberation, did the last thing she could think of to gain his attention.

She pretended to faint.

Then groaned for real as she hit the ground. Hell, that would bruise.

Naturally, Josairo droned on, oblivious, even as the crowd gasped. He was just a recording, after all.

"Kinsley!" Martin yelped.

"Shit! Is she all right?" This from Leanne, who sounded genuinely concerned.

Clammy fingers took her pulse.

Kinsley kept her eyes closed and muttered, "I'm faking. Did Raveno notice?"

"Oh," Benjamin said. The fingers disappeared from her neck. "Uh... Oh, wow."

"Yeah," Martin confirmed. "He noticed, all right."

Kinsley sat up and met Raveno's eyes. This time, he didn't look away. *Finally.* He did, however, look ready to commit murder. His chest frill was standing on end all around his head, stiff and rattling like the tail feathers of an enraged peacock.

"Does he know he's not your boyfriend?" Leanne asked.

Kinsley pointed at Shesho, or whatever his name was, and overenunciated her words in the hopes Raveno could read her lips. "He killed Josairo." And then added, "Maybe," since she didn't have any evidence beyond her own speculation. As usual.

Raveno's frill flattened against his neck. He spread his arms out and shook his head, uncomprehending.

Kinsley pointed at her mouth. *Read my lips*, she said and tried again, pointing an accusing finger at the alien in question. *Ask him who killed Josairo!*

Raveno muttered something to Tironan.

Tironan squinted at Kinsley.

Kinsley pointed again. *I think he killed Josairo*, she mouthed at him.

Tironan continued squinting, then followed her finger's trajectory to Shezio.

Kinsley held her breath.

Tironan shook his head at Raveno and shrugged.

Kinsley groaned. If she survived today, she was getting an anku implant.

"What can I do?" Martin asked.

Raveno resumed his silent treatment.

"Nothing," Kinsley said. Martin offered her a hand, and she stood, feeling the unbearable crush of Raveno's rejection break over her a second time. "There's nothing to do."

Josairo's projection swirled into a crazy growth spurt. His feet rocketed up from the platform, springing to his head like a snapped rubber band into the sky, and on impact, Josairo exploded into a dazzling blast of strobing light.

Again.

The crowd erupted into fanatical applause, screaming and whistling.

As usual.

From the opposite side of the arena, a line of havari, dressed in their gladiator best, approached. Ready for battle.

Veilon was among them. Her strawberry-blonde hair was braided at the temples, securing her princess headband across her forehead. Her scowl was as intense as her confidence. Her small, striking lime-green eyes found Kinsley in the crowd and held her gaze.

Kinsley didn't know what she was trying to communicate. Had she reconsidered their conversation? Was she still angry? Did she plan to beat the snot out of her again?

The only thing Kinsley knew for certain was that she was as alone down on this stage as Raveno was up on his dais. Even from this distance, she could see his chest flap bristling. The cut of his upturned jaw was glacial. Between his brows was a canyon of seething wrath, and the tips of his flared nostrils were nearly as pointed as his disapproval.

Kinsley bit her lip against the sick ache in the pit of her stomach. She shouldn't have blown his cover. She should have stuck out the fight and remained true to their plan.

She should have remained true to Raveno.

The lasers connecting her wrist cuffs unlocked.

Kinsley startled back to herself.

Veilon stood before her. She'd unshackled her.

In fact, everyone's shackles had been released. Martin, Benjamin, Leanne, and the thirty-two other humans had all paired off and spread out with the aliens who had selected them.

Shit, Benjamin was screwed. Granted, they were all screwed, but

Benjamin especially. His alien sparring partner was massive! Leanne didn't stand a chance either, no matter her partner, and Martin—

Actually, Martin's alien was rather small for an havarian, and matched him in height if not muscle. Martin was bulkier. Kinsley's spirits lifted. Maybe Martin could—

Martin's alien performed some sort of Matrix-level flip-kick that knocked Martin off his feet and launched him through the air. He landed flat on his back five yards from where he'd just stood. His alien politely waited for him to crawl onto all fours—coughing and groaning—and regain his feet before flip-kicking him a second time. If this was just warm-up sparring, they were all totally screwed once the real fighting began.

Kinsley winced, and suddenly, Raveno's snarled warning returned to haunt her: *You better hope you're right about Veilon, because if you're not, you've blown more than just my cover. You've blown our entire mission.*

For once in her life, she hadn't intended to *blow* anything, but when he'd said the words, even as her heart had galloped with right-eous indignation, the sentiment had rung true. Because this wasn't the first time her single-minded pursuit of a mission had backfired.

You've risked my life, yours, the lives of my people, your people, and the lives of all the future people...

What if she had put them all at risk? What if this mission ended up being a repeat of her failed prison escape because of her inability to listen to other people and act on their wishes rather than her own resolve?

She'd bullied the humans to escape before they were ready, and the mission had failed.

She'd blown Raveno's cover before he was ready, and now this mission might fail.

When had strength and confidence and persistence become weaknesses?

"Ready yourself, Kinsley."

Kinsley took a deep breath and faced Veilon. "Friends call me Switch."

Veilon nodded. "I appreciated your honesty during our private sparring session. And I will do you the same courtesy. Kinsley."

Shit. "With honesty is no understanding between us?"

Veilon shook her head. "There's too much you don't understand about Havar. Things even Raveno doesn't know. I'm truly sorry, but we can't possibly be friends."

"Damn," Kinsley said, trying to keep her cool when all she could think was, *shit, shit, shit!* "Maybe after this, I not need Avier this time?"

"Needing Avier is a blessing. It means you're still alive." Veilon's lime-green eyes were shinier than usual. If she'd been a man, surely her chest flap would have quivered. "Ready yourself."

Kinsley lifted her empty palms. "No pivz."

"I'm not armed either. No one is."

Kinsley scanned the arena, surprised. She'd been so distracted that she hadn't even noticed everyone was getting their asses kicked with fists and claws and feet and teeth alone.

"You seem like a person I might have been honored to know. Raveno certainly is taken by you, and we have always been of the same mind." She laughed, and the sound was gratingly brittle. "More than I ever knew."

"That sounds like goodbye."

Veilon bent her knees and raised her hands, one straight out and the other bent at the elbow, prepared to strike, or block, as necessary. "Ready yourself."

"It just the Sparring Ceremony."

"Ready yourself!" she shouted.

Kinsley looked up at Raveno. He was watching, murder in his eyes, chest flap going wild.

"Ready yourself!" he screamed at her.

Well, *probably* he screamed. With the cacophony of the crowd and distance between them, she could only read his lips, but his chest frill didn't flap out like that unless he was screaming.

Kinsley shook her head, feeling... She didn't know what she was feeling, but God help her, she was the furthest thing from ready.

She confronted Veilon squarely, bent her knees, and raised her arms.

Veilon's hard, scaley knuckles smashed into her face.

THIRTY-EIGHT

KINSLEY WAS BETTER THAN THIS. SHE WAS SO MUCH BETTER than this!

Raveno flinched as she took another hit to the temple without even trying to dodge it, another punch to the stomach without attempting to block it, and another elbow to the chin without any perceivable counterstrike. Instead of showing up as the competitor he'd trained, she'd become a punching post for Veilon's practice, and his dear sister, as usual—as had been stabbed into her—wasn't holding back.

Raveno skimmed over the many humans and found the three who'd shared Kinsley's cell on *Sa Vivsheth*. The three who still sought her out as if they were loyal friends who hadn't betrayed her. She might deign to converse with them, but they'd already proved in spectacular fashion that when lives were on the line, they would save only their own. Case in point, they currently had their own losing battles to fight, and none of them, not even Martin, seemed aware that Kinsley needed help. More help than they needed.

They're not trained in battle combat, Raveno reminded himself, but that logic was cold comfort as Veilon landed another jab.

Kinsley doubled over, made a sad attempt at a takedown—which Veilon anticipated—and took an uppercut to the chin.

Kinsley rocked back and hit the ground hard.

Raveno winced. *This is my fault.*

He'd been so distracted by her betrayal, so consumed by his own hurt, that he'd let himself forget that she wasn't an unstoppable force, no matter how invulnerable she seemed during their personal battles. Without him, who would remind her of fighting tactics? Without him, who would praise her strengths? Who would build her confidence? Who else had her back?

Kinsley needed him.

Veilon straddled her and commenced breaking her knuckles on Kinsley's face.

His brother leaned in. "She's better than th-this."

Raveno snarled at him.

Tironan raised his palms and stepped back.

Avier cleared his throat. "If I may—"

Raveno turned his snarl on him, but Avier only pressed forward.

"This isn't, as Kinsley says, a good look for you."

"For *me*?" Raveno waved his arm to indicate the beating below.

Veilon very helpfully allowed Kinsley to stand only to land a jump-kick to her ribs.

Kinsley hit the ground a second time, clutching her side.

Avier winced. "She's losing miserably, and her failure is a reflection on you."

Raveno glared sideways at him. "Elaborate."

"No one knows about the private sparring session that broke her confidence. No one knows how close you are to Kinsley or that you two broke up—"

"We didn't—"

"Or that she's taking the worst beating of her life the one time it counts. *They* don't know she's better than this." Avier gestured to the spectators.

Kinsley gained her feet only to have them swept out from under her with a kick she should have easily jumped over. The arena was better lit than any room they'd trained in! Nevertheless, she didn't jump in time and fell flat on her back. Again.

Raveno sucked in air through his clenched teeth. "Your point?"

"Everyone knows you wanted to select Kinsley. You made your interest clear to your crew on *Sa Vivsheth* and to the public at the Welcome Ceremony. But why would you fight anyone besides the greatest, most skilled warrior? It'll make people question your motivations for wanting to select her."

"Svik, who cares about public opinion right now!" Raveno snapped. He chopped his hand at Kinsley. "She's *dying* down there."

Kinsley caught another blow to the temple and collapsed, hitting her head a second time on the ground when she failed to catch her own fall.

She didn't get up.

Raveno inhaled sharply. She was truly dying down there.

"Veilon is taking this beyond a sparring session," Raveno murmured. "We must stop the fight."

Avier had the gall to laugh. He laughed! "And how do you propose we do that, hmmm?"

Tironan worried his knuckles. "We should do s-*something*."

"What, like leap from the dais and shield her with your own body like you did on *Sa Vivsheth*?" Avier snorted. "Protecting her from fire is easier than protecting her from the dangers of this arena."

Kinsley still hadn't moved.

Avier turned on Raveno. "Or better yet, go ahead and meet your beloved little sister in combat!"

Veilon locked her arms around Kinsley's neck in a chokehold.

"No, I have it!" Avier lifted a claw in feigned epiphany, very much like Kinsley often did. "You could distract the audience by finally publicly challenging Josairo to a frisaes without any new on- or off-world allies! A frisaes that he can't even meet because he's, once again, not physically here."

Raveno stilled. "That would work."

Tironan's vresls flapped out and quivered.

"Ha! Right." But then Avier took notice of Raveno's intensity and stilled. "No."

"It *would* work. If Josairo can't meet my challenge, then I rise to Vra Cilril s'Hvri." Raveno shrugged. "And if he does, I finally face him in a frisaes."

"Y-y-you think whoever has been posing as Josairo in his absence will l-let you rise to Vra Cilril s'Hvri?"

"No," Raveno said, beginning to love this plan. "And that's exactly what we'll count on to force whoever is behind the curtain to reveal themselves."

"W-w-what curtain?"

Avier slapped his forehead. "I was pointing out the many ways in which you *couldn't* stop the fight. Because stopping the fight is impossible."

"I am Vri Cilvril. Nothing is impossible."

"T-t-there he goes. Believing his own p-p-propaganda," Tironan muttered. "I knew it would h-happen eventually."

Avier cursed under his breath. "You can't sacrifice all you've worked toward for nearly twelve thesh and damn the entire world—svik, the entire galaxy!—to Josairo's rule for one woman."

Kinsley was still limp in Veilon's chokehold.

Veilon wasn't letting go.

And the crowd went wild, cheering for her victory. For Kinsley's death.

"I lost Cresha in the pursuit of this mission. I lost my anonymity, my left leg, my very soul carrying out what I thought were Josairo's orders. Despicable orders!" Raveno shook his head and locked eyes with Avier. "Kinsley is the one thing I refuse to sacrifice. We will save both her *and* our people, or we die trying."

"You can't just—svik, there he goes."

Raveno stepped forward to the edge of the dais and raised his arms.

The crowd silenced.

The fighting ceased.

Raveno eyed Veilon and waited pointedly for her to stop fighting too as the projectionist sprinted to him and clipped an amplifier to his collar.

For a chilling moment as Veilon stared him down, Raveno thought he'd truly need to physically intervene.

Veilon released Kinsley and stood.

Kinsley slumped to the ground, still unmoving.

Cry mercy, what if he was too late?

Raveno attempted to compose himself and faced the crowd. "I, Vri Cilvril Raveno Hoviir. Challenge Vra Cilvril s'Hvri Josairo Hoviir. To a frisaes!"

For the first time in nearly ten thesh, since he'd earned his position as Vri Cilvril, the crowd didn't cheer at his words. People glanced at one another, confused and nervous. As they should be.

At the moment, to cheer would be treasonous.

Cresha gaped at him from her seat amid the masses. Had he still known her, he'd say she looked stricken.

The only sound in the entire arena was behind him: Tironan and Avier whisper hissing.

"How c-c-could you?"

"It was an argument *against* a frisaes."

"Dear brother," Veilon said from below, but her voice projected throughout the stadium's speakers, same as his. "Our father is not present to receive such a challenge."

Raveno whipped his head, nearly as shocked to hear the word *father* from her lips as he was to hear her voice broadcasting clear and precise around him. Had all the challengers been issued amplifiers?

"Perhaps you've been off-world, serving us for too long. You've forgotten our traditions. A challenge can only be issued in person. And, as you can see, Father is not present." Veilon lifted an arm to indicate the dais. "Or have you also forgotten that the visage of our Vra Cilvril s'Hvri is merely a projection for entertainment?"

The crowd shifted, not sure what to think or how to react. A few forced chuckles echoed from the higher seats.

"I haven't been off-world so long as to forget that, traditionally, draws are considered wins. That government positions can only be earned, not given." Raveno let that sink in a moment. "That the Sparring Ceremony is meant for practice and bidding, not true combat."

The crowd succumbed to pure silence.

From the corner of his eye, Raveno saw Sheso straighten up and lean into Tironan.

"Is he talking about me and the position I was granted?" Sheso asked, wild-eyed as he blinked at Raveno. "Why is he dragging me into this?"

"Is that your true concern?" Veilon asked. "That Father changed a few traditions in your absence?"

Raveno leveled a look at her. "You know my true concern."

"Don't do this, Raveno. Please," Veilon added, and Raveno was shocked to hear her voice crack. "I can't lose you too."

"This is beyond just you and me, now, and everything our family lost. I can no longer remain complicit in his lies." He turned to address the arena. "The humans are not warriors. They did not come here of their own free will. They have not trained a lifetime for the honor of competing in the fifty-fourth Intergalactic Frisaes."

The crowd began to buzz.

"Under the direct orders of Vra Cilvril s'Hvri Josairo Hoviir, I was tasked with purchasing the humans from the Lorien," Raveno spat. "The Lorien had abducted the humans from their planet Earth without their consent. And per orders from our Vra Cilvril s'Hvri, I kidnapped them from across the galaxy. For our entertainment!"

The buzzing swelled. People were shaking their heads. Some were pointing down at the humans. Many had covered their mouths. All were murmuring at one another. Shocked. Confused. Angry. Disbelieving.

"That seems unlikely." The doubt in Veilon's voice echoed through the arena.

The crowd quieted.

Raveno faced Veilon. What was she playing at? She knew the truth. Much to Raveno's continued consternation, Kinsley had confessed everything to her. *Everything*.

Had Veilon not believed her?

But why wouldn't she believe *him*?

A projection formed in the center of the arena. Even as the figures materialized in the air before him and quadrupled in the air above for the benefit of spectators with higher seats, Raveno couldn't quite believe what he was seeing.

"Bend your knees more. *More*," his projected self said in Haveo. "Arms remain out—yes, like that—but your knees..."

"They're bent!" Projected Kinsley yelled at the ceiling, inadvertently dropping her arms, and with them, the pivz in each hand.

Her words were dubbed in Haveo.

Raveno gaped at the impossible. At that point in her training, she hadn't begun language lessons! Even now, her Haveo was much worse than this. But her image as well as her voice had been doctored in the projection. Not that anyone else would notice. One would have to know Kinsley personally to recognize that she would never sound so coy and that the timbre of her natural voice was snappier. More textured, somehow.

"Yes, your knees are bent," projected Raveno replied. "That is why I said they should be bent *more*."

Projected Kinsley scrunched her nose.

"Assume your position," projected Raveno barked.

Raveno shook his head at the drama replaying before him, stunned. From the top-down view of the camera, this was obviously security footage from *Sa Vivsheth*, but it *couldn't* be security footage. They didn't have cameras in the training room, and their footage didn't have audio.

Yet someone had obtained this footage and recreated their original conversation.

Their projected selves began sparring. This was one of their first training sessions, before they'd even struck their deal as allies. He could tell because they were training alone instead of with his full crew and because Kinsley's skills were still so raw.

His chest ached at the sight.

His projected self leapt forward, slashing down with the pivz in his right hand.

Kinsley blocked his strike with a pivot-drop, then rolled right and popped to her feet at his side, striking up hard and fast.

His block was late. He halted her pivz with a chop to her inner elbow before she could do any real damage, but she managed to slip the blade between his scales deep enough that blood poured from the wound and gloved her hand.

Projected Kinsley released the pivz and cupped her elbow, injured from the block.

Projected Raveno extracted the pivz from his scales, wet a towel, and, heedless of his own wound, carefully wiped the cloth over her palm.

"I can just wash my hands at the sink," Projected Kinsley murmured.

Projected Raveno cleaned the back of her hand, then each finger. "We should keep your elbow as immobile as possible until Avier examines it."

"Your hands are so warm."

Projected Raveno inhaled sharply, then sealed his nostril slits against the scent. "You sound surprised."

"I always am when it comes to you," she murmured.

Projected Raveno's nostrils opened. He was clearly breathing in her scent again.

Several people in the crowd huffed. Many outright laughed.

Real Raveno's ears were searing.

Projected Kinsley leaned closer, the movement minute but unmistakable. Raveno remembered how it had felt having her in such close proximity in those early days. Not much different from now, if he were honest. He'd been enthralled by her scent, by her proximity, by *her*. But he also remembered his uncertainty over her true feelings and whether he should act on his.

There was nothing uncertain about what was being projected now.

She was going to kiss him.

The projection cut.

The crowd was silent for a tense moment, unsure.

One person whistled.

Another laughed, clapping.

The sentiment sparked, caught wind, and swept through the crowd. The entire stadium whooped their excitement.

Raveno ground his teeth.

When the crowd quieted, a burst of shocked laughter pieced the arena. "Is that a woman taken against her will?" Veilon asked.

Raveno stared at Veilon and couldn't quite wrap his mind around what he'd just seen. Had she not believed Kinsley's story of being kidnapped? Was this her way of protecting him, as Kinsley believed?

Or was this the result of Kinsley having armed Veilon with the truth?

Raveno turned his back on Veilon and addressed his people. "I have the receipt of transfer to confirm the humans were bought. Under Josairo's orders, we locked them in cages aboard *Sa Vivsheth*. We currently lock them in their rooms here in the arena. We—" Raveno pursed his lips. Everyone's attention was fixed on the projection of him and Kinsley, their training session playing on loop. No one was listening.

Avier held out his hand. "The amplifier, if you will."

Raveno unclipped it from his collar and passed it to him.

Avier held the amplifier to his mouth. "I witnessed everything Raveno has described. The humans *were* bought from the Lorien. They *were* transported here against their will."

A few people in the crowd refocused on Avier's words rather than the projection, but not nearly enough.

"They *were* kept in cages. They still are. See the cuffs on their wrists? They are not leads. They are shackles!"

As Avier gestured to the humans below—the evidence of their imprisonment still fastened around their wrists—the projection reconfigured to depict Raveno's cabin on *Sa Vivsheth*. Projected Kinsley leaned into projected Raveno's neck and grazed her teeth across his throat.

Thev sa shek! A security camera was planted in his cabin? *His* cabin?

Raveno groaned at the sight of them together. Her gesture might have looked like the bonding agreement it was supposed to be had his ears not been glowing. His vresls stiffened, and as much as he remembered keeping them in check, Raveno could see with his own eyes that his projected vresls were quivering.

She wasn't kissing him, and he wasn't breathing her in, but the scorching intimacy of *not* acting on the longing between them was nearly worse.

Avier dropped his hand to his waist. "Svik."

Raveno homed in on the projectionist, but the man who'd given him the amplifier was several steps from his equipment, hands raised. Shaking his head. Frantic.

Tironan snatched the amplifier from Avier's hand. "I—I—I am witness as w-well, and c-confirm the injustices against the h-humans."

Veilon pointed at the projection between them. "You can't argue against solid proof, little brother!"

Avier snatched the amplifier back from Tironan. "This footage is only a partial truth, clipped to support someone's agenda. Should you see *all* the footage and witness what we have witnessed, you would see the rooms that lock from the outside on *Sa Vivsheth*. You would see the riot that Kinsley attempted to incite, and the human who was executed for requesting more food!"

The crowd hushed at that.

Kinsley moved. First her hand, as she cupped her head, and then her arms as she struggled to lift her own weight. She managed to push herself up from the ground into a sitting position.

Relief swept through Raveno so swift and potent, he nearly staggered.

"She's n-not dead," Tironan breathed.

"Not for lack of trying," Avier muttered.

Kinsley raised her arm, palm up, and beckoned with her fingers.

"W-w-what is she—"

Raveno felt his chest swell so wide with pride, it ached. He held out his hand to Avier. "The amplifier, please."

"She doesn't look well," Avier said, even as he passed the amplifier. "I'm not sure she'll be able to speak."

"I have no doubt she will try." Raveno tossed the amplifier down to Kinsley.

The crowd, all 200,674 people, fell completely silent.

Kinsley swayed. In another moment, she might very well be unconscious again.

Raveno's heart sank as she slumped over.

One of the humans ran to her side.

Martin. He caught her by the shoulders before she could fall and propped her upright against his side.

Another one of her cellmates—Leanne or Annie, the woman whom Kinsley had so little patience with—sprinted forward and caught the amplifier. She peered back at Martin, and he tipped his head at Kinsley. The woman rolled her eyes, clearly annoyed, but despite her reluctance, she knelt before Kinsley and extended the amplifier toward her mouth.

Her third former cellmate, the poor-sighted man mated to Annie, hovered nearby, not helping in any tangible way but clearly wanting to be a part of their effort.

"You got this," he whispered, then flinched as his encouragement echoed through the arena speakers.

Kinsley licked her lips. "One...thesh ago, Vri Cilvril Raveno Hoviir give me *his* ouk. Not for selection. For protection."

Martin lifted Kinsley's wrist to flash her glowing ankesh. Kinsley didn't flinch, but even from this distance, he could see her pain in the flex of her neck.

"Because I taken from Earth. I live in cage. I escape many times, but I fail to make freedom for my people."

Raveno couldn't tear his eyes from her, high on her courage, even as his heart squeezed with dread as she swayed. But Raveno wasn't the only one riveted. The entire stadium held their breath. Even Veilon.

Raveno did a double take. Veilon was more than just caught by Kinsley's speech. She looked as stricken as Cresha now. Raveno glanced at the other Vri Shavrili beside him. Jzoeshi looked stunned, and for all that he'd managed to politicize himself into position, Sheso only looked confused.

"I think Raveno kill me for escape. I see him kill shols for less. But he not the evil I think. He not *want* to kill us. He want justice." Kinsley pointed at their projection. "You see him train me. You see him feel for me. But his ouk not save me here. On Havar where he is law after your Vra Cilvril s'Hvri, I am not safe."

She took a moment to catch her breath, but she couldn't inhale past the wet gurgle in her lungs.

"You give me and my people chains, but we not alone." Kinsley's words—"ALONE-ALONE-ALONE"— echoed into silence. "You all wear chains."

Her breathing became ragged. She slumped into Martin's lap on a groan.

"Kinsley?" Martin whispered.

"'m fine," she croaked, but she didn't sit upright.

"To clarify," Veilon interrupted, her voice quaking. "Raveno, brother. You have...bought and trafficked people *unwillingly* from their home planet instead of escorting willing competitors?"

"Under—" *Josairo's orders*. Damn it, he needed an amplifier. He glared at the projectionist for another and blinked. The tech was gone.

"Yes," Kinsley croaked. "Raveno act...under Josairo...orders."

The barbs in Raveno's swell of pride sliced deep. *Oh, my little lilssna.*

"By your own admission and by the eyewitness testimony of your own hands, you executed one of those same unwilling victims?" Veilon asked him.

"Under Josairo orders!" Kinsley gasped out.

Raveno didn't know what pierced him more, her pain or her loyalty.

"You know that Josairo will confirm those orders," Veilon said through gritted teeth. "And will respond accordingly."

Raveno, sans his amplifier, just nodded.

Kinsley grinned. "We happy to meet Josairo...for his answer."

Allowing me to formally issue my challenge. Raveno grinned back. Even now—beaten down and defeated—the gleam of calculation sharpened Kinsley's gaze.

Strong in mind if not in body, he thought warily, thankful that she spoke for and not against him.

Veilon knelt before Kinsley and unclipped both their amplifiers. She said something. Without the amplifiers, Raveno couldn't hear her, and from his current angle, he couldn't read her lips, but whatever she said wiped that gleam clean from Kinsley's eyes a moment before she collapsed, unconscious in Martin's embrace.

THIRTY-NINE

YOU KNOW AS WELL AS I DO THAT JOSAIRO DIDN'T ORDER anyone's execution. I thought you didn't want Raveno dead.

Veilon's parting words echoed in Kinsley's mind long after she'd been carried from the stadium. She was the only human with injuries severe enough to require healing, of course, and throughout the joy of that process, worse even than yesterday—or the previous shift, whenever the hell she'd last visited the infirmary—Veilon's words haunted her.

Raveno could have let Veilon finish the fight. For the mission, he should have, and as grateful as Kinsley was to be suffering inside the healing pod rather than inside a Twoey, she hated to admit that Veilon was right. By stopping the fight and going public with the truth, Raveno risked everything: his mission, his planet, his revenge.

His life.

After eight months trying to convince Raveno to quit procrastinating and finally overthrow Josairo so she could return home, he suddenly was, and strangely, instead of feeling vindicated or excited or anticipatory, she was terrified. They were shouting the truth from the tops of their lungs, and somehow, inconceivably, no one could hear them.

If the spectators in the arena were any indication, they *did* need more on-world allies.

If Avier's grumbles at her during their long walk to the infirmary were true, they needed more off-world allies too.

If Kinsley's gut was accurate, they were completely screwed.

All because Raveno, for the first time ever—or at least for the first time since his mother had been murdered—had prioritized something over revenge.

He'd prioritized *her*.

Kinsley covered her face and screamed. She wanted to go home, damn it, but she didn't want to be the reason this mission failed!

Somehow, she wasn't sure when it had happened, his mission had become hers. She needed to see it through to the end, and not just for her personal stake in their deal. Nearly as much as she wanted to return home to Earth, she wanted to see Raveno confront whoever was behind his father's projections, find some sort of closure for a lifetime of hurt, and end this frisaes madness, once and for all.

Her healing complete, the gurney slid out of the tube, and she startled.

Raveno was hovering over her instead of Avier.

Raveno was here.

Before Kinsley could apologize or cover herself or even blush, Raveno leaned down and wrapped his arms around her to help her from the healing pod.

Blood and vomit glued her body to his uniform with a sticky squish.

Her face flamed. "I can do it myself!"

"You can't."

"Where the hell is Avier?" She scanned the room, but they were alone.

"I ordered him away."

"Of course you did," she muttered.

Raveno adjusted his hold so he could balance her on the edge of the pod with one arm and swipe her bangs from her face with the other. A hank of wet hair tried to stick to her temple, and failing that, stuck to his finger instead.

Kinsley flinched. "At least let me shower first!"

Raveno dropped his hand from her cheek, but the hand around her waist tightened. "I'm sorry."

"You? *I'm* sorry," she gushed, clinging to his neck. "You were right about my overconfidence. I should have stuck to the plan, as we agreed, and not make my own decision about blowing your cover."

Raveno shook his head. "I knew you were gravely injured, but if Veilon's wrath during your sparring was anything like the wrath I witnessed in the arena..." He cleared his throat. "I forgive you."

Oh, he smelled like oranges and eucalyptus, so fresh and tangy sweet. Which only highlighted how sour she must smell at the moment. "You do realize that between the two of us, the mission is, how would you say, a swill of svik, right?"

Raveno hissed. "When have I ever said that?"

"It's something you would say."

"Would you have preferred I allow *all* your ribs to pierce your organs? Or perhaps allow your skull to crack *completely* in half?" He held a finger aloft. "Or no, I have it. Broken bones aren't enough. You want to see them split through your soft skin!"

"Nothing's broken. I—"

Raveno tipped the healing pod's screen toward her with one hand and pointed at the outline of her body on its health summary. Her body was lit like a Christmas tree. "Everything was broken!"

"Yes, but I'm fine now."

"That doesn't make the lethality and pain of your injuries any less real in the moment. What if I hadn't stopped the fight?"

"You shouldn't have."

"What if Avier wasn't as skilled a doctor?"

"But he is."

Raveno covered her mouth with both thumbs on his right hand. "This mission no longer matters if you do not survive it."

Kinsley wriggled free of his grasp. "This mission is so much bigger than my one life. You said it yourself: this mission affects the lives of your people and all the future people who might be abducted if we don't—"

"I know what I said," he growled, his breath ragged. "But their lives do not make yours any less valuable. I will save both."

The small ridges of scales on his finger pads should have been jarring against her lips. He was different. So very different. But his touch was electric. How could a caress be so soft yet so penetrating? The burning contact began at her lips and spread through her entire body until even the tips of her curled toes caught fire.

He might have scales instead of skin, claws instead of nails, a forked tongue, fangs, and snake eyes the color of the sun, but they shared the same heart.

Rely on your instincts rather than your eyes.

The problem was, she couldn't see the truth of him beneath his flesh without acknowledging another truth, an unfathomable truth, within herself.

Raveno tightened his grip around her waist, and Kinsley realized she'd leaned her weight into him.

She hadn't been losing her balance.

"Kinsley, I—" Raveno swallowed. "I've been in awe of you since the moment we met. Your strength. Your courage. Your determination. Your dimples." His eyes skimmed across her face as he spoke. "You are my greatest strength and my greatest weakness in this mission, and earning your respect was my greatest challenge. But you had mine from the very start."

Kinsley bit her lip, unsure if their trembling would burst in a smile or a sob.

"When I saw you losing against Veilon, when I thought I might lose you, *really* lose you, I realized that nothing matters—not revenge, not allies, not secrets. None of it matters the way you matter. Before knowing you, I would have given anything to overthrow my father. But you are the one thing I can not give. Because I love you."

And there it was. The unfathomable truth. Not just lust or longing, which was, quite honestly, unfathomable enough.

But truth couldn't be made less real via disbelief.

Kinsley bridged the distance between their lips and kissed him.

Raveno sank into her for a moment—ah, heat and heaven and sin in a single lick—before jerking back. "No. You're hurt."

"I'm healed." She tried to tug him back in, but he was a wall of resistance.

"You're weak and—"

"I'm not—" Kinsley began, but she knew that clenched jaw all too well. She'd never win this argument with logic alone. She stopped tugging. "You're right."

His vresls sprang out.

"I'm so weak, I couldn't possibly shower on my own. And I need a shower. Desperately." That much was disturbingly accurate.

Raveno narrowed his blood-orange eyes, all uncertain suspicion. "You're taking advantage of my concern."

Kinsley batted her lashes innocently. "You said so yourself, I'm in a weakened condition."

"I did. *You are.* But—"

"And you can't deny that I require a shower."

"No, obviously, but—"

Kinsley winced at the "obviously," but forged ahead on a sigh. "If you can't, Avier can help me, I suppose."

Raveno stilled. "Do you want Avier to help you?"

She met his eyes. "I'm asking *you* to help me."

"Your will by my hands." He swept her from the pod, cradled her against his chest—oh, those biceps!—and carried her to the bathroom.

Or, rather, what apparently passed for a public bathroom on Havar. If Kinsley were to properly translate the room based on accommodations and not just functionality, she would call it a spa.

Raveno carried her past the vanity hallway—a row of mirrors and fluffy stools where one could sample all the lotions and potions and polishes and perfumes on display—and through the sliding doors to the more private, individual washing areas. Each shower stall was essentially its own room along the perimeter of the spa, accommodating any type of washing you might need or desire: waterfall, handheld, dual, pulsing, and high-pressure showerheads. Each had curved, in-water pool loungers, same as the three in her private bathroom.

In the center of the room were bathtubs the size of pools, complete with jets and more showerhead features, and everything—absolutely everything, from the air to the water to the soaps and lotions and maybe even the showers themselves—smelled fresh and clean and lovely. Like cucumbers and jasmine with a hint of spice. Ginger?

As if they had ginger—or cucumbers and jasmine, for that matter—on Havar.

Maybe they did. They had microwaves and fireworks, after all. Maybe—

Raveno approached a waterfall shower stall, one *without* a pulsing handheld showerhead.

Kinsley pointed to the adjacent room, which offered a dual handheld showerhead and pool lounger. "You'll need the removable showerhead."

He didn't even break stride. "This shower is basically the same as that one."

"It most assuredly is not."

He peered down at her with a side-eye. "How would you know?"

"All your planet's advancement in space technology, communication devices, and weaponry, yet your budget for improving indoor plumbing ended at roughly the same time as Earth's."

"Meaning?"

"Meaning that I can look at that waterfall showerhead and know that I would *enjoy* the handheld, pulsing showerhead more." Kinsley bit down on her smile and said, as seriously as she could manage, "I'm very dirty. And as weak as I am, I'll need your help washing *everything*."

Raveno stopped walking to fix the full bore of his attention on her. "You don't know what you're asking for."

"I know exactly what I'm asking for, Raveno. You. Now, carry me to that shower with that pulsing showerhead and wash away all the ugliness and pain and hurt of today." His expression was so beautifully torn, so she added, "Please."

"That shower is meant for more than just washing," he said roughly.

"I know."

The vein in Raveno's temple was throbbing.

"Unless..." Kinsley cursed under her breath at her own insensitivity. "If you're not ready to share your havari customs with me, I understand. I can bathe myself."

"It's not that," Raveno said, but he stared down that shower stall the way another man might an approaching army. "You're too weak to bathe alone."

"You really think that if you left me here and now, I couldn't make do? That I couldn't clean myself and shower and dry and be done with the necessity of it if I really wanted? You saw my health report. Don't make this about me."

Raveno's jaw flexed.

"You were faced with an impossible choice today: your mission or my life." Kinsley released his neck and cupped his face. "And you chose me. It was the stupidest choice you could have made for our mission, but—"

"I've already been chastised by Avier and Tironan. I don't need it from you too."

"—*but* it was the most perfect choice you could have made for me."

Raveno shut his mouth.

Kinsley caressed her thumb across the plump softness of his lower lip. "We can't control whether anyone believes you. We can't control whether they care enough to rally behind you. We can't control the outcome of this mission. But I face a choice now too. Granted, a much easier one. I could choose to focus on everything so out of our control, or I could choose to cherish the one thing very much within my grasp." Kinsley tightened her hold around his neck. "And I choose you too."

Raveno's vresls quivered.

"You gave voice to my suffering. At great risk to yourself and all your carefully laid plans, you had my back and remained my ally when I needed you most." Kinsley massaged his throbbing temple for him, and Raveno closed his eyes on a rocky exhale. "I need you again. I need you now. I need you to wash away this day, this world, from my body, and I need you to do so in that shower, knowing full well that it will be more than just a shower." Kinsley pointed to the stall in question, the one with the pulsing handheld showerhead. "*Wanting* it to be more than just a shower."

Raveno opened his eyes, and finally, he tore his attention from the shower stall and met her gaze.

"So tell me, Raveno," she murmured. "What do *you* want?"

FORTY

Water sluiced over Kinsley's skin, washing away the blood from her body along with the lingering fear knotted in Raveno's gut. She was alive, Raveno reminded himself. She was healed. She was standing on her own, healthy, if a bit weak, and, most miraculous of all, struggling to unclip the buckles of his uniform, her fingers slippery from soap suds.

"A little help here?" She gave up on the buckles themselves and resorted to yanking ineffectively on his chest straps.

He grinned. "You nearly usurped me as captain of my own ship. Don't let mere uniform buckles defeat you."

He swept a cleaning sponge over her breasts and imagined laying his throbbing, aching head upon the warm softness of her curves, burying his nose in their valley, and inhaling the sweet spice of her scent deep into himself.

Just the thought of it made his vresls quiver.

He wanted to drop to his knees before her and act on his imaginings. *All* his imaginings. He wanted to breathe in the scent of every part of her into every part of him until he couldn't determine where her scent ended and his began. He wanted...

She tugged at his chest strap so violently that he nearly slipped on his own soap suds. "Less staring and more doing!"

"I can't help myself. Your body is magnificent," Raveno murmured. He caressed the sponge down her ribs and across her belly, reveling in the puckering of her skin. "How a body can be so strong, yet so soft, is mind-boggling. Your skin, for example..." He nuzzled his face in the curve of her neck.

She shuddered.

Oh, that skin! She smelled divine: the spice of her true scent mixed with the clean soap and dulled by the water just enough that he could enjoy it without losing himself in her.

Very delicately, deliberately, Raveno nipped at her neck.

Her hands lost all focus and gripped his buckles in a sagging groan.

Her scent surged. Even under the shower spray, Raveno nearly staggered from the potency of it.

Kinsley tugged at his uniform. "Get this damn thing off already."

"Your skin..." he continued determinedly. "So easily pierced and unsuitable for combat, yet so sensitive." He circled her chest with the sponge, leaving a mound of suds on her puckered nipples. "So perfectly suitable for receiving my affection." He dropped the sponge and cupped her breast. Remembering the intensity of her reaction to his previous attentions, he mimicked the action, carefully rolling the tip of her nipple between his knuckles.

Her head lolled back on a moan.

"Your limbs, so fragile and lean." He stroked his hands over her arms, careful of his claws. But remembering the shivering rake of her own nails across his scales, he followed the trail of his touch—from bicep to inner wrist—with soft nips of his teeth. "They don't seem capable of performing the skills and strikes you've mastered."

Her fingers resumed their ineffectual mission on his buckles with a frenzy.

He moved to her ear and bit at her lobe. "So deceiving, the perfection of your body, and I am consumed by it. By you."

His uniform fell from his body in a clanking heap at their feet. "Finally! Those buckles are the worst. You—"

Kinsley froze.

Raveno jerked back, startled by his abrupt nakedness—he hadn't thought she would win the battle against his buckles without his help.

"I knew it." A grin replaced the shock on her face. "It makes a strange sort of sense, I suppose. Considering your split tongue, two thumbs, two..." She peeked up and met his eyes. "Is this what you wanted to educate me on? Your two penises?"

He choked. *Svik, she thinks I have two penises.*

"It's something different, for sure," she forged ahead when he failed to find the words. "Something I've never seen before, but it's not the only difference between us. We've seen past scales and skin, chest flaps and puberty breasts—"

"As if breasts were something to see *past*," Raveno muttered.

"Sharp claws and blunt nails, pointy ears and—"

Raveno startled anew at that. "What's wrong with my ears?"

Kinsley's eyes softened. "There's nothing wrong with any of it." She lifted herself onto her tiptoes, and when he refused to lean down as she so obviously wanted, she simply wrapped her arms around his shoulders and pulled herself up—climbing his body as she might an incineration shaft—to lick the lobe of his ear.

Raveno shuddered.

"I *prefer* pointy blue ears." She dropped back to the ground and grinned. "Because they're *your* ears."

He felt them blaze at that. Svik, he'd lost complete control of his will. "They're not *always* blue," he muttered.

"I like them," she insisted, her voice low and rough, and suddenly, he wondered if ears played a more significant role than he'd realized in human intimacies.

He thought he'd been quite thorough in his research, but obviously, he should have reviewed Zethus's report more carefully.

"Do female havari have two vaginas?" she asked.

446

Raveno staggered at that. And he'd thought himself prepared for this encounter. Ha! "No." There was absolutely no way he'd missed *that* in his review of Zethus's report. And yet... "Do you?"

"Ehrm." She coughed. "No."

"Then why ask about vaginas?" Raveno asked, exasperated.

"Well, why have a second penis if not for a second vagina?"

And here, finally, they'd come to the conversation he'd been gnawing over. "I don't have a second penis."

"Yes, you do."

"No, I don't."

Kinsley chopped at the air over his groin. "I'm looking at it!"

He studied his own penis, his *one* penis, and pointed at it. "One."

She reached under his penis and cupped his thev. "Two."

"That—" Cry mercy, the back of her thumb grazed his penis, and his knees nearly buckled. "That is my thev."

"Your thev?" she pronounced the word carefully, and without any hard trills, correctly for once.

He nodded. "It differs anatomically from my penis in that it serves a different purpose other than procreation." The fact that he could manage any words at all let alone the accurate ones strung in the correct order to make sensible sentences was a testament to his remaining will. Despite his blazing ears.

"Huh. Are you sure?" The doubt in her tone would have been hilarious had he not been in agony. Her hand was physically so close, but her attention so far.

"Unequivocally certain."

"Hmmm."

Breathe. By will alone, just breathe.

She lifted a single brow. "If it looks like a duck and quacks like a duck and waddles like a duck, it's probably a duck."

He pondered that a moment, but no, he was completely unable to understand how her words applied to his thev. "This is another of your inexplicable bird idioms, isn't it?"

"It means that if an unknown thing looks and talks and acts like something, then it probably is that something you expect it to be."

"This"—Raveno took his penis in hand under the guise of explanation. In reality, he'd simply lost all sense of restraint and decorum— "is my penis, used for procreation and pleasure. I—" Gah, the embarrassment was sharp and keen! But he must be frank. Now was the last time for *any* cultural confusion or misinterpretation between them on the subject. "I will insert my penis into your vagina during intimacies. For pleasure. For fun. For..." He was rambling. "Assuming that is your desire as well."

Kinsley stared at him for a long moment.

Raveno thought he might curl up and die if it wasn't her desire as well.

"Are you seriously giving me the birds-and-bees talk right now?" she asked. Her shoulders began to shake. She grinned, and then her cheeks dipped into deep wells on either side of her smile. Dimples, he recalled vaguely.

She was laughing.

He was contemplating death, and she was laughing!

Raveno frowned, trying and failing to work out the meaning behind her words. "The bees and— More bird idioms. Speak plainly!"

"I know how sex works." Her lips twitched. "I don't need an explanation."

"I strive only to ensure we perfectly understand one another," he said. From where inside himself he found such patience, he couldn't say, but by some miracle, his voice managed to sound calm and rational. "Learning about you and your culture can be a joy, but in this, I think, we should avoid surprises."

"That's very considerate of you. Thank you," she said, and although her tone was sincere, that smile lingered. "Now that we have established the form and function of your penis, may we commence putting it to good use?"

Yes, please! "In a minute," he began. "Beneath my penis is my thev."

Kinsley slapped her face. "Which you've already established."

"Yes. I use it to..." *Just say it.* "...urinate."

"You have a second penis just to pee?"

"*I do not have—*" Raveno began vehemently. He swiped his hand down his face and sighed. Her definition was close enough, he supposed, and it covered the mechanical basics, so... "Yes, I use my thev to pee."

"Wow." She didn't release him, disgusted, as Cresha so often had after accidentally touching it. If anything, Kinsley gave it an even closer inspection. "No wonder gladiator skirts are so popular on Havar. You'd never fit all this in pants!"

His ears could not possibly burn any brighter if they were literally on fire.

Raveno cleared his throat. "They are not always this engorged."

"But your peeing penis—"

"My thev."

"—is getting hard too, like your sexual penis."

He tried to swallow, but he no longer had any saliva. "Blood flows to that general area when stimulated, so they both grow and harden, but the sensation on my thev is not as intense as my penis."

A gleam entered Kinsley's eyes, one he knew all too well when her brain was thinking faster than his. Such an expression had never before boded well for him. "But there *is* sensation."

"Yes, there's sensation. It's just not intended for pleasurable sensation." His vresls quivered.

Kinsley glanced up at their movement. "Not *intended for* or not *actually* pleasurable?"

She stroked his thev, and her knuckles simultaneously grazed his penis from base to tip.

Raveno closed his eyes and saw fireworks.

"Well?" she asked.

He hissed something at her, but he had no idea what he said and couldn't hear his own words over his rattling vresls.

"Interesting. May I?" she asked, stroking the side of the hand with which he still held his own penis.

Svik! Please! Yes! He nodded.

She cupped him in both hands—her warm, soft, strong hands—and Raveno reached out to grip the shower wall for support before he collapsed at her feet.

"Mmm," she murmured.

"Mmm?" It was all the response he was capable of with her hands upon him.

"I find it difficult to believe that havari are so unimaginative that they haven't found a pleasurable purpose for your thev."

"It's. Not. *Intended.* For—"

"Yeah, and a tongue is intended for tasting food, but that doesn't mean it doesn't enjoy tasting other things."

Raveno hesitated, not wanting to mistake her meaning. Could she truly be saying what he thought she was saying?

She caressed his penis in her hand, offering a long pull to his tip and then stroking back down to his base.

Raveno choked. "Some havari are imaginative in that way." Breathe. Must remember to breathe in order to speak. "It's considered slightly...how would you say...I believe you might call it...*kinky?*"

"Yes, I would definitely call it that." She met his eyes and grinned with both dimples and all her teeth.

If he hadn't loved her before, he would have fallen hard on that look alone. As it was, he gripped her hands so she would cease their movement and reached behind her for the showerhead.

Her cheeks flushed pink. "I'm sorry if any of that was rude. I was just surprised."

"I am not offended."

"Human men have one organ for both procreation and urination."

Raveno nodded. "Zethus reported as much. If you have questions, ask. Before. During. After. I know I will. I want... I want to know everything. I want..." Raveno couldn't help it, soaking in her sweet, upturned face. She wasn't usually sweet. She was usually all rough edges and live wires and adrenaline highs, but that smile was the sweetest thing he'd ever seen. He smiled back. "I want everything."

"How many times do I need to tell you that Zethus doesn't know everything. It's me you should rely on for Earth intelligence," she teased, and he could tell she was teasing this time by the return of that gleam in her dark eyes. "What else did Zethus report?"

Raveno held the pulsing showerhead between them. "Would you like me to tell you or show you?"

He hadn't thought it possible, but her grin widened. "Show me."

FORTY-ONE

Zethus's intelligence on pleasuring human women was decidedly more accurate than his intelligence on corn and breast development. Or maybe human women weren't all that different from havarian women. Or perhaps Raveno was simply intuitive. Kinsley didn't care.

She just didn't want him to stop.

He laid her back on the pool lounger. Its strategically placed water sprays were heaven on her back, not to mention a few other tantalizing places, and while the jets surrounded her with constant, delicious pulsing, Raveno set the showerhead to a light, slow rhythm. The sensation was exquisite at first as he simultaneously nibbled up her neck to her ear. He flicked her lobe with that thin, bifurcated tongue—oh, but the plans she had for that tongue!—then licked his way down to the curve of her shoulder and sank his teeth into her skin. The bite hurt, but only that shivering, aching kind of hurt that made her want it again, harder and deeper.

And she wanted more.

Keeping one arm looped around Raveno's neck, Kinsley scraped her nails down his chest—which he didn't even seem to notice, damn scales—and over his abs to grip the base of his cock.

His vresls, which were already spread wide around his head like a mane, taut and trembling, began to rattle.

Oh, he noticed *that*. Kinsley grinned.

He flicked the showerhead's pulse up a level, and Kinsley's grin melted into a head-lolling moan.

No, he would not distract her!

Kinsley tightened her grip on his cock, squeezed at his base, and stroked up to his tip.

His head fell forward to rest against her shoulder. His vresls vibrated against her chest, which her nipples quite appreciated, and the hand controlling the showerhead paused in its maddening, circling rhythm. His other arm, braced against the lounger, quivered.

Kinsley grinned smugly. Men were men, whether they had scales or skin, nails or claws, two penises or one.

And apparently, women were women, because Kinsley reveled in his reaction and her complete power over him with a single touch.

She bit his ear and whispered, "Let's leave the shower and continue this somewhere we can finish."

Raveno lifted his head, which appeared to take some effort, and met her eyes. His were dazed. "You're not enjoying this?" He raised the showerhead in question.

Kinsley stopped writhing, feeling slightly bereft. "Did it look like I wasn't enjoying it?"

"It certainly smelled like you were." Despite the scales and fangs that always made him look vaguely snakelike, his grin was decidedly wolfish.

"I was."

"Then why would we stop?" Raveno re-aimed the showerhead.

Kinsley stiffened in searing, gasping, gripping pleasure. "Raveno! Please!"

He chuckled. "Using my name to beg for mercy after all."

Kinsley tried to open her eyes. When had she closed them? "I want *more*," she gasped.

"Your will by my hands." He flicked the showerhead up a notch.

"Ah!" Kinsley bucked and might have launched herself completely off the lounger if her arm hadn't been locked around his neck. "No. I want... More... Of you."

"Tell me what you want. Specifically." He leaned back slightly. "And frankly. No bird metaphors."

"Ha! Oh!" She lost herself for a moment in the thrill of that warm pulse, circling her hip so its jet stream hit in just the right place, since Raveno had completely lost all sense of aim with her hand stroking him.

Hmmm, but Raveno was certainly a man on a mission. Not that he wasn't ever *not* mission oriented, but the focus of that persistent, stubborn, goal-oriented mind was apparently to reduce her to a pile of quivering nerve endings. And unlike his efforts to overthrow his father, his persistence and stubbornness were unequivocally succeeding.

Eventually, she came up for air long enough to gasp out, "I want to feel you, not the water. I want to feel your fingers and your tongue. I'm close, and I want to feel *you* inside me when I come."

Raveno's cock vibrated in her hand at that, not dissimilar to his vresls, and Kinsley marveled at the sensation.

She most definitely needed him inside her. Now.

"You've been holding back," she accused.

"Excuse me?"

"That is no ordinary penis. First you have two—"

"I maintain I have one."

"And now one of them vibrates?"

Raveno blinked sideways. "Is that cause for alarm?"

"I'm not alarmed. I—" She coughed out a laugh. "Dry off and get inside me!"

"You seem alarmed," Raveno said dryly. "Why else would you want to leave the shower?"

"So I can fully appreciate you licking and touching and stroking inside me."

"Why would we need to leave the shower to do that?"

Zethus's intelligence and Raveno's intuition could only go so far. "Human women need lubrication in order to fully enjoy being intimate," Kinsley explained.

He nodded. "As do havari women."

"But water is not lubrication. It's the opposite," Kinsley said. Very patiently, she might add, considering the raging longing throbbing from her core.

"That's why we have this." Raveno flicked a different setting on the showerhead, and the water cut, replaced by a thick, viscous gel. He spread the gel across his thumb and held it up for her inspection. "It's a waterproof lubricant. It lasts for about an hour before being absorbed into the body like lotion."

Kinsley bit her lip. "And you're sure it's safe? For humans, I mean, considering I have skin instead of scales."

He nodded. "As you may have noticed, havari don't have scales on their intimate organs. Just skin. Like you."

"But you can't be sure. You—"

"I'm sure. I..." His ears blazed blue, and his vresls dipped back against his chest. "I asked Avier, and he did whatever he does to confirm such things. It's safe for you. As am I, in terms of sexual diseases. It's just a matter of want."

Kinsley met his eyes, torn between being touched, amused, and mortified. "Presumptuous of you," she teased. "Asking Avier about this."

"I knew how I felt, and in the hopes of your returned affection, I needed to ensure your safety."

Amusement won out. "And naturally, you just assumed that we'd end up here. In the shower. Needing lubricant."

Raveno laughed. "Where else would we end up?"

"In a bed, maybe?"

Raveno shook his head. "Never. Without the water to mute the pheromones of your desire, I would be overwhelmed by your scent and eventually, well..." He grinned ruefully. "Your scent is intoxicating. Literally."

"You would get drunk on my scent?"

He nodded.

"So instead of having sex in bed, your go-to 'normal' place of intimacy is the shower?"

"Yes."

Kinsley took in the extravagance and kinky convenience of the shower spa with new eyes. "I see."

"So?" Raveno lifted the gel on his thumb up for her inspection a second time. "May I?"

Kinsley nodded.

Raveno dipped his hand between them, spreading the gel over and around and between.

Kinsley closed her eyes and shuddered.

"Speaking of ensuring your safety..." Raveno began.

Oh, what more could he possibly need to discuss?

"I'm not a scientist, and although Avier has some theories on the subject, he could only speculate on the outcome of intimacies. Between us. An outcome, which isn't very likely, but I wouldn't want to risk..."

Kinsley sandwiched his face in her hands. "You're spiraling."

Raveno cleared his throat. "I can't imagine that we would be capable of conceiving a child, but until we know for certain, and until that is the goal of our intimacy, I propose that we endeavor to prevent conception."

"Agreed." Kinsley tapped his nose. "And in fact, I've got that covered."

"How so?"

"I have a birth control implant."

Raveno glanced down at her ankesh. "An implant?"

"Yep."

"To control...the many risks of giving birth?"

"Ha! No, although that would be inventive. It controls the risk of getting pregnant. I had it replaced for my mission to Yemen, about seven months before being abducted. It lasts up to three Earth years, so unless the implant is removed, I won't get pregnant for the next year and five months. Assuming conception between us is even possible." She snorted. "A big assumption if you ask me."

Raveno's vresls perked. "Really?"

She grinned. "Really."

"To confirm: I may insert my bare penis into your vagina without risking pregnancy?"

"Correct."

His vresls popped wide open and rattled.

Kinsley laughed at that. "Do female havari not have birth control?"

"They do. *We* do. A barrier is placed between us, so we may both enjoy intimacies while preventing conception. But we have nothing that would allow us to *forgo* a barrier."

"So." Kinsley wiggled her hips. "You planning to put this lubricant of yours to good use or just talk about it all day?"

"All *shaoz*." Raveno grinned, but instead of positioning himself over her and easing himself inside as she'd expected, he dropped to his knees. He lifted her legs so they rested high on his shoulders and breathed in her scent.

Kinsley cringed—of all places to become intoxicated by!—but before she could protest, he was kissing her. And before she could inhale enough air to sufficiently moan her appreciation, he was licking her.

And all her dreams for that bifurcated tongue became reality.

Sweet Jesus, the waterproof lubricant worked as advertised. She felt every whip-quick lick, every textured lap, every nibble and kiss and vibration of that talented tongue. Oh, but those impossible hard trills she'd never be able to physically pronounce blazed over her clitoris like lightning strikes.

"I take it back," Kinsley gasped, clinging to Raveno's neck and gaping in wonder at the lubricant-spitting, massaging showerhead in his hand. "Havari plumbing has far surpassed human plumbing."

Raveno laughed, and the rumble from his amusement flamed through her core to her nipples and toes and every tingling cell in between.

"Oh, Raveno."

"Yes?"

"More."

And Raveno proved without a shadow of a doubt that he could take orders just as well as he gave them.

Raveno hit a particularly sensitive spot—how he even managed to find a spot left unwrung after his previous onslaught was a miracle all its own, but he did—and the Y of his tongue attacked it mercilessly, swirling and lapping and rubbing and swirling and tapping and coaxing and more swirling and more tapping and—

Raveno eased back. "May I enter you?"

"God, yes! Enter me! Enter me!" Kinsley shrieked at him, completely beyond inhibition and shame.

Raveno helped her legs from his shoulders, and Kinsley wrapped them around his waist as he eased his cock inside her.

His vibrating cock.

Kinsley bucked up and moaned, clawing at his back in embarrassing abandon. "Your penis is a fucking miracle."

Raveno swayed and braced his arm on the lounger with a groan. "Say that again, and I won't need your full scent to lose all control."

"I'm serious. This is... Unreal. This is... Jesus, you're not even moving and it's—oh!"

Raveno finally moved, and his second penis—his thev—swelled just as hard if not as large and not as vibrating. It rubbed against her ass with each thrust. Not entering, just knocking. As if asking for permission.

Kinsley bit her lip and gave in to the sensation. She gripped the lounger with one hand and Raveno with the other and held on for the ride. It was everything she did on her own in the dark and didn't ask from her partners because that would be embarrassing and probably unsanitary and likely something she wouldn't like anyway. And it felt... It felt...

"If it's something you want, too..." Kinsley hedged on a gasp. "You can...your thev can...oh!"

The tip of his thev dipped inside. Just its tip and just for a moment.

Kinsley gasped. "Like that!"

Raveno stilled. "I'm so sorry. I didn't mean to. I—"

"Mean to!" Kinsley bucked. "Mean to!"

"—didn't..." He blinked. "What?"

"Please, Raveno. Don't stop." Jesus, she *was* begging.

He blew out a hard breath. "If we continue—"

"If?" Kinsley jerked back, alarmed.

"I can't— That is to say, it might— I'm so aroused, my thev will sneak in."

"I sincerely doubt it will *sneak* anywhere." Kinsley snorted. "I know you said it's kinky, and I know I was mostly half joking earlier, but right now, I like how it feels."

Raveno gaped. "You like it?"

"Yes." She wriggled her hips. "Keep going. Let your thev caress me, and if you manage to *sneak* it in, that would be amazing."

"You *want* me to sneak it in? *Deliberately?*"

Kinsley threw her head back, half exasperated and half aching— mostly aching—and banged the back of her head on the lounger. "Ouch! Yes!"

He cupped her head, concerned. "Are you—"

"If you check on my well-being one more time, you'll need someone to check on *your* well-being!" Kinsley hissed.

Raveno chuckled, then eased inside her and continued where he'd left off.

Kind of. Something was different about his movements. His thrusts were deeper, his retreats more fluid, his caressing more confident. Intentional. Uninhibited.

The pounding vibrations of his cock were like thunder inside her. His thev caressed her slickly, rubbing and pushing and teasing and finally—*finally!*— entering simultaneously with his penis. Kinsley felt that first clenching wave pulse within her.

Raveno leaned his forehead to hers. The noise that ripped from his throat was heady and raw, nearly pain-filled. "Kinsley."

Kinsley opened her eyes and met his gaze from inches away.

Oh.

The ecstasy on his face stole what little breath she had left. His pleasure was so apparent, so exquisitely sharp, her heart was pierced by it.

A second clench pulsed through her, then a third and fourth, and like a riptide, they crashed together and pulled her under.

She couldn't think. She couldn't speak. She couldn't see, only feel.

And she felt the sun.

FORTY-TWO

Water was pooling in Raveno's right ear. His left elbow was still smarting, having caught his fall after slipping off the lounger, but that pain was swiftly easing into numbness from the weight of Kinsley's body.

He should get up. He should dry and dress and brace for the repercussions of publicly challenging Josairo's authority. Svik, he needed to prepare for a frisaes and the possibility of the frisaes frenzy to come.

Raveno tightened his arms around Kinsley, wedged his nose in the valley of her breasts, and inhaled long and deep.

Even with water and soap muting her scent, his head still spun.

Her fingers had unraveled his braids, tossed his ornamental circlet aside—who knew where—and were massaging his scalp with lulling tenderness. Tingles spread down his neck and through his shoulders. He'd never felt so utterly boneless. Their mission was on the precipice of defeat, but in this moment, in her arms, he felt safe. For the first time in forever, his mind was quiet, his head blissful, his body at peace.

He buried his face in her chest and felt his shoulders heave. She couldn't possibly see his tears as they blended with the shower water, and he swore he didn't make a noise, but her arms left his scalp and wrapped around his shoulders.

She kissed his forehead, exactly where his temple was no longer throbbing.

"I like your kisses," his murmured hoarsely. "Even if that is the same mouth you use to eat and vomit."

"This mouth can be used for other things too." She tightened her hug with one hand and traced the line of his spine with her nails, raking them between his scales, just as he liked. "Things I haven't gotten around to yet."

He grinned, but as incredible as that sounded, assuming he was accurately envisioning the fantasy she was implying, he didn't move. He never wanted to move again. "Next time."

"Next time?" Kinsley huffed. "It's not like you to be an optimist."

"There are things I didn't get around to either."

Kinsley eased back, letting the shower spray pelt her face. "Okay, then. Next time."

Raveno relaxed in her embrace. He cupped the breast next to his face, encouraged it closer, and sucked its tip.

Kinsley arched her back deliciously.

"Next time could be now," he suggested.

Kinsley grinned.

Raveno pushed himself up, very gently sucking the opposite nipple into his mouth, between his fangs, and nibbled until it peaked.

His anku buzzed. "Avier to Raveno. Do you receive?"

Kinsley must have felt the vibration in his arm, because her groan was decidedly less enraptured. "What do they want?"

"I might normally ignore them, but we are in the middle of an insurrection."

Kinsley flapped her hand at him.

Raveno propped himself over her, eyeing her breast longingly. "Raveno to Avier. Signal received."

"Is Kinsley recovered from her healing session?"

His eyes swept over her luscious body. "Yes."

"We need you home. Now."

Kinsley propped herself up and bit the sensitive lobe of his unscaled ear.

Raveno closed his eyes and shuddered.

"Raveno?"

"I'm—" He cleared his throat and attempted to speak without hissing. "I'm here."

"That's the problem. We need you *here*. Both of you. We have a situation that—"

"I started a battle we're not ready for. I know," Raveno growled. "We'll be there shortly. Both of us."

Kinsley ceased nibbling and flopped flat to her back with a pained sigh.

Raveno heartily concurred. "Next time."

"There may not be a next time."

The first twinge of his returning headache flexed through his temple. "Then we must ensure there is."

"What?" Avier asked.

"We'll be there shortly," Raveno barked and ended the connection. He returned his head to Kinsley's chest. Although his ear was no longer waterlogged, it ached. His elbow was still throbbing, and his mind raced with everything they needed to do, everything that hadn't been done, everything they couldn't possibly accomplish in time.

Kinsley rubbed her eyes. "Avier, Tironan, Zethus, Dellao, and Riley are more likely to kill each other than save the world on their own."

"I'm not doing this for the world anymore."

Kinsley resumed rubbing his back.

"We could leave."

Her hand stilled.

"Cresha was right. She was crazy at the time because I'd have been forced to hunt her down and kill her, but now my cover is thoroughly blown." Raveno sat up again and met her wide, dark eyes.

"We can take *Sa Vivsheth* and leave. Without a full passenger load, I can maintain the craft with a four-person crew."

Kinsley licked her lips, and Raveno could see those cogs grinding.

"We'll return to Earth," he said. "You'll be home in less than a thesh. A year."

"What about you?" she asked.

He frowned. "What about me?"

"After you drop me off on Earth, what will you do?"

"I'll return home to Havar and face the consequences of my actions."

"Alone," Kinsley said flatly.

"With Avier, Tironan, Zethus, and Dellao."

"Alone."

Raveno scowled. "I might have been undercover, but I still bought and trafficked you and all the humans. I will face my fate. But before I do, I will see you home."

"If we leave today, you wouldn't return for two years, Raveno. How many people might be stolen and trafficked in that time for another Intergalactic Frisaes?"

"In that timeframe? Another shipful. Two at the most."

"Two shipfuls too many."

Raveno groaned into her chest, knowing she was right.

"It's not just about saving your planet, Raveno. It's about saving future planets. Future *mes* in the galaxy who don't want to fight in your death games. Future Martins and Leannes and Benjamins who don't want to be abducted."

Raveno stilled. He could see now where this was leading, and he would not abide it. "No."

"I can't leave them."

And there it was. "You damn well can!"

"I can't."

"They would leave you. They *did* leave you!"

Kinsley sandwiched his face between her hands. "And I am not them."

Raveno stared into those deep dark eyes. So like Tironan's. So like his mother's. And yet, all her own. "You're certainly not."

"We're not running from this fight. I made you a promise, and—"

"I relieve you of that promise."

"And your mission became mine."

"I'm not letting you sacrifice your life for my revenge!"

"You can't 'let' me do anything." She cocked her head. "Or are you taking away my choice entirely? Throwing me back in that cage?"

"Kinsley—"

"And besides which, even if you claim not to want it—which I know isn't true—this isn't about your revenge. It's about mine."

Raveno hung his head. He'd known from the very beginning the terrible lengths it often took to break the strong of will. Lengths he'd never cross. Not with her.

"Listen." She licked her lips. "Before we reconvene with the crew, I need to tell you something."

Raveno peeked up, wary of the sudden hesitancy in her tone. "Yes?"

"Back in the arena, before getting my ass kicked, I...had a thought."

"A thought."

She nodded, then bit her lip.

"Well?" he asked, summoning patience he hadn't even known he possessed. "What was this thought?"

"If I'm being honest, it's just more speculation against someone without evidence," she admitted.

"I don't mind speculation, assuming such accusations stay between us until we find evidence." Raveno rubbed her back. "Speak your thoughts."

"I was thinking that maybe Josairo's newest advisor is responsible for his absence. What's his name, Shezi, Sheso, Shensu?"

"Vri Shavril Sheso Zami?"

"That's the one."

Raveno barked out a laugh. "Doubtful."

"He's the only Vri Shavril who didn't earn his position. It was very conveniently granted to him by Josairo, who no one has seen in two thesh."

"I've known Sheso since childhood. We played on the same sheshzi team." Raveno shook his head. "He could barely remember his position, let alone think three plays ahead."

"Who better to usurp Josairo than someone no one would suspect?"

Raveno traced the ridges of her spine, thinking. "You no longer want to suspect Veilon," he said, not unkindly. He didn't want to suspect her either.

"I want to get this right," Kinsley insisted, and then in a smaller voice, she added, "I don't want to be responsible for another failed mission."

"After the stunt I pulled at the Sparring Ceremony, we can share blame should the mission fail," Raveno acquiesced. "But whoever may have usurped Josairo, it is not Sheso."

"Then who?"

Raveno compressed his lips, hating his thoughts. "Cresha, perhaps."

Kinsley thumped the back of her head on the floor.

"Are you—"

"Talk about wild, unsupported speculation!" Kinsley speared him with a look. "She offered to help me *escape* this planet. I doubt she was responsible for *bringing* me here."

"How better to cover her guilt?"

She snorted. "No."

Raveno scowled. "As if Sheso was such a better suggestion."

"Your argument against Sheso is based on the boy you once knew. He's a man now, and you haven't been on-world in over two thesh. People change."

"It wouldn't matter if I'd been gone two hundred thesh. Sheso couldn't grow a brain in either amount of time."

"Then how did he gain his position?" Kinsley snapped.

"How did any of this even happen?" Raveno snapped back. "How did someone have the tech to access that security footage from *Sa Vivsheth*? How did they translate the English into Haveo?"

"How did they even have that video? I thought the only security cameras on your ship were in the brig."

"That's what I thought too," he groused.

"Then who has that kind of access and technology?"

Raveno let his head fall limp into Kinsley's chest. "If I knew the answer to that question, I wouldn't be leaving your arms in favor of conversation with Avier."

She stroked his head. "Avier isn't the only one waiting."

Raveno groaned.

They dried and dressed and braced themselves for the conversation to come, but when they arrived at Raveno's private suite, it wasn't just his inner crew and Riley waiting for them.

Raveno stared at the crowd inside his suite, floored. "A warning would have been appreciated," he murmured.

"I tried. You seemed distracted," Avier said dryly. "And then you cut our connection."

Raveno chortled. "You'd have been distracted too."

His entire living suite was packed. In what he could see of the relaxation, cooking, and dining rooms, there were at least fifty people, if not more, including Jhoni, Kual, and his entire crew from *Sa Vivsheth*. The rest of the people in the crowd were familiar by face alone. He'd recall their names should someone remind him, but in terms of allies and enemies, they were strangers.

Cry mercy, people were probably waiting for him in the sleeping and bathing rooms too.

After half a lifetime of crowds chanting his name and swooning at his presence, he'd developed a sense for judging the mood of a room, and this crowd, with their wide eyes, crossed arms, bristling vresls, and flicking tongues, was nervous and edgy. Scared, even. But not unkind.

They were hopeful.

A movement caught his eye: someone stepping forward from the masses to stand on a chair.

Cresha.

Raveno fisted his hands to preventing anyone from seeing how they trembled.

A tentative fingertip traced the side of his pinky, at the very edge of where his scales ended and his skin began.

Raveno opened his hand, and Kinsley slipped her palm against his, wrapped her fingers in the spaces between his fingers, and gripped tight.

With the firm tenderness of that one gesture, a miracle occurred. His headache eased, and his trembling stilled.

She's right, he realized with some awe. *With her, I'm not alone.*

Cresha raised her arms, and the light buzz of the crowd yielded to silence. "Vri Cilvril Raveno Hoviir," she said, calm and sure and proud, as he hadn't witnessed her address him in over eleven thesh.

She clicked her heels in salute, and the entire room echoed her.

"I am here, as we all are, as family representatives," she said. "We have heard you, Raveno, and we believe what you revealed. You were ordered to transport the humans to Havar against their will." Cresha let a moment of tense silence fill the room. "Some of us are shocked. Many of us are ashamed and disgusted. But *all* of us want to hear what you plan to do about it. And learn how we can help." Cresha's eyes seared into his, as much fire and demand in her gaze as there had been all those thesh ago when she'd confronted him with a similar challenge.

This time, however, he wasn't walking away.

Cresha stepped down from her chair.

Tironan shouldered through the crowd, carrying another chair. He placed it before Raveno.

By will or wrath, this is it.

"Tell me you've secured this suite," Raveno demanded.

Tironan nodded.

"Better than you secured *Sa Vivsheth*? We can't afford another video leak."

Tironan's ears burned, but his eyes narrowed. "Y-you never asked me to s-secure *Sa Vivsheth*."

"I never asked you to secure this suite either."

"After that s-spectacle in the arena, I thought it appropriate," Tironan grumbled.

Raveno glanced at Avier.

Avier smirked. "Don't worry. I had him secure the infirmary too."

Tironan sniffed. "As if I w-wasn't already securing the s-suite when you approached m-me about the infirmary."

"True enough," Avier admitted.

Raveno patted Tironan on the back hard enough to stagger him, then stepped on the chair.

"Thank you for coming," Raveno said to the crowd. "Your presence here puts you at great risk, and I'm honored by your support. For many thesh, I've worked undercover during my missions for Josairo in the attempt to gain off-world allies to support a transition in power. Thus far, Bazail, Iroan, and Fray support my endeavor."

The crowd shifted, seeming less hopeful. They eyed one another, murmuring about Lorien, Ku, Marzes, Ioali and all of Josairo's many allies, and of course, the off-world threat never far from their minds: Haven.

"I too had hoped to gain more off-world support against Josairo, and I *will* continue working toward that goal. Assuming I still have the trust and support of my crew." Raveno turned to Kual and Jhoni and the many upturned faces beyond them. "I apologize for the deception. Until now, I felt it imperative to maintain my cover and operate under Josairo's orders. Which were abhorrent, I know. Asking you to trust me now, after I have so deceived you, is asking too much. But I ask you anyway. Will you help me overthrow Josairo?"

"Yes, Vri Cilvril."

"Of course, Vri Cilvril."

"I am with you, Vri Cilvril."

Kual nodded.

Jhoni, possibly for the first time in his entire life, didn't dive in headfirst to lick Raveno's boots. He crossed his arms, waiting.

Even without Jhoni, however, the near unanimity of this crew's support was overwhelming. Raveno felt his throat clench. Svik, his reputation was shattered enough without him succumbing to tears.

"My challenge to Josairo was in earnest, and with your support, I would happily face Josairo in a frisaes. However—"

"Nearly anyone would be a better Vra Cilvril s'Hvri than Josairo!" A male in the crowd interrupted. "Someone must win against him eventually."

"Raveno will!" a female answered. "He's never lost a frisaes!"

Another female scoffed. "Neither has Josairo!"

Raveno raised his arms for silence. "*However,* I don't believe that Josairo will rise to my challenge. Per the advice given to him by his Vri Shavrili, Josairo has hosted the Intergalactic Frisaes via projection for several thesh. I've honestly been grateful for his absence. It's been a relief not having any of my crew or our civilians targeted and executed during the ceremonies."

Many in the crowd were nodding. A few eyed one another with speaking glances, murmuring about *Sa Riluuz.* That particular execution—so many at once and many of them so young, fresh vrili newly graduated from the academy—had haunted him all these thesh as well.

"But I've recently discovered that Josairo has been conducting *all* his business remotely," Raveno continued. "It's possible that someone else is conducting his business and issuing orders on his behalf. Possibly...in his absence."

"Who?" someone shouted. "Who would do that?"

"Where is Josairo?" And quickly following that question, a hopeful, "Is he dead?"

"Why would someone kill him only to pretend to be him?" another scoffed.

"Please." Raveno raised his hands again. "I have those same questions! Tomorrow, either Josairo will meet my challenge or he won't. And if he doesn't, we will unravel this mystery and right the wrongs that he—"

"Where has he been all this time?"

"Isn't Josairo's absence a good thing?"

"Just declare him dead and take over as Vra Cilvril s'Hvri!"

"Without enough off-world allies, Haven will attack!"

I'm losing them, Raveno thought, distraught, as their mutters swelled to outright arguing.

Cresha stood on her chair again. "Please! Everyone! We're here to listen! We—"

But the crowd just shouted over Cresha's pleading.

He'd waited too long. He'd kept too many secrets. They'd only feared him, and now in absence of that fear, would they resent and distrust him? Hate him, even, just like Josairo?

Kinsley lifted her arm and waved. "Tironan, would you—"

Tironan appeared from the crowd with another chair. "Already o-on it."

"Thank you." Kinsley was suddenly standing on a chair beside him.

The entire room went silent.

"*Your* allies, the Lorien, took us. *Your* Vri Cilvril s'Hvri ordered Raveno to kidnap us. And you argue about how and why and blame?" Kinsley asked, her tone scathing.

You could pierce the tension in the room with a pivz.

"Thirty-six people in chains, but *you* not see. Thirty-six people, not warriors. Two shaoz from now, *you* have thirty-six murders."

Her words were clear, if a bit ungrammatical, but she'd never spoken with better and more precise inflection than in this moment. His heart soared, all pride. No barbs.

"I, of all people in room, have right to doubt and blame. But Raveno proves his true intent with action. *He* see chains you do not. *He* train me for battles you watch and enjoy. *He* plan to stop

471

murders. He *tries*." Kinsley paused, met each person's eyes, then took Raveno's hand in hers. "I trust him to return me home."

Some people were nodding. Others were still just frozen, as riveted as Raveno himself. Several, he noted, couldn't meet her eyes.

"What about the human he murdered?" Jhoni burst out. "How can you trust him after that?"

"Raveno did many bad things for Josairo," Kinsley said. "But not murder human."

"I was there! I saw it!"

"You saw a trick. That man lives. He here. He—" Kinsley stood on her toes and scanned the crowd. "Riley, would you please...there." Kinsley pointed, and everyone turned, wide-eyed.

Riley unfolded one hand from his crossed arms and waved. He was leaning against a doorjamb in the corner of the room, scowling, completely unimpressed by the entire proceedings and his role in it.

Jhoni stared, agog.

"That's him," someone from his crew breathed.

And then, louder, another crewmate. "That's the man Raveno executed!"

"He *is* alive!"

The collective inhalations from the room seemed to suck the air from Raveno's lungs. He refused to rub at his chest, no matter how his heart throbbed.

He'd done his job well, very well indeed, for them to believe him capable of burning someone alive. That had been the point: to inspire obedience through fear.

Why, then, did his eyes burn?

"How can we help?" Cresha asked, helping to steer the crowd.

Kinsley didn't smile, but Raveno knew her well enough to read the twitching corners of her mouth. "Raveno fights frisaes in two shifts. If Josairo here or if he not here, Raveno fights to free me and all humans. Support Raveno to support our return home."

The murmur of the crowd swelled. No one was chanting his name or swooning at his presence this time, but despite their frowns, they were nodding. Their arms were still crossed and their vresls bristling, but when they looked up at Raveno, he didn't feel their hatred. He didn't feel their unwavering support either, but he could see the determination in their eyes. For today, for saving Kinsley, that was all he needed.

Kinsley stroked her thumb lightly across his knuckles. He could barely feel her touch through his scales, yet the sensation, as minute as it was, shot like a puff of phosh straight to his head.

Raveno nearly swayed, but her strength was as anchoring as her scent was intoxicating.

He firmed his grip and held on tight.

FORTY-THREE

KINSLEY LAY IN BED WITH HER HEAD BURROWED UNDER THE pillow, attempting to block out the racket of Raveno's tossing and turning or, failing that, to smother herself into unconsciousness. They'd begun the night—third shift—cuddling, his arms wrapped around her shoulders and her head resting on the rock that was his chest. She'd inhaled his orange-fresh scent and felt—dare she even think it?—content. When the comfort of his embrace couldn't overcome her throbbing ear and crushed shoulder, she'd flipped onto her side, and he'd followed, spooning her. And just when she'd begun to drift asleep, lulled by the surrounding warmth of his bed and body, he'd rolled onto his back to brood.

Half a shift later, the pillow couldn't possibly be more fluffed, and his throat must be sore from all those hissing exhales.

And Kinsley was still wide awake.

She groaned into the mattress.

"Are you all right?" he asked.

"Me? Am *I* all right?" Kinsley laughed. "You're the one moving and huffing all shift."

Raveno grunted.

"Are you ever going to tell me what's wrong?"

Silence.

Kinsley unburied her head. "Maybe you should inhale a deep lungful of my scent and just pass out. Then at least one of us could rest."

"Don't think I haven't considered it," he grumbled.

Kinsley found his leg—his calf, she thought—with her foot and stroked it. "We're not even sure Josairo will show. In fact, he probably won't, and then *you'll* pontificate about a new world order. We'll face whoever jumps out of the woodwork to stop you, win a frisaes against them if need be, and then we're home free. In my case, literally."

"The arena is carved from volcanic rock."

Kinsley hesitated at that. "What?"

"We have no wood for anyone to jump out of."

Kinsley blew out a hard breath. "*Coming out of the woodwork* means someone emerging unexpectedly for selfish reasons. It's just an idiom."

"Hmmm. There was no mention of birds, so I didn't recognize it as such."

Kinsley rolled to face Raveno and pinned him with a glare that would have been more effective had he been looking at her and not the ceiling. "Is this about killing Josairo?"

"Is what about him?" he asked the ceiling.

"Your brooding."

His jaw flexed. He had a beautifully chiseled jaw, perfect for brooding.

Kinsley shook her head. "I know you've dreamed of revenge for a long time—"

"Eleven thesh," he murmured.

"But if you're feeling conflicted about your frisaes tomorrow, that's okay."

More staring. More jaw flexing.

"In your shoes, I'd feel anxious, angry, nervous." Kinsley waited a beat and added, "Doubt-filled."

"Then it's a good thing I am killing my father and not you yours."

Kinsley rubbed her eyelids. There wasn't enough air in the world to sigh through the frustration induced by this man.

"I will run him through with my ezil, the way he impaled my mother." Raveno peered off into the distance, presumably at the fantasy of his father's impaling. "I will meet his eyes and whisper the sealing vows, 'My will in Havar's hands.' I will liberate Havar from his rule, and in doing so, liberate myself!"

Kinsley waited.

Raveno shifted his eyes to meet hers.

She raised her eyebrows.

Raveno resumed staring at the ceiling. "Veilon wasn't here with Cresha and the other family representatives seeking the truth."

Ah. "None of the Vri Shavrili were here," she said carefully.

If possible, and she hadn't thought it was, his expression hardened. "I don't care about the other Vri Shavrili."

"It was a miracle *anyone* came. We have Cresha to thank for that show of support, you know. She rounded up everyone and encouraged them to come, to listen to *you*, her ex-husband."

"I know." His jaw unlocked, so when he spoke, he wasn't hissing through his teeth. "I thanked her."

"Another miracle," Kinsley teased, nudging his calf with her foot.

"Do you have a point, or are you just babbling for the sake of distraction?"

Babbling, indeed! "The people closest to you are not always planning to stab you in the back."

At that, he gave her his full attention. "Have you been conspiring with Avier?"

"I've been *talking* to Avier. Not conspiring with him."

"Talking to him about me without me present *is* conspiring."

Kinsley rubbed her eyelids harder. "You're being paranoid."

"How can I not be suspicious of people when someone *is* truly conspiring against us?"

Kinsley dropped her hand and met his eyes. "First, you suspected

Tironan when he was nothing more than a loyal, loving brother. Then, in a rash burst of unsubstantiated suspicion, you accused Cresha of being responsible for the IF's corruption. *Cresha.*"

Raveno covered his face with his hands and groaned.

"And now you're suspicious of Veilon again."

"She should have been here today," he muttered from behind his palms.

"It wasn't exactly a scheduled meeting."

"She beat you to a pulp during training."

"To protect you."

Raveno fisted both hands on his forehead. "She would have killed you during the Sparring Ceremony had I not intervened."

"Again, to protect you." Kinsley sighed. "At least she was honest about it."

"But she shouldn't be protecting *me.* She should be outraged by what I've done."

"She loves you."

"So does Cresha, but when *she* saw such intense injustice, she was willing to risk my wrath and her life to do what's right."

Kinsley traced a winding scar that sliced through the scales on his shoulder. "It's a novel concept for you, I know, but have you considered simply talking to her?"

"Yes," he grumbled. "She's not answering her ankis."

"I meant in person."

Raveno waved that away. "Why is she avoiding me? I am the one angry at *her.*"

"I'm sure she's pissed at you too."

"Why would she be angry with *me?*"

"Oh, I don't know, maybe for developing a persona as the murderous killing hand to your tyrannical father and planning covert, undercover missions against him without her knowledge and letting the truth blow up in her face during a publicly broadcast event in front of millions?"

Raveno crossed his arms mutinously. "I was protecting her."

"Hmm, where have I heard that before?" Kinsley tapped her chin thoughtfully.

Raveno hissed at her.

"Veilon wasn't the only person not in attendance at today's meeting," Kinsley murmured. "Zethus wasn't there either."

"It wasn't exactly a scheduled meeting," Raveno reminded her.

Kinsley joined Raveno in his ceiling staring. "He could have at least checked in."

"It's only been, what, two shaoz since his last communication?"

"Going on three." *An eternity*.

"He never connects with me that often during an off-world undercover assignment."

"What if something terrible happened? Would we even know?"

"Your sister is fine."

Kinsley opened her mouth to argue.

"*My* version of fine," he added.

Kinsley gave in to a reluctant laugh and wiped her cheeks with a swift swipe. "That didn't answer my question."

Raveno stroked his foot along her ankle.

"Well," Kinsley clear her throat. "If we're not going to sleep, we may as well do something else. Something productive."

"There's nothing *to* do," Raveno muttered. "That's why we're brooding."

"We might not be able to do anything about Veilon or Zethus at the moment, but we can certainly do *something*. Anything except lie here, not sleeping."

"Fine. What do you propose?"

Kinsley walked her fingers across his chest.

His vresls perked.

"We should go blow something up."

His vresls fell flat.

"Come on! I've been so good. I haven't touched an explosive in over a thesh. Not one!"

He faced her squarely, finally, his expression incredulous. "You blew up one of my solo cruisers."

"But *technically*, I didn't get to touch it. I only triggered the explosion, and it wasn't even an explosive of my own making."

He barked a laugh. "And you think my paranoia is a problem."

"Please?"

"This isn't even up for debate."

She clasped her hands together before him. "Pretty please?"

"Oh, the addition of *pretty* has convinced me. My mind is now changed." Raveno shook his head, but she must have been somewhat convincing, because he heaved an agonized sigh. "Even if I wanted to indulge you—"

She squeaked and tapped a drum-roll on his shoulder.

"*Hypothetically*, where would we even get—"

"The fireworks from the arena."

"Not this again," he groaned.

"You said we could 'examine explosive weaponry later,' but if we wait any longer, there might not be a later," she reasoned.

"But where would we—"

"Tell me you don't have a spot."

Raveno frowned. "A *spot*?"

"You know. That special spot where once upon a time you snuck out with your friends and got high on a girl's scent for the first time and, I don't know, escaped to get away from your younger siblings." Kinsley circled her pointer finger at him. "As a younger sibling, I know you had a spot."

Raveno scoffed. "Who has time for friends and lovers? I was training for future frisaes with my siblings, and there was no escaping that."

"Cry mercy." Kinsley tossed the blanket aside and stood. "I'll find you a spot. We'll make up for your tragic childhood with a night, er, *shift* of rebellion."

"I'm usurping my father's throne. How much more rebellion do I need in my life?" he grumbled even as he reached across the side table for his prosthetic leg.

"But you bear that rebellion like a root canal. This rebellion will be fun."

"What's a root canal?"

"It's when a doctor for your teeth drills into a tooth and cleans out its insides."

"A doctor for your teeth?"

"Yeah. On Earth, doctors specialize in specific body parts and organs and— What?"

Raveno's lip had started twitching.

Kinsley narrowed her eyes.

"'Doctor for your teeth,'" he said, giving in to his grin. "As if I don't know what a dentist is."

"You didn't know *root canal*." Kinsley smacked him with a pillow and marched to the door. "Stay here, then. I'll steal the fireworks and find some fun without you."

Naturally, the moment she told him to stay, he finished attaching his leg and followed. "We can't stay out too late, and no getting high. I have a fight to the death next shift and will need a clear head."

"You can't put parameters on fun," Kinsley complained, secretly thrilled. He hadn't unequivocally said no to blowing something up.

RAVENO HAD GLANCED AWAY FOR ONLY A MOMENT, LESS TIME than it took to blink, but apparently, that was enough time for Kinsley to unscrew two bolts from the firework with a pivz she had pulled from who knew where—she wasn't wearing a holster—and remove a control chip the size of her pinky nail. It dangled by three wires, lolling from the open panel like a tongue.

"Kinsley! What—" Raveno began and, realizing the pitch of his voice, took a moment and tried again. Calm. Rational. Sane. Someone had to be. "What are you doing?"

They were back in the arena on the stage floor, where only a scant shaoz ago Kinsley had lain bleeding—her ribs broken, her lung pierced, her skull fractured—as he'd willingly and completely blown his cover. With the seats empty, the silence calm instead of choking, and the ushelz sleeping, the memory seemed more nightmare than reality.

"This is...wow, I wasn't expecting this. Although, considering the moving display they create, I don't know what I *was* expecting." Kinsley leaned in for a closer inspection.

Raveno suspected that if she could physically manage it, she'd crawl inside the thing.

"Fascinating," she breathed, settling back with something in her hand.

Cry mercy, she'd disconnected all three wires from the firework's insides! "I thought we'd just fire off a few. Like a private show."

Kinsley placed the wires and computer chip aside and plunged both hands wrist-deep inside the explosive. Which might or might not still be armed, considering she'd just tossed its chip aside. But still...

"It has its own fuel tanks and pumps and firing chamber," Kinsley said in a tone that suggested this was something to marvel at. "It's more like a missile than a firework, but it still has a bursting charge and stars. Yet without a time-delay fuse..."

Raveno rubbed his forehead. "When you mentioned finding 'a spot,' I thought it was something we'd do together."

"The detonation must be programmed." Kinsley leaned back, rubbing her bottom lip. "We are together."

"Something romantic."

Although her eyes were fixed in his direction, he could tell her mind was still seeing the inner workings of the firework.

"Never mind." He should probably be annoyed by her absolute absorption, but in spite of his misgivings, he was charmed. "This is how you define fun?"

"This is art," she said, her tone distracted at she returned to the operation in front of her.

Teaching Kinsley hand-to-hand combat and helping her grow as a warrior was gratifying. Her accomplishments were his pride. Her failings his pain. But seeing her reunited with her passion and performing the very skill that had inspired her nickname was like witnessing a bird soar. Envy and awe filled him, and unexpectedly, more pride.

Her mastery had nothing to do with him, yet his surge of satisfaction was unmistakable.

"Why explosives?"

The near rapture in her expression soured. "I've been trying and failing to answer that question my entire life." Her nose scrunched, and her voice rose half an octave. "'Why blow up the barn, Kinsley? Why not just join the soccer team, Kinsley? Why are you ruining your life, Kinsley?'"

Raveno frowned. "I didn't mean it like that, as if you needed to defend yourself or justify your passion."

Kinsley's fingers stilled. Her eyes flicked up to meet his.

"I meant, what does it mean to you?"

Kinsley straightened.

"It seems to mean quite a lot."

"It does." Kinsley bit her lip. "Sometimes it's like a compulsion. Do you remember the rocket on *Sa Vivsheth*?"

"The lir s'flis?" Raveno snorted. "How could I forget?"

Kinsley grinned. "I saw that rocket and knew by its componentry that the explosion would be amazing. One look, and I was hooked. I just *had* to get my hands on it. By the time I finally did detonate it, I'd already fantasized its explosion a dozen times a dozen different ways. I could practically smell the lightning of it. Its heat. The power."

Her voice drifted off.

Raveno sealed his nostrils. Cry mercy, she was nearly as aroused now as when they'd showered together.

Kinsley sighed dreamily. "Witnessing the real thing was better than anything I could have imagined."

"You nearly took out our entire ship!"

She bobbed her shoulders, as unconcerned now as she'd been then. "Tironan got us out."

"Tironan's not that great a pilot."

"Apparently, he's good enough."

Raveno grunted.

"So sometimes it's like that, a fantasy come to life," she explained. "And then other times, it's like what I'd imagine having a best friend would be like. Someone who's beside you in all your good times and sticks around through the bad."

"What you'd *imagine* having a best friend would be like?"

"Yeah, but better, I'm sure, because explosions never disappoint."

Raveno opened his mouth, but before he could delve into *that*, she pushed forward. "And then sometimes, it's similar to what it's like for you when you do that." She gestured to his face.

He straightened, self-conscious. "What am I doing?"

"You sealed your nostrils shut against smelling me because you crave it too much."

Raveno felt his ears burn.

"But most often, like now, when I crack open its insides and learn the secrets of its function and see how it ticks—literally, sometimes—and rebuild it, changing it to my purposes..." Kinsley stroked a hand down the firework's outer shell. "It's not just an itch or a friend or a longing. Its finding something of me inside it."

Raveno nodded. He had no idea what she was talking about, but he could see her passion, and if there was anything he did understand, it was being passionate about something he believed in.

Kinsley's hand paused, midstroke. "We could use this, Raveno. Tomorrow, during your frisaes."

"Use what?" Why was he always a pace behind her?

"These missiles. I've worked with similar componentry—"

"You've worked with military-grade havari explosives before?" Raveno asked dryly.

She wrinkled her nose at him. "—and if your frisaes goes south—"

"The frisaes isn't going anywhere. It'll be right here."

"The outcome, not the location, Raveno! If the *outcome* of your frisaes doesn't go as expected..." Her eyes lit with that crazy glint that never boded well for him. "We need a contingency plan."

"A contingency plan."

"A backup plan. A second plan to set in motion should our first plan fail."

"I know what a contingency plan is."

"Then why did you repeat what I said?" she snapped.

"It bore repeating." Raveno rubbed his jaw. "What do you propose for this contingency plan?"

"We should reprogram the fireworks into demolition bombs and position them at all the arena exits."

One of the ushelz stirred.

"We could rig a few under the stage, too, but program those so the blast is localized to the stage hydraulics. If everything goes south, not according to plan," she clarified, "and we need to run, we blow the stage hydraulics, drop to ground level, and make a run for it. Blowing the exits will give us a head start."

Raveno eyed the lobotomized weapon between them. "Not that I doubt your skills, but..."

Kinsley raised her eyebrows, daring him to finish that sentence.

"These are dangerous, unfamiliar weapons, not one of your self-made IEDs."

"They'll be mine once I'm done rigging them."

Raveno tried to find the words that wouldn't offend her and still properly express his misgivings, but his silence spoke for him.

"You don't trust me." Her face fell. "I don't blame you after blowing your cover, but—"

"I trust you. I do," he added at her look. "But placing explosives so close to the arena spectators... I don't want to endanger more people than necessary."

"If we reprogram them and position them tonight, we can antici-pate the blast radius and ensure that area remains clear."

Raveno massaged his chin, considering. "Thanks to Cresha, we do have a considerable number of allies to aid in that effort. I could reassign the current guard, positioning our people at the entrances for crowd control. And then our allies would already be in place at the entrances should our plan 'go south,' allowing them to escape the arena before we detonate." Raveno tapped his lips. "We'll need a coordinated signal. And a reason for blocking those exit row seats. And somewhere to relocate those spectators..." Thev sa shek, could this really work? "We couldn't blow all the exits," he added. "Innocent people would need *some* way to escape."

Kinsley shrugged. "We'll leave one or two exits on the top floor open."

Raveno grinned, beginning to like this contingency plan. "Let's speculate: the worst happens and we successfully escape the arena. Where exactly are we escaping to?"

She bit her lip. "Where will we be safe?"

He snorted. "Off-planet. I'll have Avier prepare *Sa Vivsheth* for a contingency launch."

"The humans won't willingly reboard *Sa Vivsheth*," Kinsley warned. "It was their prison for nearly a year."

"We're taking all the humans with us for this contingency plan?"

"As opposed to, what, leaving them here?"

Maybe, Raveno thought, but he knew that wasn't the correct answer. "We'll post Riley with Avier, and he can encourage them on board."

Kinsley pointed an accusing finger at him. "They can't return to the brig."

"Of course not!" He reared back, offended. "The crew will swap wings with them. Assuming you don't still plan to lock us inside," he added, grinning.

She smirked back. "I can't promise anything." Kinsley picked up the computer chip and fingered it and its wires consideringly. "How will I program them to fire on a remote detonation trigger?"

Raveno opened his mouth.

"I'll need some sort of transmitter that can communicate wirelessly across a large distance," she murmured, and Raveno realized she was posing the question to herself. "Something like a cellular or Bluetooth connection. Something like..." Her eyes caught and focused on her ankesh. "Who programmed and implanted your anku?"

"Any higher-ranking officer can program and implant an anku. It's how we manage our crew's onboard and intergalactic communication."

Kinsley's smile was wicked. "Perfect. You're going to show me how that works. We'll program the anku to communicate with the fireworks, you'll implant it in my arm, and bada bing, bada boom." Kinsley rubbed her hands together. "We'll be in business."

Raveno chuckled. "You're the only person I know who would be excited over anku-operated fireworks."

Kinsley straightened. "Over what?"

"Anku-operated fireworks," he repeated, this time in English.

"I know." She wagged a finger at him. "But you called them *fireworks*," she repeated, but in Haveo as he'd said it: *lilssna*

His vresls flared. "Yes. Fireworks."

Her grin was slow, deepening until her cheeks dimpled. "You've been calling me your little firework since we first met."

"You're beautiful and explosive and..." Svik, his ears were on fire. He raised a hand and swiped his thumbs across her lips. "It's not just an itch or a friend or a longing for me either. I found something of me in meeting you, a part of myself I'd thought dead for more than eleven thesh. I will not just miss you when you return to Earth. I will..." Cry mercy, Raveno cleared his throat. "I have purposefully lost limbs before and survived. I will do so again."

Kinsley inhaled long and deep. Her breath shook. "Let's focus on surviving your frisaes. Then we'll worry about lost limbs...or preserving them."

He leaned forward and bent down, and gently—and very deliberately—pressed his lips to the pulsing vein at the side of her throat. "Agreed."

FORTY-FOUR

For the first time in over eleven thesh, since he'd battled and won his position as Vri Cilvril, Raveno stood center stage in the capital's frisaes arena, and no one chanted his name.

From the ground level through the fourteen tiers of stacked seating and every squished, standing-only pocket in between, all 200,674 arena tickets were filled: still and nearly silent. People were whispering to one another in hushed hisses, and their nervous chatter crackled through the stadium like a live, exposed wire.

Instead of a roaring crowd, the only thing deafening in the arena now was the pounding of his own doubt.

Vri Shavrili Jzoeshi, Rez, and Sheso stood on the jutting second-tier dais, all three of them outfitted, armed, and poised in tense readiness, as usual.

Dellao stood with them, Raveno's only ally positioned on the dais.

Tironan stood unmoving, to Raveno's right.

Kinsley shifted nervously beside him on his left.

Veilon was absent from public view for the moment, undoubtedly waiting in the exit tunnel along with the other competitors.

Behind him, the humans milled, untethered and confused and scared. Their muttering speculation about what might or might not happen grated on Raveno's last nerve because he too wasn't sure what to expect.

"This is decidedly less fun than previous ceremonies, huh?"

Raveno peered down at Kinsley.

"I liked it better when they were going nuts over you," she grumbled. "This silence is freaking me out."

Tironan nodded, eyeing the crowd as if he expected them to somehow rise from their seats and swarm them like a disease.

"Silence is good," Raveno said firmly, trying to convince himself as well as Kinsley. "They're confused. I'm down here with you instead of on the dais. And they're conflicted. To support me would be treason against Josairo. And everyone knows what happens to people who rise against Josairo."

Tironan tugged uncomfortably at his chest strap.

"Better to support no one until they know I'll win," Raveno assured her.

Kinsley opened her mouth to argue, obviously not reassured in the least.

A human lunged from behind and wrapped his arms around Kinsley, knocking the wind along with the argument from her lungs.

Raveno's vresls sprang out and bristled. He might have drawn his ezil had he not recognized the man's curly beard, dark skin, and less scrawny physique: Martin.

Even having recognized him, Raveno's palm itched to draw something, a two-blade at least.

"You're okay," Martin breathed.

Kinsley returned Martin's embrace, and Raveno's ears blazed.

"Good as new," she said. "Thank you for your help."

He nodded into the curve of her shoulder, but he didn't release her. "That was really bad, Kinsley."

"I'm fine now."

"You nearly died."

She's survived worse, Raveno thought, and cursed, realizing his vresls were still bristling.

"She's survived worse," someone said dryly, and somehow, the sentiment behind his own words when spoken aloud in that sour voice took on an entirely new meaning.

Two more of Kinsley's former cellmates had sidled up beside them: a woman with a dour expression leading a sunny-haired man by the arm.

Raveno frowned. Something was different about the man. Same hair and lean frame. Same smooth, beige skin. Same thin lips and long nose. Raveno couldn't identify it, but something was missing from his squinting expression.

Kinsley straightened away from Martin—*finally*—took Raveno's hand, and urged him forward, *toward* the humans.

He suddenly liked it better when her attention had been focused on Martin.

"Raveno and Tironan," she said. "I'd like you to meet...my friends. Martin, Leanne, and Benjamin."

Raveno and Tironan stared at the three humans. Martin and Leanne stared back, everyone eyeing one another the way they might a questionable, smelly substance under their boot.

Benjamin, however, looked off into the distance. "Is that Switch? She's healed?"

"Who else would be introducing us to aliens like we were attending a barbecue instead of our execution?" Leanne asked.

Kinsley cocked her head at Benjamin. "Where's your glasses?"

Ah, his seeing aids were missing! That's what was different about his appearance.

Benjamin bobbed his shoulders in answer. "They broke during yesterday's fight."

Kinsley squeezed Raveno's hand. "Do you think that's something the healing pods could fix?"

"His glasses?" Raveno asked, just to see her eyes roll.

There they went. "*His eyes.*"

Raveno suppressed a grin, shamelessly pleased. "Possibly. We will ask Avier, assuming we survive."

Kinsley nodded.

Benjamin was blinking rapidly, but whether in confusion or blindness, Raveno couldn't quite decipher. "Did the alien who kidnapped us, burned Riley alive, and nearly killed Kinsley just agree to try to fix my vision?"

"You act as if I would trust someone who wouldn't have our backs." Kinsley glared at them pointedly.

"If you trust him, Kinsley, I trust him," Martin said, even as the skepticism in his eyes said otherwise. "Whatever plan you've cooked up, I'll swallow it."

"As will I," Benjamin joined in.

Leanne crossed her arms. "This one isn't fucked?"

"Not yet." Kinsley gripped Martin's shoulder and grinned. "Thank you."

Martin returned the gesture.

Raveno didn't hiss his annoyance because Kinsley was obviously pleased by their too-small, too-late, halfhearted alliance. "How thankful I am to have your support."

Tironan coughed to hide his amusement.

"What is your plan, exactly?" Leanne asked. "I don't think I can survive another gladiator battle."

"None of us can," Benjamin added.

"None of us would," Kinsley agreed. "The plan is for Raveno to fight this time. He battles his father if he shows up, and when he wins, we go home to Earth."

"And if his father doesn't show up?" Benjamin asked.

"Then Raveno is crowned king, and we still go home to Earth."

"And if Raveno loses?" Martin asked.

"Then we run like hell, and I get to blow something up before we go home to Earth." Kinsley gestured to her glowing arm. "No matter what, we're leaving Havar today."

Martin caught her wrist and flipped it over to examine the six pulsing dots glowing in a row beneath the skin of her forearm.

Here we go, Raveno thought, and as if on cue, Kinsley grinned. "I'm a cyborg."

"A cyborg," Martin said flatly.

Tironan leaned in and whispered, "Why does she k-keep saying that?"

Raveno covered his eyes and shook his head.

Benjamin squinted at her arm. "A cyborg is a being composed of both organic and mechanical body parts often found in science fiction and superhero genres."

"Now found in real life," she said, pointing to her own arm.

"I have one too," Leanne said flashing her own ankesh. "Whoop-de-doo."

Kinsley waved that away. "That's just a branded tracking device. This—"

Leanne gaped at her own wrist, suddenly horrified. "It's *what?*"

"—is a modified communication device. Raveno uses them to order around his crew, like a two-way radio, except their technology has the range to span galaxies." Kinsley danced foot to foot, vibrating with excitement. "Instead of programming mine to communicate with other people, I've programmed it to communicate with the bombs I've rigged around the arena."

Martin blinked at her.

Leanne was no longer listening, scratching at her own wrist.

Benjamin made a deep *Hmmm* noise in the back of his throat. He pointed at her arm. "May I?"

She offered up her wrist, and Benjamin peered at it from two inches away.

"Fascinating," he breathed.

"I'm part woman, part weapon." She bit her lip. "My arm is the switch of my IED."

Martin peeked up from her arm and met her eyes.

Kinsley squeaked with glee.

Raveno didn't know whether to laugh or cry.

Benjamin straightened. "How does it trigger the bombs?"

"Each anku, each of the glowing dots, is remotely connected to each bomb quadrant. These top four"—she pointed—"trigger the exits. This one"—she tapped the middle dot—"triggers the top exit only, and this one"—she tapped the bottom dot—"triggers the bombs beneath the stage."

Leanne dropped her arm and gaped at her feet. "You put bombs beneath the stage?"

"But how do you trigger them?" Benjamin cocked his head. "I've seen the havari activate their anku. The device sits beneath their scales, but *above* their skin, so they can wedge a claw between scales to activate the device."

"That is accurate," Raveno said flatly.

"But..." Benjamin squinted up at Kinsley. "You don't have scales."

Kinsley dropped her arm on a sigh.

"The anku is under your skin."

"I know."

Benjamin frowned. "How will you active the device without hurting yourself?"

"She won't." Martin whirled on Raveno. "You let her do this?"

Raveno snorted. "There's no *letting* Kinsley do anything."

Kinsley waved an unconcerned hand. "A little jab with a pivz never killed anyone."

"That's *literally* how you kill someone with a pivz," Raveno said, and not for the first time. "You jab them with it."

"Avier will heal me up good as new afterward, assuming I even *get* to trigger them."

"If I d-didn't know better, I'd say you were h-hoping to trigger them," Tironan murmured.

Kinsley's eyes slid left. "Of course not."

Raveno rubbed his forehead.

Martin jabbed him in the chest with his finger. "Why didn't you implant the triggers in your arm?"

"I tried," Raveno growled. "She—"

Kinsley snatched her arm to her chest, as if they could undo the damage now. "They're *my* bombs. *I* made them. *I'm* responsible for them," she said, all trace of glee wiped from her face. "I trigger them."

Leanne raised her hand. "What happens if Raveno loses his battle, but we can't run?"

Kinsley sighed. "Then we fight until we *can* run."

"We've already established that we can't survive another fight," Leanne said, but all the heat and criticism in her tone was undercut by the quaver in her voice. "I don't want to die today."

"No one *wants* to die today," Kinsley said, more resistant to the quaver than Raveno. "This is happening whether you like it or not, so buck up or shut up."

Benjamin tried to put an arm around Leanne's shoulders and nearly missed.

Martin scrubbed his face with his hands and groaned.

"I begin to see p-perhaps why you were betrayed," Tironan mused.

Raveno kept his mouth sealed shut.

Kinsley scowled at Tironan.

"J-j-just an observation," he said hastily.

The projectors flew into position over the dais, as they always did when preparing for Josairo's entrance. The illuminators lining the balconies dimmed. The already quiet crowd hushed. The projectors spiraled into animation, and a thirty-foot tall, full-body projection of Josairo materialized on the dais.

His projection. Not him.

As if his son and killing hand hadn't challenged him to a frisaes.

Raveno choked back vomit.

The crowd of 200,674 people remained silent.

"How will he fight a projection of his father?" Martin asked.

"He can't, you idiot," Leanne said. "Raveno will be crowned king, and then we go home.

"Language," Kinsley chided.

Josairo smiled magnanimously, striding passed Jzoeshi, Rez, and Sheso to the center of the arena. "Two thesh and sixty-one shaoz ago, Raveno Hoviir—my son, my killing hand—embarked on a mission to greet and transport the competitors of our fifty-fourth Intergalactic Frisaes." Josairo paused a beat, and like a ghost was speaking, his words echoed into the void of frozen spectators. "Two thesh and sixty-one shaoz, we waited for his safe return. Now. Our patience has been rewarded. Now. We begin our fifty-fourth Intergalactic Frisaes Remembrance Ceremony!"

Josairo clicked his heels together, and his own heel clack reverberated back at him.

As one, 200,674 spectators shifted their eyes to Raveno. Watching. Waiting.

Anticipating.

Raveno found Cresha in the crowd. She was seated among the general population, only a few seats from the second-tier dais and adjacent to an exit, yet she was more difficult to spot than usual. For the first time in eleven thesh, since he'd battled and won his position as Vri Cilvril, her forehead was bare.

She wasn't wearing her ornamental circlet.

Perhaps she felt the burn of his stare because their eyes locked. Her lips widened into a fierce grin, and she nodded.

Yes, he could see they were ready. Several rows around each exit were cordoned off with decorative fabric and banners commemorating the fifty-fourth Intergalactic Frisaes. They were as festive as they were effective, hiding the fireworks and keeping spectators free of their blast radius.

Cry mercy. For the first time since he began this mission all those many thesh ago, failure might not necessarily be a death sentence.

"Now, on the eve of our fifty-fourth Intergalactic Frisaes. Let. The Remembrance Ceremony. Begin!"

Josairo raised his hands as his voice resounded through the stadium and kept them raised even as his words dissipated into heavy silence.

A normal leader might look rattled or, at the very least, *concerned*, but not Josairo. He remained proud and confident. He was only a prerecorded projection, after all. Raveno's heart ached as the truth stabbed hilt-deep. His all-seeing, larger-than-life tyrannical father, the ruler Raveno had blamed for everything wrong in his life and on Havar, was an illusion.

Josairo's projection elongated, then launched from the dais and into the sky, where it disappeared without the usual fanfare of fireworks.

The crowd watched, then as one entity, they turned their attention back to the stage.

To Raveno.

From the opposite side of the arena, the competitors approached, dressed in their uniforms and armed for a ceremony that shouldn't require battle.

"Showtime." Kinsley reached up, gripped his chest strap, and urged his ear to her lips. "Whatever happens," she said in Haveo, "you have this, you have me, and Josairo's rule ends this shift. Now."

Her attempted Haveo was beautiful, soft trills and mispronunciations and all, issuing from her lips. He believed her. He could hardly believe this was happening, but he believed her.

Kinsley kissed his cheek, flicked on his amplifier, and released her hold on him to face the approaching competitors.

Veilon was among them, as he knew she would be. Her circlet was secured across her forehead by neat, tight braids at her temples. No one could find fault in Veilon's appearance or question her standing, the way they did Tironan. She'd earned her position, as Raveno had, with blood and sacrifice. He'd given his leg. She'd given her ears. In Veilon, he'd always seen a reflection of himself: the strength, grit, and courage to overcome great odds. The will to survive. The wrath to see justice served.

He watched her approach now and wanted to scream. How had they come to this, standing on opposite sides of the arena?

She halted in front of Kinsley, as each competitor approached their vri sa shols.

Sheso cleared his throat. "Our Fifty-fourth Intergalactic Remembrance Ceremony honors the lives of the brave warriors...who competed in..."

Sheso's voice faded in confused hesitation as the thirty-four havari competitors stepped past their marks and about-faced to stand beside their vri sa shols. As Raveno was standing beside Kinsley.

Veilon stiffened. Her eyes narrowed on Raveno, then dropped sharply to glare at Kinsley.

"Uh..." Sheso coughed. "Who competed in our past fifty-three Intergalactic Frisaes and..."

On an inspired whim, Raveno unsheathed two of his pivz and offered them to Kinsley.

Kinsley was already armed, but her mind was as sharp as her blades. She accepted the weapons and held them aloft for all to see: She was armed, she would fight, and she would not be fighting on her own.

The thirty-four havari competitors all unsheathed a pair of pivz and offered them to their vri sa shols.

Veilon shook her head, stunned.

"Thank God we'll be armed this time." Leanne seized her pivz as if the offering might be snatched away as a prank.

Martin accepted his weapons with grim determination.

"Ouch!" Benjamin yipped, instantly cutting himself on the blade despite being offered the pivz handle-first.

The other humans took their weapons with similar trepidation and inexperience, but their skill, or lack thereof, wasn't the point.

"Um..." Sheso tugged at his chest strap. "And who have sacrificed their lives for..."

"How are we honoring those who have sacrificed their lives by sacrificing more lives?" Raveno interrupted, and Sheso shrank back from the dais's edge, clearly relieved by the interruption. "The honor was in testing our skills against others in a warriors' battle, but as you saw during the Sparring Ceremony, this wouldn't be a battle. This would be a slaughter!"

"Then why did you bring them here?" one of the spectators shouted.

The crowd murmured, nodding.

"I shouldn't have!" Raveno bellowed. "But I was under Josairo's orders. When have I ever not completed a mission for Havar? When have I ever been less than a loyal Vri Cilvril, as is my position? A position I earned in an honorable battle with a willing warrior! But..." Raveno waited, letting his words ring for a moment. "This is an order I cannot fulfill blindly. This is an order that breaks my loyalty, and for that, I ask the unthinkable. I ask that it also break yours."

Veilon's expression darkened to resignation.

The crowd remained silent for two lurching heartbeats, and then...

"Take them home!"

"They deserve to return to Earth."

"You can't keep them imprisoned here!"

Raveno inhaled, and the relief that swept through him was staggering. "I will take them home! But before I leave, I must ensure that in my absence, the Intergalactic Frisaes will not continue. Before I leave, I must ensure that this will never happen again."

The ushelz lining the perimeter of the stadium perked at that declaration and rotated their buds toward Raveno.

"To terminate the Intergalactic Frisaes and return these vri sa shols home is a direct violation of Vra Cilvril s'Hvri Josairo Hoviir's orders!" Veilon reminded everyone.

Raveno whipped to face her. Thev sa shek, he'd specifically told the projectionist not to give Veilon an amplifier! "Then I encourage my Vra Cilvril s'Hvri to charge me for my crimes and meet my challenge for a frisaes in person! So we may settle this point of contention now and before all."

A low rumble of encouragement emanated from the crowd.

"What about the competitors?" Veilon asked, her eyes growing round with desperation.

Why was she still pushing this?

"They paid good vit for the right to battle!" she argued.

Raveno addressed to the crowd. "I will personally compensate their monetary loss."

A dull roar, like a retreating tide, swept through the arena. Everyone was nodding.

Raveno struggled not to grin. He couldn't have dreamed this would go so well.

"Monetary loss isn't the only compensation required!" Veilon countered, her eyes darting sideways.

Raveno followed the trajectory of her gaze. The ushelz we snapping at each other and bristling. What was their problem?

"What about the glory of competing in a frisaes?" Veilon continued. "What about—"

"What glory can be had against battling untrained civilians?" Raveno asked, but by now, no one was listening to Veilon or her complaints. The crowd was shouting, at Raveno, at Veilon, at each other:

"How soon can you leave?"

"How could this happen?"

"Who cares about compensation?"

"What about compensation for the humans?"

"Where is Josairo? He should answer for this!"

Veilon clenched her jaw so hard that, with the amplifier in place, he could hear the crack and pop of her teeth grinding.

Raveno raised his hands.

The crowd quieted.

"We will return the humans to Earth as soon as possible, after I ensure the Intergalactic Frisaes is permanently terminated. We will provide compensation for the humans as well. I'll need input from them on acceptable terms, if any can possibly be made for the time taken from their lives and the terror they experienced."

The crowd rumbled in cheering, nodding assent.

The ushelz ceased bickering with one another and refocused on the stage.

"As for Josairo," Raveno continued, "I demand explanation from those who have been with him during the two thesh I was away. His Vri Shavrili." Raveno chopped his arm up at Jzoeshi, Rez, and Sheso on the dais. "Where is our Vra Cilvril s'Hvri?"

The crowd shifted their accusing eyes to the dais.

Jzoeshi, Rez, and Sheso ceased squabbling amongst themselves and, as one nervous unit, glanced down at Veilon. For direction.

No.

Raveno refocused on his sister before him, but all her sneering animosity was for Kinsley.

Tironan edged closer. "V-V-Veilon?"

Raveno flicked off his amplifier. "By will or wrath, what the svik is going on?"

She flicked off her amplifier too. "You don't know what you're doing."

"He do right!" Kinsley shouted at Veilon in Haveo. Then under her breath, she added in English, "I take back everything I said about you being paranoid, Raveno. Your sister is in on it."

Veilon crossed her arms, her ankis a flashing glow between them. "What is *it* that I'm in on?" she asked in Haveo.

Kinsley looked at Raveno, her eyes huge and speaking, but for the life of him, he had no clue what they were trying to say.

"That's what I thought." Veilon laughed. "You don't know shit, little girl."

"Don't talk to her as if her opinion isn't valid!" Raveno snapped.

"Don't talk to me as if your opinion is!" Veilon snapped right back.

"Excuse me?" Raveno hissed.

"Have you been here for more than ten shaoz at a time for the last eleven thesh?"

"I—"

"As you flit from planet to planet, deciding what orders to follow and what orders to rebel against, who remained here on Havar with our dear father?" she asked Raveno, then whipped her eyes sideways to blast Tironan. "Who served his will and wrought his wrath, shift after shift after shift, on my own?"

"We—"

"And now, here you are, after all those thesh *not* here, demanding we cease the Intergalactic Frisaes without any thought to the consequences!"

"No consequence matters more than doing what's right!" Raveno shouted, shocked that he had resorted to shouting. At Veilon!

"Oh, suddenly, the consequences don't matter when it's convenient for you. *Now*, you decide to stand up to injustice. But guess what, brother, you're two thesh too late!"

"How is any of this *convenient*?" Raveno asked, baffled.

Veilon eyed Kinsley. "I see the convenience."

Tironan worried his knuckles, his vresls flexed on end.

Mustering the greatest force of will in his life, Raveno remained calm. "When faced with such a grievous wrong, I can't just stand by, complicit in inaction."

Veilon laughed, incredulous. "You were perfectly content to stand by, complicit, when Mom was murdered."

Tironan flinched so hard, his vresls retracted, then snapped out again.

"Josairo won a frisaes, legally and fairly, with our mother's willing consent," Raveno forced out, the words ash on his tongue. "She knew the risks of challenging his position."

"As Josairo should meet your challenge," Kinsley said, then added to Raveno in English, "Your mom showed up for a losing fight. Guess she was the only one with balls in the family."

Raveno gaped, taken aback that she'd ever say such a thing, even if it was true, and nearly missed Veilon's lunge forward. "Don't you *dare* speak of our mother that way!"

Raveno had shouldered between them, not sure who he was more exasperated with, when he noticed Kinsley's grin.

She nodded sideways at Veilon. "We have our English-to-Haveo translator."

Tironan staggered back, stunned, but Raveno could only manage to blink as frigid, inevitable resignation swept through his veins.

Kinsley snatched Veilon's wrist and tugged it forward. "Isn't that right?" she asked in English.

Veilon's ankis glowed and vibrated, exactly like his anku while receiving a transmission.

Was this what people meant when they described a heart as breaking? This aching, wrenching, tearing, agony inside his chest? To think, he'd considered his headaches insufferable.

"You hacked into the video footage on *Sa Vivsheth*," Kinsley said, completely giving up on Haveo in favor of rapid, crude, accusing English. "You translated our English and doctored our conversations into Haveo for that spectacle yesterday."

Veilon yanked her glowing, vibrating arm from Kinsley's grip, seething.

"It wouldn't have taken much hacking," Raveno said numbly. "Cershys was commissioned to install the cameras and maintain the monitoring system."

"That's right, she owns her own business!" Kinsey pointed a finger at her. "If I studied your financials, would I be able to justify the profits of your business?"

"Yes." Despite being caught, Veilon suddenly looked baffled.

"I wouldn't find small deposits—labeled as donations, perhaps—from civilians who either don't exist or have no recollection of making such donations?" Kinsley crossed her arms. "And I wouldn't find that the total of those combined donations correlates with the profits made from the Intergalactic Frisaes?"

Veilon turned to Raveno. "What is she talking about?"

"Don't pretend to misunderstand!" Raveno shouted, completely beyond will. "I know your ankis is translating her words for you!"

"I understand her words, but I don't understand their meaning!" Veilon shouted back "What does Cershys have to do with anything?"

"Are you or are you not using your company as a front to hide Intergalactic Frisaes profits?" Raveno roared.

"What profits?" Veilon laughed. "We're trafficking people from across the galaxy and *still* providing prize money to the winners. Do you know how much that costs? We're barely breaking even!"

"Lies!" Raveno pulled his ezil from its sheath and pressed its barrel flush against Veilon's chest.

"N-n-no!"

Tironan lunged forward, but Raveno blocked him with a stiff arm to the chest, not taking his eyes from Veilon. "Confess!"

Veilon stopped laughing, but even with Raveno's ezil pressed between them, her smirk remained. "You didn't kill Josairo after he murdered our mother. You won't kill me now."

Tironan ceased struggling against Raveno.

"You..." Raveno tried to steady his nerve—he couldn't impale his little sister by mistake on a worldwide broadcast—but no matter how deeply he breathed, his hand shook. "You knew the Intergalactic Frisaes was corrupt and not only allowed it to continue, you became a party to it!"

Veilon narrowed her eyes. "I was under orders, brother. Same as you."

Kinsley tugged on his arm. "Raveno, we have a problem."

"When was the last time Josairo issued an order to you in person?" Raveno asked and half squeezed the trigger, just hard enough to pierce Veilon's scales. To get her attention. To get her to *see*.

Tironan jerked as if *he'd* been stabbed.

Kinsley stepped back.

Veilon stared down at the ezil piercing her chest, and the agony in her eyes cracked open Raveno's heart.

"You *would* kill me," Veilon murmured, shuddering. "Over *her*."

"I would kill anyone who betrayed me," Raveno forced out, hemorrhaging inside.

"Lies," Veilon whispered.

"Don't test my word, Veilon." *Please.*

"Had you been willing to kill Josairo," Veilon said, "I wouldn't have had to."

FORTY-FIVE

As fascinating as Veilon was becoming at the moment, nothing was more pressing, in Kinsley's opinion, than the slow, inexorable approach of the—flock, pack, swarm?—of Twoeys converging on them. Their mood had soured during Raveno's speech, and as Raveno and Veilon began arguing in earnest, the Twoeys turned the focus of their aggression from each other to the stage.

"Y-y-y—" Tironan swallowed, staring at Veilon as he might a ghost. "W-what?"

Raveno had been shaking his head going on three minutes now, since he'd first aimed his ezil at Veilon's chest, as if trying to convince himself not to kill her.

Kinsley couldn't tell if Veilon was about to laugh or cry.

Now was obviously not the ideal time to interrupt this multi-car pileup, but the Twoeys weren't taking into consideration the fact that the Hoviir siblings were beyond dysfunctional at the moment.

Or perhaps that was exactly what they were considering.

"Explain," Raveno hissed at Veilon. The vein in his temple wasn't just throbbing. It was engorged to the point of rupture.

"I..." Veilon sucked in a loud breath. "I was meeting with Josairo to discuss Cershys's latest advancements, quarterly budgets, and customer satisfaction scores. The usual. One of my designers, Heila, was really performing, and I'd included a promotion for her in my proposed budget for the next thesh. Which Josairo denied." Veilon laughed, dislodging a tear from her eyelashes. "He was more interested in discussing the financial benefits versus the agricultural risks of expanding Cershys's production centers. I wanted to invest more in translation tech—but *surprise!*—he didn't like my recommendation. We debated for a time, as usual, and then I thought to myself, *why?*" Veilon lifted her arms out. "Why was I waiting on you?"

Raveno's affliction must have been catching, because Tironan was shaking his head now too.

The Twoeys were steadily closing in, their toothy buds smirking.

"You'd just accepted your mission to 'escort' shols from Earth. But by then, I'd finally hacked into Mom's mission records, detailing her efforts to find off-world allies. Her intelligence was nine thesh old, but in that time, Earth's inhabitance couldn't have advanced fast enough to achieve intergalactic communication. They hadn't invited you. They weren't even expecting you. They certainly weren't willingly sending you contestants for the Intergalactic Frisaes. And for the first time, I saw *you* clearly," Veilon said, trembling. "You weren't just surviving. You were completing Josairo's missions. Following his orders in earnest. His will *truly* by your hands."

"As if I could defy him outright without consequence," Raveno gritted out. "To free Havar from Josairo without plunging us into another war with Haven, I needed to win Bazail and Fray and his other allies as my own. My loyalty was an act to fool Josairo just long enough to betray him."

"Well, it was the act of a lifetime," Veilon agreed. "You fooled me."

Raveno's jaw flexed.

Veilon let her arms drop to her sides with a slap. "When Josairo leaned in for a lasvik, I pierced him in the neck with my fang and shoved my pivz through his heart."

Raveno's forehead vein hadn't ruptured, but its throbbing was the only movement in his entire body.

"V-V-Veil—"

"By the time I drew my ezil, he'd already dropped to the floor. Josairo would have died eventually, but I gutted him. Just like he deserved. Just like he'd gutted *her*." Veilon laughed, a little hysterical. "Mom got justice, I got my translation tech, and Heila got her promotion."

That tore Kinsley's attention from the approaching plants. "And you've been running Havar ever since? For *two thesh*?"

Veilon met Kinsley's gaze.

"Josairo didn't project himself because of an increase in profits or viewership." Hell, now even Kinsley was shaking her head. "You projected him so no one would know he was dead."

"So no one would know I murdered him," Veilon corrected. "I killed him in the moment, filled with so much hate and resentment and rage I couldn't breathe! It was only afterward that I considered the consequences, that killing him could result in another war with Haven." She laughed again, and it hiccupped into a sob. "It was only afterward that I discovered why Josairo thought the Intergalactic Frisaes was so necessary."

"H-h-how did no one n-n-notice his absence?" Tironan asked, gaping.

"Of course they noticed! Two thesh without a single public execution? Svik, people were *happy*!" Tears poured over Veilon's sneering lips. "Josairo's sudden preference for issuing orders remotely and conducting digital meetings and projecting at public events was a relief no one dared question. And *you*," Veilon scoffed. "You were away on assignment. Once I surrounded myself with people who listen and don't question, who could stop me?"

Ah, Sheso.

"But you let the Intergalactic Frisaes continue," Raveno said, anguished. His grip on the ezil tightened.

Veilon winced as blood oozed from around the blade.

"Even after you killed Josairo, you still had me continue my mission. *You* allowed me to purchase the humans. *You* let me traffic them from across the galaxy against their will to fight in a competition they weren't trained in compete in."

Veilon's lips compressed into a tight, straight line.

"Even now, knowing I was plotting to overthrow Josairo, you still kept all this from me and chose instead to *host the Intergalactic Frisaes!*"

"They need to eat *someone!*" Veilon shouted. "My efforts to cull the ushelz failed! My efforts to eradicate them failed! What else could I do? I can't watch them consume someone I love! Not ever again." Veilon gripped Raveno's ezil in her hands, and suddenly, it seemed that Raveno was the one preventing his weapon from stabbing deeper as Veilon leaned in. "No matter the cost."

They? Kinsley scanned the arena, and sure enough, the Twoeys had completely surrounded the stage. *Fuck.*

Martin edged closer. "Are those plants about to eat us?"

"Probably," Kinsley snapped. "Let me think."

Leanne twirled the pivz in her hand, impressively nimble-fingered as she familiarized herself with its weight. She tossed it in an arch, caught it by the handle, and pointed the blade alternately at Raveno and Veilon. "I thought they were chummy?"

"They're siblings," Kinsley murmured distractedly.

"Ah," Leanne said in complete understanding, as if she and her siblings regularly held each other at sword point.

Kinsley rubbed her forehead. She had a group of thirty-five trained, armed warriors, thirty-five untrained, armed civilians, three siblings about to murder each other, and live explosives rigged at the exits and under the stage hydraulics.

The stage.

Kinsley looked up at the dais and found Dellao.

"Lift the stage," she shouted at him.

He pointed to his ear and shook his head, then gestured to the crowd.

Shit. She'd been so focused on Veilon's confession and the creeping plants that she'd forgotten about the crowd, the very people this entire show had been intended for.

The entire stadium was in an uproar.

Kinsley snatched Raveno's microphone from his ear and stuck it in her own.

"Dellao," she said, and her voice echoed through the stadium.

Dellao's vresls popped out around his head.

"Lift the stage to the dais, and get us the hell away from these monsters before they eat us!"

Dellao tensed, but hesitated, unsure. His lips were moving. Repeating her words.

Translating.

Damn it! "Lift stage," she tried in Haveo. "Before we plant food!"

Dellao nodded—finally!—and sprinted to the AV tech console. A moment later, the stage began to rise.

"Should the stage be moving with bombs attached to it?" Leanne asked warily.

"Switch is a trained professional," Benjamin said. "I'm sure she wouldn't—"

The stage trembled, strained, and, with a terrible cranking screech, stopped moving as they hovered eleven, maybe twelve feet in the air.

"What the fuck was that?" Kinsley asked, then winced as her voice echoed through the stadium. She flicked off the microphone.

Leanne crossed her arms. "Trained professional, hmm?"

The stage struggled to rise and quaked with another cranking screech. Something was breaking.

"It's the ushelz," Veilon said. "Thanks to your public announcement, they think we're not continuing the Intergalactic Frisaes."

Raveno stared. "The ushelz."

"Their young are hungry for hosts, and their parents were already angry after waiting nearly an entire thesh for a measly thirty-six shols." Veilon skimmed her gaze over the Twoeys in despair. "You were supposed to bring over two hundred."

"Who's hungry?" Martin asked. "What did she say?"

Benjamin tried to push his glasses up his nose, realized they weren't on his face, and dropped his hand. "Why did we stop?"

Raveno extracted his ezil from Veilon's chest with a wet, suctioning pop. "Explain!"

Veilon flinched. "Why else would I continue this charade? Certainly not for the fun of it!"

Kinsley ran to the stage's edge, lay on her stomach, and peered under the platform. Shit, the Twoeys *were* to blame. They'd knotted their roots all around the lift hydraulics, and if the continued quaking and screeching of gears was any indication, in a battle of plant vs. machine, the plants were about to win.

The Twoeys that weren't attempting to tear down the stage had flooded the ground below, forming an undulating sea of seven-foot-tall Venus persontraps, all with their mouths wide open. Four neat rows of clear, needle-thin, serrated teeth haloed the bodies inside their gullets.

For a moment, Kinsley couldn't look away. She didn't know what was worse, the dozens of dead bodies who gaped at her, revealing their rotten gums and watching with their zombie-blind eyes, or the hundreds of Twoeys whose open mouths revealed nothing but hollow stems.

"The ushelz have rooted themselves everywhere," Veilon explained. "What was once a lovely decoration evolved just as we did. As Haver's atmosphere became less stable, we became more dependent on core power rather than solar. We moved our civilization underground. Our eyes adjusted to the dark. We adapted, and so did the ushelz. Without the sun as a food source, they became completely dependent on a carnivorous and parasitic diet. They grew their heart roots and adapted to hunt their new food source. Us."

"That was centuries ago," Raveno growled.

"W-w-what does that have to do with w-w-what's happening now?"

Kinsley stood and met Dellao's eyes. She pointed down at the stage and sliced her thumb across her throat.

Dellao nodded, and the stage creaked to a shuddering halt.

Kinsley blew out a breath—*think think think*—and returned to Raveno. "Let's just light 'em up."

Raveno's eyes flicked to Kinsley. He opened his mouth.

"Yeah, I know. 'Explain,'" she hissed in mocking impersonation. "We evacuate everyone and use the fireworks I didn't rig to bomb the Twoeys."

Veilon laughed, then winced and put pressure on her chest wound. "Are you seriously suggesting that we kill the ushelz?"

Kinsley whipped around to face her. "You have a better idea?"

"Any idea would be better!" Veilon yelled. "You think I haven't thought of a hundred ways to rid us of those parasites? A hundred failures! We can't kill them completely."

"Why not? Do they have fire-resistant scales too?"

"Eradicating the whole crop would destroy their root system."

"That would be the point."

"If I could destroy the ushelz so easily, don't you think I would have done so instead of trafficking people from galaxies away and hosting death battles? *Like my father?*"

Kinsley lifted her arms and laughed. "At this point, I have no idea what you would and wouldn't do!"

Veilon rolled her eyes. "Without the need to remain rooted for nutrients, the ushelz began stalking their prey. Healthy civilians were apparently disappearing by the dozens back then, according to Josairo's records. That's why he initially began the Intergalactic Frisaes, to give the ushelz something to eat and keep the public distracted while he attempted to fight them with pesticides, with fire, by physically chopping them down. We can kill the ushelz individually, but we can't risk killing them en masse. Or so Vriusheli advises."

"That's why you've been investing in them—the botanical

company that specializes in ushelz." Kinsley stared. "You haven't been caring for the Twoeys. You've been researching them for the past two thesh."

"We were more than just researching them. We were trying to eradicate them, so we could eventually stop the Intergalactic Frisaes," Veilon said shakily. "But they've entrenched their long roots within our infrastructure, embedding themselves into the very support system that keeps our walls from caving in. If we kill them, they'll bury us, and we'll die with them."

"Instantly?" Raveno asked. "Would it take time for the root system to die, or—"

"Or would they knowingly crush the infrastructure out of spite, knowing they were dying anyway?" Veilon finished, shaking her head. "Care to find out?"

They'll bury us. Kinsley forced herself to inhale through the sudden constriction in her throat.

"In English!" Leanne yelled.

Martin gripped her shoulder. "Kinsley?"

"Why can't we blow them up like you suggested?" Benjamin asked.

Breathe. Just breathe. "You should have just abandoned ship and found a safer planet," Kinsley muttered.

"Because uninhabited planets capable of sustaining life are so easy to come by." Veilon laughed. "Havar is our home! Haven couldn't take her from us, and neither can the ushelz!"

Raveno ignored his sister to address Martin, Leanne, and Benjamin. "If we bomb the ushelz—the Twoeys, as you call them—the resulting explosion may cause a cave-in." He hesitated, glancing at Kinsley. "We would be crushed." He scanned the stadium of thousands. "We would all be crushed."

Kinsley closed her eyes.

Breathe, damn it.

The stage shook, whined, then tipped sharply to one side.

"Svik!"

"Fuck!"

Half the havari and all the humans slipped off their feet. The few havari who managed to keep their balance scrambled to catch the fallen before they slid off stage. Tironan lunged for Benjamin. Dellao caught Leanne by the wrist. Veilon grabbed Martin. Raveno had his arms around Kinsley before she'd even lost her feet, and all the havari competitors snatched a hold of their Vri Sa Shols.

Two of the havari who'd slipped didn't manage to find a foothold.

One latched on to a fellow havarian with one hand and her shols with the other.

The other havarian didn't.

Both havarian and human fell off stage, screaming, and plummeted into the waiting gullets of two wide-open Twoeys.

The plants closed their mouths.

A few moments passed—an eternity—and the screams ceased.

"We're gonna die," Leanne whispered. "We're all gonna die."

"Whatever we do," Martin gasped, hanging tightly to Veilon's neck, "we need to do it now!"

"How many of the ushelz are here in the stadium?" Kinsley asked.

"At a glance?" Veilon shook her head. "The majority, if not all of them. Like I said, the young are starving and their parents are desperate. We've held them off with snacks, but they need real nutrients to survive."

"Okay. We can't kill them without committing mass suicide, right? So let's evacuate everyone out of the stadium, then blow my rigged charges. That'll seal the exits, trapping all the plants inside."

"How does that help?" Veilon adjusted her hand on her chest with a wince, but more blood seeped from between her fingers. Martin, obviously feeling grateful for the quick save, helped her apply pressure. "Eventually, they'll either suffocate or starve. Their roots will die, and *then* our entire civilization will cave in."

"*Eventually,*" Raveno growled. "While they're trapped but not dead, we can evacuate."

Tironan stared at him. "T-t-the entire planet?"

"We have an entire fleet of carrier vessels at our disposal," Raveno said ruefully. "We survive today and live to fix our planet tomorrow."

Everyone just stared at him.

Kinsley could kiss him.

Raveno flipped on his microphone, faced the spectators, and ordered, "Everyone! Your attention please. I know you're scared. I know you're confused and angry. But everyone must evacuate the arena. Single-file march. Calmly but quickly. This is not a drill. Evacuate and meet at your district's carrier vessel. Now."

By will or wrath, thousands of spectators stood and began to evacuate. More than a few people tried to run, inciting a spike of panic through the crowd, but with Raveno's allies already positioned at each exit, they maintained a semblance of order.

Raveno activated his anku. "Vri Cilvril Raveno Hoviir to Vri Zyvril Avier Risan. Do you receive?" Raveno paused. "Prepare all carrier vessels for departure. Yes, all of them." And then he squared off with the filming drones, broadcasting the event to living rooms across Havar. "Viewers watching from home. I repeat, this is not a drill. Board your family or solo cruiser, if you own one, and meet your nearest carrier vessel off-planet. If you require transport, notify your district's Fyvrili, and meet them at their assigned carrier vessel. Immediately."

"Maybe I missed a word or two between all the Haveo being tossed around," Leanne shouted over the stampede of marching feet, "but how exactly does this plan help *us*?"

"The spectators will be safe," Benjamin chimed in. "And the plants will be trapped, giving the havari time to figure out how to safely exterminate them."

"That's all great and dandy," Leanne said, elbowing Dellao away from her, "but unless we evacuate too, we'll be trapped with them."

Raveno hefted his ezil in both hands. "No. We most certainly will not."

All thirty-five havari competitors unsheathed their ezils and assumed the ready position.

Kinsley wasn't ready, not by a long shot, but she gripped her pivz tight. After eight months of training with Raveno and two ass kickings from Veilon, she was as ready as she'd ever get.

"Switch?" Benjamin squeaked.

"We're going to fight our way out," Kinsley said, "And once we've evacuated too, *then* I'll blow the exits and trap the plants inside."

Martin straightened from Veilon and nodded.

Benjamin clung to Tironan tighter. "Fight?"

Leanne faced Raveno. "Promise me that you meant it when you said you'd return us home. If we win against those...those..."

"Ushelz," Raveno said.

"Plant monsters," Leanne corrected, "you'll take us back to Earth?"

"Yes, I promise," Raveno said gravely. "I'll personally escort you safely to Earth myself."

Leanne studied Raveno's expression like one would a contract—a deal with the devil—then nodded. "Okay, then. Let's get this fight over with."

Martin's jaw dropped.

Benjamin squinted.

Kinsley laughed. Witnessing Leanne willingly agree to kick ass lifted Kinsley's spirits like nothing else could. "Who are you, and what have you done with Annie?"

Leanne scowled. "Excuse me?"

"The last time I asked you to fight for your freedom, you refused to leave your *open cell*."

"No, last time, you asked me to crawl through an incineration shaft so you could *hopefully* trap the murderous aliens in the brig and *maybe* navigate us home on a spaceship you'd never flown by yourself before. Those odds sucked. Having an alien prince promise to fly us home on his ship is something I'm willing to fight for."

Raveno met Kinsley's gaze and flicked his tongue.

Kinsley pointed a finger at him. "Don't. Not one word."

"I didn't say anything!"

Martin grinned. "You'll learn that, with human women, just thinking something can get you into nearly as much trouble as saying it."

"H-H-Havari women are n-n-not so different."

"I'm so dead," Benjamin whispered, squinting out at the sea of plants around them.

"No, you're not." Raveno turned to the havari competitors. "The humans are civilians, not trained fighters. We need to form a circle around them and maintain that barrier to protect them as we fight the ushelz."

They clicked their heels. "Yes, Vri Cilvril!"

"Get into formation!"

They did. With a few running leaps, the havari on stage surrounded the humans, ezils drawn.

"Ready yourselves!"

The havari bent their knees and raised their weapons.

The humans held on to each other.

Just as Kinsley braced to activate her sixth anku, Raveno wrapped his arm around her waist, lifted her up, and slanted his lips over hers in a sharp, searing kiss.

Kinsley's blood hummed—from his lips, from his arms, from all the explosive potential between them and just below their feet—but with startling, stunning clarity, she realized that pressing a button and watching the sparks fly wasn't the most exciting thing in her life anymore.

"Do it," he whispered against her lips, still holding her against his chest and off her feet. "Blow the stage hydraulics."

FORTY-SIX

RAVENO BRACED HIMSELF—KNEES BENT, EZIL GRIPPED IN HIS left hand, Kinsley tight in his embrace, his face buried in the curve of her neck as he held his breath against her scent and their doom—as she detonated the bombs beneath their feet.

The bombs beneath our feet. Svik, this was insane!

But the fireworks didn't explode, not quite as he'd expected, anyway. When functioning normally, they zipped across the sky, releasing bursts of color to create moving stories in light. They were gorgeous and brilliant from miles away when gazing at them from the safety of the ground, so having them burst beneath the stage directly under his feet, he half expected to lose his other leg.

The explosion was only a pop, not a blinding blaze.

The hydraulic stage supports broke, not their bones.

The stage fell to the ground without bursting to bits or blowing them sky high.

Raveno grunted, landing hard on both feet. The surging relief at finding himself still whole and hale was staggering.

He nearly didn't recover fast enough to block the ravenous jaws of the nearest ushelz.

He definitely—probably—would have, but Kinsley raised her arm, pivz in hand, lunged into—*into*—its mouth, and jabbed her blade through the sensitive flesh of its upper jaw. Her pivz tore through the roof of its mouth, splitting its leafy head in two and rendering it unable to bite.

Raveno blocked its second attack and swung his ezil in a wide arch, neatly decapitating it in one strike. Its bud, with its gaping maw and gleaming rows of sharp, needle teeth, spun midair and fell to the ground next to its downed, flapping stem.

And out spilled a body.

The man's vresls were tattered. His scales were flaking, the exposed skin a sickly white. His eyes were open, and through the film clouding them, he peeked up and saw Raveno. He *saw* him. His mouth opened. He inhaled a racking, wet breath, and then stilled, just like that, midbreath, midlook, midstruggle. He died on the ground, covered in ushelz saliva, beside the corpse of the very creature that had imprisoned him and fed from his body for who knew how long. He died here, now, in this moment.

Which meant he'd been alive inside the ushelz.

Which meant that Kinsley was right.

Which meant...

"Where's its brain?" Kinsley asked.

Raveno stared at the man's body. Cry mercy, he might vomit.

Kinsley pinched the ushelz's upper jaw and wrinkled her nose as she lifted it to peek into its split maw. "It's just a mouth inside folds of petals. I don't— Raveno!"

Kinsley lunged in front of him, pivz slashing.

Raveno startled from his stare. Another ushelz had attacked from the front, and two more were converging on them. Raveno quickly dispatched the two on either side with one neat swipe of his ezil, hearing the double *whump whump* of their decapitated heads hitting the ground. Two more bodies slipped from their stumps. Like the first, they gaped at him and gasped their final breaths. Raveno deliberately ignored what or who had just died at his feet and lunged forward to save Kinsley, only to stop short, panting.

Kinsley was, well—Raveno smiled—Kinsley was fierce as only Kinsley could be. The ushelz chomped, attempting to swallow her whole, but Kinsley dropped into a familiar block-pivot, rolled right, and popped to her feet at the ushelz's side, a little closer than he'd advise but in perfect striking distance for her shorter arms. She jabbed hard and fast and *through*, just as he'd taught her, seeing beyond the plant's exterior to the true target of her aim: the vulnerable organ beneath.

The ushelz threw its head back and writhed.

Two more ushelz charged from the sides, and Raveno swung his ezil left then right—*whump, whump*—but his impressed gaze was consumed by Kinsley.

The ushelz didn't really have organs to pierce so much as a hollow stem, some of them filled with a rotting body—zombie?—so when Kinsley jabbed her pivz into the stem above the body's bulge, the momentum of her strike carried her arm through the stem and out the other side, impaling the ushelz on her arm, shoulder-deep.

She tried to step back and tug her arm free, but the ushelz's increasingly violent wiggles only locked her arm in place.

Raveno lifted his ezil to finish it off for her, and—

And Kinsley used her impaled arm and her own weight as leverage to rip the ushelz from its roots and drag it to the ground. Its entire body flailed from bud to root, trying and failing to buck Kinsley off, but in its desperation, it only tore itself from the inside out, scrambling its innards on her pivz. Kinsley managed to stand and brace her weight with both feet on either side of the ushelz's stem, pinning it in place even as it whipped and struggled at both ends. She ripped her arm free.

Gore sprayed the air and Kinsley. A body belched from the yawning hole she'd left in its gut. It slid on the ooze of ushelz saliva to die at her feet.

Raveno lowered his ezil.

Kinsley peered over her shoulder and scowled. "You gonna help or just—shit!"

Raveno followed the trajectory of her horror-filled gaze and cursed. The line of havari protecting the humans had broken, and several ushelz were feasting.

Raveno whipped around and charged, a beat behind Kinsley.

The ground was saturated with blood and bodies: the preserved fallen of past frisaes spilled among the freshly dead: ushelz, havarian, and human alike. Raveno leapt over several, refusing to see their faces. He wasn't sure which was worse, the potential of seeing someone he knew or seeing the many who weren't even havari. The Lorien who had traveled to Havar of their own volition, long before his time, when competing in the Intergalactic Frisaes had been revered as the highest honor. The Bazaili, Iroanio and Frayans who had come as spies and willing sacrifices to help his mission when the IF's legitimacy had been compromised.

His mother.

Raveno swung his ezil overhead—*whump, whump, whump*—taking out three of the ushelz that had breached the line of havari. Kinsley stabbed at a fourth, trying to yank a human free from its jaws. The woman was already waist-deep, head first inside the ushelz, but her feet were still kicking.

Raveno couldn't decapitate the ushelz without splitting the human in half.

The blade of a pivz stabbed *out* from the ushelz, carving its own hole in the stem from the inside.

Raveno rushed forward to widen the hole and gripped a pair of wrists.

Kinsley pushed the woman's feet deeper *into* the ushelz, and Raveno yanked her out from the hole they'd carved in the ushelz's gut.

She popped free, and Raveno fell back under a saliva-slicked Leanne.

The ushelz flopped, dead, beside them.

Kinsley offered Leanne a hand. "The incineration shafts seem pretty great right now, huh?"

"Smug isn't a good look on you," Leanne wheezed, but she took Kinsley's hand to gain her feet.

Kinsley grinned. "Whereas Twoey guts look fantastic with your complexion."

Raveno lunged up from his back in time to decapitate another two ushelz.

"Annie!" Benjamin screamed, rushing forward to embrace Leanne, the idiot, and Raveno dove sideways to decapitate another ushelz before it could gobble him whole.

"Stay behind Veilon!" Leanne snapped at him.

"You okay?" He gripped her shoulders, shaking.

Another ushelz rose up for Benjamin's head.

Kinsley whipped around and stabbed it through its lower jaw, trapping its mouth closed with the bar of her arm.

"Get off!" Leanne wriggled free from Benjamin's embrace and helped Kinsley finish off the ushelz with a long slice down its stem. She jumped back from the spill of guts, and the spray hit Benjamin full in the face.

He screamed.

"Stay in position," Leanne snarled.

Martin yanked him back behind Veilon as Benjamin wiped his eyes. As if he could see with them open anyway.

Raveno filled the breach left from the fallen, sealing the line of havari with the humans protected inside.

"How are they attacking us without a brain!" Kinsley shouted, then grunted as the ushelz she'd just killed smacked her across the face in its death spasm.

"Plants on Earth have brains?" Raveno asked, breaking formation to block an ushelz about to chomp Kinsley's head off.

"I got it," Leanne said, and with a quick stab and slice, indeed she did.

Kinsley blocked another attack. "Plants on Earth stay firmly anchored in the ground and only sometimes eat flies! Not people!"

"Instead of a b-b-brain and spinal cord, the ushelz have a non-centralized n-nervous system," Tironan explained between ezil swings.

"Dumb it down!" Leanne tried to jump into another mouth.

Raveno caught her by the waist, and Kinsley gutted it instead. "Tear it open from the *outside!*"

"It's too fast!"

"Follow Kinsley's lead and cover her!"

"No brain or spinal cord?" Benjamin asked, focusing, of course, on the science.

"P-p-precisely. Their motor movement is controlled by a net of nerves and electrical pulses throughout the b-body."

"Do they not feel pain, then?" Martin asked. "Is that why they're so silent?"

"Is feeling pain dependent on having vocal cords?" Veilon asked.

The ushelz under Raveno's blade writhed in agony.

An ushelz snaked through a breach in their line, consumed a warrior in one bite, snagged a human by the arm, and tossed him, screaming, into the air.

A young ushelz directly under the human opened its maw wide.

"Dellao!" Raveno pointed at the falling human with one hand while decapitating three ushelz with the other.

But Dellao had two of his own ushelz to deal with.

The ushelz swallowed the human whole, cutting his screams short.

A rush of ushelz widened the breach and swarmed the humans.

"Fuck formation!" Kinsley screamed. "Buddy up!"

"Pair up!" Raveno shouted in Haveo. "Find a human, and get them out!"

Tironan scooped up Benjamin and ran, ezil slashing.

Veilon tossed Martin over her shoulder, which was spectacular all on its own, and tore through the battle, hot on Tironan's heels.

Dellao reached for Leanne.

While his back was turned, an ushelz reared over his head. Leanne tossed her pivz with her free hand, blade over handle, and struck the ushelz through its cavernous mouth. It reared back, choking, giving Dellao just enough time to whirl around, and decapitate the plant in one swing.

Leanne kicked its limp mouth wide and retrieved her pivz.

"I, well..." Dellao swung and decapitated another charging ushelz. "Thanks."

"Anytime." Leanne hitched a thumb toward the exit. "I'll cover you?"

"Let's go," Dellao agreed, and blazed a path forward, Leanne keeping pace at his side.

Kinsley glanced over her shoulder at Raveno. "Is everyone out? We—"

An ushelz reared up over her.

Raveno charged forward. "Behind you!"

Kinsley dodged its snapping jaws a second before its strike, so instead of swallowing her head, it clamped onto her arm, shoulder deep.

"Kinsley!" Raveno swung at the ushelz, slicing low on its stem to avoid Kinsley's arm. Too low, because its jaw didn't release her. It swung its head side to side, in agony, dragging Kinsley along for the ride.

Kinsley stabbed at it, but it whipped her to the left and slammed her to the ground and flung her to the right and dragged her across the gravel. She couldn't land a solid blow.

"Fuuuuu—" Her scream cut short into a groan as it pounded her into the dirt.

Raveno aimed his ezil, waiting for a clean strike. "Get out of the way!"

"If I could extract myself from it, I would!" she yelled.

"Your body is shielding it!"

"Not on purpose! I—"

The ushelz lifted her high overhead and slammed her flat to the ground.

Her head whipped back with a sick thud.

Her body slumped, limp.

The ushelz released her arm and widened its jaws to consume her whole.

Raveno swung.

His ezil sliced the ushelz in half, roots to bud. It spasmed before finally collapsing to the ground.

Kinsley cradled her arm to her chest and rolled to her side, keening.

Raveno lunged in front of her, blocking a charging ushelz, his heart throbbing through his throat. "Your hand! Let me see it!"

"It's okay!" she gasped out. "It's just my left arm!"

Just. Raveno peeked down and immediately returned to fighting. The four ushelz about to converge on him were a better sight than the shredded, bloody travesty that was her limb. "Your arm is not okay!"

"But the remote detonator in my right arm is!"

Whump, whump. Another two decapitated heads hit the ground as Raveno swung his ezil. He dropped, rolled, and lunged up swinging. *Whump, whump.*

Four more ushelz were neatly dispatched, but even as he spotted another three to his right and two to the left, Raveno still seethed. *Just.* As if the near certain dismemberment of her left arm was *just* anything!

Beyond her life, the possibility that the remote detonator might have been compromised hadn't even registered.

"Did everyone make it out?" Kinsley asked, squinting through the fray. "I don't see anyone."

Whump, whump. "That's because it's just us." Raveno spun and jumped over Kinsley.

"Kual and Jhoni too?" She tried to sit up. "I haven't seen them since they broke formation." She flinched back, gasping.

"I'm not sure." *Whump, whump.* "At this point, I think it's safe to assume they either made it out or died trying."

"We didn't make it out, and we're not dead," Kinsley countered.

Not yet, Raveno thought, but he didn't say it. He couldn't. He lost his breath at the cold truth of an entire sea of ushelz homing in on Kinsley.

She was the key to their demise, and the ushelz weren't going to let her out of this arena alive.

Raveno tightened his grip on his ezil.

Bully for them. He wasn't going to let her die.

FORTY-SEVEN

Kinsley watched Raveno battle, part terrified, part in awe, and part annoyed. He hadn't just gone easy on her during training. He'd been flat out faking.

Raveno decapitated three Twoeys with one controlled stroke of his ezil, dodged a fourth plant, and while he sliced its head clean off with his left hand, he loosed two pivz with his right. The pivz spun through the air, embedding hilt-deep in the Twoeys approaching at his back. He decapitated two more in front of him, then flipped over Kinsley and faced the two he'd just wounded. One swing of his ezil later, the plants were writhing on the ground. He'd retrieved his pivz and was releasing them on the two plants converging on his left while he side-rolled to block the Twoey attack on his right. Another wide arch of his ezil—*whoosh*—and he took out the Twoey in front of him *and* behind him in one smooth spin.

Kinsley shook her head. Raveno wasn't just skilled or experienced or lucky. He was a machine.

How she'd ever managed to sneak past his guard and stab him with a pivz that one time was baffling. Insulting, really. He must have been daydreaming from pure boredom while sparring with her, because nothing could sneak past him now. The weapons were merely extensions of his body. His blows never wavered, and his aim never faltered.

But the plants just kept coming.

Kinsley struggled to regain her feet.

"Stay down," Raveno hissed.

He can't possibly keep this up by himself.

"Don't tell me what I can't do." Raveno threw two pivz consecutively with his left hand while swing the ezil with his right. "I'll do what I must."

Kinsley winced. She hadn't meant to speak out loud. But now that she had... "You're holding them off but not making any forward progress."

"I would appreciate any solutions you might suggest." Three more pivz throws. A backflip. Four more decapitations. "Not statements of our current position."

"It's a bad position," Kinsley muttered.

"Another example of an unhelpful statement," Raveno said, but he was only angry because it was true. They were grossly outnumbered. No one, not even Raveno, had the stamina to fight all the Twoeys surrounding them.

It was only a matter of time.

"You could fight your way to an exit if it weren't for me," she murmured.

"Tironan fought his way out with Benjamin over his shoulder." Flip. Decapitation. Side roll. "Anything he can do, I can certainly do," Raveno said, then undercut all that indignant confidence by missing a pivz throw.

A Twoey reared up behind him.

Kinsley closed one eye so there was only one plant to aim at and stab-dragged her last pivz through its gut.

The Twoey fell to the ground, spasming wildly before slumping into death.

Raveno whipped around, eyes wide. "Thank you."

Shit, the stadium spinning around her was fading into starbursts. "You should go."

Raveno resumed his losing battle. "Cease speaking."

"You'll make it if you leave now. The stadium's empty. I'll blow your exit last."

"The stadium is not empty. You are still here." Two decapitations. A backflip. Three pivz throws.

Kinsley gritted her teeth against the sour truth. "We can't let the plants leave the stadium. This is our one chance, while they're all here and the explosives are rigged. We *must* trap them inside."

"Yes, we must." Raveno slashed five plants with two powerful arcs of his ezil, his muscles flexed and gorgeous and seemingly unstoppable. "Trigger the detonators. All of them."

Kinsley froze. *Not again. Never again.*

"Kinsley—"

"I'm not blowing all the exits with you still inside. You'll be trapped here."

"*We'll* be trapped." Another decapitation.

"No."

"You said it yourself. We must." Another backflip.

"*I* must! *You* go!"

"I'm not leaving you," he said. He hadn't growled it, yelled it, or hissed it. He was just so fucking calm because that was that, and there was no point freaking out about something that just was.

Kinsley stared at Raveno—his talent, his stubborn resolve, those pointy blue ears and flexed vresls and his unfailing determination in the face of overwhelming odds—and believed him. He wouldn't leave her. He would *die* before leaving her.

He would die.

An irrational calm settled over her too. "I love you."

Raveno swung his ezil and, for the first time—maybe in his entire life—missed his target.

He might die before leaving her, but she wasn't saving the world if it meant losing him.

Think, think, think.

"How dare you," Raveno growled.

She wasn't going rogue to commandeer an alien spaceship. She wasn't the last remaining survivor of a classified mission gone south in the heart of Yemen. Raveno might be as self-sacrificing as Brandon at the moment, but—Kinsley scrutinized the empty stadium, considering—this wasn't about her escape anymore.

"You say that now because you've given up." Raveno dodged sideways, re-aimed and took out six plants, four by ezil, two by pivz. "We are not dead yet! I—"

"Pass me the microphone."

Raveno glared at her.

"Pretty please."

Raveno's tongue lashed out on a long hiss, but between decapitations, he tossed it to her.

By some miracle, she caught the damn thing, not its double image, and flicked it on.

"People of Havar, if you still near arena, I beg you hear," she intoned in Haveo, her voice echoing through the stadium. "I Kinsley Morales." She hesitated, then added, "Vri Sa Shols to Veilon Hoviir."

Raveno rolled his eyes midswing of his ezil. "They know who you are."

"Raveno Hoviir and I are trapped on stage, surrounded by Two—"

"Ushelz!"

"Plants," she corrected smoothly. "I can trap plants inside, so they not attack your people. But I not want to trap me. I want to go *home*. To Earth. So I need your help." Kinsley paused, then added, "Raveno need your help."

"Cry mercy," Raveno muttered. "No cares about me anymore, not after everything my family has done."

"You severed your own foot to meet your father's unattainable standards. You're the poster child for everything wrong with this world, and still, you sought to make it right," Kinsley insisted.

"Your own people didn't remain loyal to you on *Sa Vivsheth* when you had their best interests at heart." Raveno missed two of his pivz throws and only managed to decapitate one of the three plants rearing over him. "Svik!" he panted. "Remaining loyal to me is the last thing I can expect, or deserve, from my people now."

"Your people know what you've sacrificed for them. After all these thesh, they know your heart, as do I, no matter how hard you tried to keep it hidden."

Raveno grunted, barely landing his backflip in time to slice and dice the Twoey behind him.

"With enough people working together, risking together, *seeing* together," Kinsley said, switching back to haveo and speaking faster now that Raveno's stamina was visibly flagging. "We fight the, the ushelz and escape. Once everyone clear, I trap the ushelz inside."

"Kinsley—"

"*Cease speaking!*" Just by the tone of his voice as he uttered her name, she knew she didn't want to hear the tail end of whatever he was about to say.

"Just pull the trigger."

"I can't."

"*I* can't—" Raveno released a low, desperate hiss. His voice hitched. "I can't hold them off much longer."

"Then run for it."

"I'm"—three pivz throws—"not"—a backflip into another decapitation—"leaving you."

Kinsley flicked off the microphone. "If they don't help us, then the entire planet and all its citizens can zombie rot inside the Twoeys!"

"This situation isn't their fault!" A plant bit his shoulder.

Kinsley covered her mouth to seal in her scream. Her distress would only distract him.

Even with a plant biting him, Raveno still decapitated two other ushelz before—finally—fighting off the one latched to his shoulder.

Deep breath. "Your people accepted prize money after winning death battles against unwilling victims, kidnapped to fight in the Intergalactic Frisaes, did they not?"

"They didn't know—"

"Because it was convenient not to know. But they should have! They should have opened their eyes and cared," Kinsley snapped. "And now they have no excuse. Either they care or they don't. They have a choice, and no one can say it was anyone's choice but theirs. They can save us, and in doing so"—Kinsley flashed her five pulsing anku at him—"save themselves."

Two plants attacked, converging from either side, as a third slithered up to confront Raveno directly. Raveno missed both pivz throws and managed to decapitate only one Twoey. The other two sank their thin needle teeth deep into both of his shoulders.

He dropped his ezil.

"Raveno!"

"Kinsley, I—"

A plant reared up behind him, its jaws wide open over his head.

Kinsley scanned the ground for something, anything, to help.

Nothing was within reach.

The plant dove down to consume Raveno.

No!

A pivz embedded itself hilt-deep in the plant's mouth.

The Twoey reared back, flailing.

Cresha cut through the wall of Twoeys and, with one smooth strike, decapitated both plants clamped onto Raveno's shoulders.

Raveno fell to his knees.

Another four Twoeys converged on him and Cresha.

A sea of strangers burst through the plants, swinging ezils and lobbing pivz and—Kinsley blinked, unsure if the hitch in her throat was a laugh or a sob—carving a path through the Twoeys.

They were here.

They were all here.

The citizens of Havar surrounded Kinsley and Raveno, forming a barricade between them and the Twoeys.

Cresha knelt in front of Raveno, examining his shoulder with an indelicate poke.

Raveno flinched, and despite her own agony, Kinsley grinned.

Cresha poked harder. "Are you—"

"I'm fine." Raveno picked up his ezil, stood, and met Cresha's eyes. "Thank you."

"I'm sorry." Cresha tossed two pivz, ordered someone to fill a crack in their barricade, then turned back to Raveno. "I don't know exactly when, but somewhere along the way, I stopped believing in you."

"I know." The vein in Raveno's temple throbbed. "I'm sorry I gave you reason to."

He raised his hand and skimmed both thumbs across Cresha's forehead.

Kinsley felt jealously like a backdraft blast to the face. For a moment, she couldn't even see past its unreasonable, unbearable heat until she realized: her *bare* forehead.

The corner of Cresha's lip quirked down. She whirled away sharply, her pivz ready, but there was nothing to aim at. Together, everyone was staying strong and holding the plants at bay.

Raveno ran to Kinsley.

"You okay?"

"No." Kinsley smacked his chest. "What the hell was all that Mortal Combat acrobatic hero shit?"

He knelt, reaching out to cradle her body. "What does excrement have to do with my fighting skills?"

"They stink like deception, that's what," she muttered, then cried out as his hand brushed against her raw forearm.

"That would be exertion and pheromones." Raveno hesitated, eyeing her mangled arm uncertainly. "How should I pick you up?"

"Quickly."

Raveno scooped Kinsley into his arms and stood with a grunt. Considering he could curl a minivan... Kinsley winced as she got an up-close view of his own shredded muscles beneath the armor of his scales.

Cresha sprinted for the exit, and Raveno followed. "Retreat!" she ordered. "Steady and synchronized! Maintain the barricade!"

As one unit, the havari defending them retreated toward the exit, still slinging pivz and lopping off heads. Kinsley would have been thoroughly impressed if Raveno's every step didn't launch a jarring stab of agony through her arm.

At the exit, Cresha stepped to the side.

Raveno drew up beside her.

She tapped one of the fighting havari on the shoulder as he backed toward the exit. "Out!"

He dropped from the barricade, and the havari beside him stepped in line to close the gap.

Raveno met the man's eyes. "Thank you."

The man nodded, then sprinted down the exit tunnel.

Cresha tapped the next in line. "Go!"

"Thank you!" Raveno added.

"For you, anything," the woman said, then ran.

Cresha continued encouraging their retreat until one last havarian held the plants at bay. "You ready?" she asked.

Raveno clenched his teeth and nodded.

She tapped out the last fighter. "Run!"

The three of them sprinted down the tunnel.

Kinsley watched over Raveno's shoulder as the Twoeys tried to follow. They were bottle-necked by the narrow exit, their stems and roots tangled from all the fighting, none of them willing to step back to let the others through first.

"I'll miss you," Cresha said.

Kinsley glanced at her, but Cresha was looking straight ahead.

Raveno scoffed. "As if I haven't been gone for thesh at a time before."

"For me, you've been gone eleven thesh," Cresha managed

between breaths. "Since the moment you left on that first mission to Bazail. I always thought, *hoped*, you'd return to me."

She took a moment—she was winded after all—but Kinsley suspected she still would have hesitated even had they not been running for their lives.

"But now, you're gone for good," Cresha finally forced out. "I'm happy for you, but...I'm sorry, and I'll miss you."

"I may return to Havar." Raveno peered down at Kinsley. His vresls stiffened. "Or you may visit wherever I am."

"I can't follow where you're going, and we both know it." They stopped at the end of the tunnel as it branched into the residential wings. Cresha leaned in, brushing one fang across the curve of Raveno's neck. "Goodbye, Raveno."

Raveno leaned in and brushed his fang over her neck in return. "Take care of Havar."

"Take care of each other." Cresha faced forward and met Kinsley's eyes. "The way we didn't."

"Thank you." Kinsley bit her lip. "And good luck," she added. The slithering stampede of enraged Twoeys had managed to squeeze through the exit.

Cresha unsheathed her ezil. "Nothing I can't handle. Take cover."

Raveno ducked into the nearest unlocked room, kicked the door shut with his foot, and promptly collapsed back against it, panting.

"Do it," he gasped, burying his face in the curve of her neck. "Now."

Kinsley reached for a weapon. Her holsters were empty. "I used all my pivz during the fight." She offered up her wrist. "You'll need to do the honors."

Raveno glowered at her proffered arm, the pulsing glow of five anku flashing blue across his face. He closed his eyes for a moment, pained.

"It's okay." Kinsley grabbed his hand and positioned his fingers, one claw aligned over each blue dot.

Her skin dimpled as he squeezed, but he still didn't puncture her skin.

"Svik," he whispered.

"Pull the trigger, Raveno."

He met her gaze.

"End it. Once and for all."

Raveno's lips pinched, grim. Determined.

His claws pierced her skin.

The fireworks exploded.

Kinsley didn't need to see it to know that the blast would fracture the supporting arches. The volcanic rock would splinter with spiderweb cracks and then—there it went. The ground shook as walls collapsed, sealing the exits. Debris and dust would burst through the tunnel. The dozen or so plants that had escaped the arena before the blast would meet Cresha's blade in a single line, and she would dispatch each, one by one, until their bodies and the bodies they'd fed from spilled across the hallway in a wash of slime, guts, and dust.

The remaining Twoeys would be trapped in the arena.

Kinsley blew out a trembling breath. "It's gonna be quite the mess out there in a few days. Once the Twoeys die, they'll destroy your entire underground infrastructure."

"We would need to rebuild anyway, even if it wasn't destroyed. And I'm glad of it," he murmured.

Kinsley met the promise in Raveno's eyes, and her world stilled.

The blast was everything she'd always loved and craved and had sacrificed being "normal" to have—that larger-than-life rush of excitement and accomplishment and danger—but for the first time in thirty-two years, she felt all that, everything she'd ever wanted, without having to watch the sparks fly.

For the first time, the sparks ignited her from within.

EPILOGUE

SEVEN MONTHS LATER.

Kinsley stared out into the stretch of unending space before them, halfway between Earth and Havar, and couldn't decide if she was more excited for or dreading the return home. Leaving Havar far behind and finally returning to Earth was one thing.

Facing her sister again was another entirely.

She brushed her fingertips over her favorite pulsing orange button without pressing it as she reached to flip the next switch in their daily systems cross-check.

Raveno's eyes homed in on her movement behind his sunglasses. "Don't—"

"I didn't!"

"—even think about it."

"I wasn't." Kinsley grinned. "Not with serious intent, anyway."

Raveno adjusted their flight path to avoid the comet tail they were approaching, two shaoz out. "That's how it always starts."

Kinsley wrinkled her nose at him.

His anku vibrated, and Raveno pressed a claw into its flashing dot. "Signal received. One moment, and I'll connect you to our control room's projection system."

"Another diplomat?" Kinsley whispered, tucking a few flyaways back into her braids. "Did Dellao finally make contact with Marzes? I thought he was still several shaoz out."

"It's not just another diplomat. It's your *favorite* diplomat," Raveno said, synching the projector and his anku with a few keystrokes. "No need to spruce up. You're exquisite, my lilssna."

Kinsley peeked up at him doubtfully. "I don't have a favorite. They all suck equally."

"Which is why you're not our diplomat." Raveno leaned down and kissed her forehead. "It would require you to be diplomatic."

Kinsley stuck her tongue out at him, which of course, was when the projector completed its sync.

Cresha's projection flashed on screen, and seeing the two of them, she laughed. "Glad to know that nothing has changed since our last meeting."

Kinsley grinned, and where Cresha couldn't see, kicked Raveno under the instrument panel. "Never."

Raveno grunted, then nodded to Cresha. "Vra Cilvril s'Hvri Cresha."

She nodded back, her smile lingering. "Vra Cilvril s'Hvri Raveno. How goes your journey?"

"It progresses as planned. Uneventful."

Kinsley huffed. "I'm sure we'll endure events enough to last us a lifetime once we reach Earth."

"Undoubtedly," Cresha agreed.

"And you?" Raveno asked. "Any updates on or off Havar?"

"Reconstruction efforts on Havar remain slightly behind schedule," Cresha admitted. "Several support systems we'd hoped would survive the ushelz were unsalvageable. Our engineers are... How would you say in English? Starting from scabs?"

Kinsley smirked. "That suits, but the proper phrase is 'starting from scratch.' Did any of the ushelz survive?"

"A few," Cresha confirmed. "Construction crews still have a few more districts to excavate, but in those locations, it seems unlikely."

Kinsley focused on keeping her breath deep and even, trying not to feel the horror that must have been their final moments under the rubble.

Raveno squeezed her knee under the control panel. "And off-planet?" Raveno asked Cresha. "How is morale on the other carrier vessels?"

"Morale remains shaky, but genuine. Reestablishing our education system and workforce as you suggested helped tremendously. And I've implemented the solo cruiser initiative, so citizens can visit other carrier vessels to meet new people, if they wish. Additionally, Iroan delivered another shipment of supplies and foodstuffs. We're well stocked for another eighty shoaz, at the least."

"Has anyone else shown interest in temporarily relocating to Bazail or Fray?" Kinsley asked.

"Not since our initial outmigration," Cresha said. "But both Bazail and Fray are keeping their planets open indefinitely for our refugees, as long as renovation on Havar remains an ongoing effort."

Raveno nodded. "Thank you, Cresha."

A muscle in Cresha's neck flexed. "Veilon requested a transfer."

Kinsley glanced aside at Raveno.

"Where?" Raveno asked, his voice clipped.

"*Sa Vivsheth.*"

"Request denied. Anything else to report?"

"Raveno—"

"Anything else, Vra Cilvril s'Hvri Cresha Zami?"

Cresha sighed. "No, Vra Cilvril s'Hvri Raveno Hoviir."

"Thank you. Signal—"

"Bye! Talk soon!" Kinsley said, waving.

"Terminated," Raveno finished, and the screen cut Cresha off midwave.

Raveno scowled down at her.

Kinsley batted her lashes at him, feigning innocence. "What?"

"Permission to speak freely regarding our revised flight path, Raveno?" Benjamin shouted from across the room.

Raveno inhaled a long-suffering sigh and swiveled to face the room at large. "No permission needed."

"If you loop around planet Ku from the opposite direction," Benjamin suggested, "we can circumvent the comet tail and shave approximately seventeen hours and thirteen minutes from our journey."

Martin caught Kinsley's gaze and raised his eyebrows. "Approximately."

Kinsley grinned.

"Benny. Babe. Why don't you come into the room instead of shouting from the hallway?" Leanne crooked her finger at him.

Benjamin stepped even farther back and examined the screen without squinting. "It's *still* crystal clear!"

"You could stand across the entire ship, if the ship had no walls, and still read that screen. Assuming we kept the lights blazing, as you prefer," Avier said, only fueling Benjamin's enthusiasm.

Of all the havari, Avier was the most dashing in his "dimmers."

Tironan's fingers danced over the keyboard with flawless accuracy, triple checking Benjamin's calculations. "S-seventeen hours and *nine* minutes," he said. "But he's correct about it being the f-faster route."

"Did you take into account the fourth moon's gravitational pull?" Benjamin asked.

Tironan nodded. "D-did you take into account the extra fuel we'll pick up from the s-space station?"

Benjamin nodded back. "Did you—"

"Did either of you take into account that Ku is within Lorien territory and in range of their sentries?"

Benjamin's cheeks turned bright red.

Tironan's ears turned bright blue.

Raveno grunted. "We avoid Ku and circumvent the comet per *my* calculations."

Jhoni raised his hand.

Raveno massaged his calf and pretended not to see him as he studied the system's cross-check report.

Kinsley suppressed a laugh. The younger crew members had enthusiastically adopted a few human gestures during English class.

"If you'd allow the crew to upgrade their anku, Jhoni wouldn't ask so many questions," Kinsley muttered without moving her smile.

"That would be cheating," Raveno murmured back. "And knowing Jhoni, he would still ask questions."

Kinsley raised her eyebrows. As if Raveno didn't occasionally use a translator.

His vresls stiffened. "Technology is not infallible. It can malfunction, and translators are only as good as their linguists."

"I've updated the program myself," she reminded him, vaguely offended.

"The program doesn't detect tone and sarcasm."

"Oftentimes, neither do you."

Raveno leveled her with a look. "What if Veilon contaminates the translations?"

Ah, the heart of the issue. "Veilon is in protective custody on Cresha's carrier vessel now until the end of time. How would she—"

"She ruled an entire planet under the guise of our father's projection for two thesh after killing him. She's capable of anything!"

"She's also your sister, and—"

"I will not have her influence on this ship or in my life."

"I know how it feels to be the sister in the wrong," Kinsley insisted. "To feel your older sibling's hate and disgust. And I just... I don't want that for you."

Raveno lifted his hand and caressed the edge of her jaw with both thumbs. "Just because I will not forgive my sister for her egregious wrongs doesn't mean that your sister won't forgive you."

"Yes, well..." Kinsley cleared her throat. "I guess we'll find out soon enough. Have you heard from Zethus yet?"

Raveno shook his head. "Not since he skipped our last meeting."

Kinsley bit her lip.

"As I said, technology is not infallible. His anku is most likely malfunctioning." He urged her close and pressed his forehead to hers. "And as *you* said, we'll find them soon enough."

She leaned up to kiss him. Just a peck. Just enough to enjoy and not get him too dizzy on her scent.

Even so, his vresls quivered.

Kinsley grinned, feeling more comforted by that one involuntary reaction than by anything he could say.

Martin coughed.

Riley gagged.

Jhoni wiggled his raised hand.

Raveno jerked his eyes to that impatient hand and back to Kinsley.

"Yes, Jhoni?" Kinsley asked, putting the poor boy out of his misery.

"What is gravinationpool?"

"It's pronounced gravi-tation-al pull," Kinsley enunciated in English.

"And it means *sheknash*," Raveno said in Haveo.

"I know how it translates," Jhoni said, so earnest. So eager. "I meant, what is the definition of sheknash?"

Raveno blinked sideways. "We have such a long way to go," he muttered to Kinsley.

She glanced at everyone in the control room around them, not having to strain her eyes to see because Kual, Jhoni, and all the havari crew were wearing sunglasses in the well-lit room. Benjamin took another step back without squinting, and Avier was loving it. Leanne rolled her eyes but was fighting a grin. Riley was still sullen but free. Martin was content as friends, even if he often studied the control panel with more concentration than was warranted. Tironan was comfortable enough to voice his opinions. No one was armed, not with pivz, ezil, or svirros.

Raveno dropped his head into his hand and massaged the side of his forehead. His bare forehead.

"We might still have a long way to go." Kinsley took his hand and squeezed. "But we're further along than I'd ever dreamed."

HEARING HAVEO: AUDIO LINGUISTICS PROGRAM
TRANSLATIONS BY: KINSLEY MORALES

ankis (noun): a one-way receiver and translator implant for the hard of hearing. Similar in function to a cochlear implant.

anku (noun): a two-way transceiver implant, functional at any distance.

ankesh (noun): a tracking implant used for branding shols.

avish (noun): a form of cryptocurrency on the planet Havar.

bresha (noun): an occupation that involves helping people obtain the resources they need to live; a social worker.

Cershys (noun): an engineering company that produces advanced hearing aid technology. (noun): sonar.

Dorai (noun): a formal, polite address for the Lore'Lorien to show respect. (noun): Madam.

eussh (noun): an eating utensil fashioned like a glove to fit over havarian claws.

ezil (noun): a handheld weapon, two-feet in length and hollow, like a decorative kaleidoscope, with expandable spear and scythe. Typically worn across the back.

frisaes (noun): a gladiator-style duel to the death by which havari earn military or political ranks. Also for entertainment purposes.

Haveo (noun): the modern version of the language spoken on Havar.

Havar (noun): an Earth-like planet with a nitrogen-oxygen atmosphere, three moons, and one sun, inhabited exclusively by nocturnal creatures and carnivorous plants. (noun): hardened lava. (verb): to burn with no flame; to smolder.

havari (noun): the people who inhabit the planet Havar. Singular: havarian.

hevrch sha (noun): a congenital deformity in which an infant's foot or hand is turned inward, similar to club foot on Earth; twisted limb.

Hvrsil (noun): the traditional language spoken on Havar.

lasvik (noun): A gesture of good faith used for greetings, farewells, and to bind deals, similar in meaning to a human handshake. Instead of clasping hands, havari brush their fangs against each other's throats.

lir s'flis (noun): an explosive used for space combat, similar in form and function to a missile.

lilssna (noun): an explosive used for celebration, like a firework, employing the componentry and precision of a missile to create moving images of light in the sky.

Lorien (noun): the name of the planet inhabited by lorienok; referred to as a spirituality, like Mother Earth, to be praised and respected.

Lorienok (noun): the people inhabiting Lorien.

losths (noun): a sweet, pancake-like dessert.

ouk (noun): a family symbol used to brand Vri Sa Shols.

phosh (noun): a gas that induces inebriation-like side effects in havari.

pivz (noun): a handheld weapon similar to an ice pick, with a hilt on one side and a skinny, sharp, pointed blade, designed specifically to spear between scales. Typically worn at the hips.

riluuz (verb): to end something's existence. To destroy.

rhef (noun): a sweet, flaky puff, similar to a croissant or bun, made from powdered seeds.

shaoz (noun): a measurement of time on Havar equivalent to approximately one day; more precisely, 25 hours.

sheknash (noun): gravitational pull.

sheshzi (noun): a recreational sport played on Havar.

shetn (noun): preserved blue eggs with a consistency and taste similar to pinto beans.

shols (noun): competitors in the Intergalactic Frisaes.

svik (noun): A rude, curt explicative, similar in usage to *shit* or *damn*. Derived from the shortened form of the word *lasvik*, implying that a deal has been broken or a bond has been severed.

svirros (noun): a sedative used in patients undergoing intense healing.

tashis (noun): a long voyage often undertaken with many people for a specific purpose. (noun): expedition.

thesh (noun): a measurement of time on Havar equivalent to approximately one year; more precisely, 336 days or 350 shaoz.

thev sa shek (noun): a rude, sexual explicative translating to "urethra fucker," similar in usage and vehemence to mother fucker.

thev (noun): a penis-shaped external organ of the male havari anatomy located beneath the penis, utilized for expelling urine from the body.

ushelz (noun): a carnivorous plant, similar in form and function to a Venus flytrap but five feet tall with sharp needle teeth in its gaping maw. Primary diet: people, indiscriminate of species.

vespirs (noun): A bird, similar to chicken or turkey, commonly eaten on Havar.

vit (noun): a form of cryptocurrency on Havar earned during the Welcome Ceremony in preparation for bidding on shols.

vivsheth (verb): to chase something with purpose. (noun): pursuit.

vresls (noun): an external organ of the male havari anatomy consisting of six spines around the neck connected by a thin, sensitive webbing. The spines lay relaxed around the collar and react reflexively to emotion.

vri sa shols (noun): a shols that has been selected by an havarian for the "honor" of a frisaes.

Vriusheli (noun): a botanical organization dedicated to the research of ushelz; a hand of ushelz.

yensha (noun): a handheld digital device with timekeeping, scheduling, computing and filing capabilities that syncs with a ship's mainframe and its crew's anku; a tablet.

Havar Military Ranks

Vra Cilvril s'Hvri: The killing hand of Havar.

Vri Cilvril: A killing hand.

Vri Shavril: An advising hand.

Vri Zyvril: A healing hand.

Fyvril: A helping hand.

Vrili: Many hands; military crew. Singular: vrilis.

ALSO BY MELODY JOHNSON

Love Beyond Series

Beyond the Next Star

Sight Beyond the Sun

Night Blood Series

The City Beneath

Sweet Last Drop

Eternal Reign

Day Reaper

Anthologies

Romancing the Holidays, Vol. 1

Romancing the Holidays, Vol. 2

Romancing the Holidays, Vol. 3

ABOUT THE AUTHOR
MELODY JOHNSON

MELODY JOHNSON IS THE AWARD-WINNING AUTHOR OF THE "out of this world" Love Beyond series and the Night Blood series published by Kensington Publishing/Lyrical Press. The New York Times and USA TODAY Bestselling Author, Lynsay Sands, "laughed out loud" reading Beyond the Next Star (Love Beyond, book 1), and Kirkus Reviews praised it as, "an engaging and unusual otherworldly tale."

Melody graduated magna cum laude from Lycoming College with her BA in creative writing and psychology. Throughout college, she wrote contemporary love stories, but having read and adored the action and dark mystery of vampires and aliens her entire life, she decided to add her fingerprint to the paranormal and sci-fi genres.

When she isn't working or writing, Melody can be found swimming at the beach, hiking with her husband, and exploring her home in southeast Georgia. Keep in touch with Melody on social media or sign up for her newsletter to receive emails about new releases and book signings. Website: authormelodyjohnson.com

facebook.com/authormelodyjohnson
instagram.com/authormelodyjohnson
goodreads.com/authormelodyjohnson
amazon.com/author/melodymjohnson

CPSIA information can be obtained
at www.ICGtesting.com
Printed in the USA
JSHW081009141022
31405JS00006B/6/J

9 781735 149943